W9-BKR-913

WITHDRAWN
BY
WILLIAMSBURG REGIONAL LIBRARY

Miss Kopp's Midnight Confessions

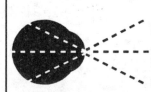

This Large Print Book carries the
Seal of Approval of N.A.V.H.

A KOPP SISTERS NOVEL

MISS KOPP'S MIDNIGHT CONFESSIONS

AMY STEWART

THORNDIKE PRESS
A part of Gale, a Cengage Company

GALE
A Cengage Company

Farmington Hills, Mich • San Francisco • New York • Waterville, Maine
Meriden, Conn • Mason, Ohio • Chicago

LIBRARY OF CONGRESS CIP DATA ON FILE.
CATALOGUING IN PUBLICATION FOR THIS BOOK
IS AVAILABLE FROM THE LIBRARY OF CONGRESS

ISBN-13: 978-1-4328-4249-9 (hardcover)
ISBN-10: 1-4328-4249-8 (hardcover)

Published in 2017 by arrangement with Houghton Mifflin Harcourt
Publishing Company   ·

Printed in the United States of America
1 2 3 4 5 6 7 21 20 19 18 17

To Masie Cochran

"You try to help your prisoners, then?"

"Certainly. Often a little help is all they need to get back on the road to straight living — sometimes help against others, but very often help against themselves. They come to me often at midnight, after I have gone to bed in my cell. At midnight a woman will tell almost anything if she finds one who is sympathetic to tell it to."

— Miss Kopp, Naming Six Requisites for Detective, *New York Evening Telegram*, March 5, 1916

1

On the morning of her arrest, Edna Heustis awoke early and put her room in order. She occupied the smallest of Mrs. Turnbull's furnished rooms, nothing more than an alcove under the eaves, with just enough space for a bed and a wash-stand. A row of iron hooks on the wall held the entirety of her wardrobe: two work uniforms, a Sunday dress, and a winter coat. The only decoration was a picture of a sailboat, furnished by Mrs. Turnbull, and for reading material her landlady had issued her a history of the Italian lakes, a guide to Egyptian art, and a general's wife's account of Army life on the western plains. Those sat on a hang-shelf, alongside an oil lamp — although Edna preferred to do her reading in the parlor, under the single electrical light offered for that purpose.

Absent from her possessions were any portraits of her family or mementos of home. She'd left in such a hurry that she hadn't thought to bring any. She'd been inquiring at factories for weeks, and when the women's superintendent at the DuPont powder works in Pompton Lakes agreed to hire her on, she dashed home, gathered up only that which she could carry, then slipped out the back door while her mother was occupied in the kitchen.

Edna might have been a quiet and serious girl, but she'd been raised among boys and had a fine sense of adventure about her. The war in Europe had reached its boiling point, and every American boy was eager to join the fight. If there was work to be done for the war, and women were allowed to do it, Edna was impatient to begin. She left the briefest of notes on the day she left: "Gone to work for France in Pompton Lakes. I have a place in a good house and you needn't worry."

It was true about the good house. Mrs. Turnbull only rented to girls from the powder works and maintained a strict policy about curfews and church attendance on Sundays. She was in many ways a tougher task-master than Edna's mother had been, but Edna didn't mind about that. She believed the regimen of living in a boarding-house to be similar to that of the Army, and liked to imagine that the daily making up of her room (tucking in the sheets, folding down the coverlet, stowing her bed-slippers and nightgown, arranging her brush and comb in an even row alongside the basin) might resemble, in some way, the orderliness of military camp life, of which her brothers were so eager to partake.

But France seemed very far away that morning as Edna stepped into her work dress, washed her face in the basin, and ran down the stairs for breakfast. In the cramped butler's pantry that served as a dining room, Mrs. Turnbull had put out porridge and stewed apples. Edna sat, as she did every morning, in comfortable silence among the five other girls who roomed there: Delia, Winifred, Irma, Fannie, and Pearl. Their conversation ran along familiar lines:

First Delia said, "There's a ladder in my stocking so far beyond mending that I might as well go bare."

Then Fannie said, "Albert's good for another pair."

To which Irma replied, "Then it's a shame she threw off Albert and went with those men from the Navy, who don't need to supply a girl with stockings before she'll go to a dance hall with them."

11

Then Pearl said, "Delia, you didn't go with all of them, did you?"

And Delia retorted, "You couldn't expect me to choose one!"

This kind of talk had embarrassed Edna terribly the first time she heard it. Before she left home, she'd allowed a friend of her brothers' to pay a little attention to her, but she could never imagine stolid and steadfast Dewey Barnes buying her a pair of stockings or taking her to a crowded and noisy dance hall and then letting her stumble home, as the girls at the boarding-house did, dazed by liquor and cigarettes, with a sort of swollen and bruised look about the lips that they wore like a badge until it faded.

It wasn't that Edna disapproved of their feminine vanity, or their wild ways. She just couldn't do what they did. She didn't know how to make herself up and put herself on display. Dancing was a foreign language to her: she felt foolish trying to work out the Kangaroo Hop or the Peabody, and never could master Delia's trick of kicking her heel back when she turned to make her skirt fly up. She practiced with them because they insisted, but more often than not she took the man's part, maneuvering woodenly while the other girls practiced their flourishes.

Only once did she allow herself to be dragged along to a dance hall with them, and there she found herself entirely out-matched. Over the whirl of laughter and music, the other girls chatted gaily with any man who came into their orbit. They had a knack for making the sort of easy, meaningless chatter that would lead to a turn on the dance floor, then a sip from a bottle secreted away in a man's pocket, a taste of his cigarette, and a kiss just outside the door, sheltered under a dark and discreet night sky.

But Edna hadn't any idea where to begin, and wasn't sure she wanted to. Every dance step, every smile, every laughing word exchanged with a man was like a piece of machinery that she didn't know how to operate. Instead she held her friends' purses, and went home at midnight with all of their keys, rattling them in every doorknob so that Mrs. Turnbull might hear the sound of all six girls returning home at once.

The others didn't mind that Edna stayed home from the dances after that, and for her part, she'd grown accustomed to their ways. She was sitting placidly among them that morning, listening with some amusement but relieved, as always, that they didn't expect her to join in.

"You remember Frank, don't you? From the train station?" Delia whispered.

Pearl leaned in and said, "The one with the walking stick filled with whiskey?"

"Yes," Delia said gleefully. "That one. He asked me to Atlantic City for the weekend. How am I going to get away? I'm all out of sisters with birthdays."

"What about an elderly aunt in a state of decline?" Fannie offered.

"What about inviting me?" Irma complained.

"Oh, Frank would like that, but he's to register us as man and wife, and who would you be?"

"I'll be the sister with the birthday! Or the elderly aunt. Just take me along."

They were all laughing at that when heavy footsteps stormed the porch and someone pounded the brass knocker hard enough to rattle their saucers. Every girl leapt up at once, flushed and guilty, as if they had, improbably, been overheard and caught. Mrs. Turnbull, having just come up from her lodgings in the basement, bustled past and admonished them to finish quickly and wash their own bowls.

But not a single girl moved, and not a single spoon clanked against a dish, as the

14

door swung open and a policeman's brusque voice demanded to see a Miss Edna Heustis, who was to be put under arrest on a charge of waywardness and taken without delay to the Hackensack jail.

2

The female population at the Hackensack jail consisted at that moment of a conniving fortune-teller who, among her more colorful aliases, insisted on being called Madame Fitzgerald; a practical nurse named Lottie Wallau, convicted in the overdose of her elderly patient; and Etta McLean, a stenographer who sold company secrets to her employer's competitor and lived so conspicuously well off the proceeds that she was easily found out. They were housed alongside Josephine Knobloch, who had been arrested for rioting at the Garfield worsted mill (and could be released if she paid a six-dollar fine, but the strikers were united in their refusal to do so). On a cell block by herself sat an old Italian woman, Providencia Monafo, contentedly serving a sentence for murder. She'd aimed for her husband but shot her boarder instead, and thought it a distinct advantage to live for a time behind

16

the jail's protective stone walls, where Mr. Monafo couldn't take revenge.

Constance Kopp, the deputy in charge of the female section, usually oversaw eight to ten inmates, but in the dark, cold days following Christmas, women — even criminally inclined women — simply weren't out and about and were therefore less likely to be seen and arrested. It was true among the male population, too: there was always a drop in January and February, when the weather was simply too disagreeable to bother about stealing a horse or knifing a fellow drinker at a saloon.

It was, therefore, something of an occasion to receive a new inmate. Sheriff Heath announced it from the entrance to the female section. "There's a girl downstairs. An officer brought her over from Paterson. He insisted on speaking to me —"

"They all do," Constance put in.

"I told him that we have a deputy for the ladies and he must tell it to you," the sheriff said.

"I hope she isn't terribly old," Etta called out as Constance turned to go. "We could use another hand in the laundry." All of the inmates did chores, but Constance tended to save the light work for the older women — in this case, Madame Fitzgerald and

17

Providencia Monafo — which left the younger ones to work the wringer and the steam press.

"I just want a fourth for bridge," Lottie said. "Madame Fitzgerald cheats."

"Don't bring us any more strikers," Etta added. "They're so *earnest.*"

If this was intended to incite a response from Josephine, it didn't. Constance agreed, privately, that strikers tended to be grimly single-minded and didn't make particularly good company.

She locked the gate and followed the sheriff down the stairs. Once they were alone, he said, "The girl looks to be about as wayward as my left shoe, but I leave that for you to determine."

"I wish it could be left to me." It irked Constance to put a girl in jail who didn't belong there, even temporarily.

As this was a conversation they'd had many times before, Sheriff Heath merely waved his hand in acknowledgment and went back to his office, leaving Constance to contend with the officer.

It came as something of a relief to Constance that she and the sheriff had developed their own shorthand, and that he so often seemed to know what she was thinking before she said it. She'd never had a proper job before, and hadn't any idea what it would be like to take orders from anyone, much less a lawman. What if he'd had a temper, or an animosity toward the criminals under his roof, or merely lacked any concern for the welfare of his inmates — or his deputies? Surely such things happened in jailhouses around the country.

But Sheriff Heath was an even-tempered and fair-minded man who seemed to have run for office for all the right reasons. He campaigned for better treatment for his inmates and believed that by directing charity and education to the poor, crime could be eradicated. Although his office put a tremendous burden upon him — inmates had died in his arms, murderers had gone free, and he was often the first to the scene of every form of human suffering imaginable — he managed to maintain his dignity.

And — she wouldn't hesitate to admit it — she admired the fact that he'd seen something in her that no one else had. He saw that she was strong-willed, with a keen sense of justice and a sharp eye, and that she knew how to put her size to an advantage. A lack of physical strength had long been an argument against hiring women officers, but Constance had plenty of that and wasn't afraid to use it. Sheriff Heath recognized in her the qualities that make a good deputy sheriff, regardless of sex, and offered her a job on that basis. For that she'd owe him a lifelong debt.

Constance had expected her work for the sheriff to land her in the middle of feminine versions of the same sorts of cases the men handled: thieves and pickpockets, drunkards, brawlers, and the occasional murderess or arsonist. There was nothing stopping her from going after a male criminal, either, and she had, whenever it was called for. She was taller than most of the men she tackled, and heavier than some. Furthermore, it didn't hurt that Constance had a certain recklessness about her when it came to physical confrontation: she'd been known to hurl herself down a city street and leap on top of a fleeing suspect, with no consideration to the unyielding pavement that would rise to meet them. This habit had left her with a broken rib and more than a few nasty bruises and sprains, but it had also earned her Sheriff Heath's respect, and that meant more to her than a bloodied kneecap.

But lately, there'd been less rough-and-tumble and more moralizing. This bothered her, as jail was rarely the best place for a girl gone wrong. The steady uptick in morality cases coming before her was one of the more troublesome aspects of her position as deputy sheriff and jail matron. In the last few months she'd seen a parade of girls brought in under charges of waywardness or incorrigibility: Rosa Gorgio, reported by her own father for keeping late hours with men; Mabel Merritt, caught following a man out of a drugstore; and Daisy Sadler, arrested at Palisades Park for indecent dress.

These girls tended to linger in jail for weeks, awaiting trials for which they had neither preparation nor adequate defense. Often their parents were the ones to accuse them. It was not uncommon to see mothers testifying against daughters, and fathers standing up in court and begging judges to take their unruly girls away. It had become all too easy for parents to turn to the courts when their daughters grew too willful and headstrong for them to manage.

Some of the accused served their sentences there at the Hackensack jail, and others went off to the state prison, but she couldn't think of a single one who'd been found innocent of the charges and released. Young women were being locked up for months, and possibly years, over offenses that amounted to little more than leaving their parents' home without permission, or carrying on with an unsuitable man.

Constance couldn't help but notice that the unsuitable men were never arrested for their part in the crime.

And now here was Edna Heustis, huddled in the corner of a bare, windowless interviewing room on the jail's ground floor. She was wrapped in a floppy quilted coat entirely unsuited to the weather (thrust upon her by one of the other girls as the officer strong-armed her onto Mrs. Turnbull's porch), and wore no hat. Her hair rested in black ringlets about a pale and heart-shaped face that would have seemed listless but for something sharp in her eyes and a determined set to her pointed chin. She looked to be about the age of the youngest Kopp, Fleurette, although there was no trace of Fleurette's vanity about her. By the way she held herself, she gave the impression that she was accustomed to hard work, to which Fleurette, Constance would readily admit, was not.

Officer Randolph of the Paterson police force was sitting heavily in the room's only chair, resting his meaty forearms across a little table that held the ledger-book. This was where the deputies registered every inmate brought to them.

"The chair is for the deputy in charge," Constance said crisply, when he did not rise. This earned the slightest hint of a smile from Edna, and a groan from the officer as he staggered to his feet and pulled the chair out in an exaggerated gesture of chivalry.

"We picked her up at a boarding-house out in Pompton Lakes," the officer said when Constance was settled. He turned his head so Edna Heustis wouldn't see, then hoisted an eyebrow to underscore the menace to young girls found in such places. His skin hung in loose folds under his eyes and beneath his chin, bringing to mind an old hunting dog that still enjoyed the chase.

Constance wished very much to explain to him that a girl renting a furnished room was not immediately a cause for suspicion, but she knew that if she started down that line, he'd be likely to walk out without finishing his recitation of the facts, and she'd be left with an inmate whose case would be all the more difficult to unravel. The act of holding her tongue was a sort of tactfulness that did not come naturally to her.

"For what crime was she arrested?" was the question Constance settled upon. She allowed her hand to levitate over the column in the ledger-book where this particular bit of history was to be recorded.

"Her mother came in after Christmas to

make a charge of waywardness. We only just now had reason to be in Pompton Lakes, and thought why not pick this one up if she's still there."

Edna pressed her lips together in a frown at the word *waywardness,* or perhaps it was the word *mother.* Constance knew that particular strain of defiance; she'd practiced it herself at a younger age. She nonetheless tried to sound strict with Edna when she said, "What were you doing by yourself at a boarding-house?"

Edna squared her shoulders and looked directly at Constance, her hands clasped in front of her the way a schoolgirl addresses her teacher. "Working, ma'am. I found a place for myself at the DuPont powder works."

Well, of course she had, Constance thought but did not say. What else did Officer Randolph think she'd been doing there?

"And how old are you? Tell the truth, or we'll find out easily enough."

"I passed my eighteenth birthday just before Christmas."

"There's no law against a girl of eighteen finding work and a place for herself." Constance leaned back in her chair and folded her arms across her chest the way Sheriff Heath did when he made a pronouncement on a legal matter. "Why would your mother report you as wayward?"

Officer Randolph shifted and sighed, tugging at his belt as if adjustments would have to be made if he were to stand there much longer. "Wouldn't this be a matter for the judge?" he put in. "Or the sheriff?" He pushed open the door and looked with faint hope down the corridor, but no sheriff appeared.

Constance's sense of restraint abandoned her. She wiped her pen and said, "Officer, you've brought me a girl who has not, to my knowledge, committed any crime, nor has she any connection to Bergen County that I can see. She lives and works in Passaic County — at least, I hope she still works there. Dear, does anyone at the factory know where you've gone?"

Miss Heustis sniffed — although this might have been more for show, as she had already sensed in Constance a co-conspirator and felt she had a role to play — and said, "I asked to write a note for the girls' superintendent, but the officer said it wasn't allowed."

Officer Randolph tried to protest, but Constance interrupted him. "That's fine. I'll see to it myself. I take it your mother lives here in Bergen County, which is why you've been brought to me?"

Edna nodded. "Down in Edgewater."

At last Constance discovered the most tenuous of reasons for a law-abiding young woman to be carried against her will to the Bergen County Sheriff's Department. She made a note of it in the ledger-book, alongside Edna's name, her birthday, and the charges against her.

Suspected waywardness, she wrote, underlining the first word. Although anyone placed under arrest is, at first, only suspected of the crime, she felt the need to put an emphasis upon it.

Once her particulars had been recorded, Constance stood and took Edna by the arm. "Thank you, Officer. I'm sure you're eager to get back to Paterson."

"I — yes, ma'am, thank you." He looked briefly in the direction of the jail kitchen before he left. On gray and miserable days like this one, officers liked to linger around the jail, accepting a deputy's offer of a cup of coffee and a little conversation before going back out on patrol. But Constance thought they'd had about as much of each other's company as they could stand and sent him on his way.

"I don't like the looks of this," Constance said when he was gone. "Did Officer Randolph ask your landlady about you before he took you away?"

"No, ma'am."

"And what about your employer? Did it seem to you that he'd stopped first at the powder works to make any inquiries about you?"

"He didn't, ma'am. He didn't know where I worked."

Constance took a step back and looked her over. "Tell me something. Is there any truth to your mother's accusation? Have you been staying out late at dance halls and movie palaces, or going around with a different man every night? Have you done anything at all that would give the judge cause to lay a charge of waywardness against you?"

Edna gave an embarrassed little smile, thinking of Delia and the others, and shook her head. "No, ma'am. Mrs. Turnbull will tell you. The other girls will, too. I'm the dullest one in the house."

"You're not dull," Constance said. "You only wanted to work, and to pay your own way. Is that right?"

Edna nodded. She seemed to Constance to be a modest and serious girl who wouldn't know what to do inside a dance hall.

"My mother doesn't think I should be allowed to go away on my own," Edna said, "but I never knew she went to the police over it."

"Your mother isn't the one to decide," Constance assured her. Constance's own mother had tried to keep her from working, but that was before there were lady telephone operators and women reporters, much less female deputy sheriffs. It was a different age now. Parents had even less cause to try to keep their daughters from doing as they pleased.

What she didn't want to tell Edna was this: *A judge will decide. And the judge won't be shown the facts, because no one will bother to go and gather them.*

This was precisely the problem. The prosecutor's office was in charge of proving that a crime had taken place, and that the arrest was proper. For evidence they would present Edna's mother, who would say whatever mothers said when they wished to complain about their daughters.

But who would put up a defense for Edna? She couldn't afford an attorney. The prosecutor wouldn't bother to disprove the charges. In fact, the prosecutor's office seemed to be growing ever more fond of these cases, and liked to see them written up for the papers. It showed that they were doing something about immorality and vice.

The fact that the charges had no merit mattered little to anyone — except the girl accused.

That's why Constance made a rather rash promise, one that she had no authority to make and no means to carry out. "Edna, I believe I'll go myself to speak to your landlady and to the superintendent at the factory. The judge will listen to what I have to say about it."

Constance had a very definitive way of speaking and tended to state a thing as fact even if she wasn't entirely sure about it. Her job demanded this sort of bravado: one could never hesitate in front of an inmate. As far as she knew, she had no authority to intervene in a criminal charge or address the judge on an inmate's behalf. But something had to be done for the girl, and she was impatient to do it herself.

"Leave it to me," she told Edna, "and try not to worry over it."

"I'm not worried," Edna said. In truth, she wasn't. Upon passing into the custody of Deputy Kopp, Edna felt a great good fortune come over her. She'd never seen such a formidable-looking woman, and she knew that any woman who took on such

29

unusual work would surely be sympathetic to Edna's case.

In fact, she wondered if Deputy Kopp had considered war-work herself and thought she might like to ask her about it. Here was a woman who wore a revolver as easily as a string of pearls, commanded a powerful voice that could bark out an order, and possessed the disposition to go along with it. With a name like Kopp, she might well be German, but Edna suspected that her loyalties resided in New Jersey and not with the Kaiser.

She was about to burst forth with all of this when Constance said, "Now, Edna, I'm going to put you in a quiet and clean cell and bring you something hot for lunch. I'll go out to Pompton Lakes this afternoon. This entire mess will make a good story that you can tell your friends when I take you home tomorrow."

"Tomorrow! You don't mean that I'm to spend a night in jail?" A note of panic rose in Edna's voice. She planted her feet and refused to take another step unless she was towed, which Constance could have done but didn't.

Edna had never even spoken to a police officer, much less been arrested by one. She couldn't say with any certainty that she'd so much as seen the county jail before today. How was she to survive a night behind bars, surrounded by vagabonds, drunks, and criminals?

Constance bent down awkwardly to look Edna in the eye. The girl's lips were starting to waver and she looked as though she might cry.

"Listen to me. I'm your friend in this. I'm going to get you settled, and then I'll go right to work on setting you free. There's no law against having a job and living on your own."

"The officer didn't seem to know that." Now the tears did come, in a rush of dread and shame.

"But the judge will. I'll see to it. I'm going to speak to the sheriff right now, and he'll be on your side, too. You can't lose, can you, with the two of us in your corner?"

Edna didn't know a thing about the sheriff, but what choice did she have? "I suppose not."

With that, Edna went along trustingly to her jail cell, and Constance went to tell Sheriff Heath that she had just decided upon a series of improvements to the way criminal justice was carried out in Bergen County.

3

It was not unusual for Sheriff Heath to be rousted out of bed in the middle of the night over a train accident, a country house robbery, or some other calamity. He rarely enjoyed anything like a full night's sleep, and he carried eggplant-hued shadows under his eyes to prove it. He spent mornings in his office, reading the mail and attending to business, which is where Constance found him after she settled Edna in her cell.

His office was a plain room with nothing adorning the wall but a fire insurance calendar. There was a glass-fronted bookcase, a desk for him, and an oak table that was always piled with inmate records, correspondence, and case files. Across from his desk sat two battered old chairs for visitors. On the other side of the room was a little blue-tiled fireplace that he kept kindled all winter long, making it easily the most hospitable place in the jail.

She walked in and went to stand in front of the fire, intending to launch immediately into the subject of Edna Heustis's future, but she was derailed over a newspaper story.

"I've just had a look at Miss Hart's latest," he said, rustling the paper in her direction. "She paints quite a picture of Hackensack's girl sheriff."

"Wasn't that the idea?"

Carrie Hart was a New York City reporter who'd helped her with a case the year before. She was tired of writing about society luncheons and had persuaded her editor that a profile of New Jersey's first lady deputy would be of interest to readers.

Sheriff Heath had allowed it, thinking that a story about the unfortunate women who came into the jail, and the ways that a female deputy could advise them, would win support for his ideas of rehabilitation and reform. His detractors believed that jail should be a grim and miserable experience, thus deterring criminals from doing the sorts of things that might land them there. The sheriff had to fight for decent hygiene, wholesome food, and simple medical care for his inmates. He was even criticized for offering them improving books to read and church services on Sunday. To persuade the public, he was willing to let a reporter into the jail.

Constance had agreed to the interview although she disliked the way the papers talked about her. Every newspaper in the country had a women's page in need of comedic and dramatic filler, which meant that a story about a cop in a dress might circulate for months all over the country, always with creative alterations from enterprising copyeditors, until she hardly recognized herself in the headlines.

Owing to the flurry of stories about her last case, in which she wrestled with an escaped fugitive on the subway steps in Brooklyn, Constance was subjected to a barrage of letters from lonely men and enterprising employers. She'd had a marriage proposal from a doctor in Cuba, an offer of a job as a factory foreman in Chicago, and a set of keys to a jail in El Paso if only she'd consent to come out West and run it.

Her sister Norma took great pride in answering those letters. She spent hours composing sharp-tongued retorts and reading them aloud. Under her pen, the rejection of impertinent propositions had been elevated to an art form.

Constance had a feeling that this story

would only bring more letters her way. The sheriff held up the paper to show her the headline, then cleared his throat and read aloud.

GIRL SHERIFF, A REAL LECOQ, DETECTS CRIME IN A NOVEL WAY

"A woman should have the right to do any sort of work she wants to, provided she can do it."

Miss Constance A. Kopp, Under Sheriff of Bergen County, N.J., took a reporter back into the women's ward of the county jail at Hackensack, carefully locking the door, and into one of the light and airy cells before she would talk. And Miss Kopp works: she was busy when the reporter arrived at the appointed hour. It was an hour later before the Under Sheriff could stop long enough for an interview.

"Some women prefer to stay at home and take care of the house," she continued. "Let them. There are plenty who like that kind of work enough to do it. Others want something to do that will take them out among people and affairs. I always wanted to do things from my early girlhood years."

Sheriff Heath put the paper down. "Was this to be a story about jobs for women, or about our inmates?"

"The inmates, of course," Constance said. "But she had to paint a picture for the reader. She warned me about that."

"No one warned me," he said, reading on. "She says that you took her around, introduced her to the inmates . . . Ah, now she gets to it."

"The inmates are free to come see me at any time," said Miss Kopp. "Besides being out on active work in connection with the duties which fall upon Sheriff Heath, I am matron of the prison. I am always friendly with the women. That is the way to win their confidence. In the end they always tell me the truth. They have learned that this is the only way I can help them."

"You try to help your prisoners, then?"

"Certainly. Often a little help is all they need to get back on the road to straight living — sometimes help against others, but very often help against themselves. They come to me often at midnight, after I have gone to bed in my cell. At midnight a woman will tell almost anything if she finds one who is sympathetic to tell it to."

"That's exactly why you hired a matron, so don't complain about it," Constance put in.

"Oh, but there's more to it. And you haven't seen the pictures."

"Pictures? You know I didn't agree to —"

He held it out to her. A sketch artist had drawn a slimmer and more fashionable version of Constance in two scenes: comforting a crying girl, and wrestling a fugitive.

"I never saw an illustrator, and he obviously never saw me," she said.

He read down a few more lines and said, "It says here that Miss Kopp has no desire to give up her work for matrimony, in spite of the proposals that have come to her from the newspaper publicity which her office has given her. She wants an active life."

"If only that were enough to put a stop to the proposals."

"Refusing to speak to reporters would put a stop to them," the sheriff said.

"You asked for the interview!"

"I wanted a story about our good works."

"Is that all of it?"

"I didn't read the part where she wrote about your fetching appearance," he said.

Constance groaned. "You might as well."

He cleared his throat and read, " 'Miss Kopp is a young woman of abounding energy. She is large of build but . . .' " He faltered, and couldn't look at her. She snatched the paper away from him and read, to her utter dread:

```
    . . . large of build but well-
formed, and carries off her size
regally, as the novelists would
say. Her eyes are the velvety
brown shade which matches her
hair in color, again giving the
novelist a chance for a page of
descriptive matter.
```

She threw it back at him. "I can't believe Carrie wrote that."

He took the paper up again. "You haven't seen the list of 'Miss Kopp's Ideas on Detection of Crime.' Are you planning to write a book? This looks like a table of contents."

"What are my ideas?"

He leaned over it and said, " 'The requisites for a woman who wants to do police work are determination, fearlessness, persistency, sympathy, love of work, and the ability to throw one's self into the lives and feelings of the prisoners.' "

"You must admit it's a fine list."

He turned to yet a third page and scanned the last few paragraphs, which were tucked at the bottom corner below an advertisement for rubber gloves. "Why, here's the bit about reform, at the very end, after everyone has stopped reading."

Much has been said during the last few years about prison reform and making such institutions reformatory rather than punitive, but none of them has worked out a more comprehensive scheme than the one devised and followed by Miss Kopp. Fortunately, she is supported by a progressive sheriff, Robert N.

Heath, who has been a close
student of modern prison manage-
ment since he was appointed
under sheriff five years ago and
despite opposition, he has
helped to work out these plans.

Now he looked up at her in utter despair.
"I wasn't aware that I was the one who
helped you with a prison reform program."

"You know I never said that."

He sighed and ran a hand across his
forehead. "I think we'd best put a stop to
these stories. They write anything they
please and we never have a chance to answer
to it."

"It's fine with me," she said. "I never
wanted to be singled out like this. It doesn't
sit well with the other deputies. None of
them have their pictures in the paper every
time they catch a man. And not a one of
them has to answer to the kind of correspondence I do."

"Then don't answer it, if you don't like
it," the sheriff said.

"Oh, it keeps Norma occupied."

"There's a bit here about your salary, too."

The question of her salary had come up
recently at a meeting of the Board of Freeholders. There was nothing unusual about

the sheriff being raked over the coals regarding his expenses, but this was the first time they'd thought to scrutinize the cost of hiring a lady. She was paid a thousand dollars a year, the same as every other deputy. Although Constance hadn't attended the meeting, she'd heard plenty about it since then. Suddenly everyone in town had an opinion about her wages.

"Go ahead," Constance said, miserably.

"She's quoting me. At least it resembles what I actually said."

"This office is a business office, conducted on business principles. We needed a matron to look after the women prisoners, to take the insane to Morris Plains, and for other duties. There are many cases in which a woman can succeed in trapping a criminal where a man can't. It is therefore a part of the business efficiency of the office to have a woman under sheriff, and I offered the position to Miss Kopp because of the splendid work she has accomplished in that line."

"I don't suppose my splendid work persuades the Freeholders," said Constance.

"Nothing ever does, but don't bother yourself over it. I hear more complaints every day about the girl troubles in this county. I can't do a thing about it unless I have a lady deputy."

Constance saw her opportunity at last. "Which is why we need to talk about the girl who came in this morning. You were right. She doesn't belong in jail. But what am I to do about it?"

Constance knew exactly what she was going to do, but thought it best to give the sheriff a chance to suggest it first.

"Most of these constables are volunteers. They get almost no training in the law," Sheriff Heath said. "It isn't just the girls. They'll arrest a man simply because he speaks no English and looks suspicious."

"What do you do about that?"

"Oh, I turn them loose. I'm not putting a man in jail just because he's Polish."

Turn them loose? Constance was shocked by how casually he said it. It had never occurred to her that she could simply walk a girl outside and set her free after an officer brought her in. In fact, she was entirely certain that she could not. This was obviously a privilege reserved only for the sheriff.

"Then what about my girls? Some of them are arrested just because they happen to be female and look suspicious."

Sheriff Heath leaned back in his chair, his arms crossed, in the posture of a professor considering a question of philosophy. "How can you be sure there's no cause?"

She didn't bother to point out that he had no way of knowing for certain what the suspicious-looking Pole had been up to, either. Instead she said, "I know you don't like to go against the police officers, but what if I went around and did a bit of investigating to see if there's any merit to the charges? So many of these cases should be dismissed without ever going to trial, but there's no one in a position to say so. Wouldn't it save an awful lot of time and trouble if some of these girls could simply be released under my supervision?"

The steam-pipe shuddered in the corner and the sheriff leaned over to knock it, a useless procedure that nonetheless allowed him to feel that he had the upper hand. "They're doing something like that in California. A girls' delinquency court."

"There's no need to be as formal as all that," she hastened to say, knowing that a new court would take years to bring about. "Just give me a chance to look into the charges and go before the judge. Wouldn't they like to save the taxpayers the expense of locking a girl away in a state home?"

"They might. But the prosecutor won't like anyone meddling in his morality cases."

"The prosecutor doesn't like anything I do. But if he insists on putting innocent girls behind bars, I might have to call a reporter I know." Constance's feud with the prosecutor's office went back more than a year, when Detective John Courter failed to do anything about a man who was harassing her family. She went to the papers and shamed him publicly over it. They'd done little but hiss and spit at each other since.

"Let's try to stay out of the papers for a week or two," Sheriff Heath said. "But go on up to Pompton Lakes and see what you can do about that girl. Morris can drive you."

4

It was an inconvenience to Constance that she didn't know how to run a motor car, but having grown up in an era of slow-moving carriages and horse-drawn trolleys, she didn't believe herself to be suited to it. Very few roads were adapted to the needs of machines and, as a result, they'd become so rutted and pitted that they tended to fill with water in the summer and snow in the winter, turning common by-ways into creeks and gullies. The drivers of automobiles were forever having to go round up a few strong men and a horse to disentomb their machines from the mud. And the autos required constant attention: it was not at all unusual for the sheriff himself to have to stop his wagon and tend to a pulley, a crank-shaft, or some other errant bit of metal and rubber.

As she preferred not to be made a fool of by an unruly machine, she left the driving to the other deputies and made do with trolleys, trains, and the sheriff's wagon when someone else was driving it, as was the case that afternoon, when Deputy Morris was at the wheel.

He was, at that moment, Hackensack's longest-serving deputy. He'd been at his post well before Sheriff Heath was elected sheriff deputy and had served a distinguished line of sheriffs of both political parties over the years. Morris was one of the deputies who'd been stationed to guard the Kopp sisters' house when they were being harassed by a wealthy factory owner. He'd become a friend of the family as well as a trusted colleague.

"It wasn't much of a town before the powder works opened," Morris said as they rolled past the train depot in Pompton Lakes. "Now they've got rooming houses and a new school, and a carnival in the summer. Lots of girls working here."

It did have the look of a formerly shabby town that had been spruced up: the roads had gone from dirt to macadam, electric lighting-wires were strung along the main street, and the druggist advertised fine soap and toilet articles.

"I wouldn't think they'd hire so many girls to make gunpowder," Constance said.

"They put them on the fuse line," he said. "It's textile work, really. No different from the mills."

They stopped first at Edna Heustis's boarding-house, which was neat and freshly painted and bore a hand-lettered sign advertising no vacancies. The landlady who answered their ring was exactly the sort of character Constance expected: a stout, gray-haired woman who wore a striped house dress and answered the door with a rag duster in hand.

"Which one are you after?" she asked wearily, when she saw their uniforms.

Constance started to explain their business, but the landlady interrupted. "Edna Heustis does fine. She pays her rent on time and she don't cause no trouble. I keep a curfew and I turn a girl out if she comes in late even once. I won't have it. But Edna never goes out in the evenings. I keep an electrical lamp in the sitting room and she's down here almost every night with some old book. Go and find a bank robber to arrest, that's what I told the policeman. There's no trouble with my girls."

It seemed to Constance as though she'd delivered that lecture before. "Thank you, Mrs. —"

"Or you can come inside and help with

the dusting, if you intend to be here all day. It's Turnbull."

"We don't intend to be here all day, Mrs. Turnbull," Constance said quickly. "If I may just take a peek into her room, I'll file my report and we'll have Miss Heustis back to you right away."

She sighed and waved her duster at Deputy Morris. "He stays outside. No gentlemen. Rules of the house."

"Yes, ma'am," Deputy Morris said, and sank down on a wooden bench on the porch with evident relief. It was colder in Pompton Lakes than it had been back in Hackensack, but he seemed to prefer the weather to another scolding from Mrs. Turnbull.

She handed Constance a passkey and sent her up the carpeted stairs to Edna's room, which was one of four on the second floor. Constance inspected everything closely, but saw only the trappings of an ordinary, well-run boarding-house: a handwritten bathing schedule posted on the bathroom door (Edna had Monday, Wednesday, and Saturday nights), a coat-rack with an oval mirror, and a mop hanging out of an open window at the end of the hall to dry.

Edna occupied a tiny room under the eaves. Constance found it to be neatly kept and entirely unremarkable. She felt under the girl's pillow, reached into the pockets of the dress hanging on a peg, and paged through the books on the shelf. Seeing nothing of a suspicious nature, she went downstairs and thanked Mrs. Turnbull.

"I'll hold the room until the end of the week," the landlady said.

"Please do."

Deputy Morris's chin had dropped into his collar. Constance closed the door a bit too loudly and he jumped.

"This arrest was nonsense. We'll stop at the factory, and then Edna Heustis is going home," Constance said.

"And I can go home," Morris said. "Sheriff's had me on guard duty three nights in a row. We have a weeper on the third floor. Kept all of us awake."

"He'll settle down." It was well known to all the deputies that only the men sobbed loudly enough to be heard all over the jail. Women inmates tended to be practiced in the art of crying themselves silently to sleep. But a man on his first night behind bars, overcome by shame and remorse, was guaranteed to keep everyone awake.

They arrived at the powder works plant in the middle of the afternoon shift. The factory itself was surrounded by several long brick buildings, each one newer and larger than the last. One was under construction at that very moment, and men were running back and forth with wheelbarrows full of cement and lumber. Smoke stacks discharged black billows into the sky. From every building came the rattle and clank of machinery. There were hundreds of workers in their broadcloth uniforms, running pushcarts along tracks from one building to the next. It was like a miniature city, entirely devoted to the manufacture of ammunition for the war.

Constance found Mrs. Schaefer, the girls' superintendent, in a low-slung office building on the other side of the dining hall. She was a tall, wiry woman of about fifty, with a beaky nose and a thin mouth that was naturally inclined to turn down. She nodded briskly when she saw Constance and seemed to guess at the purpose of her visit. "Edna Heustis? She's a good worker, but we can't have our girls getting hauled away by the police."

"I wasn't sure if you knew," Constance said. "She asked the officer to be allowed to send a note, but there wasn't time."

"Oh, I knew. The girls in the fuse room were gossiping about it all day. What's she done?"

"Nothing, as far as I can tell. I believe it

to have been a simple misunderstanding with her mother. The police never should have been involved. I intend to speak to the judge myself. Please just hold a place for her. She seems to me to be of good character and a hard worker."

"She is," Mrs. Schaefer said, "but the machines don't run themselves and her place is sitting empty."

"She'll be back," Constance promised, and very much hoped that she was right.

5

"Pretty, Vivacious, & Versatile" read the bills posted all over Paterson. "May Ward and Her Eight Dresden Dolls — The Most Elaborate Girl Act in Vaudeville, Employing Beautiful Costumes and Special Scenery — Open Auditions February 15. Public Invited."

Fleurette pasted a copy of the hand-bill on the front door so that Constance wouldn't miss it when she walked in. She believed it would bolster her cause to create a sense of occasion, and for that reason had chosen a blue nautical dress with a clever sailor's collar that she hoped would inspire in Constance the idea of a voyage — one that neither Constance nor her other sister, Norma, would be invited to join.

The possibility that an actress of May Ward's caliber would come to Paterson personally to hold auditions was so precisely the sort of thing Fleurette dreamed of that she could not, at first, believe that it had actually happened. The news had been delivered by Mrs. Ward's husband and stage manager, Freeman Bernstein, who presented himself at her dancing class the previous Wednesday to make the announcement.

"Girls, I bet you've always wanted to go on the stage!" he called out, smacking his hands together as he took long strides across the dance studio. "Will your mothers agree to it? If you're under eighteen, we'll have to have their permission. Mrs. Ward intends to give every last one of you her most thoughtful consideration, and we don't want her to waste her efforts on girls whose mothers aren't prepared to say their good-byes the very next week."

The very next week! Fleurette suddenly considered her age — a few months past her eighteenth birthday — to be a sort of golden ticket that would win her admittance to a realm that she'd only ever inhabited in her feverish imagination: one centered around the theater, carpeted hotel rooms, high-ceilinged restaurants, rumbling black automobiles, and fancy shops, all so far away from the New Jersey countryside that the lowing of the dairy cows and the stench of the chicken coop would never again find her.

If permission had been required, Fleurette would've had no alternative but to forge a signature and hope for the best, a scheme already underway for more than half of her class-mates. It had taken a good deal of wheedling and pleading to simply persuade her (staid, antediluvian) sisters to allow her to attend Mrs. Hansen's Academy in the first place, and another delicate negotiation, a few months later, to win the freedom to take employment as the school seamstress, thus allowing her to earn her own tuition and buy the odd bit of ribbon and silk. That much her sisters could tolerate. But leaving home to join a vaudeville troupe was, as Norma would have said, not at all on the Kopp family program.

It was fortunate, then, that Fleurette didn't need their permission. She required only their money, and this was much simpler to come by, as Constance was the one who earned it, and was favorably disposed toward slipping it to her if she presented her case properly. There was a small fee to enter the audition, and, once that was secured, something extra for the expense of costumes and stage decorations. She knew better than to ask for all of it at once. Today her ambition was fixed, modestly and singularly, on the price of admission.

Thus the hand-bill posted to the door, and the pretty blue dress, and the apple jumbles timed to come out of the oven as soon as Constance walked in. Her plan went off perfectly: she was in the kitchen letting fly a dusting of cinnamon sugar across the top just as the front door opened and her sister called hello.

Constance was still standing in the doorway, reading the notice, when Fleurette skittered across the room and helped her off with her coat.

"Can't you just see me as a Dresden Doll?" She put an arm around Constance's waist as she said it, and looked up at her with an expression that she hoped Constance found beguiling.

"I generally try not to," Constance said quite truthfully, "and I've never heard of a Broadway actress coming all the way to Paterson to hold auditions. Has New York run out of singers and dancers?"

Norma — who had until that moment been ignoring Fleurette's preparations for Constance's arrival by pretending to be fixed on the household ledger-book (which she had recently seized control of, after Constance neglected it too long) — came up behind them and supplied the answer before Fleurette could.

"It's not a legitimate audition. It's a con, and Fleurette would've been lured right in. May Ward proposes to charge these girls five dollars apiece for the privilege of standing on the stage and singing a song in her presence. In return, none of them are chosen and all they take home is an autographed picture that can't cost more than fifty cents to print. The public is invited, just as the bill says, as long as they buy tickets, which the bill fails to mention. It's a way to make money in the theater without actually going up on stage and doing anything. Close that door before the fire goes out."

There was a rather frigid northeastern wind blowing into the foyer, bringing with it a few spiny burrs from the sweet gum tree that overhung the barn. Constance shut the door against the onslaught and unpinned her hat. Fleurette tried to take it from her. "Let me do something with this old thing," she said. "I could at least have it blocked and put on a new ribbon."

"Don't." Constance liked her hat exactly the way it was and always resisted Fleurette's efforts to improve it. She hung it on the very top of the hat-rack, where

Fleurette couldn't reach it. "I've never heard of having to pay a fee to audition. Does Mrs. Hansen know about this?"

"Of course she does," Fleurette said. "May Ward's husband came to class himself to invite us. He's her manager."

"I should've known there was a Mr. Ward behind this," Norma said.

"His name is Freeman Bernstein," Fleurette said, sounding terribly modern. "He and Mrs. Ward live right here in Bergen County, down in Leonia near the moving picture studios."

"Freeman Bernstein." Norma said the name as if she was auditioning it. "He sounds like one of those Broadway theater hucksters. When he's not running this scheme for his wife, he's probably down at the Grand Central Station selling tickets to Central Park to the out-of-towners. Mrs. Hansen ought not to have let him through the door. I'll write her a note and tell her so."

"She doesn't read your notes," Fleurette said.

Constance, already weary of this talk, sank onto the creaking old divan, whose stuffing had long ago surrendered to her form. Norma took up her spot in a leather armchair to which the years had similarly not been kind. Fleurette rushed into the kitchen and returned with the apple jumbles and a pot of tea that she'd been keeping warm on the stove.

Constance was being worked over, and she knew it. The truth — the hushed-up, never-mentioned truth — was that in Fleurette she had not a pretty and spoiled younger sister, but a pretty and spoiled daughter, the result of a long-ago liaison with a salesman. By unanimous family concurrence, Fleurette would never be told. As far as anyone knew, she hadn't ever suspected. The three of them lived together easily enough as sisters despite the difference in their ages. As often happened in such families, Constance and Norma had settled — sometimes awkwardly — into the roles of older sisters rather than mother and aunt, and had grown practiced at playing them.

"Did you arrest anyone today?" Fleurette asked kindly, while she poured the tea.

"No, but I tried to set a girl free," Constance said. "All she wanted was to go to work, but her mother filed a charge of waywardness and the police took her to jail. Can you imagine that?"

Fleurette shook her head. She wore her hair in dark, loose curls that floated around when she moved. "Do you suppose that if our mother were alive, she would report me to the police for going to work?"

Constance reached over to smooth a lock of hair away from Fleurette's forehead and said, "I doubt it, but only because she was terrified of the police. But she would've found some other way to put a stop to it. She always did."

"Now you're the police, and you're the one to tell mothers that their daughters have a right to go to work," Fleurette said happily. She thought it extraordinarily supportive of her cause to have such a statement spoken aloud and agreed to before the audition.

"I know what else Mother wouldn't have approved of," Norma said, returning to the subject of the audition.

"Mr. Bernstein apologized for the fee," Fleurette said. Constance couldn't help but notice that she'd dressed herself up in the most charming manner, and worn a little cameo of the deceased Mrs. Kopp's that looked endearing on her. "He wishes he didn't have to charge it at all, only the expenses involved in renting the theater and arranging for the lights and accompanists are just too high. And we must perform in front of a full house in order for him to see how we'll really do. He was very kind about it, and humble."

"So he's a trained actor, too," Norma put in.

"Helen's father doesn't seem to mind," Fleurette said. She was speaking directly to Constance, knowing her to be the easy mark. She picked up her collection of sheet music and sat nestled alongside Constance, paging through all the songs May Ward had made popular. "My Little Red Carnation" and "The Bird on Nellie's Hat" were all too well known in the Kopp household, as Fleurette sang them incessantly.

May Ward's picture adorned the covers. Constance thought that she must have been an English girl, or perhaps Irish. She wore her frizzy, dusty-colored hair down around her shoulders in a style that Constance regarded as unbecoming, but what did she know about the theater, or hairstyles?

There were other pictures of May Ward tacked to the wall of Fleurette's sewing room, alongside her other idols. This was a woman Fleurette had admired for years. She and her troupe traveled all over the country performing what was referred to as "polite vaudeville," which was meant to suggest a light comedic performance that any respectable person might attend without fear of embarrassment. What harm, Constance reasoned, could come from letting Fleurette sing a song for her?

At that moment, neither Norma nor Constance felt any alarm over the possibility that Fleurette might actually be chosen to join a vaudeville troupe. The two elder sisters were in perfect, unspoken agreement that the auditions were a sham. The only difference between the two of them was that Norma wanted nothing to do with it and was particularly reluctant to part with the five dollars, whereas Constance didn't see a reason to deny Fleurette that which she had fixed her heart upon.

"Are you sure Helen's going?" Constance asked.

Norma tried to kick Constance, but she was just too far away. Instead she said, "I only wish you weren't quite so predictable."

"Of course Helen's auditioning," Fleurette hastened to answer, "and so are all the other girls in my class."

There! Constance took that as further evidence that these so-called auditions were harmless. Not a single mother had objected, so why should they?

Fleurette pressed on. "I'm the only one in my class who hasn't paid the fee."

"You're the only one who hasn't any money," Norma said.

Fleurette rolled her pretty, pleading eyes over to Constance but didn't say a word. She didn't have to.

6

That night Edna Heustis found herself under the care of the night guard, who didn't offer anything in the way of care but did walk past her cell four times before dawn, rattling his keys to announce himself in case any of the female inmates happened to be in a state of immodesty. On his first time through he told her that he'd be by every two hours. Edna took some comfort in that, as it helped to mark the passage of time. She did not sleep, but when he passed she pretended to. He only stopped long enough to make out her shape on the bunk, and then moved on.

The cell in which she found herself was even smaller than her room at Mrs. Turnbull's, with a concrete floor and white steel bars that looked out onto nothing but the wall opposite. What passed for a bed was merely canvas webbing stretched across a frame, and in the corner sat a toilet, uncovered and lacking any sort of curtain for privacy. Deputy Kopp had lent her a few things from her own cell, which she took to be a privilege not ordinarily accorded to inmates: an old flannel quilt, an embroidered pillow, a magazine, and a comb.

"How can you bear to spend the night here?" Edna had asked, before the deputy left for Pompton Lakes.

"I don't mind at all." Constance sounded terribly forthright and self-possessed. "I live in the countryside and it's too far to go every night. Besides, I want all the inmates to know that I'm just like them, and that they can trust me."

"But . . . you mustn't be just like . . . all of them," Edna said, dropping her voice to a whisper. "Aren't some of them thieves, or murderers?"

Constance smiled at that. "They are. But I try to think about the circumstances that brought them here. One of our inmates put a gun on her husband after he gave her reason to fear for her life. I won't say that excuses it, but doesn't it say something that she feels safer in here than back in her own home? She didn't even try to put up a defense."

Edna found this line of talk fascinating, as she had never met a murderess, and wondered if she would be allowed to. She tried to think of her night in jail as a sort of social experiment that might prove enriching in some way. But after Deputy Kopp left, she saw no one but the night guard, and had only the noise of the jail for company: unseen voices, coughs, grunts, the clanging of metal bars opening and closing, the sweep of footsteps, and the clattering of steam-pipes.

In the darkness her courage deserted her, and she sank into the very despair that a jail cell is designed to instill in its inhabitant. Her liberty had meant nothing to her until it was taken away. The ability to wander down to the kitchen in the middle of the night, or to open a window, or rummage through a closet for another blanket — these were the smallest of privileges, but to have them taken away was an enormous loss. The confines of her cell pressed in on her and she feared she might choke. She was obliged to sit up and force herself to breathe. At that moment an oddly comforting thought occurred to her: *It's worse at the front.*

Edna had come to rely on this idea any-time her work on the fuse line started to seem too oppressive. It was tedious to stand for long hours on a hard wooden floor, elbow to elbow with the other girls, the machines all humming and clattering, the spools of thread spinning on the rack above her head. It was impossibly dusty work owing to the fibers that flew about, but there was no time to stop and dab at one's eyes or nose, as a single dropped thread could throw the machine out of joint and she'd have to unravel and start again. There was nothing to do but to let one's eyes and nose drip. Sometimes she'd look up at the girl across, and see that they were both crying for no reason other than the lack of a free arm with which to wield a handkerchief, and they would both start to laugh at once, which only made the tears worse.

On her first day at the powder works, she asked the girl sitting next to her how one stopped the machine to go to the lavatory. She didn't know it at the time, but in asking the question, she'd entered into a rite of initiation that every new hire suffered.

"Oh, just ask Mrs. Schaefer," the girl said, never once looking up from her work.

Edna waited until the superintendent passed by, and turned briefly to make the inquiry. In the second she looked away, her foot pedal slowed and the fine fuse she'd been weaving collapsed into a tangled mess.

The other girls knew better than to laugh under the watchful eye of their supervisor.

Edna asked her question and was pointed sternly in the direction of the privies. The need to go left her suddenly, but there was nothing to do but to run out, red-faced, already terrified that she'd broken some unspoken rule and lost her place, and would have no choice but to return home that night, defeated after only one day at work.

When she found the women's privies, she understood the trick that had been played on her. The toilets were nothing but boards with holes them in, placed atop a trench, all housed in a slapdash wooden shack through which flies buzzed in and out. There was no paper — she was meant to bring her own, but how could she have known that? — and no one inside except two arthritic old women who, Edna would later learn, stole into the bathroom at intervals throughout the day and perched on the edge of the wooden boards to get some relief for their aching feet.

A woman of advanced years might be excused for taking a lavatory break in the middle of her shift, but Edna would never take one again. None of the girls used the factory toilets if they could help it. The rush to get out the gate at six o'clock, she soon learned, was a rush home to use a clean facility. The men knew it and liked to congregate around the gate, walking slowly with their arms locked, to impede them on their way home. (The men, apparently, had no qualms about their facilities and found them suited to their needs.)

By the time Edna returned to the boarding-house that night, the other girls knew all about what had happened and commiserated with her over dinner.

"You had to find out for yourself," Delia said. "You wouldn't have believed it otherwise."

"If you're nice to Mrs. Schaefer, she'll take you to the one in the office building. But only if you're sick," Pearl added.

"At least it isn't a trench," Fannie said.

"A trench? Why, there's a trench underneath! I saw it," Edna said.

Delia laughed. "No, silly, she means a trench in France. Where the soldiers live. Their living quarters are nothing but a muddy old dugout in the ground. Think about that when you finish off your fuses. They'll be sent to some boy in France who hasn't seen anything as nice as a factory privy in months."

That proved to be a useful thought to Edna, and a heartening one. Whatever discomforts she might endure, they couldn't compare to the hardships of a trench in the

Argonne. The idea stayed with her, as she grew more accustomed to the tedium of a factory job, the long hours on her feet, her red and swollen fingers, and the dull ache behind her eyes from staring at those spinning threads all day. Her brothers were eager to go overseas and endure far worse. Surely she could bear it for their sake.

And while there was nothing patriotic about a night in the county jail, she could bear that, too, if she thought of the boys in France. Still, she couldn't comfort herself enough to ever once close her eyes. All night long she stared through the bars. She kept Deputy Kopp's comb pressed tightly into her fist until morning.

7

"We never used to see young ladies on trial," Judge Seufert told Constance when she brought Edna into his chambers the next day. "It's unseemly."

The judge was a man of advanced age with a ridge of bluish veins across his forehead and hands that trembled when he shuffled through the papers on his desk. He sat rigidly upright, in a trim striped suit and a crisp bow tie, and looked down kindly on Edna from his high desk.

"She looks respectable enough to me," he pronounced, squinting down at her from underneath the rims of his spectacles.

Constance found this enormously promising. Judge Seufert tended to be friendly toward the sheriff's office, and moved by the sight of a girl in distress.

The prosecutor's office was represented by the very same Detective John Courter with whom Sheriff Heath and Constance had feuded in the past. He was a stout man with a head that, when uncovered, most closely resembled a duck's egg. His mustache formed an upside-down V that gave him the appearance of a perpetual frown. He kept his chin high, as if to lower one's chin was the first step into moral turpitude. There was a self-righteousness about him that irked Constance, particularly when he took on these morality cases.

In a chair next to Mr. Courter sat Mrs. Monvilla Heustis, Edna's mother. Constance wanted very much to be angry with her over the trouble she'd caused, but her irritation dissipated at the sight of a tired-looking woman of about fifty, with a pinched mouth and dull hair fading from watery brown to gray. She wore a wool coat whose cuffs had been replaced recently, and a pair of high leather shoes unsuited for walking in the snow.

Here is a woman who does not have much, thought Constance, and now she doesn't have her daughter. Mrs. Heustis's downcast appearance stabbed at Constance, bringing to mind the way her own mother had once clung so fretfully to her, contriving to push the world away and keep her stiflingly close by denying her an education, a profession, and friends, even. Mrs. Heustis had done much the same thing — only she had involved the police, and brought humiliation and the possibility of a criminal record down on her daughter.

As Constance and Edna took their chairs, Mrs. Heustis sat stoically and kept her eyes on Judge Seufert, refusing to even greet her daughter. He looked up at them with great animation, but then gave a little sigh when he saw Mrs. Heustis's grim eyes fixed upon him.

"Very well. I suppose the prosecution has something to say."

Detective Courter stood and put one hand inside his vest pocket. "Mrs. Heustis filed a charge of waywardness with this office on January 4, 1916. I alerted every police department in five counties, and yesterday the girl was found living in a furnished room and arrested. We ask that she be sentenced to the state reformatory until she's twenty-one, upon which time she may be released to her mother's care."

Edna nearly jumped out of her chair. Constance reached out to put a hand on her arm.

Judge Seufert looked down at Mrs. Heustis. "I'd like to hear from the mother. Ma'am, what led you to go to the police?"

Mrs. Heustis rose to her feet and answered

in a wavering voice unaccustomed to speaking in public.

"She went off without a word and without the permission of her mother and father. We just knew she must've gone bad. I was afraid she'd turn up in a furnished room somewhere, and now she has." She dabbed at her nose with a handkerchief and sat down.

"Has Miss Heustis anything to say on the matter?"

"Your Honor, I don't see —" interjected Detective Courter, but the judged raised a hand to silence him.

Constance had seen to it that Edna's dress was pressed and clean, and gave her some time with her comb and mirror to fix her hair. She was as simple and honest-looking a girl as had ever appeared before the judge. She took a little breath and said, "Only that I've found a steady place at the powder works and a room in a good Christian house. Miss Kopp says it's my right to do so and I needn't stay at home just because my mother wants to keep me there."

Judge Seufert raised an eyebrow at that. "I've been made to understand that Deputy Kopp undertook her own investigation."

Detective Courter slapped a stack of papers on the table. "Your Honor, it's irregular to have anyone from the sheriff's department investigate a police matter. The sheriff may hire a jail matron if he wishes, but she hasn't any involvement in this case other than as a jailer. She has no education in the law and no authority to conduct an investigation, if it can even be called that."

"I know more about Miss Heustis than the officer who arrested her," Constance shot back. The detective snorted.

Judge Seufert sighed and said, "I believe the sheriff hired a matron — excuse me, a lady deputy — precisely because these cases come before us and no one seems to know what to make of them. Is it the wish of the prosecutor's office that perfectly respectable girls be locked away at the public's expense for years at a time?"

"No, sir. But in this case, we have the mother —"

"Yes, and who looks into the mother's claims to decide if there's anything to them?"

Detective Courter looked as though he'd swallowed a chicken bone. He coughed and said, "Anyone charged by this office may engage an attorney for his defense."

"An attorney? Miss Heustis, how much do they pay you at the powder works?"

Edna was so alarmed that she could hardly speak. "Seven dollars a week, sir," she croaked.

"Seven dollars. And what do you pay for that furnished room?"

"Five dollars a week, sir."

Judge Seufert seemed taken aback by that. "Five! Does it include board?"

"Yes, sir."

He sat back in his high-caned chair. "Well. When I was a law clerk, I paid sixty cents a week for room and board, but never mind about that. Detective, how do you expect this girl to engage an attorney? No, don't answer. I'd like to hear from Deputy Kopp."

Constance was indignant on all fronts by this time, and spoke assuredly. "Your Honor, I visited the powder works yesterday, which, to my knowledge, Detective Courter did not. They tell me that Miss Heustis is a fine worker and they'd like to have her back. The boarding-house, to which Detective Courter has likewise not paid a visit, is clean and well-run. The landlady only rents to DuPont girls who come recommended."

He nodded. "That's fine . . ."

But she wasn't finished. "I am fully convinced," she continued, aiming her remarks at Mrs. Heustis, who kept her eyes cast down to her lap, "that the girl is high-minded and of good character and that her only desire in leaving home was to go to work and earn her own living. Detective Courter would agree with me if he'd only bothered to go to Pompton Lakes and see for himself, before throwing a girl's future away."

The detective jumped to his feet. "I won't listen to this girl instruct me —"

"That's enough, John," the judge said.

Constance pushed on. "Furthermore, it was selfish of her mother to want her back. She bore a good reputation in Pompton Lakes, and as for her being wayward, I can't believe it's true."

"It wasn't selfish!" Mrs. Heustis cried. "She's gone off on her own and left me by myself all day while her father is at his office. I haven't anyone to help with the washing and cooking, and nothing but an old beagle for company. What am I to do?"

Judge Seufert dropped his chin into his hand, but not before giving Constance a glance to let her know that he hadn't missed the intention of her scheme. She wanted Detective Courter to reckon with the fact that he was putting innocent girls in jail. More importantly, though, she wanted Edna to hear, in front of all of them, that her mother might miss her daughter's company, but she didn't really believe Edna to be morally corrupt. No girl, Constance believed, should have to bear the burden of a mother's shame just for leaving home.

"Mrs. Heustis," the judge said, "is it your idea that a housewife should call the police when she gets lonely or tired of her work?"

"No, sir." Mrs. Heustis kept her eyes down.

"And did you honestly believe that this girl's character was of such a low standard, after all your years of raising her, that she'd get herself into some trouble the minute she left home?"

Mrs. Heustis looked briefly at her daughter and shook her head.

"Then would it be all right with you if we allowed Miss Heustis to return to her position, and for us to return to ours? I believe there are still criminals to be caught and put to trial, and Deputy Kopp and I would like to proceed with that business. I don't know what the prosecutor's office might get up to next, but I suppose I'll find out."

Mrs. Heustis nodded mutely and the judge dismissed the charges, but not before asking Constance to look in on Edna once or twice to be sure she wasn't causing any trouble.

Detective Courter could hardly contain his indignation. "Am I to understand that the lady will be serving as a probation officer?"

Judge Seufert sighed and gave the detective the weary smile of a man who had seen every kind of subordination in his courtroom. "Yes, I suppose it will be something along those lines. Does that meet with your approval?"

Mr. Courter tapped his papers on the desk officiously and said, "The prosecutor's office will expect a copy of her reports weekly."

The judge rose and waved them all away. "Go back to your office, John. You'll get your reports when she writes them. Deputy, please take this girl back to Pompton Lakes before she loses her place."

Constance thanked the judge and rushed Edna and her mother out of the room before Detective Courter could say another word. They went outside and down the courthouse steps, where they were set upon by a small platoon of reporters who'd been lounging there, smoking cigarettes and slapping their notebooks against their legs, idly watching both the courthouse and the jail next door for any sign of an arrest, an arraignment, or any other small scandal they might write up in time for the morning edition.

Every last man jumped to attention when

he saw the three of them. The reporters liked nothing better than to put Constance's name in a headline, especially in connection with a girl in trouble. It gave her a great deal of pleasure to announce that they'd have to look elsewhere to fill tomorrow's papers.

"Just a mother who misplaced her daughter's new address," she told them, giving Edna's elbow a squeeze. "You couldn't even get a paragraph out of it." That was enough to make them wander off.

Constance was of the opinion that Edna was owed an automobile ride back to Pompton Lakes by the Paterson policeman who'd brought her there, and said so, but Edna insisted on taking the train. "I'd rather not be seen again with the police, miss," she said.

Constance let her go, but not before extracting a promise that she'd visit her mother of a Sunday now and then. Edna allowed her mother to clutch her briefly and awkwardly, then she ran off to the station. Her coat flapped behind her, and the weak winter sunlight cast a little amber into her hair. Constance saw something fine and determined in the girl, and was glad to see her go free.

Her mother watched her go, too. The lines

in her face fell into hardened resignation.

"Mrs. Heustis," Constance said, after Edna rounded the corner out of sight, "you know you must call on us if you ever believe the law's been broken. But your girl's done nothing wrong. Does her father even know you reported her?"

She shook her head and looked away. "He encouraged her. She's our only girl, and he told her how to go off and find work just like her brothers did."

"There's nothing wrong with that," Constance said.

"They all want to do something for the war."

At last Constance had come to the heart of it. Her boys were eager to go to France, and now she was losing her daughter, too. She opened her mouth to answer and just then heard Sheriff Heath calling for her from the side entrance to the jail.

"We all want to do our part," she said quickly. "But she hasn't gone far. You could go up and pay her a visit, too, you know. Bring her a little something from home."

Mrs. Heustis didn't look satisfied with that, but she nodded and turned toward the train station. As she left, Constance couldn't help but wonder if she'd treated her too harshly. Her daughter was leaving her behind. It would happen to Constance, too, someday. But she'd be more dignified about it.

Wouldn't she?

8

There was a kind of buoyancy about Sheriff Heath as he strode across the frozen lawn to meet Constance, but she couldn't guess as to its cause. He saw the reporters watching from the courthouse steps and slowed to a walk. When they met, he nodded at the departing figure of Monvilla Heustis.

"Well, Deputy? Did things go your way this morning?"

"Of course they did. It was nothing but a mother who didn't want her daughter thinking for herself."

"That's not a matter for the law."

"Judge Seufert agreed, so we sent them both home." Constance was surprised that her scheme had worked as well as it did. It had been almost too easy to get Edna released. Was this really all it took?

"Well, it's a fine way for one of my deputies to spend the morning," the sheriff said, "but it's better than keeping a young lady in jail who has no cause to be there. I don't suppose the prosecutor's office had anything good to say about it."

"No, but I saved us all needless work. They should give me a medal."

Sheriff Heath was just standing there, looking at her oddly.

"What is it?"

He rummaged around in his coat pocket and pulled out something folded in brown paper. "This came for you."

There was no mark on the package. She took it from him and turned it over. "What do you mean, it came for me? What is it?" After all the strange letters she'd received, she was suspicious of packages.

He shrugged and cast his eyes up and over to the spire atop the courthouse dome. "Don't open it if you don't want it."

That's when she felt the metal point under the paper.

"It couldn't be." She unwrapped it and let it drop into her hand.

There it was. She had her badge at last.

The sheriff didn't go in for eagles or stars. All of his men wore a plain shield with the words "Bergen Co." engraved along the top, and "Sheriff's Deputy" at the bottom. In the center was the county seal, which was impossible to make out at such a small size but consisted of an Indian and a Pilgrim shaking hands under the talons of an eagle in flight. It was heavier than Constance thought it would be, and strangely warm, from having been in the sheriff's pocket.

Hers wasn't silver like the others. "This isn't gold, is it?" she said, catching his eye for the first time since he'd handed it to her. It occurred to her that he must have come straight from the jeweler's. The metal shone cleanly, like it had never been touched.

The sheriff looked embarrassed over the extravagance and said, "It's only plated in gold. It'll rub off the first time you get into a scuffle."

"What will Norma say when she sees me in a gold badge?" She looked down for a place to pin it.

The sheriff fumbled with his gloves and took it from her. There is nothing more awkward than having a man pin something on a woman's coat, but occasions do call for it and she stood with her hands at her sides and let him. He slid the clasp together and lifted his head and there they were, staring evenly at each other.

"Well, Deputy Kopp," he said, clearing his throat. "I suppose —"

But he never got to finish, because the

reporters spotted them.

"Miss Kopp!" called a skinny young man, running up behind her. "Is that a badge or a corsage?"

"Have you the backing of the Freeholders on this one, Bob?" asked another, although he must have already known the answer. Sheriff Heath never had the backing of the Board of Freeholders on anything.

"What exactly are the duties of a lady deputy?" asked a third, panting as he tried to keep up with the other two without turning loose of his cigar. "Has she the authority to arrest a man? Will she go on patrol alone or will she require an escort? Have you issued her a gun and handcuffs as well?"

The sheriff shifted his hat and turned to face the men gathered in a half-circle around them. "Roger, you know that Deputy Kopp carries a police gun and handcuffs and used them to capture a dangerous fugitive only a couple of months ago," he said calmly. "She's been in all your papers, so don't pretend that you don't know about it just to get a fresh quote from me. There was some delay in having a badge engraved, owing to the metal being in short supply, but it's done now. As to her duties, Deputy Kopp has charge of the women in my jail and I will continue to deploy her as I do any man under my command."

It was just then that Constance noticed Carrie Hart stepping off a streetcar. She was wrapped in a smart green coat and wore shoes to match. From the brim of her hat stood a single black ostrich feather, which waved about in the wind like a weather-vane. She waltzed up behind the scrum of reporters just as the sheriff was dismissing them.

"Go on, boys," he said, and they wandered off morosely. "Good afternoon, Miss Hart."

"Sheriff. Deputy." She laughed. Her lips were painted a bright geranium red.

"What did you do to get sent all the way to Hackensack?" Constance asked.

She raised an eyebrow and looked back at the reporters, who had returned to their posts on the courthouse steps. "I told my editor I wanted off the club luncheon track. After three stories about a lady deputy in Hackensack, I thought I could handle the city crime pages. He said I could, as long as the city wasn't New York. I had my choice of Hackensack or Trenton."

"And you chose us."

"Of course I did! Take me up to the top of that jail and introduce me to all your dangerous dames. One of them must want to tell her story to the papers."

"Oh, they might want to, but I won't allow it," Constance said. "Do you know the kinds of letters I've had because of your stories?"

"Those girls might like a letter from a handsome stranger," Carrie said.

"And what was that about my velvety brown eyes giving the novelists a page of descriptive matter?"

She gave a shrug and a false little frown. "My editor put that in himself. He said no male reporter would've neglected the lady deputy's good looks."

Carrie glanced over at the sheriff, who had been standing by impassively with the air of a man who knew better than to come between two sharp-tongued women. Then she looked back at Constance's coat. "Say, how about that pretty little badge?"

"It's an ordinary badge," Constance said. "No different than —"

Carrie leaned in close to examine it. "Oh, it's far from ordinary! There's nothing stopping me from writing about it, is there? You're wearing it out in public, after all."

"So does every man with a badge," Constance said. "It's never made the papers before."

"We've never had a girl deputy before," Carrie said brightly. "I'm sure I can get a paragraph out of it. Watch these pages, as they say."

"You can't mean to put me in the papers again," Constance said. "I don't think I can endure another marriage proposal."

She and Sheriff Heath watched as Carrie ran to join the reporters on the courthouse steps. She looked like a bright exotic bird that had just landed among tree stumps.

"Reporters go along with the badge," the sheriff said resignedly. "You can give it back if you don't like it."

She wasn't about to give it back.

9

"Oh, you make such a handsome fellow," Fleurette said as she draped a length of striped navy serge around Helen Stewart's shoulders. "Put your hair up under the hat."

Helen laughed and did as she was told, pushing a knot of red hair beneath the brim of a battered old bowler.

Fleurette took a step back and sang out in admiration. "I'll marry you tonight!"

Helen shook off the hat. "You're supposed to refuse."

"No, *you're* supposed to refuse."

"Oh, I will, at first."

The two of them were squirreled away in Fleurette's sewing room to make their preparations for the audition. Surrounding them was an empire of luxury goods: the newest pattern-books, spools of silk ribbon, jars of buttons and hooks, an entire library of pin-books, including the kind with the pearls, both silk and muslin flowers, glittering buckles and hat-pins, dress nets, feathers, braids and trimming, and endless lengths of lace. Bolts of fabric towered nearly to the ceiling along one wall and spoke of every whim that had ever taken Fleurette's fancy: oriental patterns of peacock flowers and water lilies, lengths of purple silk embroidered with Napoleon's gold bees, dizzyingly tiny prints of miniature roses, sheer emerald-colored chiffon, polka-dotted satin, georgette and crêpe de Chine, and velvet and silk in whatever yardage and hue she could charge on the account that Constance kept for her at Schoonmaker's.

With Norma now in custody of the household ledger, it was incumbent upon Constance to hold a little back from her weekly pay and to distribute it among the various merchants around town to whom Fleurette was indebted. In addition to the dry goods and clothiers, there was a ribbon shop where they knew her by name, a shoe store that kept a supply of beaded slippers in her size alone, and a millinery that should have hung her portrait in the window, in honor of its benefactress. They could not all be paid at once, but Constance managed to put a little toward each in turn, and to save a few extra coins and bills in a tin box in her dresser (where, she mistakenly believed,

Fleurette wouldn't know about it) in case funds were needed and Norma refused to relinquish them. These extra expenses put a strain on their finances, but Constance seemed to enjoy sharing a secret with Fleurette, and Fleurette couldn't think of a reason to deny her the pleasure.

With so much finery around them, it was nothing but an adventure for Fleurette and Helen to pin together their costumes. They didn't dare rehearse the song at home for fear of being overheard — the sewing room was one of those awkward windowless chambers so often situated off the parlors of old country homes, originally intended as a fainting room, a place to lay out the dead, or some other antiquated purpose — so they were forced to run far out into the shorn and snow-covered hay meadow to sing and to choreograph their dance.

But the day had been too bleak and miserable to rehearse out-of-doors. They were far more content indoors, and found themselves making all sorts of plans for their future as two of May Ward's Dresden Dolls.

"Have there always only been eight of them?" Helen asked.

"As far as I know, but I think May Ward will want *more* Dolls when she sees us. I'll be the ninth and you can be the tenth,"

Fleurette said.

"But the other eight already have their parts. They hardly need two extra, except for the chorus."

"They'll write new parts for us." Fleurette stood and tucked another ruffle into her skirt, raising the hem halfway to her knee. She wondered idly if it was possible to rig up some kind of cord that would raise the skirt when she left home and lower it again when she returned, like the canvas blinds in a shop window.

Helen watched her from the little embroidered stool where she sat. "I don't know how you persuaded them to let you join the troupe. My father would never agree to it. I had to promise him that I was only going through the pretense of auditioning because you wanted to put on a duet."

Fleurette pushed aside a dress-maker's dummy that blocked her view of the mirror. She kept it angled a bit in its stand, which had the effect of making her appear taller.

"Oh, I haven't persuaded them, exactly," she said, and turned around to admire her backside. "I told them I'm only auditioning because you are."

Her reverie was interrupted by the rattle of an engine in the drive. She smoothed her skirts and whirled around to Helen. "Hand me that jacket," she said, waving at a pile of gray wool behind her friend's stool. "You can help me with the fitting." Helen took up the garment and they burst out of the room and into the foyer, where Constance was just hanging up her coat.

"Who brought you home?" Fleurette asked.

"Deputy Morris."

"Oh, and he's gone already?" Fleurette ran to look out the window. Deputy Morris and his wife lived in Paterson near Mrs. Hansen's Academy and had taken on the role of adopted grandparents to Helen and Fleurette. After their lessons, they could often be found at Mrs. Morris's kitchen table or at her sewing machine, making last-minute changes to costumes.

When she turned back to Constance, she spotted the badge.

"Isn't there to be a ceremony?" she cried, slipping the badge off Constance's coat and holding it up to the light. "I thought we'd all be going down to the courthouse to watch you make a vow."

"It's a bit late for that," Constance said. "I've been doing the job in some capacity or another since July. The badge is only the final formality."

"But I like formalities. We never have any

93

sort of occasion around here."

Constance hardly had a chance to reply before Fleurette snatched the jacket away from Helen and held it up with a flourish.

"And look at what we have for you to pin it on! Helen helped me with the epaulettes."

Constance took it from her gingerly and turned it around. It was a smart new Norfolk jacket, styled like a man's, but with just enough darts where it counted. There were deep pockets in the front, a wide belt, commanding epaulettes on the shoulders, and a heavy silk lining inside.

The sheriff's department had no provision for a woman's uniform. After the newspapers photographed her in a hastily assembled ensemble of borrowed clothes the previous year, Fleurette insisted on outfitting Constance with a proper uniform. The jacket was the final piece.

Constance slipped it on and immediately felt more authoritative. Fleurette had been making her clothes since she was old enough to work a sewing machine, it being nearly impossible to find anything in Constance's size from the catalogs and shops. Fleurette hadn't taken a measurement in years and seemed to know innately where to place a button or a dart so that no seam was ever stretched, no collar too tight, and no sleeve too short. Her clothing was solid and wonderfully made.

"You should always wear a jacket," Helen said, going in a circle around her and tugging at the sleeves. "You look so smart."

"I do feel smarter, and I feel about six inches taller," Constance said.

Fleurette reached up to brush a thread away from her collar. "Well. We don't need you any taller. There's a pocket inside for your revolver, and one for your handcuffs."

Constance slid her hand inside and found them stitched into the lining at exactly the spot she might naturally reach for them. "It's just perfect."

"Only I might have run up the account at Schoonmaker's," Fleurette said lightly, as she checked the buttons and clasps.

"Don't worry about it," Constance said. Before she could add another word, Norma came in from her pigeon loft and all talk of paying on accounts ceased.

Norma wore a grubby barn coat adorned here and there with gray and white feathers, a leather bill-cap with flaps on the side, and a split skirt that Fleurette had cobbled together from a pair of old tweed suits on the condition that Norma would never wear it farther than the barn.

The three of them stood staring at her.

95

Fleurette tried very hard not to laugh. Norma looked like a tramp in those old clothes, but it must be admitted that the sort of outdoor work an old farmhouse required had to be met with suitably sturdy clothing. As neither Constance nor Fleurette volunteered to do the more difficult chores, it seemed only fair that Norma should outfit herself as she pleased.

"You've had another letter," Norma said as she peeled off the most disagreeable of her outer garments.

"I wish they didn't know where we lived," Constance said.

"They don't. They write nothing on the envelope but 'Girl Sheriff, Hackensack,' and it makes its way to us."

"Do they really propose marriage?" Helen asked.

"Always," Fleurette said. "They don't know what to do with her other than to marry her." It irked Fleurette that her sister — she of the pontoon-sized feet and the figure of a telephone booth — enjoyed the romantic attentions of men she'd never met. The men who laid their hearts down in front of Constance got nothing but a curt reply from Norma, which seemed to Fleurette like a wasted opportunity.

This was why Fleurette was so eager for

her tour on the stage, and her own notices in the paper. Then the letters would come to her. She would never reject them out of hand: she would invite her suitors to audition for her affections, and she'd let them bring her gifts.

Norma went over to the writing desk and sliced open the envelope.

"Oh, you'll like this. A fellow wants you to run his ranch in Wyoming." She made a surprisingly convincing imitation of a bachelor rancher as she read his letter aloud.

Dear Miss Constance,

  I can't offer much to a lady who likes her hair washed at a parlor and gets bothered over a little dirt under her fingernails, but an energetic woman who is accustomed to hard work and quick with a rifle can make a success of herself in Wyoming. I am unmarried, as are most of the other men around this place. It is an uncommon woman who can put her shoulder to the wheel alongside one of us. Out here a rancher's wife knows how to stretch a potato and butcher a hog, and doesn't mind sleeping for a night in the barn alongside the cows when they're calving.

Strong as a horse and pretty as one, that's all I ask. If I don't suit you, there are a dozen other fellows who will. You might as well come out and have a look at us. Write to me with your answer and I will send a train ticket, but don't wait too long. There's fields to plow in March.

Expectantly,
Old Jack Dobbs

"Old Jack!" Fleurette shrieked. "Did he really write that?"

"He's been called it so long that he's forgotten it wasn't his given name," Norma said.

"We haven't seen him yet," Fleurette said. "His mother could have named him Old Jack when she first laid eyes on him."

"What do you intend to tell him?" Constance asked.

Norma looked over the letter again and pushed at the spectacles slipping off her nose. "I'll say that it pains me to admit that you look nothing like a horse, and that you do like your hair washed on Saturday, which renders you unfit for service."

"Old Jack's going to be disappointed," Fleurette said.

"Everyone in Wyoming is disappointed," Norma returned.

Constance pulled out a handkerchief and took a swipe at Fleurette's mouth. She looked like a porcelain doll, with cheeks and lips painted on.

"I hope you're not going anywhere looking like that," she said.

"Helen and I have a run-through at the theater tonight. It's for the audition."

"But I don't see why you have to put it on before you leave the house. You'll only call attention to yourself on the train."

Fleurette raised an eyebrow to let it be known that calling attention to herself on the train was precisely her aim. A horn sounded in the drive and she ran to look.

"It's only Mrs. Borus," she said, "come with some urgent business pertaining to birds flying about in the sky. You're all due at my show on Tuesday, so don't forget about it. Invite Mrs. Borus if you want, and anyone else who hasn't defected from your pigeon club."

"No one's defected," Norma called as

Fleurette went to gather her things. "We're on winter hiatus."

Norma ran a pigeon club, which she insisted upon calling the New Jersey Society for the Deployment of Messenger Pigeons to Aid in Civic Affairs. It had dwindled from a membership of a dozen or so pigeon-keepers to just a few civic-minded women eager for a worthwhile project. This wasn't seen as much of a surprise by Constance and Fleurette, after Norma installed herself as the club's entire slate of officers and ran its affairs in her ruthless and autocratic style. Not a single man remained. Norma ignored Fleurette's suggestion that perhaps they didn't like to take their orders from her, insisting instead that the men never intended to join in club activities, and had only been hoping to pick up new breeding stock with the aim of selling more birds for a higher profit. But the trade in messenger pigeons had never been brisk, and the men found other things to do.

Apparently the women who stayed around felt that they had enough to run in their own lives and didn't mind Norma taking charge. It was really the only way to get along with Norma, and wasn't too different from how Fleurette and Constance had managed all along.

Carolyn Borus was the most steadfast of the women who remained. She was a widow of some means and quite the sportswoman. Before her interest turned to pigeons, she had hunted with a pair of dogs, and she once raced a horse. She ran an auto with perfect ease, but was just as likely to show up on a saddle-horse if the weather was fine.

Norma went to greet Mrs. Borus and brought her back to the kitchen, which was the warmest room in the house in winter, thanks to an enormous old cast-iron stove. Constance followed and was relieved to find a pot of potato soup with bits of sausage submerged within it. She built a fire under the burner. Carolyn went right over to warm her hands.

"I love a country home," she said cheerfully, looking around at the old kitchen, which hadn't changed since Mrs. Kopp bought the place eighteen years ago. The floors were made of broad planks covered in a painted floor-cloth whose fleur-de-lis pattern was nearly worn away. The wall was spattered with grease for three feet around the stove, and Constance wondered, as she considered it from the perspective of a guest, why none of them had ever thought to wash it down and paint it.

"You're smart not to bother with a refrigerator," Mrs. Borus continued. "My sister just bought one of those new ammonia-cooled models, and the whole house stinks of it. No one can stand it except the bugs, who come from miles around to take up residence behind the milk bottles."

"How do the bugs get in?" Constance asked.

She dropped into a chair beside Norma and sighed. "Would you believe they insulate these refrigerators with cattle hair? The bugs adore it. They chew right through it, and the next thing you know, you reach in for the eggs and butter, and come away with a handful of beetles instead."

"I object to the idea of a motor inside the home, even without the beetles." Norma turned her attention to the neatly typed list Carolyn had set before her. "Twelve volunteers? Are you sure?"

"Oh, yes. They were all quite eager when I told them we were taking their birds on long-distance flights for the war effort."

Norma and Mrs. Borus had, of late, affiliated their pigeon society with the American Pigeon Racing Association, which had announced its plans to set new world records in speed and distance flying, in an effort to convince the War Department of the necessity of deploying pigeons overseas when the

Americans went (inevitably, as Norma regarded it) to France. They intended to help in this endeavor by sending their own pigeons on increasingly longer train trips — five hundred miles, seven hundred miles, even a thousand miles — so that they could select and breed the most competitive flyers.

"I thought this was just a demonstration," Constance said. "How does it help with the war?"

Both Norma and Carolyn looked at her pityingly.

"It's a national effort on the part of pigeon-keepers to supply the War Department with the training and equipment they will so desperately need," Carolyn said, in the manner of a woman accustomed to making a speech. "They don't yet know how badly they need pigeons, because they haven't yet seen what they can do. We aim to change that."

"That sounds just fine," Constance said quickly, not wanting to seem unfriendly to the first person she'd ever met who enjoyed Norma's company.

Norma went back to studying the list. "I have my doubts as to whether these birds have been properly conditioned."

Constance was trying to keep quiet, but

she couldn't help herself. "How do you condition a bird to fly? Isn't that what comes naturally to them?"

"Oh, not at all," Carolyn said brightly. "Your sister has the very best method for acclimating them to long flights, one that has been enthusiastically adopted by our club. It begins with a short course of flights from the east, of increasing lengths from one mile to ten. Then the same course is attempted from the west, and then the south. Then they must be taken for a flight of twenty miles, followed by a day's rest and a diet of mealworms, and then fifty miles. After their first one-hundred-mile flight, they take a week of rest, and then they are shipped to a two-hundred-mile station. It proceeds along those lines until —"

"What a fascinating program you two have put together," Constance said, rising quickly before she had to hear the rest of it. "The War Department will be delighted."

"There's nothing delightful about war, but we do our part," Carolyn said, before Constance could escape the room entirely. "Now I only wish you'd help me convince your sister to come along on the train when we take our pigeons to the five-hundred-mile mark. We're only going as far as Columbus, and I'd like to make an outing of it."

Norma hated to travel but didn't like to admit it. "Why don't you start with a conditioning program?" Constance said. "Begin by taking her ten miles east and see how she does."

"You can go on back to jail now," Norma said.

"I'm home for the night," Constance said, "but I'll take my soup in the other room and you can draw up your plans in peace."

As she left, she heard Carolyn say, "I wish I had a sister."

"I can't think why," Norma told her.

10

There was about to be another female inmate admitted to the Hackensack jail over a morality charge, but the girl in question didn't know it yet. Minnie Davis was sleeping soundly in her own bed, in the early gray hours of the morning, when the police pounded on the door.

The events of the night before came back hazily at first. Tony and Minnie had quarreled — there was nothing new in that — but she'd won a round, for once, and forced Tony to take her somewhere on a Friday night.

There was no denying that Tony and Minnie had grown tired of each other. No love was left between them, if there had ever been any. But they were forced to live under the same roof — forced by circumstances of Minnie's own making, if she wanted to admit it.

They used to go places together. Minnie

didn't see any reason why that should change, even now that things had soured between them. It was terrible to spend their evenings in a drab furnished room, under the dim light of one electrical bulb, with Tony pretending to be interested in a newspaper and Minnie making a half-hearted offer of a game of cards. Why couldn't they ride the ferry across to Manhattan and visit one of the glittering dancing palaces she'd seen from the trolley on their first night together, or dine at a high-ceilinged restaurant with yellow light pulsing from the steamy windows? But Tony never had anything like that on offer.

"You're always after me about the rent," he complained, "and then you want to spend a week's pay on Broadway. Maybe you picked the wrong fellow."

She most certainly had, but what was she to do about it? If they were stuck together in their dismal room over the bakery, wasn't he obligated to take her with him when he went out on a Friday night?

So she kept after him until he finally relented and said, "Fine. Get your coat."

Tony's idea of an evening's entertainment turned out to be a card game at a house a few blocks away. Minnie put on a polka-dotted dress anyway, and rubbed her finger

107

around an empty perfume bottle with the hope of finding something to dab behind her ears.

When they reached the house, she knew she needn't have bothered. These were the men with whom Tony worked on the steamboat in the summertime. The card game was merely a continuation of every game they'd ever played below-decks. They only looked up from their cards long enough to slap him on the back and make room for him around the table. "The girls are in the kitchen," one of them hollered, jerking his thumb down the hall.

Minnie went dispiritedly, having lost all hope of a fancy party. In the kitchen she found half a dozen women draped around the table or perched on the drain-board, all of them older than her and none of them dressed for any sort of evening out.

She never bothered to learn their names and they didn't ask hers. "You're Tony's girl!" one of them shrieked. The others gave vigorous nods of understanding. One pulled out a chair for her.

"We're having gin and lemonade," said the woman nearest the icebox, "unless you'd rather have gin *or* lemonade."

Minnie spoke boldly. "I'll take them both, and I wouldn't mind a cigarette if you can spare it."

That was the right way to answer. Both were offered to her, and soon Minnie was at her ease, leaning back in her chair with a practiced air, grateful to have both hands occupied. The drink was sweet but bracingly strong: with the first sip, she told herself to go slow, and with the second, she forgot to. Although she never smoked in front of Tony, she'd had plenty of cigarettes along the boardwalk back in Catskill and knew what to do with one. The talk flowed around her, and she didn't even have to bother over what to say.

These women, it developed, all worked at the sorts of jobs that Minnie used to dream about before she left home. They were office girls or clerks in department stores, and one took tickets at a moving picture theater, which was the very position Minnie hankered for the most. Another worked at a flower shop, and one — incredibly — poured the chocolates at a confectioner's.

"I come home covered in sugar and cocoa powder," she said, "and you can imagine what Stanley makes of that."

"Stanley!" the others shrieked. "Don't make us imagine it."

But it was too late. The picture floated before Minnie's eyes, and she wondered which of the men in the other room was Stanley. Tony might have gone in for something like that, at one time, before their troubles, but he hardly bothered with her anymore, and Minnie didn't miss it. She was tired of his rough searching hands and his lazy mouth, and the way he never looked at her or paid her a compliment when he pulled her dress up. She hated to share her small bed with him afterward, but he was paying the rent, and didn't someone have to pay it? She never had enough money, not on a factory salary. She either had to share a room with Tony, or with another girl in a boarding-house, where she would have to live under a curfew and hand over all her wages to the landlady, leaving her without a dime for herself. She chose Tony — for now, anyway.

Her glass seemed to stay full all night. The talk in the kitchen grew wilder and more wicked, even drawing the men away from their card game a few times to see what the commotion was about. Tony never appeared in the doorway. She only heard his voice once, when he called for more beer.

That voice didn't do anything to Minnie when she heard it. She wanted to ask the others if they still felt any sort of a flutter at the sound of their fellows' voices, or when they saw them again at the end of the day, but what difference would it have made if they did? There was something sick and poisoned between Tony and Minnie. She could live with it or she could go home to Catskill. She had ideas about running off, but she hadn't gone yet, and what did that say about her?

Somehow the rest of the night slid away. Without her quite realizing how it happened, the laughter had subsided and most of the girls had gone. She found herself being pulled out of her chair and grabbed around the waist.

"Can't you even walk home?" asked a voice that belonged to Tony.

She couldn't see him. She tried to turn and look, but his face was somewhere else, floating up high near the ceiling or drifting around behind her where she couldn't get a fix on it. Next they were in the ruined parlor, where the card table was turned over on its side amid a swarm of brown bottles, and then they were on the stairs, which were dark and terribly cold. The shock of it threatened to make Minnie sick. She lurched and put a hand over her mouth.

Someone was behind them on the stairs, calling down to Tony. It was a man's voice, and he was making some sort of rhyme about liquor that she couldn't follow. Tony gave an equally insensible answer, they both laughed, and then the man said the only thing capable of working its way into Minnie's befuddled mind and staying there.

"A girl in every port!" he hollered.

Tony laughed and took them out into the hard and unrelenting cold. Minnie gasped and choked on the air, and thought she might be sick right there, on the darkened street. Then she was.

Somehow she made it home, walking on her own now, following Tony's murky shape down the wooden sidewalks along Main Street. The shops were all shuttered — it was well past midnight — and there wasn't a sound, save for a bird making some lonely call from a branch overhead, and the low rumble of a train at the other end of town.

Minnie knew better than to say what she was thinking. The idea was packed in cotton anyway, buried in some part of her brain that she couldn't quite reach, but she knew it was there, she could feel the shape of it, and she knew she wouldn't forget it come morning. It was this: *You've been doing the same thing I did. You're no better than me.*

Those words were still with her in the morning, when the police came and pounded at her door. She felt around in the bed for Tony, but he was gone, and the room was flooded with light because they'd forgotten to close the curtain when they went (unspeaking, unsmiling) to bed a few hours before.

Another splintering knock, and a man shouted to open the door. Minnie was still wearing her polka-dotted dress, but it was too terrible to show to anyone. She wrapped a blanket around her and stumbled across the room, tripping over her shoes and cursing at them. The lock was temperamental and she had to rattle it a few times to open it. When she did, a blue-suited constable pushed into the room and looked around.

"What's your name?" he bellowed.

His voice knocked around inside her head. She thought she might be sick again.

"Minnie Davis."

The constable looked at his note-pad. "Davis? Says here this place is rented to a Mr. and Mrs. Anthony Leo."

11

"Who's the girl?" Constance shouted over the whipping of the wind.

They were riding in the sheriff's motor car, one of those soft-topped machines that offered very little in the way of warmth, even when the fabric was pulled overhead. Unless it was raining, the deputies didn't bother with the top and just suffered in the open air. In the back were kept two ancient raccoon coats that they all shared, along with a pile of lap rugs. Constance kept one of the rugs over her legs as Sheriff Heath drove them south toward Fort Lee.

He fumbled for a paper in his coat pocket and said, "Minnie Davis. She turned up by accident during another investigation. The police down there were following a report of shots fired in an alley. In the course of asking questions, they found a couple living in a furnished room above a bakery, posing as man and wife. The police chief ordered them arrested on a charge of illegal cohabitation. He'd like us to come and take the girl away while he works on the shooting."

"Then it's another waste of our time," Constance said. She disliked everything about an illegal cohabitation case: the woman's crushing shame, the man's blustery defense, the inevitable newspaper headlines. Nothing was ever a scandal until a third party found out about it and told a fourth party, and that's exactly what the papers liked to do.

"There might not be a case against the girl at all," Sheriff Heath said. "She's from Catskill."

The engine gave a loud report and they both jumped, but it settled back down again. They were in the countryside outside of Hackensack now, rolling past bare fields and frozen ponds still fringed in black cattails.

"What does Catskill have to do with it?" Constance asked.

The sheriff gave her the mildly tragic expression he deployed when he delivered bad news. "It means he took her from New York to New Jersey. The idea is to jail him for transporting a woman across state lines for immoral purposes. We'll only be holding her as a witness."

Constance groaned. Everyone in law enforcement had an opinion about the Mann Act, which made it a crime to do exactly what the sheriff had just described. Some were of the opinion that any man and woman who drove, took a train, rode a bicycle, or walked across a state border together must surely be acting with immoral intent and deserved the most severe (and public) prosecution. Others — and Constance counted herself among this group — believed that the Mann Act was only meant to put a stop to kidnapping and forced prostitution. Two consenting parties out to break their marriage vows — or to dodge the institution of marriage entirely — might be punished by shame and guilt, but didn't deserve to go to jail.

The sheriff was entirely familiar with Constance's views on the subject, but she nonetheless said, "Is it truly a case of white slavery, or have we merely uncovered two naïve young people pretending to be married?"

"The girl's only sixteen. Do you suppose she went of her own free will?"

Constance shuddered at that but said, "Well, she's old enough to be married."

"Then she should have. They wouldn't be on their way to jail if they were married."

"They shouldn't be on their way to jail regardless."

They stopped at a train crossing, and he turned to her with a look of exasperation that suggested he was out of his depth. There was always something askew about him: either his bow tie or the brim of his hat was usually out of kilter. He grimaced in a way that made his wide mustache lift up at one end. "This isn't another strong-willed girl off to work in a factory and her mother doesn't approve. These two were . . . living as man and wife."

He couldn't bring himself to delve further into the unspeakable act, but she understood it well enough. She also knew why the police had to do something about it. The mothers and fathers of Bergen County expected someone to go to jail when immorality was discovered, and they would hold the prosecutors to account.

"Even if that's true," Constance said, "I'm sure we can do something better for her than bring her to court on an indecency charge. Judge Seufert seems to agree with us. He calls these cases unseemly."

They sat together in discouraged silence for a minute. The idea of a sixteen-year-old girl caught in a furnished room with a man worried Constance as few other cases could.

She'd been trying to relax her hold on Fleurette, and to see her launched into the world in a manner both respectable and responsible. Under no circumstance did Constance wish to turn into a woman like Edna Heustis's mother, who called on the police to rein in her daughter's independence. But Edna knew how to stay out of trouble, and now they were on their way to pick up a girl who clearly did not. Fleurette, she felt, might land somewhere in the middle, and the idea unsettled her.

Constance had been trying not to make a fuss over the auditions for May Ward's troupe, but as the train clattered on interminably in front of them, her resolve weakened. "What do you know about a show promoter named Freeman Bernstein?"

Sheriff Heath looked over at her, puzzled, and lifted the brim of his hat the way he did when he was thinking about something. "Bernstein. I've seen his name on posters. He brings prize fighters through town. Used to manage a theater in . . . Bayonne, maybe. Friend of yours?"

"Not at all. And he's made an enemy of Norma."

"Maybe I should take the fellow for a drink, offer my sympathy."

"He's going to hold an audition in Paterson for girls who want to join his wife's vaudeville act. Have you heard of her? May Ward?"

He shook his head. "I don't follow the theater, unless Miss Fleurette is performing."

"That's just it. He charges each girl five dollars to audition, and you can be sure Fleurette wants to go. Norma thinks it's a con."

At last the caboose went by and they drove on. "She could be right about that. If he has no intention of choosing a girl, then it's like any other game of chance. He'd have to give them something of value in exchange for their money."

"He's giving each girl a signed portrait of May Ward."

He laughed at that. "Then it's perfectly legal. He's a clever man."

"But harmless, I hope. I gave Fleurette the five dollars."

"And what happens if she's chosen?"

"I'm counting on the auditions being a sham."

"They don't sound legitimate to me," he said. "I wouldn't worry about it. Oh, would you look at this mess."

They had just arrived in Fort Lee and pulled into a short stretch of shingled and gabled shops clustered around the corner of Main and Hudson. Half the town seemed to have turned out to watch the police at work. Every man in the barber shop had stepped outside, half-shaved and shorn, and three delivery boys leaned against their carts, pointing and whispering. Constables were stationed up and down Main Street. Constance saw John Courter among them. "How did the prosecutor's office get here before we did?"

"It wasn't the report of gunfire, I can tell you that," the sheriff said. "Courter's been making more noise about moral crimes. He stood up at an Odd Fellows' meeting last night and said he intended to close every disreputable house in Bergen County."

"How many disreputable houses do we have?"

"A better question is why he hasn't closed them already, if he knows so much about them."

The sheriff nosed his motor car to a stop along the curb. Constance spotted a girl she took to be Minnie Davis standing with a police officer in full view of all the spectators.

"I hate to see girls paraded around like that. Couldn't they have kept her inside so the neighbors wouldn't gawk?"

"They don't think about it that way," the sheriff said.

Constance elbowed through the crowd to take possession of her inmate. Minnie was a tall and broad-shouldered girl who wore her dresses a little too snug. Constance kept a wool blanket in the sheriff's automobile to wrap around girls who weren't properly clothed, or who were sick or injured, and that seemed to be most of them. It was such a brisk day that Minnie took the blanket without protest.

"I work for the sheriff," Constance told her, "and I'm here to look after you."

"I don't need looking after," Minnie said impatiently. "I was doing nothing wrong, and those cops had no right to bust in on me like that."

"Then you can tell me your side of it," Constance said, "and I'll do what I can to help."

"I already told him, and he didn't listen." Minnie rolled her eyes at the police officer assigned to watch her, a tired-looking man with stooped shoulders and a skinny neck that left his collar sagging. He handed the girl over to Constance and spoke directly to Sheriff Heath.

"We've still no idea about the shots that were fired, but while we were looking, we

121

found this one in a furnished room that was supposed to be rented to a married couple. We'd already picked up the fellow sneaking down the alley. Says he never quite got around to marrying her. It's the usual story."

"I'd like to hear the story anyway," Constance said. "Couldn't we go inside?" The gray slush was already starting to seep into her boots. Minnie wore little buttoned oxfords that did nothing to keep out the snow. With both police and sheriff automobiles parked on the street, they were attracting an even larger crowd.

"Take her to the jail and you two girls can talk all you want," the officer said.

Constance didn't like the way the man was speaking to her and was about to tell him so when Sheriff Heath intervened. "Deputy Kopp will take Miss Davis upstairs while I go see about the man."

Constance had a firm grip on Minnie's arm. "You've no right to drag me around," the girl complained.

"I'm doing you a favor by not putting handcuffs on you in front of everyone," Constance said, a little gruffly. "Do you live above one of these shops? How do you go in — through the alley?"

Minnie tried to pull away, but only half-heartedly. Constance dug her fingers into the bones around the girl's elbow and she sighed. "Yes, it's down here."

They walked down the street and around the corner, into a little alley of the sort one finds behind any downtown district: narrow and muddy, lined with ashcans, empty wooden crates, and old push-carts. There were puddles behind the restaurants where the cooks threw out the dishwater, and here and there were chicken bones, moldy bread, and potato peelings being picked through by seagulls.

Three Fort Lee police officers had a man in handcuffs behind the bakery. He was a good-looking Italian fellow of about twenty-five, with a head of thick black hair and a fine cut to his coat. Minnie made some small sound when she saw him, but he didn't look over.

"Wait here," Sheriff Heath said. Constance pulled her under a porch roof behind the hardware store while he went to talk to the man.

"What's your name, son?" Sheriff Heath asked, but got no answer.

"Anthony Leo," said one of the officers. "Goes by Tony."

"Tony, is that your girl?" The sheriff pointed at Minnie.

Still the man wouldn't answer. He was

looking down at his shoes, which were of a scuffed leather in need of a good polish.

Sheriff Heath said, "If she's not your girl, then I suppose we'll have to charge her with breaking and entering, because the police found her inside a room rented to you and your wife. Where is Mrs. Leo?"

"That's her," he said at last, glancing briefly at Minnie. "We were all fixed to get married. I even got the license. I'll show it to you."

That drew a snort from Minnie. Constance nudged her to stay quiet.

Detective Courter came around from the street with two other men from the prosecutor's office. He stopped only briefly when he saw Constance, then turned very deliberately away and said to the sheriff, "We've had reports of several men going in and out of the young lady's room. She's been seen with new jewelry and other little trinkets of the sort a man might give to a girl after an evening together."

"That's a lie!" Minnie cried. "Tell them, Tony!"

"I don't know nothing about that," Tony mumbled. The other officers stared at Minnie with a mixture of pity and disgust.

"I've heard enough," Constance said, just loud enough for Courter to hear it. She led

Minnie to the back of the bakery.

The detective continued as if nothing had happened. "I don't like to think what part this fellow Leo played in it," he announced, as if in a courtroom, "but I've got an idea about that."

Minnie stiffened beside her and Constance thought she might run. "Go on," she said quietly, and let Minnie show her the way up the back stairs to her room, which sat at the front of the building, looking out over Main Street. There was another room in the back of the building, and a shared toilet between them.

The police had left the door to Minnie's room open. When they walked in, Constance let go of the girl's arm, and she went over and sat on the bed. There was a silkoline cover over the mattress that would have been pretty once, but it had started to fray. All around the room, Constance saw evidence of Minnie's attempts to make it a home: the rosebuds painted on an enamel teapot, the lace hung over the window, the picture of a winter scene in Central Park cut out of a magazine and pasted inside a frame.

But nothing could hide the fact of her impoverishment. Minnie had only a single work dress and sweater hung from a peg on the door, and Constance saw nothing to eat but a box of crackers and a tin of potted meat. There was a sour smell of sickness in the room that Constance now realized came from the front of Minnie's dress. She would have gone to sit with her on the bed, but in light of that fact, she kept her distance and let Minnie stretch across the bed with a blanket over her.

"I'm sorry that the detective said those things in front of everyone," Constance began. "Suppose you tell me what really happened."

Minnie slid around on the bed and looked at her from behind a tousled head of hair. "It's a lie."

"What part of it?"

"All of it." She rolled over to face the wall and ran her hand idly along it.

Constance had to remind herself that the girl was only sixteen and probably didn't grasp the extent of her troubles. It was also true that Minnie didn't seem to be at her sharpest: she looked to have had a wild time the night before and was probably suffering a nasty headache. Still, the girl had to say something if she wanted to help herself.

"The police seem to think the two of you were posing as man and wife. Is that right?"

No answer.

"I expect they'll prepare a charge of illegal cohabitation."

Minnie's hand paused in its route along the wall, but she said nothing.

It was the other charge that worried Constance the most. "I don't know if they can prove that you've had other men in this place, but —"

Minnie sat up suddenly. "I haven't! You'll tell them that, won't you? Can't I go to the toilet? I feel rotten."

"Go ahead," Constance said, and Minnie shuffled across the room with Constance's blanket still wrapped around her, and into the little hall bathroom. Constance stood guard outside.

Minnie put her head right into the sink and ran water over it. The cold water wasn't as restorative as she'd hoped it would be, but the sound of the water splashing around gave her the cover she needed. She reached under her dress and pulled out the little fabric-covered parcel she'd managed to extract from under the mattress while Constance questioned her. It was a risk to leave anything in the bathroom, but she seemed to be on her way to jail, and she'd have nowhere to hide it there.

The ceiling was made of thin shiplap planks that had worked loose in the dampness. She pushed at one and it gave way slightly, yielding just enough room to slip her bundle between the boards. Before she did, she opened it and fingered its contents: A hat-pin with a real pearl on the end, a fragile gold chain with the tiniest possible chip of diamond suspended from it, a silver bracelet, and a comb that she believed to be made of real ivory. There was also a ring holding what she thought might be a ruby or a garnet.

It didn't amount to much. But she'd been clinging to those trinkets against the day when she might need to sell them quickly and get away. Apparently that day had come, only she didn't get away fast enough.

The lady deputy knocked at the door. Minnie pushed her bundle up between the boards and took a pin out of her hair to draw them closed again. She ran a towel over her head, took a hasty drink of water from the basin, and called, "I'm ready."

12

Minnie took offense at the jail's de-lousing regimen and laughed at the flannel house dress and battered old buttoned shoes she was expected to wear upstairs.

"Next you're going to come after my dainties," she said, lightly, as if the whole situation were a farce. She looked down at her corset, which sat limply on the floor of the shower room. It was stained yellow with sweat, and the lining had worn away, leaving naked a section of boning.

"I'll pack it away for you," Constance said, and rolled it into a bundle with Minnie's dress.

"Do you mean that I'm to go bare?"

"It's only women on the fifth floor," Constance assured her. "The sheriff hasn't been able to persuade the Freeholders to pay for corsets, but I did manage to put in a supply of sanitary aprons when it's your time —"

"I'll be gone before then." Just the idea of rubberized jailhouse sanitary goods made Minnie shudder.

Constance settled her into the cell recently vacated by Edna Heustis and offered to bring her lunch.

"I couldn't look at food," Minnie said.

"You'll feel better if you try," Constance said. "What about coffee?"

Minnie sat gingerly on the edge of her bunk and looked with distaste at the bare toilet next to her. "Is there such a thing as toast?" she asked, resignedly.

"I'll find out."

Downstairs, Constance passed Sheriff Heath in the corridor. He'd already been out on another call, and his coat was splattered in mud and straw.

"Horse thief?" Constance asked.

"Goats," he said. "I have a note from Detective Courter. That marriage license of Anthony Leo's looks to be a fake. It's two months old, and obviously just for show. I don't think this is his first time to try it with a girl."

"That's quite a trick," Constance said. Under better circumstances, she might have argued that the couple should be given a stern lecture and left alone for a week or two, so that they might marry and right the situation themselves. But when she tried to imagine Fleurette living in that cheap furnished room, with the lingering stench of gin, and a man who would go so far as to trick her with a false promise of marriage, she knew what she would want. She'd want every lawman in the country kicking down the door to rescue her.

"What does Miss Davis have to say about it?" the sheriff asked.

"She refuses to talk, except to say that the police are telling lies."

"What did she tell you about this business of her running around with other men?"

"Nothing," Constance said. "She denies it all. Who accused her?"

"A constable heard it from the landlord," the sheriff said.

"The landlord? Is that the baker downstairs?"

"Apparently so. But Anthony Leo says that she's a good girl, and that if we'd set him free, he'd marry her."

"Well, he would say that if it would get him out of jail. I suppose this means we're back to illegal cohabitation, and they're both guilty," Constance said.

"I don't know about that. It looks to me like she was conned," Sheriff Heath said. "I wish she'd tell you if she was."

"I just don't picture this as a white slavery case," she said.

"What do you picture?"

"Well, you read about girls locked in bedrooms or drugged and draped about on chaises, and a man at the door deciding who can go in."

"That might be how it is in the Sunday magazines, but this is what it looks like in Fort Lee," Sheriff Heath said. "This girl obviously had no money and no one to turn to, and Mr. Leo saw an opportunity. We're going to treat her as the victim until we're told otherwise. Put her on the witness's meal plan."

Constance didn't think that an extra sausage with her dinner would be of much comfort to Minnie, but she made a note of it. "Has anyone spoken to her parents?"

"That's for you to do. They reported her missing months ago."

13

Eugene and Edith Davis made their home in one-half of a plain, flat-fronted clapboard house at the unfashionable end of Catskill. The larger homes had all been turned into summer cottages for New Yorkers, which left the year-round factory families to make do with what was left. Every house on the Davises' street was similarly carved into two or three apartments, with front doors added where windows once were, and kitchens tacked on awkwardly in the back, under low roofs that served as porches where one might, in fair weather, climb out a bedroom window and take the night air.

Some of the houses had little shops on the ground floor offering services to the summer crowd — shoe repair, laundry, tailoring — but they were all closed for the winter. With no one around to pass judgment on the appearance of the place, brooms and shovels sat on porches and gray wash-rags fluttered from second-story windows. The entire neighborhood looked as if it wasn't expecting company.

Mrs. Davis had been watching from the window and opened the door before Constance could knock. She was one of those women who was as wide as she was tall, which is to say that it took some effort for her to lean back and take Constance in from head to toe.

"Ooooh!" she sang out at the sight of her. "You're taller than my girls."

"Is Minnie Davis one of your girls?" Constance asked.

She stood back and surveyed her again. This time her eyes landed on Constance's badge. "She was, until she run off."

"Your daughter's been found, ma'am, and she's safe and well. I work for the sheriff in Hackensack. Might I come inside?"

"She's safe, is she?" Mrs. Davis screeched. "I thought she had the devil inside of her."

Constance took a step back in shock and looked up and down the street, certain that half the neighborhood had heard her. She could only assume that Mrs. Davis was partly deaf and wondered if she might be only partially sane, too.

"I couldn't say, ma'am. I've come to ask you a few questions, and to talk about what we might do for Minnie."

Mrs. Davis gave a resigned shrug and stepped aside. Constance found herself in a place that was immediately familiar: a seamstress's work room. If Fleurette had taken in mending from the neighbors, rather than sewing costumes for the theater, her sewing room would have looked just like this. There was an old treadle machine with a pile of crumpled work-shirts to one side and a stack of folded, mended trousers on the other. On the floor were boxes of fabric scraps and a heap of old coats in need of fresh sheepskin. Along every window-sill were jars of buttons and pincushions stuck all over with rusty pins and needles.

Mrs. Davis dropped into a wooden chair outfitted with a sagging cushion she'd made herself from scraps. Constance pushed a roll of wool batting off an armchair and sat across from her.

"I take in mending," she called, as if trying to make herself heard across a great distance. "Washing, too, in the summer, when the city people get here."

Constance thought it a strange way to begin, considering she'd come with news of her daughter. "You must've been terribly worried about Minnie all this time."

"Worried? She done wrong, and she knows

it. She was too ashamed to even tell us directly. Couldn't do nothing but send a letter. And that was only after we went down to the police, thinking she'd fallen in the river."

She was still nearly shouting. Constance had to force herself not to draw back.

"She wrote you a letter?"

"Her father wanted to burn it, but Goldie snatched it from him. She's a bad girl, too."

"Is Goldie . . ."

"His other daughter. She's older than Minnie and should've known better. Ada's the only one of them worth anything, and she's married and gone. She belongs to my first husband, bless his soul, so that tells you something."

She crossed herself at the mention of the man's soul and sat back in her chair with an enormous, deflating sigh.

"I take it that you and Mr. Davis were both widowed?"

"That's right. He had to raise mine, and I had to raise his. Don't ever do it. Other women's children are always trouble."

"Is Mr. Davis expected home soon?" Constance entertained an unreasonable hope that Mr. Davis might be easier to talk to than his wife.

Mrs. Davis sat up straight and patted her

136

hair, which was gray but streaked in black, and of such a coarse texture that it was impossible to see where she'd pinned it up. It seemed to mass together of its own volition at the back of her head.

"He'll be along. He works down at the brick factory. Goldie's at the knitting mill. You'll hear the whistle shortly."

Constance wasn't sure how to keep a conversation going with Mrs. Davis, but she soon discovered that she didn't have to. While they waited, Mrs. Davis delivered a monologue about the job prospects available at the various factories in town and which ones were best suited to Mr. Davis's failing knees and trembling hands. The brick factory was the worst place for him, she explained, but there wasn't anything left. His fingers shook so that he couldn't do the fine work required of textile labor, nor was he fit anymore to be a machinist.

"That's why we need the girls to work," Mrs. Davis pronounced. "Because he can't no more. But Minnie spent every penny she made down at that boardwalk, and still expected me to keep a bed for her and food on the table. I told her I could rent that bed to the girl sitting next to her at the mill and collect more money in rent than Minnie brought home. She told me to go right ahead and try. Have you ever heard of a girl talking to her mother like that?"

From the little Constance knew of Minnie, it sounded exactly like her. But before Mrs. Davis's line of questioning could run on much longer, the door flew open and Goldie ran inside. She was the mirror image of her sister: tall and broad-shouldered, with a firm chin, a strong nose, and hair a shade too dark to be considered gold, although it might've had more shine to it in the summer.

"They told me on the corner the police were here. Are you police? Is it Minnie?"

"You already know what happened to Minnie," Edith Davis snapped.

Goldie didn't even glance at her stepmother. She took Constance by the hand and led her through the kitchen and into a little room behind it that was not much more than a sleeping porch.

"Go on and tell her your lies!" Mrs. Davis shouted from her chair.

Goldie pulled a curtain closed and Constance found herself in a room so small that she stumbled over the bed. There were heavy blankets over the windows, giving the place a gloomy, greenish cast. Having nowhere else to sit, Goldie dropped onto the bed, and Constance did, too. In this way they found themselves settled on a ratty chenille bedspread like two sisters sharing confidences. Goldie and Minnie must have done exactly that, Constance thought, before she disappeared.

"Did you share this room with your sister?" she asked.

Goldie nodded and jutted her chin at the wall. "That's her side."

The wall above the bed was covered in magazine pictures, some of which they had colored themselves. Goldie had a liking for etchings of scenes from antiquity: Roman palaces, Egyptian queens along the Nile, and statues of Diana with her dog. Minnie preferred the Manhattan skyline and elaborate interiors of theaters, with curtained balconies and gilded ceilings. She had also pinned up a picture of last year's spring dresses from Paris. It gave Constance a ragged little pain to see that Minnie and Fleurette longed for the same life.

She thought it better to start by letting Goldie talk about herself, so she said, "You've taken an interest in the classics."

"I used to have a teacher who read mythology to us, and Virgil. It seemed like another world. I couldn't believe any of those things really happened right here on this Earth." She flashed a wide and winning smile, and just as quickly took it away again. Here was a girl who was too pretty to work in a factory, and too poor to study the classics. Constance could imagine her and her sister, sleeping side-by-side, each wondering how she'd ever get out of that room.

Then one of them did.

"Minnie must've thought New York was another world," Constance said.

"She's more practical. And brave. She just went."

"Did she tell you where she was going?"

Goldie laughed and shook her head, tossing her hair around. "She didn't have to tell me. Everybody goes down to that boardwalk. I was there, too. I saw her with Tony."

"What happens at the boardwalk?" Constance asked, even though she had a fairly good idea about it.

"Why, the pleasure boats come up the river! Who do you suppose steps off those boats?"

"People from the city," Constance offered. She could just imagine how romantic that must be to girls in a small town. An image came to mind of Fleurette at the age of nine or ten, when she kept an album of pictures of fashionable people in pretty places. There was a newspaper drawing she particularly liked of debutantes strolling down the

Catskill boardwalk under their parasols. She had a little paint set and she colored in all the dresses, making them as bright as peacocks while the world around them stayed newsprint gray and drab.

"Yes, people from the city," Goldie said. "Rich people. Young men handing out cigarettes and offering to buy the town girls a drink. We all go down and wait for them. If we spend our own money in the arcades and shops, there won't be anything left over. But a man from the city has plenty to spend."

"And what does a man like that expect in return?"

She smiled again, and a little color came up in her cheeks. "Plenty."

The rest of it came out easily enough. Minnie hated her job at the knitting mill. For two years she'd been sitting alongside a few dozen other girls, running a hosiery machine all day long. It was a better place to work than one of the silk factories in Paterson: it was cleaner, the wages were higher, and the girls could sit at their stations, rather than stand over a loom all day. But it was monotonous work that gave Minnie little reward, as every dime she earned was supposed to go home to her parents.

There was no thought of Minnie finishing her schooling. Mrs. Davis told the teacher she was needed at home, and that was the end of her education. She was locked into a life of factory work and house-work.

Around the time Minnie turned sixteen, she realized that there would be no end to it unless she got married. But she knew that if she married a Catskill boy from one of the factories — and who else would she marry, but one of them? — nothing much would change. She would stay at the knitting mill until she had a baby, and then she would keep house in another small and dingy set of rooms just like the ones she'd always lived in.

When Goldie put it like that, Constance couldn't blame Minnie for running away. Anyone might run away from a life like that.

"What about you?" Constance asked. "Weren't you tempted to go off to the city the way she did?"

"I might've gone with Minnie, if she'd asked. But she wasn't just tired of this old life. She was tired of me, too. Anyway, there's a foreman at the brick factory. We're to be married in the spring."

"Congratulations," she said, and Goldie gave her that bright smile again. Then a door slammed and she said, "Daddy's home."

"Wouldn't he like to have Minnie back?"

"Go and ask him yourself."

Eugene Davis did not like to hear any news of his daughter. In fact, he didn't hear much at all, which explained, at last, why his wife was in the habit of shouting the way she did.

He was a decrepit man in late middle age with a pot belly and wobbly knees. He sank into a chair, still in his dust-covered dungarees, and put his hands out to rest on top of his legs very gingerly, as if they required special handling. Constance couldn't help but stare at them, as she'd never seen hands so scarred and mangled. One index finger had been sheared off at the top knuckle, and a pinky finger on the other hand looked like it had been worn down to a useless stub. They trembled helplessly and seemed, just as Mrs. Davis had claimed, entirely unsuited to any kind of work.

Constance explained the purpose of her visit and said, "We have your daughter at the Hackensack jail, but please understand that she hasn't been charged with a crime. She's being held as a witness. That's why I've come to see you. If you can speak to the judge, it would go a long way in helping to get her released and brought back home. I'm sure you'd all like to put this behind you."

Eugene Davis spoke in a hoarse voice, worn down from years of shouting over the noise of a factory floor. His lips moved a little before any words came out. "That girl's not coming back here, if that's what you mean to say."

Constance hadn't come prepared for such heartlessness. "It would take nothing more than a word with the judge . . ."

"I've had a word with the judge." Mr. Davis jerked his arm up and pointed a finger heavenward. "She needs to speak to my judge if she wants to get right."

Goldie kept her eyes on her lap. Edith Davis was leaning forward and nodding encouragingly at her husband as he spoke.

"County jail might be the best thing for her," he said. "Any Bibles in that jail?"

"Of course," Constance said. "And services on Sunday."

"That'll do just fine."

"But you must understand that the judge won't release a sixteen-year-old girl on her own. Someone would have to take her in."

Mr. Davis acted as though he couldn't hear, although she'd shouted at him just as his wife did. He leaned forward, and Mrs.

144

Davis rushed over to help him up. "We're going to get on with our supper," he said by way of dismissing her.

"It's nice that you can," Constance snapped. "Your girl has nothing but a jailhouse supper waiting for her tonight."

Mr. Davis huffed and turned away.

"Take an address, at least, so that you might write when you have a change of heart."

But the Davises were unmoved. Mrs. Davis pointed her in the direction of the train station and sent her on her way. Before she went, she pressed her hand into Goldie's and left the jail's address in her palm. Goldie made no expression as she pocketed it.

Once outside, Constance picked her way down the dark and pitted street. Here and there, a faint yellow light fell out of kitchen windows. Even in the thin February air, a few boys ran up and down the street with a leather ball. At the bottom of the hill, a tattered newspaper was caught in a bare tree, snapping in the wind like a flag.

When the breeze hit her, she took an enormous breath, relieved to be out of the Davises' stifling sitting room. There was no point in staying longer anyway: she couldn't have put those two before a judge and trusted them to say anything that would cast

Minnie in a favorable light. Even Goldie couldn't help, as she was possessed of knowledge of her sisters' dalliances with out-of-town men and might — if questioned sharply and compelled by a judge to speak truthfully — see no choice but to confess what she knew.

Constance reached the edge of town and walked along the boardwalk, where she could perfectly imagine Minnie going to wait for the boats. Even with the operation shut down for the winter, it wasn't difficult to picture the carnival atmosphere that would have prevailed in the warmer months. There were wooden booths, shuttered and locked, that advertised pretzels and beer. A wide shingled shed offered three shots at a target for a chance to win a set of ruby glass. At one end stood a bandstand, with benches in a half-circle around it.

The wind came up off the gray river. Constance gathered her collar around her neck and turned her back on the place. It held the promise of merriment, even though there was none to be found.

14

Up in Pompton Lakes, installed once again in her little room under the eaves at Mrs. Turnbull's boarding-house, Edna Heustis turned over a pamphlet that someone had dropped in the train station a few days earlier.

On one side was a picture of a woman in a smart gray uniform, standing on a hill. Behind her lay a ruined, smoking battlefield. It read:

Are you going to help us win this war?

Answer not with words and cheers, but with shells, ships, food, and bandages.

Is the work heavy, you ask?

Not so heavy as the soldiers' work.

Are the hours long?

Six days and nights in the

trenches are longer.

On the other side was the announcement of the Women's Preparedness Committee's weekly meeting at the church, with this call to join:

Just as our young men are not waiting for their nation's orders to go to France, so can women take up the call and follow them. In hospitals and shipyards, in aeroplane sheds and railways, in homes and workshops, there is work overseas right now for American women who are willing to do it.

Edna turned the paper over again and looked at the woman sketched in pencil, with just a few lines to suggest dark hair tucked under her cap, and a single mark along her jawline to show a strength of purpose. She wondered how she would look in a uniform like that. She'd never met a woman who professed an interest in boarding a ship for Europe and serving alongside the men, but she'd read about it in the papers. Women were volunteering for the Red Cross and the Ambulance Service.

They were serving as nurses, cooks, and secretaries.

She wondered if her brothers would meet women like that when they went to France. All four of the Heustis boys were ready to depart as soon as President Wilson gave the order. Early last year, they'd each gone out to join in some sort of war-work to prepare themselves, which their father heartily encouraged. Charlie had taken an orderly position in a hospital with the hope of joining an ambulance service in France; the twins worked at the munitions depot on Black Tom Island; and Davie, the youngest, apprenticed himself to an automobile mechanic, thinking that he might drive his brother's ambulance, even though he grew dizzy at the sight of blood.

There had been such high spirits among the boys when they left home. Her father hardly noticed the gloom that settled into the empty rooms her brothers had vacated. He was out every day but Sunday, conducting his business, making the rounds of factories and shops that kept their money at his bank, and he found reasons to call upon his sons' places of employment often enough that he felt satisfied with their progress and secure in their success. But Edna and her mother were alone, quite suddenly, and Edna found the solitude unbearable.

Her brothers' patriotic talk had stirred her. Wasn't there something she could do? A few of her school chums had taken up with the Red Cross, rolling bandages and knitting socks. But she found that sitting in a church basement with a knitting bag in her lap was as stifling as sitting at home. Anyone could knit. Surely there was more to war service than that.

Another group was putting together little comfort bags for the soldiers — playing cards and handkerchiefs, and short notes meant to cheer them in the hospital — and she made fifty of those to help fill a barrel, but that wasn't enough, either.

It was her father who'd given her the idea to go to work in a munitions factory. One night, as she paged listlessly through a pattern-book, he glanced up from his newspaper and said, "Would you look at this? They're hiring girls on the fuse line. Says here those tiny fingers are just the thing. Let me see your tiny fingers, Miss Edna."

Edna did, in fact, have narrow, delicate fingers. They also happened to be steady and strong. She raised them up between her face and her father's. He looked right past them and into her eyes. "You see there?

Even the ladies can serve."

Her mother, who'd been sitting across from them with a box of buttons in her lap at the time this exchange took place, cried out at the suggestion and went into a sort of nervous chatter about all the ways in which women serve their country already from the kitchen and the wash-room. She rattled the buttons for emphasis as she spoke, but it was too late. Her father's suggestion was all the encouragement Edna needed. Over the following weeks, she inquired at every factory within a train ride from Edgewater until she found a place for herself and left home.

Until her arrest, factory work had satisfied her. What could be more heroic, and more useful, than to put her shoulder to the wheel at the powder works, where the very instruments of war rolled out of the factories and onto ships, to supply the British and Canadian soldiers rushing to fight? Soon enough the Americans would join, and a fuse that left her fingers would go into the hands of her own countrymen. Every strand she wove would, she hoped, shield them from harm.

The factories were filled with women giving their all for France. It should've been enough for Edna. And for a time, it was.

But during the final few hours of her one

and only night in the Hackensack jail, while Edna waited for Deputy Kopp to return with the results of her investigation into the unimpeachable life she'd been taken from, and to release her back to it, Edna began to wonder if she wasn't meant to do more. As she sat in the very picture of deprivation — what could be more cruel and cold than the bars of a jail cell? — the shape of this new thing came to her.

Europe. If her brothers could go, why couldn't she?

It was nearly morning as the idea crept in, and with it the realization that she had survived a night in jail. If she could endure that, couldn't she endure a hundred times worse?

It must be said that Constance Kopp was, in part, to blame for this idea. In arresting Edna, Officer Randolph had put her under the care of a tall woman in a uniform, with a gun strapped to her side. Deputy Kopp hardly even seemed real to Edna at first. She seemed like a vision of an entirely different kind of woman, one who would be capable of doing far more for the war than rolling bandages. Not every woman had the temperament for war, but some did, surely.

When Deputy Kopp came for her in the morning, Edna looked up at her and just nodded, calmly, and thought to herself, Yes, certainly. Why hadn't I thought of it before?

The little pretense of a trial that morning — her mother's quiet protests, the words of the judge — none of it made much of an impression on her. In her mind, she was already venturing across the Atlantic.

When that pamphlet slipped out of some-one's coat pocket and fluttered to the ground at the train station, Edna wasn't at all surprised to see it. Something about the call to serve — the need to answer the cries coming daily from France as the Germans advanced — something in that call went directly inside of Edna and fit like a key in a lock.

Women were going to France, and so could she. Here was her ticket.

15

With Constance so thoroughly occupied, Fleurette found herself free to do as she pleased. Norma did keep something of a watch on her, grumbling if she came in too late or made too many demands to be run down to the train station in their buggy, but in general, Fleurette enjoyed her liberty and devoted every minute to her preparations for the audition.

She had, of late, come to see the frivolity in the little shows put on by Mrs. Hansen's Academy — the Christmas concert, the spring chorus, the fall drama — in a way that had not been apparent to her only a few months before. While she'd once been delighted to play the part of a farmer's daughter in a musical about a giant pumpkin, she now saw such roles as childish and knew that they did nothing to prepare her for an audition in front of a woman of May Ward's caliber. Those performances were, she suspected, merely a showcase to demonstrate to parents that their tuition payments weren't being wasted. As long as each student could be paraded before an audience of mothers and neighbors at regular intervals, and showered with applause, enrollment at Mrs. Hansen's would look like money well spent.

She was, furthermore, coming to understand that she hadn't been properly prepared for the career on stage she'd envisioned for herself. Most of the other girls saw dancing and singing as a diversion from an otherwise stultifying life and had, from a young age, enrolled in classes at girls' academies merely to amuse themselves. Drawing, dancing, flower-pressing, elocution, and embroidery were all equally suited to that purpose: they kept the girls busy but not harried, entertained but not exhausted, and instilled in them a few social graces and decorative impulses that never threatened to go so far as to foster anything in the way of ambition or independence.

On the other hand, the dancers who toured with May Ward — her Eight Dresden Dolls — couldn't possibly have come out of academies like Mrs. Hansen's. Fleurette had been twice to watch May Ward's act, in the company of her teacher and classmates, and had glimpsed a species of performer unlike anything she'd come across before. May Ward and her chorus girls moved as if they'd done nothing but dance all their lives. They sang out in powerful, clear voices over which they had perfect mastery. Never once was there a misstep or a mistake. They seemed to have been born backstage, to have danced before they could walk, and to have spent their formative years in rehearsals, not nodding over a history book.

Fleurette came to believe that her childhood had been wasted. She'd been schooled at home and taught such useless subjects as grammar and arithmetic, with music and dance treated as secondary to her education.

Surely May Ward's chorus girls hadn't suffered such a pedestrian upbringing. One could tell by looking at them that they didn't sleep on horsehair mattresses, or sit down at night to a dismal supper of cabbage and potatoes, or go around in an old duster on Mondays, picking up after themselves. They seemed to have alighted from some remote and exotic island, peopled only by long-limbed girls in satin slippers. Why hadn't Fleurette been given admittance to their world already? She felt a pang of regret at what she'd missed. She was now desperate to make up for the time lost.

The audition provided exactly the opportunity she needed. While the other girls chose pretty frocks and songs they'd performed many times on stage already, Fleurette recruited a small ensemble of half a dozen girls, choreographed a clever dance, and chose a song and a way of presenting it that was entirely outside the confines of Mrs. Hansen's prosaic imagination. She rehearsed it everywhere: in the barn, in the meadow behind the house, in her bedroom when everyone else was away, and in the empty dance studio at Mrs. Hansen's Academy, anytime it wasn't in use. Only she and Helen had dance steps to rehearse, as nothing was required of the rest of her cast but walk-on roles. This they had also accomplished in secret, swearing each girl to secrecy. Everything about their performance was to be a surprise — and so much more than that.

Fleurette felt sure that May Ward would see it as a revelation. She wouldn't be expecting such polish and sophistication on a stage in Paterson. She would demand to know Fleurette's name. She would write it down and take care to spell it correctly (Fleurette hated to see her name misspelled), and would ask to see her after. She would invite her to the join the chorus without delay. Fleurette would become her protégée. She imagined the two of them spending their afternoons together in empty theaters, where May Ward would teach her everything she'd failed to learn in Paterson.

"You're ready for New York," May Ward would tell her, panting after some particularly vexing dance steps one afternoon. "Get some rest. We leave tomorrow."

But she wouldn't rest. She would be tireless. Some other Dresden Doll would probably lose her place to make room for Fleurette, but that couldn't be helped. The theater business was ruthless that way. Fleurette already felt a little world-weary as she thought of the constant striving and the endless jostling for position that would characterize her new life. It would never be easy, her stage career, but it would be the only life for her.

And tonight it would begin.

Constance arrived late to the audition and rushed to take her seat alongside Norma. She was surprised to see the theater nearly full: usually the families of the students didn't occupy half the place.

"Why are there so many people here? Is May Ward expected to perform?" she whispered.

"If she doesn't, we'll have a riot," Norma said.

A few piano notes from behind the stage curtains brought the audience to silence, and then to applause. Constance didn't recognize the melody and the piano cut off abruptly before the song could begin. After some deliberately awkward fumbling with the curtain, a tall man in a smart suit and a high silk hat took the stage.

"Ladies and gentlemen!" he called. "So good of you to come see me!"

That got a groan and a few cheers. He looked around in mock surprise.

"What, you didn't buy tickets to get a look at Freeman Bernstein, manager of vaudeville's most famous girl act?"

"Then it *is* him," Norma said grimly, as if his appearance confirmed everything she'd suspected of him.

There were more jeers. A few small cabbages pelted the stage — obviously planted — which Mr. Bernstein dodged gracefully, to the delight of the crowd.

"Hey, now! Do you mean to say you didn't line up around the block for old Freeman Bernstein, husband and manager of the renowned comedienne May Ward?"

He ducked this time and peered out

anxiously from behind his hat to make sure there were no raw eggs forthcoming. Now the audience whistled and shouted and demanded May Ward.

He put out his hands to silence the crowd. "Now, you know Mrs. Bernstein — excuse me, she'll punch me if I don't call her Mrs. Ward — you know that my wife has a very important job today, and that is to see for herself the talent here in Paterson, and to decide if there's a girl in this town who's ready to join her on the stage. What do you think about that, folks? Are we going to find our next Dresden Doll today?"

There came another roar from the crowd and then, without any further preliminary, May Ward strolled on stage with the light, rhythmic stride of a dancer. She held her arms out in that peculiar way that performers have. When Mr. Bernstein took her hand, she gave a graceful twirl that raised her pink skirts and showed her kid slippers, along with quite a bit more. Norma grunted as May Ward's knees — clad in white stockings — were revealed to an appreciative audience.

Constance elbowed Norma in the ribs. "She's only dancing."

"We used to know how to dance and keep our skirts down at the same time," Norma

160

said, without taking her eyes off Mrs. Ward.

"I don't recall you ever knowing how to dance. I'm sure they're to be judged on their abilities, and nothing more."

"They're to be judged on their ability to pay the five dollars. You still haven't admitted to giving her the money."

Constance pretended not to hear and leaned forward to get a better look at May Ward. She had always seemed, in the pictures Fleurette had pinned to her wall, to be a surprisingly ordinary-looking woman: fair-skinned and fine-featured, with thin lips, a frail nose, and eyes neither large nor expressive. With a good deal of paint on her face, anyone could be made to look striking, and Mrs. Ward did indeed look striking on stage. Her eyebrows were penciled into a state of comic curiosity. Her lips were stained a loud strawberry red. When she fluttered her eyelashes, they could not only be seen but counted from the back row. Every gesture she made — every turn of her wrist, every lift of her chin — had an air of theatricality about it calculated to make the audience understand that she was not at all like the rest of them.

As the applause died down, Mr. Bernstein turned to the pianist and said, "Jerry, do you think we can make this bird sing a few notes?"

The pianist resumed the song he'd begun earlier. May Ward pretended to protest and wave him away, but then she did give a verse, taking up a coquettish pose and singing in what was meant to be her good-girl voice.

There's a little bit of bad in every good little
   girl
They're not to blame
Though they may seem like little angels in
   a dream,
They're naughty just the same.
They read the good book Sunday
And snappy stories Monday
There's a little bit of bad in every good little
   girl
They're all the same.

One verse was all they were meant to hear, to the raucous displeasure of the audience. As everyone around them cheered and stomped their feet, Freeman Bernstein took his wife's hand and raised it high. His jacket fell open, revealing a red-and-white-striped vest.

"Now, you know we'd take every girl in this theater with us if we could!" Mr. Bernstein bellowed. "But there's only room for one more Dresden Doll, and I just know we're going to find her tonight. What do you say, Mrs. Ward? Shall we give them an audition?"

16

A little bit of bad in every good little girl? It could have been Constance's personal anthem. Sorting the good from the bad had become her main occupation of late. Even as she tried to take her mind off her work and give her attention to the auditions, she couldn't help but scrutinize each girl and wonder what might someday become of her.

A cherub-faced creature with ringlets of curls in a halo around her face sang "Daddy Has a Sweetheart and Mother Is Her Name" in a voice that had obviously received much adoration in her mother's parlor and always would. A lanky girl decked out in a motoring costume tried to put some sauce into "Keep Away from the Fellow Who Owns an Automobile," but it came across as shrill and condemning, which met with much approval from the parents in the audience. One aspiring actress dared to step out in a bathing costume (an old-fashioned one, the kind with the heavy skirt and the woolen stockings) to sing "By the Beautiful Sea," and Constance just knew that she longed to roll off those stockings and show her beautiful legs but didn't dare. Another attempted "In the Heart of the City That Has No Heart," but she sang it so cheerily that it lost its sense of the melodramatic, and there seemed no danger of the city ever showing this particular girl how heartless it could be.

But when Fleurette took the stage, both Constance and Norma squirmed in their seats. It was obvious that something unusual, and possibly scandalous, was about to take place, and that it would have the Kopp name attached to it.

Fleurette skipped out in an elaborate ruffled gown, with an enormous satin bonnet on her head and a pink silk poppy behind her ear. Helen Stewart ran out after her, costumed in a man's baggy suit, her thumbs tucked into suspenders and a top hat nearly covering her eyes. Above her lips she had painted on a black mustache, and she kept a pipe tucked between her teeth.

It was the very picture of practiced vaudeville. When Helen turned to the audience and doffed her hat at them, her red hair came tumbling down around her shoulders.

A roar of laughter was her reward. She straightened her tie and took the first verse.

I'm a pushing young man that's been
    pushed
My heart has been cannoned and crushed
I've heard about some people falling in love
Ah, but I didn't fall, I was pushed.

Fleurette gave Helen a shove that sent the girl tumbling backwards and scrambling for her hat with the comedic exaggeration of a veteran showman.

Helen tried to stand up, but got only as far as her knees before Fleurette leaned an elbow on the top of her head and took the chorus, singing in the mock accent of a working-class city girl.

I pushed him into the parlour
Pushed the parlour door
Pushed myself upon his knee

Helen fought her way back to her feet and sang in a deep voice, hands on hips:

Pushed her kisser in front of me!

By now the audience was roaring and clapping and stamping their feet. Never had

166

a crowd gone wild for such a silly song before, but then again, they'd never seen it done quite like this.

Fleurette took Helen's hand and dragged her around the stage. Two young actresses stepped out into the lights, dressed according to their professions: first a jeweler with a monocle and a pile of costume jewels on a pillow, and then a minister in a black collar. Both girls were greeted with more laughter for their convincing masculine costumes.

Helen reached a hand out to the audience as if begging for help, and sang in an ever more frantic voice as Fleurette pulled her around.

She pushed me round to the jewelers
Near the Hippodrome
Pushed me in front of the clergyman
And then she pushed me home.

Constance could hardly hear the rest of it for all the applause showered upon poor beleaguered Helen, with her empty wine bottle and the rent past due. Even Norma shook all over and dabbed at her eyes with a handkerchief. When Helen sang, *"I now push three kids in a pram"* and wheeled out an enormous pram with three girls inside, their legs kicking, everyone in the theater was on their feet, and Helen and Fleurette took their bows together.

A few more performances followed, but they were light and frothy and quick to dissipate, like meringue. Constance hardly noticed them, so stunned was she by what she'd seen. Fleurette had only ever taken part in ensemble performances before. She'd sung a few solos, but she'd never taken command of the stage like that.

The youngest Kopp, Constance saw all at once, was becoming someone else entirely. She had ideas Constance never heard about, ambitions that exceeded her grasp, and friendships she wasn't a party to. Fleurette thought of jokes but laughed about them with someone else. She was inventing a different version of herself, one Constance had no part in.

She had to take herself quite firmly in hand at that moment. Let Fleurette make herself unrecognizable to the very people who made her, she told herself. Isn't that what she's supposed to do? Isn't that what we all do?

17

Backstage, the air was electric. Young actresses came running off after their final call, so giddy that they couldn't stop and had to dance around in a circle. The unmistakable fragrance of the theater rose up in their wake: waxy face paint and curling cream, rice powder and stolen cigarettes, and an undercurrent of nervous sweat.

Helen and Fleurette found themselves in the middle of the commotion, accepting squeals of laughter and congratulation from all sides. Fleurette pressed palms and held her cheek out to be kissed, and patted at her hair to ensure the integrity of its elaborate arrangement — but she never took her eyes off the stage door.

When the door finally opened, and May Ward breezed in, followed by her husband, Fleurette lifted her head and inhaled an enormous draft of air in an effort to calm herself. She tried to remember to be modest and grateful, and to introduce Helen right away, and to call out to the other members of their small ensemble in the way a true professional would.

But there was no chance for any of that. May Ward rushed right into the very center of the flock of girls, her arms outstretched, a shriek of delight issuing from her painted lips. She wore a hat festooned in turquoise feathers and a gauzy wine-colored velvet frock coat with a frothy white fur around her shoulders, looking every bit like a picture in a magazine.

"I've never seen anything like it, and I don't know when I will again!" she squealed. Mrs. Ward was, for some unimaginable reason, not looking directly at Fleurette as she said this, or at Helen, but twirling around and clutching at all the outstretched hands offered to her. "We ought to snatch up every last one of you and take you all with us."

This gave rise to a great deal of giggling and whispering. The air was extremely close, and everyone was red-faced and damp from exertion. Fleurette, being at the very center of the crowd and half a head shorter than most girls, felt a little faint.

"I wish we could, darling," Freeman Bernstein was saying from somewhere far away. "I wonder what their mothers would think if we took them on a spin through Philly and Boston."

"We haven't any mothers." It was Helen who found her voice first. Fleurette's head snapped up, and she slipped over to stand next to her friend.

Mr. Bernstein gave an exaggerated gasp. "No mothers! You don't mean to say that you're two poor orphan girls! Did you meet in the orphanage? Have you thought about working up an act about that?"

"We're not from an orphanage," Fleurette put in. "It just so happens that Helen's mother passed on last year and mine did, too, the year before. My sisters used to look after me, but I don't need looking after any longer."

"Oh, we all need looking after," Freeman said airily. "Now, listen here, girls, the theater is no kind of life. Take it from me. It's a rotten existence. Nothing ruins the voice faster than singing in drafty old halls."

"That's not all we do, Mr. Bernstein," Fleurette pressed on. "We've had lessons in dancing and elocution, and I play the piano and Helen knows the violin. We could show you."

"Aren't you gracious," he said. "Now, don't forget that your teacher has a signed portrait for each of you."

"But what about the audition?"

"Mrs. Ward and I will talk about it tonight, and if the lucky girl was here today, she'll hear from us. Now, if anyone would like an autograph, I'm sure my wife wouldn't mind giving a few."

The crowd pressed in on Mrs. Ward, every girl holding out a pencil and a ribboned autograph book. Fleurette looked around at them in disgust. How could they be so easily placated? Was this nothing more to them than a chance to meet an actress and collect a signature?

Just then May gave a little squeal, and all the girls around her stepped back.

"Oh, I'm so sorry," someone said.

"Is it torn?" said another.

"She didn't mean to," said a third.

Fleurette looked down and saw a length of satin ribbon ripped from the hem of May Ward's dress, dangling from the cheap and lazy running stitch that held it on. She had a sudden impulse to slap the dress-maker who couldn't be bothered to do better.

May Ward mumbled something to her husband, and Mr. Bernstein said, "That's enough for today, girls. I'd better get Mrs. Ward back to the hotel for a change of clothes."

"No, no! Wait right here." Fleurette darted away and returned almost immediately with a needle and thread. As she ran, she could hear the other girls assuring the actress that it would be made good as new.

"She'll put it back just the way it was, ma'am," one said.

"You won't ever know the difference. Look at what she did to my buttons."

"She makes the most even little stitches. It'll be better than before."

Fleurette dashed back with her kit and dropped to her knees. Her fingers held perfectly steady, and she didn't doubt for a second that she could make the neatest, fastest repair Mrs. Ward had ever seen.

When she finished, she stood up and shook out Mrs. Ward's skirts, then walked in a circle around her to check her work. She was met with a little round of applause and a handshake from Mr. Bernstein. Mrs. Ward leaned over and whispered her thanks into Fleurette's ear, and those near enough to hear laughed and applauded again.

After the autograph books were signed, and the little portraits of May Ward distributed in their brown envelopes, there came a winding-down of the excitement, and a gradual disbursement of the girls gathered around. Even Helen drifted toward the dressing-room. Mr. Bernstein patted his coat pockets with the air of a man gathering himself together to leave.

Fleurette saw, with a rising sense of panic, that the evening was ending and she hadn't been offered a place as the next Dresden Doll. The situation seemed so entirely out of keeping with her program for the audition that she wasn't entirely sure, at first, that she had her facts straight.

The words came out before she could stop herself. "But, Mrs. Ward," she called after the actress's retreating figure. "What about me?"

A hush fell over the girls still lingering backstage. May Ward stopped and spun around on one heel. Freeman Bernstein crossed his arms and leaned back in the pose of an amused spectator.

Fleurette fought back her mortification and stared May Ward down. Now that the two of them were facing one another directly, Fleurette saw the creases around the actress's mouth, lined in face powder, and the fatigue behind those brightly painted eyes. Her collar was ill-fitted and wrinkled from having been stretched and pressed too many times. Fleurette realized with a start that May Ward was as old as Norma, and possibly even as old as Constance.

Mrs. Ward allowed a smile to break across her face. "Yes? What about you?"

Fleurette looked around, wishing for Helen beside her, but Helen was frozen in the corner. There was nothing to do but to blurt it out. "Well — wouldn't you like me to join the Dresden Dolls? And my dancing partner? Didn't you — didn't you think our song was so perfectly suited to . . ."

Her voice deserted her. Mrs. Ward spoke slowly and kindly, the way one talks to a child. "We've seen so many auditions, darling, and there are more to come."

Fleurette found herself reduced to begging and wheedling. "But — what about an understudy?" She knew she would hate herself later for talking like that, but she was under some sort of spell and quite unable to walk away or to laugh and pretend she hadn't meant it.

Mrs. Ward glanced over at her husband and said, "Oh, that's the reason we have eight girls on the chorus. We can always do with six or seven if we need to."

Fleurette saw at last that Norma had been right: they hadn't any intention of offering a spot in the troupe to a student. Her five dollars had gone directly into Mr. Bernstein's pocket, and that was the end of it.

But what was she to do now? Go home as

if nothing had happened? Start rehearsals for the spring variety show? At the very thought of it, something sank inside her.

"Besides," Mrs. Ward went on, lightly, carelessly, "you don't mean to make a career on the stage, do you? You know that my chorus girls must all be five feet and four inches. That makes them two inches shorter than me, but no more. You see, they're chorus girls, and they must be —"

"The same," Freeman Bernstein put in. "It's the very idea of a chorus."

No one had ever said a thing like that to Fleurette. She didn't dare to look over at Helen — perfect, five-foot four-inch Helen. Had May Ward really just informed her that, for want of four inches in height, she had no chance whatsoever with the Dresden Dolls?

If they wouldn't have her, what was she to do?

She didn't have time to wonder. May Ward was about to walk away. She might never again be in the company of her idol.

Even if she was propelled by humiliation and desperation, at least she was propelled.

"Of course, ma'am," Fleurette called. Her voice was clear and strong, and she felt in command of herself again. She even stood a little taller. "But that dress of yours is about to fall apart. You've been cheated by your dress-maker, and I suspect the chorus girls' costumes are in even worse condition. What you need is a seamstress, and from the looks of that collar, you need one tonight."

18

When Constance returned to work the next day, she was still feeling quite unmoored by Fleurette's performance. To see her step so easily away from her familiar familial self and into a bold new public persona that represented the woman she was to become — it was dizzying, and terrifying. Here was the girl who slept late and dipped her finger in the sugar bowl, and complained about sewing on buttons but insisted that no one else did it properly, and sang snatches of song over the wash-tub. How could she be so brash and worldly on the stage? How could she command the attention of every pair of eyes in that theater, this tiny creature?

She understood how a mother must feel when she sees her son in uniform for the first time, or in his office, or with his stethoscope, practicing medicine. Mothers go about constantly wondering: How did this child of mine become a man — or woman — of the world?

Perhaps Constance could even understand how Eugene and Edith Davis felt. *We don't know Minnie anymore,* they seemed, in hindsight, to be saying. *She couldn't possibly be one of ours.*

Minnie had begged Constance for a little company and was rewarded with a move to another cell block. Now she was next door to Lottie, the nurse who didn't like to talk about why she'd been arrested, and Etta, the stenographer who was all too happy to tell about how easily cheques could be forged, money moved around, and secrets sold.

Both were eager for some new topic of conversation and listened to Minnie's story with rapt attention.

"You didn't really think he'd marry you," Lottie said, with the grim sensibility that came with her medical training.

"You never want to marry a man who deals cards on a riverboat," Etta said.

"Of course not," Minnie said carelessly.

"The only question I have," Lottie said, "is how are you going to get out of this?"

Lottie and Etta leaned forward, eager to hear what Minnie had in mind. When she said, "Why, I'll just tell them the truth — I

179

don't see why I shouldn't," they both burst into laughter.

"The truth will get you locked up until you're past childbearing age!" Etta said. "Ask Lottie here. She's seen it."

"Oh, I suppose you've seen everything, if you're a nurse," Minnie said. "But there's no reason to keep me in jail."

Lottie had thin lips and a beaky little nose. She pushed those features together in an expression of distaste and said, "A girl of low morals is thought to be a hazard to our fighting men. They don't want to weaken America's forces right before we're called to war, if you know what I mean."

Minnie didn't know, but she wouldn't have admitted it. "I'm not worried about it. When I get into a fix, I always find a way out."

"You're lucky we have a lady deputy," Lottie said. "There was another factory girl in here before you. Brought in on some kind of waywardness charge. The judge let her go because Miss Kopp said so."

"Then why hasn't she set you two free?" Minnie asked.

They both laughed. "We've had our trials," Etta said. "We're guilty, darling."

"I'm only guilty of an accidental overdose," Lottie said by way of correction. "I didn't mean to kill the old dear. I suppose I'd be off at the state prison if they thought me guilty of murder."

"But you won't be a nurse again," Etta said.

"I might start over out West."

"Oh, I'd like that, too," Minnie said.

They passed the rest of the day with that kind of companionable talk. Minnie found that she quite liked the company of lady criminals. There was a fearlessness to them, as if the very fact of their arrest, and exposure of their secrets, liberated them of the need to cower and pretend. Etta and Lottie were resourceful women who had made their own way in the world quite successfully until they were caught, and Minnie admired them for it.

She went to bed with considerably lighter spirits after spending the day in their company. Around midnight the sound of footsteps along the cell block jolted her awake.

"Is everything all right, Miss Kopp?" Etta whispered. The deputy had been away all day on a case.

"Ladies, if you don't mind, I'm going to take Minnie back to my cell for a little talk," Constance said.

"Miss Kopp's all right," Etta said as Minnie was led away. "You can tell her."

"Tell me what?" Constance asked, but Minnie was too sleepy to answer. She stumbled along the concrete floor and around the jail's central rotunda to the cell block where Constance slept.

"How are you getting on?" the deputy asked once they were out of earshot of the others. In Constance's cell was an oil lamp, but they didn't light it. They sat together on her bunk, in the purple darkness, under only the faintest light from a half-moon that shone through the high-domed window above.

"Jail's not too bad," Minnie said, with what little swagger she could muster at that hour.

It really wasn't so terrible. Apart from the boredom and the drab, shapeless uniform, it didn't particularly bother Minnie to spend her days and nights in jail. She'd been wondering for some time how she might get out of the mess she's made with Tony, and now she knew. The most pressing of her worries — eviction and penury — had been eliminated through the provision of a bunk and three tasteless meals a day. She wondered mildly what might become of her, but assumed she'd be given a chance to tell her version of events to a judge, upon which time she'd be released.

And after that? She didn't know exactly where she would go or what she would do, but she was counting on her cache of jewelry to secure a train ticket and a fresh opportunity in a city where she could start again, under a new name if she had to. It wouldn't be easy, but it wasn't impossible.

It was in that almost carefree state of mind that she submitted to Constance's questioning. She didn't believe the others when they told her that she could tell Constance everything — she was, after all, a deputy sheriff and on the side of the law — but Minnie had assembled a version of the truth that she felt reasonably sure would be accepted.

Constance spoke in a voice just above a whisper. "It appears the prosecutor is preparing to bring a white slave charge against Anthony — against Tony."

"Because of me?" Minnie protested. "That's ridiculous! I wasn't exactly snatched from the sidewalk, if that's what you mean to say."

"That's exactly what the prosecutor wants to say. He intends to make a case that Tony carried you across state lines for an immoral purpose."

Minnie found the very idea insulting. She'd heard of girls going to jail over debauchery charges, but as the nature of their offense was never described, she'd imagined an act far worse than anything she'd ever done.

"But surely you've told them otherwise," Minnie insisted. "He didn't have to kidnap me at all. I wanted to go. I hated Catskill. Did you go and speak to my parents?"

"I did."

"Then you know why I left. Wouldn't you run off to New York, if you lived with them?"

Minnie could see that argument made an impression on Constance. "I probably would have, at your age," she admitted, "but I want you to understand the difficulty you'd be in if you put it that way to the judge."

"What difficulty? It's the truth."

Constance cleared her throat. "Well . . . I know the judge would appreciate your honesty. But if a girl is found to have . . . to have gone around with men, especially if she so freely admits to living under the pretense of marriage . . . well, she might not be set free."

"But what else could they possibly do with me? I haven't robbed a bank. Why would they keep me in jail?"

"They wouldn't keep you in jail. They'd send you to a girls' reformatory."

A reformatory! The very word brought to mind girls in white uniforms being made to march in straight lines and memorize Bible verses. "But I'm not in need of reforming," Minnie complained. "I just need to break away from Tony and find a place of my own. What's wrong with that? You could let me go today, and I'd never make another spot of trouble. You just helped another girl get out of jail, didn't you? Why can't you do the same for me?"

Constance sighed and leaned against the wall. "Hers was a very different case."

"I don't see why."

"Because Miss Heustis — Edna, the girl you've heard about — had done absolutely nothing to attract suspicion. That isn't the case with you and Tony, and you admit it. Besides, Edna is eighteen. I'm sorry to put it to you so bluntly, but in your case a judge will see a sixteen-year-old girl who dis-obeyed her mother and ran off with a man she'd only just met. He might think her a girl of low scruples for pretending to be the man's wife when she wasn't. A girl like that is in need of reforming." She turned and looked at Minnie. "That's what the judge might think."

"And you couldn't tell him otherwise."

"I could try," said Constance. "But it

would help if I had something in the way of evidence. Isn't there anyone who could testify as to your character? A landlord or —"

"There was some trouble with him," Minnie said morosely.

"What about your job? Could I speak to your boss?"

"I didn't get on very well there, either."

It was starting to dawn on Constance that her success with Edna Heustis had come a little too easily. Not every girl who got arrested came with character references. "Well, you won't be released unless someone is willing to take you in and vouch for you. Are you sure you can't write a letter of apology to your parents, and make things all right with them?"

"You know I can't."

"Isn't there anyone else? An aunt, or a cousin?"

Minnie shook her head. "I never knew my mother's family, and my father — well, you can imagine what his people are like." She found it difficult to speak as her predicament became clear to her.

"And is there anything at all you haven't told me? You heard what the prosecutor said the day you were arrested, about men going in and out of the place. Is there any truth in

186

it? I can't help you if I don't know what really happened."

Minnie forced herself to look Constance in the eyes.

"Of course there weren't other men," she said. "It was just me and Tony, and I thought we were to be married. There's nothing else to tell."

19

What Minnie missed most about her old life was perfume. The inmates were allowed nothing but tar soap in the jail, which smelled like hospitals. But perfume! It spoke to her of a life she'd held in her hand, however briefly.

She never did spray the fragrances liberally around her — she believed that to be uncouth — but instead she would allow the donor of the perfume to choose his favorite spot, and there she would apply it for him, every time: the crook of her arm, the underside of her neck, behind her knee. One man liked it on the very small of her back, and she wore it there just for him: their little secret.

She didn't know enough to ask for parma violets and crushed white roses from the perfumeries in New York, but she did enjoy a few good imitations from the druggist in Fort Lee, with names like Dreams of the

Orient and Empress' Bouquet, names that hinted at their ability to transport her to another place, another time, another life.

Tony never asked her who bought the perfume. He wasn't the kind of man to notice a little thing like the particulars of a girl's toilette, nor was he attentive enough to remark on the fragrance behind her ears.

He wasn't even particularly interested in her, but she only came to understand that later, in the solitude of her jail cell. When she went down to the dock that day in late September, she'd already decided that she wasn't going to spend another winter in Catskill. She just didn't know how, precisely, to pull it off. Tony was her opportunity. Why should he fall under the spell of her perfume, much less love her, if she saw him chiefly as a means of transportation?

It was near the end of the season for the pleasure boats that went up and down the Hudson. The men with whom Minnie had spent her summer evenings — the college boys and idle wealthy who took Catskill as their leisure grounds in July and August — had all retreated back to the city, to campuses and offices by day and theaters by night, forgetting all about their afternoons of lawn croquet and evenings with the local girls along the boardwalk. There was no one left, really, but the boys who worked on board the boats, and soon they would vanish, too, before the winter's ice made the Hudson impassable.

She'd seen Tony before but had never spoken to him. He was older than her, and a natty dresser (the striped vest and red tie was a uniform, as he worked at the card tables, but she thought he made the most of it). He seemed to prefer the company of the steamboat's crew to the locals who wandered the boardwalk, and as such had not shown any interest in her.

But that night, she saw him on deck by himself, just looking out idly over the river, and took a chance. "Do you know I've lived here my whole life," she called, "and I've never set foot on one of these boats?"

He turned around and grinned at her. "What's your name, sweetheart?"

He had an easygoing voice that Minnie couldn't resist. A friendly man, bestowing the bright light of his attention on her, could suffuse Minnie with a feeling of contentment that she so rarely knew any other time. It filled a certain hollowness inside of her and lifted her off the ground a few inches. She would live her whole life inside those moments if she could.

There was something substantial about

this man, something in his shoulders and the line of his jaw, that made Minnie feel more solid herself. She gave her name with a little laugh and accepted his outstretched hand when she stepped on board. He took her around to see the red-carpeted card room and the restaurant with its white tablecloths and chandeliers. Then he introduced her to the captain, who touched the bill of his cap and bowed a little. It made her feel like a girl in a play. She didn't ever want to stop feeling that way.

Then, all at once, it was time for the boat to leave, and Tony turned to take her back to the dock.

"Oh, but wouldn't it be nice to take a little ride down the river?" she asked wistfully. "I've always wondered what it might be like." She looked at him with all the longing that lived within her — longing for a new life, a new place, a new city, a new job, a new man. How could he resist?

He almost did resist, and perhaps he should have. Some kind of calculation hung in the air between them. With some reluctance he looked around at the empty saloon below-decks and said that there would be no harm in her riding along, and that she could get off at the next town and take the train back if she didn't like it. She gave him a bright smile and kissed him on the cheek. He put his hand up to the place her lips had been as if he wasn't sure what she'd just given him.

In a few minutes, the boat was set free of the dock, and she was watching Catskill grow smaller and smaller. That strange disassociated feeling of being a girl in a play grew even stronger. The curtain had risen on the rest of her life. A scene was in motion, and Minnie was at the center of it.

The boat was bound for Manhattan. Minnie had never been, but she had plenty of romantic notions about it. Tony talked about the city in a way that made him sound like a man of the world: he knew all about the shops and the theaters and the lights in Times Square, and the all-night restaurants and the glittering dance halls. He said that the leaves on the trees in Central Park would be turning orange, and that from above, from some bejeweled rooftop at sunset, it would look like the city was on fire, but beautifully so.

Tony made the coming winter in New York City sound like an evening at the palace, with all the shop windows lit up in the snow, and fashionable girls ice-skating on the pond. There would be restaurants and Champagne. Minnie had never eaten at a real restaurant, much less tasted anything with bubbles in it beyond soda.

Tony wore a nice wool coat and a cashmere scarf. He was all wrapped up like a Christmas present. She wondered aloud how a girl might go about exploring New York City on her own, and Tony didn't hesitate to offer to escort her around town. There was a delicious charge between them by that time. In Tony, Minnie saw the promise of a new life, freedom, a way out. What did Tony see in Minnie? The promise of a memorable night, at least. She could offer him that much.

As the boat drifted along, they sat belowdecks and talked about the city, and where they might go first when they went ashore. She sat comfortably alongside him in one of the empty passenger lounges, with his coat over her legs. In the dim hours before morning, New York City rose up over the bow of the boat like a mirage, and she knew for certain that she had left home forever.

But she didn't tell him that at first. She let him give her one perfect day in Manhattan. They saw the Menagerie in the park and the sheep grazing, and he bought her a warm roll and a packet of cheese from the little dairy. They rode in an open-air trolley downtown, which rolled slowly along but still didn't leave enough time for Minnie to take it all in. At sundown they had dinner in one of the all-night restaurants on Broadway.

Still Tony didn't know that she planned to turn that day into the rest of her life. He was ready to take her to the train station and send her home. By the time she arrived back in Catskill, she would've been gone a little over twenty-four hours. She'd be scolded if she told the truth and punished if she tried to lie, but Tony simply assumed that her parents would take her back, and that her life would go on as it had before.

When she told him that she wasn't going home — "Wouldn't you like me to stay a night?" was how she put it to him — he looked down at her with a little half-smile and thought about it for a minute, making another calculation. Then he said that she might as well come with him to the home of a distant cousin who lived down on Mott Street. He slept in a chair, and she took the only spare bed, but she went to him in the middle of the night, or perhaps he found his way to her bed, but one way or another, by morning they were something more than two strangers who'd run off to the city for a day.

Next came the delicate question of what

Tony's obligations toward her might be. Minnie wasn't going home, but she hadn't any other place to lay her head. She'd been hoping that Tony kept a little room somewhere and would let her stay for a week or two. She was surprised to learn that he lived in his parents' basement in Fort Lee and worked in their restaurant during the winter until the steamboat hired him back on in the spring. He couldn't very well bring Minnie home to live in the basement.

Minnie did her best to look a little helpless and love-struck, and perhaps she was. Tony seemed struck dumb by the obligation he found himself under, after what had transpired between them. She expected far more than he was prepared to give, but what was he to do about it?

After some sly suggestions on her part, one or the other of them proposed that they take a furnished room in Fort Lee, posing as husband and wife. She couldn't remember, later, exactly how it came about, but it was precisely the sort of situation she'd been hoping for. He promised to save every penny toward "something better for us," which might have meant marriage and might have meant nothing at all, and Minnie didn't mind either way. He told her that if she could take a job herself, they'd have enough money to go into New York from time to time. There would be dances and cabarets, and new dresses for Minnie, dresses that her sister had never once worn.

What girl wouldn't want a life like that? She would never see the inside of a knitting mill again, or share a bed with Goldie in that drafty room behind the kitchen. She'd be a woman of the world, with a home in New York — or near it, anyway, almost in sight of it. She would go to work just as Tony had asked her to, but it would be something droll and lighthearted. She would make bouquets at a flower shop. She would sell tickets at a moving picture house. She might even take the ferry across and have a little secretarial job in Manhattan like the girls she'd seen at the lunch counters.

Everything went as she hoped it would — almost. They rented a room above a bakery on Main Street in Fort Lee. Minnie couldn't find work in a theater or a flower shop, and it cost too much to go by ferry to New York every day, so she took a job as a carder in a jute mill, which was considerably dustier and less pleasant than the knitting mill back in Catskill. It was disagreeable work compared to running a knitting machine, and within a few days her fingers were always red and swollen from handling the rough material.

She found out that living near New York wasn't at all the same as living in New York, and that their plans to visit the city never quite came together. She only went once in the fall, and that was to mail a letter. Tony had insisted that she send word to her parents — otherwise, he argued, they'd send the police after her, and she could be forcibly taken back home, which would be so much worse for her. After some arguing, she wrote the letter, explaining that she was well and engaged to be married. (There had been no further talk of marriage, but what else could Minnie have said?) She insisted they go to New York to post it so that she couldn't be found by the postmark.

"I'd rather be the girl who ran away to New York than the one who ran away to Fort Lee," she told Tony, and he indulged her and took her to the downtown post office in Manhattan. She'd dressed for lunch and an afternoon in the shops, but Tony wouldn't pay for anything more than a sandwich at the train station. They rode back together in silence, Minnie despondent, Tony distracted.

He spent most nights at his parents' house so that they wouldn't suspect him of wrong-

197

doing. Although he wasn't paying rent at home, he never did seem to have any money. He claimed that he was saving it, that he had to be frugal, that he had expenses of his own. It fell to Minnie to pay most of the rent and to stock the kitchen with the little that she earned. There was nothing left for new dresses and theater tickets. After the initial thrill of playing at husband and wife wore off, Tony didn't come around as often. Sometimes she didn't see him for a week, sometimes two. There was no real bond between them — there never had been — and Tony probably wished to be relieved of any further obligations toward her.

Could she be blamed if she got lonely? What was there to do, all alone in her little room at night, but to read a library book or play a game of solitaire? The old emptiness had found her again. It practically roared in her ears. She couldn't stand her own company anymore and grew to hate the worries that ran in circles in her head: Was anything to become of her and Tony? Would she ever get out of the jute mill and on to another life? Had she only traded one factory and dingy room for another?

Minnie had always hated being poor and thought it unfair that such things as blue fox collars and emeralds and meringues existed if she couldn't have them. There wasn't enough money to go to town, much less to buy anything, and sometimes she could hardly afford to eat. She was bored and lonely and already tired of her new life and longing for another one.

One evening, when the rent was a week late, and she'd had a few too many dinners of tea and toast (the toast salvaged from the bakery's day-old bins downstairs), and she couldn't stand to be alone in a room with herself for another night, she walked out of the jute mill and nearly ran into a man who was lingering there, fumbling with a cigarette. He backed away and apologized, and looked down at her with a bemused and crinkly smile.

"Say, you look like a girl my sister used to know. What's your name?"

Minnie wanted nothing more in the world at that moment than to hear him say her name, so she gave it to him.

20

Constance went downstairs to look for Sheriff Heath but found Mrs. Heath in his office instead. She was seated at his desk, going over some papers, as if it were the most ordinary thing in the world for the sheriff's wife to occupy his place. Constance was so startled by the sight that she entirely forgot the reason for her visit.

If she could, she would've turned around and left. She never knew how to behave in Mrs. Heath's presence. All her efforts to stay in Cordelia's good graces left her feeling exhausted and insufficient.

But it was too late; she'd been spotted.

"Miss Kopp!" Cordelia called out, extending to Constance the genteel smile that she always presented to the public. There was an aristocratic fragility in her appearance, like tissue too fine to touch. On this occasion she wore a blue velvet suit with a jacket that flared just below the waist, and a tamo'-shanter hat to match. It was the uniform of a busy socialite. This, Constance realized, was a woman with an agenda.

"I'm sorry to bother you, Mrs. Heath."

"I know you were looking for my husband, but I want a word with you before I run out. I've taken charge of Bob's campaign —"

"Campaign?"

"Ah, yes. It's an election year — didn't you know that?"

"I —"

"Well, I'm arranging for a photographer, and a schedule of lectures throughout the summer and fall, and a few advertisements in the newspapers. Which brings me to you. Now, Bob assures me he's spoken to you about this already, but you must know how important it is to stay out of the papers during an election year."

"I suppose so," Constance said, although she hadn't thought at all about how she ought to behave in an election year. She wasn't accustomed to having to pay attention to such things, and Sheriff Heath certainly didn't encourage it: he told his deputies to ignore political skirmishes and to do the best job they could without worrying about what the voters might think. But their jobs depended upon Sheriff Heath winning his election, so it mattered a great deal.

Cordelia pressed on. "I can't seem to stop him from lecturing the Freeholders, or feuding with the prosecutor's office, or turning a lady deputy loose on the streets, but I can try to keep it out of the papers, can't I?"

She didn't bother to apologize for the remark about the lady deputy, as she'd made her views entirely clear already and there wouldn't be any reason to pretend otherwise. Constance, for her part, didn't bother to take offense. She thought it a waste of her time to cosset and fuss over every fresh injury Mrs. Heath tried to inflict upon her.

"Yes, ma'am. You needn't worry. I'd be perfectly happy to stay out of the papers. You wouldn't believe the letters I've had."

Cordelia laughed brightly. "Bob told me! Marriage proposals! What kind of man wants to marry a woman in uniform?"

"I can't imagine," Constance said agreeably. "There won't be any trouble about the papers."

To her relief, Sheriff Heath's footsteps came down the hall. She was still standing in the doorway, and when he spotted her, he called, "I heard there was quite a crowd in Paterson for Miss Fleurette's show."

She started to answer, but then he came around the corner and saw Cordelia. "Dear, if you sit at my desk, people will think you're running quite a bit more than my campaign."

Cordelia stood up and cleared her papers away. "I haven't any other place to work."

"We'll find you something. Did Miss Kopp tell you that her youngest sister had an audition with May Ward?"

Cordelia wrinkled her pretty little nose. "Isn't May Ward a sort of vaudeville act?"

"She is," said Constance, "but it's what you might think of as light comedy. It wasn't really an audition. It was more of a talent show with May Ward in attendance. The girls had a good time and there was no harm in it."

"Then they didn't offer Miss Fleurette the part?" The sheriff took his seat behind the desk as his wife moved away.

"Of course not. Just as Norma suspected, there were no parts on offer. But what I came to tell you is that I have been to see the Davises. It wasn't at all what I expected."

Cordelia took a seat, gingerly, as if she hoped no one would notice that she was still there. But both Constance and Sheriff Heath turned to look at her.

"This is the white slave case, isn't it?" Cordelia asked.

Mrs. Heath wasn't in the habit of putting herself in the middle of her husband's business like this. Constance could see that it annoyed him. There was an uneasiness between the sheriff and his wife that Constance wished they would keep behind the closed doors of their residence.

Sheriff Heath very deliberately turned away from his wife and said, "Tell me what happened up in Catskill."

"They're very strict," Constance said. "I believe they think Minnie's gone and ruined herself. They don't want her back."

"And what does Miss Davis say?"

"Well, she knows she's not wanted, and she wants nothing to do with them either. She seems to think she can make a clean breast of it with the judge and go free."

"The prosecutor expects her to testify against Anthony Leo. Is she prepared to do that?"

"She doesn't want to," Constance said. "She insists that she wasn't coerced. I suppose she has some affection for Tony — Mr. Leo — and doesn't think he's to blame."

"Well, someone's to blame," Cordelia put in, with a nervous laugh.

The sheriff sighed and dropped a pencil

on his desk. "I thought you had quite a busy day, dear."

Cordelia twitched a little at that but stood up gracefully. "These are exactly the kinds of cases that could hurt your campaign. If you're against arresting girls over morality crimes, then what are you for?"

The sheriff rubbed his forehead and pushed his hair back. "It's not as simple as that."

"It will be for the voters. But I won't interfere." She swept out of the room without another word. Constance allowed herself a flutter of relief: every word she said sounded wrong in Mrs. Heath's presence. But perhaps Cordelia's caution was well-founded.

"If the election changes things with this case —" Constance began.

"It doesn't. But Miss Davis is the victim in this, even if she doesn't see it that way. She's sixteen and she was misled by a false promise of marriage. Try to get her to see it that way."

"Minnie isn't the kind of girl who likes to change her mind, but I'll try," Constance said. "I'd also like to go down to Fort Lee and speak to her landlord."

"That's fine. The prosecutor hasn't even filed charges, so nothing's going to happen this week. You have time."

"Would you mind if I spoke to Tony? If he cares about the girl at all, he might know someone who'd speak on her behalf."

"Mr. Courter will think you're interfering with his case," the sheriff said, but Constance could tell he rather liked the idea of that.

"Then come with me," she said, "and you can make sure that I don't."

Tony looked up at Constance and the sheriff suspiciously, but then rose from his bunk and went over to the bars of his cell. Constance hadn't seen him since the day of his arrest. Even without his nice suit and his hair pomade, he still had the easy good looks that a girl could fall for.

In fact, he turned his eyes on her with the kind of affability that must have worked on many a young lady. "I remember you," he said with a grin. "You're the girl cop who took care of Minnie that day. How's she getting on? Did they let her keep that sweet little place above the bakery? It always smelled like sugar up there."

Constance said, "Mr. Leo, she never did go back to that little room. She's right upstairs in her own cell, up on the fifth floor. We're holding her as a witness in the case against you. Didn't you know that?"

He took a step back, stunned. "She's in jail? My girl's in jail? I thought you'd take down her story and let her go."

"We didn't," said Sheriff Heath.

"But she hasn't done anything wrong! She's never done nothing wrong in her life. She shouldn't be held on my account."

"She refuses to testify against you," Constance said. "She insists that neither of you did anything wrong."

He grinned. "That's my girl. You tell her I said so."

Sheriff Heath said, "Son, we're not here to pass messages between you two. Now that you know Minnie isn't making any accusations against you, we'd like to know if you can help her."

"We need someone who can speak on her behalf," Constance said, "and testify as to her character."

He put his shoulders back and said, "Yes, ma'am. It would be my honor."

She couldn't help but smile at that. "Not you, Tony. Someone else. A landlord, a neighbor, someone she knew at work? Maybe someone in your family."

Tony shook his head. "My family didn't know nothing about her. And I — well, Minnie and me had our troubles. I'm sorry,

207

but I wasn't around much. And when I was . . . well, we stayed in most nights. We didn't go out and see people. I don't think anybody in Fort Lee knew her."

Constance said, "Tony, don't you see? If she tells the judge she went willingly, it doesn't look good for her. He won't release her if he thinks she's prone to running off with any man she meets."

"She doesn't run off with any man! She . . ." But he faltered as he saw the reasoning behind it. "That's not fair," he added, weakly.

"It would've been fair of you to marry her, but you didn't," Sheriff Heath said.

"Aw, Sheriff! Why can't she go back to the jute factory, or home to her mother?"

"Her mother and father won't take her back now," Constance told him, "and no judge is going to release her on her own. He's going to want her under someone's care, a girl of sixteen."

"Bah," he said, the corners of his mouth turning down. "She never told me she was sixteen."

Sheriff Heath leaned in closer. Tony looked at him with the sorrowful eyes of a stray dog. "Listen to me, son. I know you must meet a lot of girls on that boat."

He shrugged and glanced over at Constance, embarrassed. "Some."

"Of course you do. And I bet Minnie isn't the first girl you took down the river for a night."

"Well. There might have been a few. But they wanted to go, Sheriff! Honest. I never forced anybody."

He nodded sympathetically. "I know you didn't. The trouble is, these girls start to get ideas about marriage and children, don't they?"

Tony let out a long breath. "That's just it, Sheriff. They don't want to go home to their mothers! What am I supposed to say about that?"

"Well, you can't marry all of them, Tony. And you weren't going to marry this one either, were you?"

He didn't answer that.

"We have a forged marriage license that we found in your pocket. The prosecutor is bound to turn up your lease, and I'll bet it says that you and Minnie presented yourselves as man and wife. Do you know what that adds up to?"

He put his head down a little. He looked like a child who'd just been scolded.

Sheriff Heath leaned forward and said, "Look at me."

Tony did.

Sheriff Heath said, "It means a white slave charge."

He stepped away from the bars and looked back and forth between the two of them. "I'm no white slaver. I never drugged a girl and I never kidnapped nobody. Let me out of here and I'll marry Minnie tomorrow. I'll marry her right now, with these chains on me, if you'll take us to the courthouse."

"It doesn't work like that, son. The prosecutor's drawing up the charges now. The only question is whether Miss Davis testifies against you or refuses to."

"She won't say a word against me because she loves me," Tony said, a little boastfully. "She was never forced. Do you want her to lie and say she was?"

"It doesn't matter what we want," Constance said. "Only — she's taking the hard road. If she tells the truth, well . . . we just can't say what might become of her. If you can think of anyone who could speak on her behalf, please tell us."

Sheriff Heath turned to walk away and Constance followed. Tony shouted after them, "Can't you do something for her, miss? She doesn't deserve to be mixed up in all of this, a kid like that."

He sounded sincere about it. She almost felt sorry for him.

21

John Courter was waiting for the sheriff downstairs. He couldn't be bothered to nod at Constance, as there was no civility between the two of them.

"I need the key to the female section," the detective said, without any preliminaries.

"It's customary for the guards to bring an inmate downstairs for questioning," Sheriff Heath said.

Mr. Courter was the kind of red-faced man for whom beads of sweat bloomed constantly across his forehead. Constance felt quite cool and collected by comparison.

"It's time for me to speak to that poor unfortunate girl of yours. Isn't that where you have your little fireside chats? Upstairs, in the ladies' cells, where you girls drink your tea and do your embroidery?"

"Miss Davis hasn't anything new to say," Constance told him, "and if she did, she'd say it to me."

He took a step closer to her and spoke in the manner of a schoolmaster speaking to a young student. "I blame the sheriff here for not explaining to you how a criminal prosecution works. He might've thought you didn't need to know, seeing as how you're only here to look after the girls. But since he hasn't told you, I will. I interview the witnesses. I file the charges. You're the jailer. All you have to do is to hold them in those little cells upstairs until I decide what happens to them. Do you think you can remember all of that?"

Constance was not a woman who was troubled by the idea of shoving a man, or throwing one down on the ground. When she was angry, a certain vigor flowed quite easily into her limbs and made itself ready for a demonstration of might. The only difficulty was keeping it in check.

"Every week I'm seeing girls brought up on frivolous charges," she said. "Someone has to speak up for them."

He snorted. "We have people called lawyers who come before the judge to explain the criminal's side of things. You aren't pretending to practice law now, too, are you?"

Sheriff Heath said, "John, you know a sixteen-year-old girl can't pay a lawyer."

212

"What I don't understand," he said, "is why she would need one, if she was dragged away by a white slaver. For that matter, why did that Heustis girl require any intervention, if she was innocent of the charges? And why haven't I seen a report on her? The judge released that girl on your word. I can have her arrested again if I'm not convinced that she's meeting the terms the judge set out. Or didn't Sheriff Heath explain that to you?"

"You'll have your report," Constance said.

22

With a sigh Edna straightened her collar and walked up to the door of her parents' house in Edgewater. It wasn't her home anymore, and for that reason she hesitated before she walked in, wondering if she ought to knock first. Her brothers never did: they simply bounced inside and hollered out to whoever might be within earshot. But her brothers all acted as though they belonged anywhere and everywhere, while Edna wasn't sure where she belonged anymore. She certainly didn't belong at the little yellow house in Edgewater.

She was about to raise her hand and knock when she heard a familiar voice behind her.

"They told me you wouldn't miss your old dad's birthday!"

Edna turned around and found herself nearly in the arms of Dewey Barnes. She stumbled on the porch step, and he laughed and caught her by the elbow. "I never swept a girl off her feet before," he said, a little too loudly, in the manner of someone hoping to be overheard.

Edna righted herself and stepped back to get a look at him. He was a man of soft features: round, unsuspecting eyes, a bulbous nose, wide lips, and a dimple on his chin like a finger pressed in dough. He was not an altogether unpleasant-looking man, but he didn't make much of an impression.

"Hello, Dewey. How good of you to stop by."

"You're awfully formal, Miss Edna." He leaned over to place a kiss on her cheek, but it landed awkwardly near her eye and Edna had to resist the urge to wipe it away.

"Your brothers invited me," he continued, as if nothing strange had happened. "I wouldn't miss a good Sunday dinner." He reached around and knocked on the door, settling the question of how Edna was to gain entrance.

Because they walked in together, her brothers had the idea that they'd arrived as a couple, and treated them as such.

"There they are!" Charlie called, jumping to his feet and pumping Dewey's hand. "We wondered where you two had gone off to."

Edna wanted to correct the idea that she'd

215

been anywhere with Dewey, but everyone was talking at once and she couldn't. All four of her brothers were crowded into the parlor, which seemed so small now that she'd been away. Her father sat happily among them, wearing a silly crown of crepe paper that the boys must have forced on him.

Only her mother stayed quiet. She hovered uneasily around the edge of the room, darting in and out of the kitchen at intervals. Edna knew that she was expected to disappear, too, and help tend to the roast or peel the potatoes, but she didn't. She settled right between her two eldest brothers, and joined into their talk of work and war.

"They finally gunned down a zeppelin," her father said. "Can you believe it? They were firing from an automobile."

"I wouldn't have thought you could take a zeppelin down with a bullet," said Fred, one of the twins.

"Oh, they didn't," Edna said. "They have a special sort of shell that explodes against the aluminum. They held enormous searchlights on it the entire time. It came right down in the countryside, and every single bomb it was carrying went off at once in a farmer's field. But it didn't get to Paris, and that's what matters, isn't it?"

The men in the room looked at her in astonishment. Her younger brother, Davie, said, "You haven't taken up with a soldier, have you? That might come as news to old Dewey here."

Edna's brothers had been teasing her about marrying Dewey for years. He'd been at school with the twins and hung around the house with them on Saturdays, and seemed to act as though a match with Edna were a foregone conclusion. And what was wrong with that? He was one of those perfectly dull, solid, mild-mannered men who would ask nothing more of a wife than a comfortable chair and a newspaper to hide behind. He would go unquestioningly to his office, his club, and his church every week, and to his mother-in-law's house for Sunday dinner. A fishing camp along a river would be his idea of an adventure, but even that would lose its appeal after a few years, and he would spend his Saturdays in the garage, tinkering with an automobile or an old clock.

Edna could see Dewey's entire life written across his placid face. Maybe at one time she had encouraged him — just a little — but now it was glaringly apparent that he had nothing on offer that Edna wanted.

"I haven't taken up with anyone," she said,

avoiding Dewey's eyes. "I read the papers, that's all. We make some of those bullets and bombs up at the powder works. Why shouldn't I want to know about it?"

Her father reached over and patted her knee. "That's just fine. You're doing your part. Be sure to carve your initials in one or two of those bullets, and maybe your brothers will see them in France."

Mrs. Heustis had been coming down the hall from the kitchen as he said this. She gave a little sob when she heard him and ran back to her oven. Edna had no choice but to go and comfort her, and to roll out the biscuits and put the potatoes on. No one else was going to do it.

She didn't say a word to her mother, or to anyone else, about the Women's Preparedness Committee recruiting volunteers to go overseas. It was one thing for her to do her duty in a factory; it was another entirely to board a ship to France. But the notion was gaining traction with Edna. She hadn't said a word out loud to anyone about it, but already the possibility had turned into a plan, and the wild idea had hardened to resolve.

23

Fleurette bought her train ticket at the station agent's window. She had to fight the urge to lift it to her lips and kiss it.

I did it, she thought. She'd found the money, she'd contrived a reason to send Norma to town (Constance seemed to be very busy on a case and hadn't been home at all), packed her trunks in secret, and bribed a man from the dairy to take her to the train station. She managed every bit of it so beautifully that it was a wonder she'd never run off before.

Now there was nothing to do but to wait for May Ward and her troupe, who would be boarding in Leonia, down south. She was to join them when the train stopped in Paterson.

Fleurette had seen no reason to tell her sisters that she was leaving. She was tired of having her whereabouts always known. She wanted very much to be out of sight of her family, to be on a train or in a hotel or on a sidewalk in some distant city, so that no one who knew her — not a single soul — could say, with any certainty, exactly where she was or what she was doing.

What a novelty it would be! Imagine walking into a shop where she'd never been seen before, and having her own money to buy things, not an account under Constance's name. Imagine sitting in a lunchroom on her very own, with the rest of the world around her, people whose lives held secrets she couldn't guess, people who spoke languages she couldn't understand, people whose afternoons rolled out before them, filled in whatever manner that other, more interesting people filled their days. Fleurette would never know until she left home to find out about them.

Even if May Ward wouldn't let her on the stage — and she would, she would, once she saw what Fleurette could do — at least she had a ticket out of town.

Mrs. Ward had been delighted with the idea of a full-time seamstress to travel with the company and put her wardrobe in order — it was such a bother, she said, to send things out at the hotel — but Freeman Bernstein insisted that it couldn't be done. It would be impossible, he explained, with lighthearted regret, to add the expense of another girl to a tour already settled.

"People don't buy tickets to watch a seamstress," he said. "If you're not on stage, you're not paying your way."

"Then that's what I'll do," Fleurette told him, still animated and half out of her mind after the audition. "I will pay my way. You won't owe me a thing until the end of the first week. If you like what I can do — if Mrs. Ward is pleased (for Fleurette knew that it was Mrs. Ward who had to be persuaded, and she would persuade her husband), then you'll put me into the company. If not, you'll send me home."

Fleurette and May Ward proved to be a formidable opposition to Mr. Bernstein's objections. After a hushed conference, he agreed and gave Fleurette the date and time of departure.

"You'll buy your own train ticket," Mr. Bernstein said. "I'm holding you to it."

"I expect you to," she answered, feeling terribly bold and brash.

Of course, there was the problem of putting her hands on the money. She could sell a few things — there was always something in her wardrobe she could part with — and she was owed for dresses she'd made for her fellow students. But that wouldn't be enough. She needed twenty dollars, at least. She didn't dare come right out and ask Constance for such a large sum.

But that didn't mean that Constance wouldn't have been willing to give it to her, if she'd understood the situation properly, did it? Besides, it would all be repaid. Fleurette imagined herself, after she'd made a success on the stage, stopping in at banks to have money sent to her spinster sisters in the countryside. When the papers wrote about her, they would all say that she was generous to her family, and that she never forgot that first twenty-dollar loan that gave her the start she needed. She would laugh with the reporter over the circumstances under which she'd "borrowed" the money, and how easily her sisters forgave her, once it had been returned many times over.

With that in mind, Fleurette had behaved, on the night of the audition, exactly as Norma and Constance would've expected her to. She didn't want to give any hint of what had actually happened backstage, or of what was to come.

"May Ward said we stole the show," she told them, with the easy confidence of someone who had, in fact, triumphed on stage that very night. "Mr. Bernstein said it was the best performance he'd ever seen at one of their auditions, and they've done them all over the country."

"Of course they have," Norma said. "The only easier way to make money would be to print it oneself, and I suppose he's tried that, too."

Constance gave her praise, measured and steady as always, for the clear and beautiful singing, the cleverness of the choreography, and the sheer perfection of the costumes. "May Ward couldn't help but think you were the best," she said. "We all did."

But it was dull to hear the same old praise from Constance. Being held in Constance's high regard did nothing for her. She wanted the admiration of theater critics, and show managers, and tasteful people sitting in boxes.

When the talk turned away from Fleurette's theatrical accomplishments, she allowed it to drift. It wouldn't do to make too much of a fuss about the evening. Over the coming days, she'd have any number of secretive preparations to make, and it would be better for her if the events of the evening were allowed to recede slightly, and for Norma and Constance to return to whatever usually occupied their minds.

Fortunately, a packet of letters had arrived earlier in the day, and Norma took them up as soon as they returned from the theater.

"I regret to inform Deputy Kopp that she has caught the attention of an attorney in St. Louis who wishes to interest her in a legal matter." Norma held up a sheet of creamy rag paper. Constance squinted at the three immaculately typed paragraphs and the elaborate flourish of a signature underneath.

"Does he want me for his wife or his secretary?" Constance asked.

"Both," Norma said, and read it aloud.

My Dear Miss Kopp,

I feel as though we are already acquainted through the many charming portraits of you that I have seen displayed in our Sunday papers. I would enclose a copy so that you could see how celebrated you are in our city, but I have pasted mine into frames and could not bear to part with them. They hang in my office where I may gaze upon them in the morning and whisper good-night to them in the evening.

After a long and careful consideration, I feel that I

must give voice to what lives in my heart and tell you of the decision that I have, at last, come to know as the right one for both you and I: We must be wed in the fall, and you are to take up residence in St. Louis and carry on with all the duties of an attorney's wife, a legal secretary, and mother to my four children, left bereft after the unexplained disappearance and presumed death of my wife several weeks ago.

You will find that I live, breathe, and sleep by the law. Its principles guide my every step and even the stirrings within my soul. Now that we have found that our hearts beat, practically speaking, as one, I take it that we may safely assume that we are engaged to be married. Under such blissful circumstances as these, I think it wiser for you (and incidentally even for me) that we should place our happy matrimonial contract upon a firm and rigid footing, so that in the future there may be no unseemly wrangling in case we should fall out (as all true lovers will) in the interval which must elapse between now and our nuptials.

Therefore, this letter, my own dear bride-to-be, according to law, is a business contract. I have copied it into my office letter book. Please send your affirmative reply, or indicate your consent by signature below, for which I enclose a stamp and my affectionate regard.

Please believe me to be —
Yours in perpetuity subject
to the above —
Edwin G. Bagott, Esq.

" 'Subject to the above'!" Fleurette shrieked. "What kind of man sends a woman a contract and a demand for a signature?"

"Are we obligated to reply," asked Constance, "or is the lack of an acceptance considered a refusal?"

Norma scrutinized the page again. "With

no terms given, I feel that we must refuse in all good speed, and preserve a copy for our office letter book, too, before you find yourself legally bound to Mr. Bagott."

"Mrs. Constance Bagott!" said Fleurette. "Mother of four."

"I do wonder about the mysteriously vanished former Mrs. Bagott, who apparently saw no other way out of her contract," Norma muttered, and took up her pencil to compose the first draft of what was to be a carefully considered and legally binding reply.

"This is Carrie Hart's fault," Constance said. "That story of hers must be going all over the country."

As Norma wrote and crossed out and muttered to herself, Fleurette imagined boarding a train. She often imagined boarding a train when Norma spoke, but now that the idea was to be made manifest, it gave her an extra thrill. She wondered what the Eight Dresden Dolls were doing at that very moment, and marveled at the fact that none of them were sitting in a parlor with two stiff older sisters, dreaming up clever ways to reject whatever proposal of marriage, job prospect, or other chance at a new life came their way.

It occurred to her, for the hundredth time,

that other people didn't pass their evenings this way. Other people — May Ward, in particular, and probably her Dolls, as well — would be intrigued by a letter from a stranger, and might hazard a friendly reply, and thereby find a new world — or at least an interesting correspondence — unfolding before them.

Norma's lips worked furiously over her composition. From time to time a word escaped: *presumptuous, unconscionable, iniquitous, abhorrent.*

She took a breath and continued: *indecorous, opportunistic, unprincipled, opprobrious.*

Fleurette had been right not to breathe a word of her plans to her sisters. Nothing — not a tour with a theater troupe, and certainly not an offer of marriage — stood a chance against Norma's formidable vocabulary of refusal.

24

Now she had her ticket in hand. There were three benches on the platform, one of them empty. Fleurette lowered herself gingerly, not certain at first that she could even make contact with the wooden slats. Nothing seemed real at that moment. Either she was intangible or the bench was, but it didn't seem possible that they were both still solidly of this Earth.

Even the air had changed. It was thin mountaintop air, too insubstantial to keep a person alive. She felt a little dizzy, as if she were looking down upon her life from a great height.

Perhaps this was how everyone felt the first time they left home: insubstantial, transitory, adrift. Fleurette remembered that when her mother died, she was made to wait in the hall, having been banished from the room when her mother started to make a sound like she was drowning. After a long and horror-filled gasp, there came the most restful silence, and Fleurette knew that she was gone. She took a long, deep breath in the hallway, and the air was just like this: cold and alien. It was the air of another world, the one that she would have to live in without her mother.

And now this — this was the world she would live in without her home, and without her sisters.

A tall man in the most ridiculous purple suit came whistling down the platform and dropped onto the bench next to her. "You made it," he said. "Are these your trunks?"

She had Freeman Bernstein to thank for breaking the spell. No longer was she walking in a dream, through her sisters' parlor, past her mother's sick-room. Freeman Bernstein might have been far-fetched, but he was undoubtedly real. He smelled of brandy and cigarettes and faintly of cloves, from the red carnation in his button-hole.

"I hardly brought anything for myself," Fleurette said. "That's my sewing machine, and some buttons and ribbons and things."

Mr. Bernstein grinned and rubbed the stubble on his chin. He wore a massive gold ring with a nest of diamonds in the middle. "I expect they'll have buttons and ribbons and things in Pittsburgh, Florabelle."

"It's Fleurette. But you're supposed to call me Miss Kopp."

His eyebrows popped up for just a second and he said, "I'm going to call you Flora-belle, and you're going to like it."

"I never will. Although if you put me on the stage, I might change my mind."

Fleurette had never felt so bold. If only someone were around to hear the way she traded barbs with May Ward's husband! What would her sisters think?

The thought made her turn around suddenly and sweep her eyes across the station. She hadn't yet left her old world behind. It wouldn't be that unusual to come across Constance in a train station. She shuddered at the thought of it: her formidable older sister, with that gold star on her coat, and that chunk of blue steel on her belt. What would Constance do if she could see Freeman Bernstein now, jumping to his feet and holding out his hand to Fleurette as the train rocked into the station?

It didn't matter what Constance thought, because it was time for them to go. He ushered her on board and tipped a porter to follow them. Fleurette felt quite grand as she led the way to the rear of the train, where Mrs. Ward and all eight of her Dresden Dolls occupied half of a rail-car.

Fleurette walked breathlessly up to May Ward and made ready with some witty remark about reporting for duty, but before the actress could even look up from her magazine, Freeman Bernstein whisked her past and deposited her among the chorus girls.

"Ladies, Miss Florabelle here is our company seamstress! Don't teach her your wicked ways."

An outburst of laughter was his reward. He scampered away, leaving her to make her own introductions and to correct, once again, the pronunciation of her name.

The Dresden Dolls were accompanied by a stern-looking older woman who had something to do with helping the actresses with their hair and costumes (although Fleurette couldn't imagine what that might be, as the woman seemed to have no sense of style herself), and an absolute brick of a man who acted as a sort of company porter, taking charge of the various trunks and hat-boxes. He was also appointed to stand guard against unwanted male attention as the troupe went in and out of theaters and hotels.

Fleurette was introduced to those two by Charlotte, the youngest and friendliest of the Dolls, as Mrs. Ironsides and Mr. Impediment. They seemed to answer to those names and not to mind them terribly.

"If you so much as take a scrap of paper from a man, I'm to wrestle it away from you, miss," said Mr. Impediment, in a merry voice that suggested he took great pleasure in his work.

"I enforce the curfew," said Mrs. Ironsides in a decidedly less pleasant tone. "There's a train ticket with your name on it if you skip out in the middle of the night."

"She means it," said Charlotte. "I took the place of the last girl who missed curfew."

The others snickered at that but didn't contradict her story.

With the exception of Charlotte, who couldn't have been a day past eighteen, the rest of them were at least five years older than Fleurette, some ten. They looked girlish, almost childlike, on stage, but in person, without their costumes, they seemed to Fleurette like world-weary sophisticates.

Two or three of them glanced up from their magazines and card games long enough to offer their names to Fleurette and to suggest the three or four costumes most in need of repair.

"Do the 'Garden of Love' dresses first. They're in tatters. She's been doing that number since 1909," said Eliza, as she smoothed her copper-colored hair in the window's reflection.

"Oh, 'The Cash Girl' petticoats are the worst. She's been doing that number since 1809," said Bernice. She had a low voice scratchy from overuse.

"I can put another dart in that dress, too, if you like," Fleurette offered to Bernice, whose dress hung awkwardly around her shoulders.

"It's not mine, so you'd better not," Bernice said, "but you can have a go at every single thing in my trunk once you're finished with the costumes."

Fleurette might have agreed a little too eagerly to tackle what was sure to be a mountain of tattered frills, but at that moment, as Mr. Bernstein waved a hasty good-bye to his wife and hopped off the train, and she felt the rail-car shudder and jerk forward, she had no doubt that she could do it. Her stomach might have lurched a little as the station slid past her window and the familiar city streets fell away, but she swallowed that fluttery feeling and bestowed her most winning smile on Charlotte, who'd settled in next to her.

"I've never been to Scranton before," Fleurette offered.

"You haven't?" Charlotte said, in mock

surprise, as it was perfectly obvious that Fleurette hadn't been anywhere. "Well. It has its diversions."

25

"Sorry, ma'am. Police wives don't ride free."

Constance stared down at the trolley car driver. "It's a sheriff's badge. And it's mine. You're new on this route, aren't you?"

"I know the rules. Free fares for sworn officers only. Not wives and stenographers and the like."

Constance was in no mood to argue. She opened her coat and showed him her gun and handcuffs. He startled and leaned away from her when he saw them.

"Lady, that's an awful lot of trouble for a free ride. You ought to give those back before someone gets hurt."

"It's trouble for you, if you give me any nonsense about my badge again."

Constance took her seat, which, she reasoned, gave him no choice but to allow it. He was a short, scrawny man who couldn't have thrown her off the trolley if he'd tried.

Her spirits did not improve when she arrived at the jail and saw Sheriff Heath and Carrie Hart walking toward the courthouse.

"The prosecutor's office is holding a press conference on the Minnie Davis case," Sheriff Heath said. "Miss Hart was kind enough to come and tell me, because no one else did."

"Have they filed charges?" Constance asked.

"You might as well come along and find out."

For once, the courthouse steps were devoid of reporters swapping stories. They had all filed into a large meeting room on the second floor, one of those dignified, high-ceilinged affairs with tall windows and mahogany panels. A series of judges' portraits, painted in oil, hung between the windows. Detective Courter stood at a lectern in front of an American flag, the yellow New Jersey flag, and a wall plaque bearing the Bergen County seal. Alongside him was his boss, Prosecutor Wright.

Sitting near the front, at an angle so that she looked out over the assembled crowd, was Belle Headison, Paterson's lady police officer. Mrs. Headison was a woman of strict moral codes who kept a sharp eye on train stations, dance halls, and amusement palaces, always on the lookout for girls at risk of being led astray. She did manage to catch a criminal every now and then: last year, she caught a man advertising for girls in the newspaper, under the pretense that he was looking for a housekeeper who might also like to audition to be his wife. Constance and Sheriff Heath were called in to help with the arrest. Such cases needed to be brought to light, and Belle Headison, fueled by righteous outrage over the continued assaults to feminine virtue she saw perpetuated all around her, was the woman for the job.

Constance nodded at her from the back of the room, and Mrs. Headison gave a stiff smile of recognition. Constance knew that she made Mrs. Headison uncomfortable: the policewoman had been shocked to see Constance arrest a man and to otherwise carry out the responsibilities of her job the way a man would.

Prosecutor Wright had just finished some preparatory remarks as they walked in, and now Mr. Courter began.

"Last week, constables in Fort Lee were investigating a report of gunfire when they found twenty-five-year-old Anthony Leo, of Fort Lee, and sixteen-year-old Minnie Davis, formerly of Catskill, New York, in a furnished room above a bakery. They posed as man and wife when they rented the room, although they were not married and Mr. Leo apparently had no intention of remedying that situation. He was found with a forged marriage license in his pocket."

There arose from the crowd a series of gasps, murmurs, and the scribbling of pencils. Detective Courter paused and spelled the names of the two parties.

"The source of the gunshots was never found and does not pertain to the business of which I speak today. Here we have a white slave case. Anyone who is familiar with the laws of this country will readily see that Mr. Leo transported Miss Davis across state lines for an immoral purpose. Her parents reported her missing months ago. The prosecutor's office has learned that Mr. Leo worked on board a pleasure boat plying the Hudson River in the summertime. We believe he coerced Miss Davis on board and employed such deceptive means as might be necessary to keep her there until the boat was bound for New York City. She obviously had no means of escape short of jumping overboard. When she found herself in a big city such as she had never seen before, penniless and lost, she fell entirely under Mr. Leo's control and was forced into a disreputable house in Fort Lee, where witnesses report seeing her entertain a series of male visitors in the evenings."

The room erupted then, with reporters all talking at once and shouting out questions. Constance looked over at Carrie, who rolled her eyes and shook her head sorrowfully. Sheriff Heath stood stiffly, without expression, as he always did in a place like this one, where so many people would be watching for his reaction.

Detective Courter went on with the fervor of a preacher. "It's well known that in every large city in the world, thousands of women are so set aside as outcasts from decent society that it is considered an impropriety to speak the very word which designates them. Now this disgrace has come to the respectable small towns of Bergen County. The commerce in white slaves was first seen in this country as coming from abroad and involving the importation of immigrant girls who spoke no English and possessed no means of escape. The Immigration Act made that illegal in 1907, and in large part, the practice has stopped. But an even more vile menace has risen up in its stead. This new depravity comes from within our own shores, as girls are lured away from their homes by these traffickers and drawn into a life of debasement from which there is little hope of rescue or recovery."

Mr. Courter mopped his forehead with a handkerchief. The reporters gave murmurs of assent.

"Can you tell he's running for office?" Carrie whispered.

"I should've guessed," Constance muttered. It gave her a sinking feeling to think of him building a campaign on morality crimes that rarely amounted to anything.

"Congress passed the Mann Act so that we could put a stop to this scourge within our own borders," Detective Courter continued. "But the laws are of no use unless the violators are caught, punished, and paraded before the public as a warning to sinister forces from a decent society. Every day I speak to fathers who say they would go to any length of hardship and privation rather than allow their daughters to go into the cities to work or to study. Who can blame them, when even the ordinary ice cream parlor — or a steamboat on the Hudson — may be used as a spider's web for her entanglement?"

Reporters were shouting out questions now, demanding the name of the steamboat and any other particulars involving ice cream parlors that Mr. Courter might wish

241

to divulge. He waved them away and continued with his speech, which had taken on the cadence of a sermon and no longer had anything in the way of a press conference about it.

"This is why I've invited Mrs. Headison from over in Paterson to be here today." Mr. Courter turned and gestured to Mrs. Headison, who stood and nodded at the audience. "Mrs. Headison does fine work in Paterson by looking out for wayward girls. Seventeen young women have been sent to the reformatory on her watch, and she hasn't been on the job a full year. Imagine what could be done if we had someone here in Hackensack to do it."

Constance's mouth fell open. Sheriff Heath gave her a sharp jab. "Steady," he whispered. It was just one word, but it was enough to make her compose herself. John Courter was trying to rattle her. She wouldn't allow it.

He wasn't finished. "There are some things so far removed from the lives of ordinary, decent people as to be simply unbelievable by them. The white slave trade now plying its ghastly business right here in Bergen County is one of those incredible things. Mothers and fathers, I put you on notice that you are placing your girls in danger if you're too trusting of them. You must all be on guard against threats to your daughters' virtue, which may strike wherever she goes, be it a train station, a secretarial school, or a place of amusement. The prosecutor's office has vowed to close down every vice resort and disreputable house in Bergen County.

"Our prosecution of Anthony Leo is only the beginning. We believe that through his arrest, we've uncovered a white slave ring operating along the Hudson River, and we will be working with the New York authorities to break it up. Who knows how many other victims like Miss Davis we might discover? We will restore this once-peaceful county to safety and security, and we want you, the public, to hold us to account as we do."

After such a speech Constance wanted nothing more than to escape that room and go outside to take in some clean, cold air. She noticed that Carrie never did write down a word.

"I've heard this speech before," Carrie muttered. "And you notice that he didn't say a thing about the actual case, because he doesn't have one. It's not much of a story."

"This is a press conference," Constance

said. "You're free to write it up."

"It's garbage, and there's a girl's name attached to it. I won't. The others will."

"You're not going to get far in crime reporting if you don't want to put a wronged girl's name in the paper," Constance said, although she was relieved.

As the reporters shuffled past, a few of them gathered around the sheriff to ask if Anthony Leo was in jail and whether he was allowed visitors. Sheriff Heath calmly refused to answer a single question and said that he was only there as a spectator. Mrs. Headison was still at the front of the room, speaking quietly to Mr. Courter, which was just as well, as Constance hadn't anything civil to say and would rather not be forced to try.

Carrie, Sheriff Heath, and Constance walked together back to the jail. As soon as the metal door closed behind them, Carrie said, "This isn't a criminal case. It's a political campaign."

"I wouldn't mind that if there wasn't a girl in jail over it," Constance said.

They were in a narrow corridor of cement floor and whitewashed brick. Their words made an echo as they walked.

"Can't you do one of your tricks in front of a judge and spring her loose?" Carrie

244

asked.

"It isn't a trick," said Sheriff Heath. "The girl has to be willing to help herself, and so far, this one hasn't been. If she was forced, she'd better say so, and quickly. I don't like this talk about men coming around in the evenings, even if Leo did force her into it. There's not a judge in New Jersey who would set her free if she had that kind of history. They'd want her in a reformatory, at least."

"Do you think it's true?" Carrie asked Constance. "It's not as unusual as it might sound. A girl doesn't have a dime for her own lunch, so she lets a man take her to a restaurant. Then he invites her to walk through the park, and —"

"That's enough!" Constance said. "I think we all understand the situation."

"I'm trying to say that sometimes she doesn't know she's done anything wrong. He buys her dinner and theater tickets, he gives her a bracelet. They're just little gifts, but the girl gets used to it, and she gives something in return."

She turned to Sheriff Heath, who had grown suddenly very interested in watching his feet as he walked. "Excuse me, Sheriff."

"Yes, well . . ."

"It's only that I see it all the time in New

York. These girls don't have their own money. Of course the men are going to pay for things, and if a girl wants to have any kind of a life at all, she'll let him. Are you sure Minnie didn't just slip into that sort of . . . arrangement?"

They both turned at once to look at Constance. A scandal along those lines would ruin this girl. Even being cast as the victim in a white slave case would cast a cloud over her life. Her parents would never take her back in either case. And who would marry her, or give her a job, if they knew?

"She insists it was only her and Tony," Constance said. "But it wouldn't do her any good to say otherwise, would it?"

"I'm afraid not," the sheriff said.

They were met at the door to Sheriff Heath's office by a bailiff of the court. He handed the sheriff an envelope.

"Transport orders," he said. "Minnie Davis has been transferred to the state reformatory in Trenton."

26

"They can't put her in a reformatory. She hasn't had a trial." At the very idea of it, Constance thought her heart might come out of her chest. Had she done nothing for this girl?

Sheriff Heath dismissed the bailiff and read over the order. "It's a transfer, not a final sentencing. She's to be held at the State Home for Girls until trial."

He looked up and seemed surprised to find Carrie still standing there. She was awfully good at slipping through doors and insinuating herself into circumstances to which she had not been invited. "Miss Hart, I'll ask you to keep this to yourself as it was not made public."

"It's turning into quite a story," she said, "but I'll hold it for now. Has she no recourse?"

"Not really. It's a temporary transfer of custody. It's not too different from transferring a feeble-minded inmate to the Morris Plains asylum until trial, or sending an epileptic down to Skillman. The idea is to put an inmate where they might be best served. Only I'm usually the one to request it. I suspect Detective Courter wants to keep Miss Davis away from any interference."

"Then this is because of me?" Constance said, alarmed.

"We knew Courter wouldn't like a lady deputy involved in his cases. I can try to speak to him, but —"

"Can't you put a stop to it? Once she's there, they'll never let her go."

"Oh, she'll have a hearing eventually," Sheriff Heath said. "I imagine he wants to prosecute Tony first."

"I don't know why Tony doesn't go to a reformatory," Constance said. "He admits to a different girl every week."

Carrie laughed. "They don't have reformatories for grown men who go around with girls."

"Well, this girl's being deprived of her liberty when she hasn't broken any law."

Sheriff Heath said, "If she's done nothing wrong, Deputy, I know you'll be the one to prove it."

She could feel the sweat under her collar.

248

"When does she have to go?"

"Today."

"Then let me take her. We'll go on the train."

He shrugged. "You're the matron. It's your job."

"I'll be back tonight." After she returned, she would sleep at the jail again. She felt she deserved another night in a jail cell, having failed to do a thing for Minnie.

Constance was under orders to keep her inmate handcuffed on the train, but she hated to see the girl embarrassed in public. She loaned her muff to Minnie and unchained her long enough to allow her to slip her hands inside before locking her wrists together again. At least no one on the train would see.

It was a ride of some three hours from Hackensack. Minnie didn't care to read a book or look at a magazine, but Constance put a newspaper across her lap regardless. She ignored it and stared out the window.

Once the train was going and the noise of the tracks muffled their conversation, Constance said, "I'm sorry. I hadn't any idea this was coming."

She sniffed at that and didn't answer.

"Just because you're going to Trenton

doesn't mean I'm going to forget about you. I will keep working on your case and I'll try to get you released. I still have some hope that your parents will come around."

"They won't," she said in a hard voice.

At least Minnie was speaking to her. "Well," Constance said, "sometimes parents change their minds after they've had a little time."

Minnie kept her face turned toward the window. They rode out of town and past open fields. The grass was all brown and stippled with snow. "I ought to have listened to you, Miss Kopp," she said. "You tried to tell me what to say and I wouldn't listen. I didn't really think they'd send me to a state home."

"I never meant to tell you what to say. You want to tell the truth, and that's the right thing to do. This isn't a punishment for refusing to testify against Tony." Although as she said it, she wondered if it was. Was Detective Courter trying to scare Minnie into playing the victim?

Minnie sighed and slumped back in her seat. "What's it like at the reformatory?"

"I've never seen it. You're the first one I've — the first one who's had to go there."

"I'm the first one you've lost. That's what you were about to say."

"I haven't lost you." But of course, she felt like she had.

She let Minnie eat a sandwich on the train, believing there to be little risk of her escaping on a passenger car moving fifty miles per hour. It took some fumbling behind a curtain of newspaper to unlock her handcuffs without the other passengers noticing. After she finished, Constance kept the chains in her handbag and let Minnie enjoy something that resembled freedom, at least superficially.

They rode directly through Trenton and out the other side, into what was once field and forest but was now giving way to homes and small factories. There was no missing the State Home for Girls: a sign on the iron gate proclaimed its purpose, and behind that was such a hodgepodge of buildings that it couldn't have been anything other than a state-run institution.

The train stopped half a mile past the reformatory and they walked back. Minnie complained of the cold in spite of the fact that she was wrapped in Constance's good coat, which dragged the ground and picked up mud and leaves. The jail had no sturdy outdoor clothing for the inmates as they had so little use for it.

At the entrance, a tall, thin woman in a

white apron ran out to meet them. She had hair the color of butterscotch and an oblong face with a wide mouth and two square teeth that jutted out in front.

"I'm Miss Pittman," she said. "The sheriff telephoned about you."

Constance introduced Minnie, who could only nod and stare at her. There was not another person in sight, only a collection of forbidding buildings surrounded by an open expanse of lawn. She noticed that there was nothing in the way of trees or shrubs, the idea being, presumably, that they might be used to conceal contraband or runaways.

It became clear to Constance that she was expected to say her good-byes and board the next train. But it didn't seem right to leave Minnie so abruptly.

"Would you mind showing me the place, as long as I'm here?" Constance asked. "I should have some idea about what my inmates can expect."

"Of course." Miss Pittman led them toward a rather large white home perched awkwardly between two low brick buildings. "The two on either side are the dormitories. They've been here the longest." She spoke in the manner of a tour guide. "In between them, this strange creature was placed, entirely without any consultation from us."

The strange creature was a stately white home of three stories, with four columns in front and four chimneys in back. Miss Pittman explained that it was built for the Jamestown Exposition in 1907 and meant to look like George Washington's headquarters at Morristown. Having nothing better to do with the building once the exposition concluded, it was brought here and put down between the dormitories to serve as offices and lodging for the staff.

Miss Pittman explained that the superintendent was away for the day to attend the trial of a girl in their custody. "She's to be sent to the state farm for the insane, or so we hope," she said. "She set a fire under the eaves of one of the cottages. A few children were locked inside and nearly burned alive." She gave a piercing look to Minnie, evidently believing it her duty to tell the most frightening stories she could in order to subdue the girl. "When you come around back, I'll show you where it happened. You can still see the burn marks."

Constance didn't like the way this was going at all. Inside the great hall of the white house, she relieved Minnie of her handcuffs. The girl rubbed her wrists and asked if she could keep wearing the muff, which Constance permitted. Miss Pittman laughed when Minnie slipped her hands back inside. "You won't see any mink around here."

"It's only rabbit," Constance said sharply.

A dinner-bell rang outside and Miss Pittman said, "It's lunchtime. I'll show you where you'll be eating."

"We had sandwiches on the train," Minnie said. Her voice was arrogant and defiant, but Constance knew what she meant by it. Taking a meal in this place would make it permanent. It would make her a part of everyday life at the reformatory.

Miss Pittman turned and looked at her coldly. "Come along and do as you're told."

Constance took Minnie's arm but she shook it off. They followed Miss Pittman out back and across another expanse of lawn to a long, low-slung dining hall. There they saw three lines of girls on the march, each being led by a matron. The girls in the first group were all about Minnie's age and dressed in ordinary cotton house dresses. Several of them looked over. Minnie straightened her shoulders and returned their curious glances directly.

Constance couldn't help but admire the way Minnie was holding up. This was not a girl who showed fear. A little strength would serve her well in a place like this.

Next came a line of girls who couldn't

have been more than ten years old. "I didn't think they'd be so young," Constance said to Miss Pittman.

"We take them from the orphanages as young as eight, if they're ready to work."

"What happens when they grow up?"

"Oh, they'll stay until they're twenty-one. How old are you?" She turned around to Minnie, who tossed out her answer as if it didn't matter. "Sixteen."

Third in line for lunch was a group of colored girls of all ages, each carrying a wooden chair out in front of her. Constance started to ask, but Miss Pittman was all too ready to offer an explanation.

"We weren't prepared to receive colored girls until they built a separate cottage for them three years ago. The state gave us one chair for each girl. It didn't occur to them that the girls required chairs in their rooms and also in the dining hall. They'll have to carry them back and forth until the legislature sees it our way."

"But they haven't, in three years," Constance said.

"We make haste slowly." Miss Pittman gave her a knowing look, perhaps hoping for sympathy, as every institution kept a long list of needful things that weren't being supplied.

But Constance just held her breath and watched a little girl carrying a chair that was almost as big as she was. The girl would be carrying that chair for the rest of her life, in one way or another.

"Well, come along and see the dining hall," Miss Pittman said, once all the girls had gone inside.

They marched along behind her. Minnie walked briskly, her chin up, with the air of an inspector who was only there to make a report and leave.

Inside was exactly what anyone would expect: long wooden tables, platters of potatoes and ham, baskets of rolls, and pitchers of milk. The girls were seated with their matrons in an arrangement that was obviously the same every day: the older girls at one end, the children in the middle, and the colored girls at the other end. They were all chattering loudly and paid no attention to their visitors.

Constance still couldn't get over how young some of them were. "Won't any of them go back to their families?" she asked, nodding at the youngest ones.

"A few of them," Miss Pittman answered. "But most are here precisely because their families are so unsuitable. You must see those cases. Father keeps a still in the basement and mother hides a trunk of stolen goods under the bed. The children are taught shop-lifting instead of school-work."

Constance nodded vaguely. An older girl turned around and caught Minnie's eye.

"Did she take you up to the attic?" she called above the din of plates clattering and girls talking. She had dirty blond hair and sharp, glinty eyes.

"No, why don't you tell me about it?" Minnie called back, daring the girl to try to scare her.

Another girl — this one nearly as tall as Constance, with broad shoulders and a booming voice — turned around and said, "It's an iron cage, and they put you there if you've been especially awful."

"That isn't true, Dora." Miss Pittman's voice was low and controlled. "Don't tell a lie."

The first girl said, "It isn't so terrible up in that cage except when the rats crowd around. Of course there's rats in the rafters. That's not a lie, is it, Miss Pittman?"

Minnie snorted and rolled her eyes.

Constance knew a troublesome girl when she saw one, and so did Miss Pittman. They turned away at once, and Constance led her inmate outside. The wind had picked up, but it came as a relief. She and Minnie each took in an enormous gulp of air.

Miss Pittman led them next into a long, low brick dormitory. They followed her down a hallway, past a series of small, dark rooms, all of them empty. "I'm bringing you in the back way, but you might as well see where we put the girls for misconduct. It isn't a cage in the attic."

She switched on a light in one of the rooms. They stared into a windowless space whose walls had been nearly destroyed. Some former inhabitant had picked away at the plaster until there were gaping holes in the center of every wall, exposing wood crossbeams everywhere except the corners where the plaster hadn't yet been torn out. The bare lathe and horsehair made a dismal sight. It called to mind the work that enormous rats might do, if such creatures existed.

Minnie and Constance turned to Miss Pittman in shock, the question evident on their faces.

"The girls do it," she said. "One started it. She was a lunatic and never should've been sent here in the first place. We took her to the asylum after only one night, but it was too late. She'd taken such a hole out of this wall that we couldn't patch it without tearing the whole thing apart. So we left it alone for the time being, and when the next girl saw it, she took up the idea. Now every one of them picks up where the last one left off. All the punishment rooms are like this now, and we've long since given up on replastering. The superintendent wants iron rooms built, but the money has to come from the state."

"How do the girls misbehave?" Minnie tried to sound disinterested, but she was starting to waver.

Miss Pittman turned off the light and led them out. "Fighting, mostly. Setting fires. Running away."

The girls' dormitories were downright luxurious compared to what they'd seen so far. They were sparsely furnished with a single cot and chair for each girl, and a hook above each bed for clothes. At the end of each room was a tiny, high window with iron bars across it. "Twelve girls to a dormitory," Miss Pittman said, "and a night matron making the rounds every thirty minutes."

They passed a set of classrooms, but Miss Pittman explained that they were hardly used owing to a lack of students from the teachers college willing to come offer lessons for free in the summer. "The state doesn't like to spend money on literature," she said. "It isn't their aim to run a finishing school."

There was a sewing room and a large kitchen. Miss Pittman said, "The girls are instructed in all manner of domestic work. Each girl cooks for a small group of eight, rather than work as part of a crew making dinner for the entire population. That way, they'll learn what it is to cook for a family. When they leave here, they'll be placed in service in respectable homes. Most of our girls were never taught their duties, or refused to do them. Our aim is to raise them ourselves, as their families failed to do."

Minnie pretended not to have heard that, but Constance said, "Minnie's family did just fine by her."

Miss Pittman gave a high and superior sort of laugh. "I don't believe they did, or she wouldn't have been sent here. Now, most girls stay on probation after they leave, and we make sure they keep to the job they've been given. They're allowed to marry only with our approval. You see, Miss Davis, we'll help prepare you for a quiet and comfortable home life. We'll see that you make a good marriage, and teach you how to be of use to a family."

"She's only here temporarily," Constance said briskly. "She hasn't been sentenced."

She bristled at the idea of Minnie being made to spend five years in a place like this over one poor decision. Some of these girls might have done wrong, but surely some were just independent and strong-willed. It was cruel to force all of them into domestic service, and wasteful to deprive them of an education and some brighter future.

Their next stop on this most demoralizing of tours was the infirmary, which was housed in one of the two brick buildings they'd passed earlier. When they stepped inside, Minnie took a sniff and said, "I know all about this." The infirmary used the same naptha soap to rid the girls of lice that was used at the jail.

They followed Miss Pittman into a small wood-paneled room with an examination table, several cupboards of instruments, and a shower room attached. "As soon as the nurse finishes her lunch, you'll have a complete examination and a Wassermann test." She gave Minnie another one of her foreboding looks, and Constance was obliged to bend over and whisper into the girl's ear that it was a test for venereal disease.

"We only just started last year," Miss Pittman said, as she handed Minnie a dressing-gown, "and it's a good thing we did. Over half of the girls test positive."

Constance felt Minnie's fingers dig into her elbow. Miss Pittman noticed and said, "I'm sure you're eager to get back on the train, Miss Kopp."

"I'll stay until the nurse comes," Constance said. The least she could do was to see Minnie through the examination. Miss Pittman didn't seem to like it, but she spun around on her heel and left them alone.

27

When they were alone, Minnie said, "Why on earth would they think I have a *disease*?"

Constance perched on the edge of the examining table and told Minnie to sit next to her. The girl sat perfectly upright and kept her eyes fixed on the wall opposite. She couldn't look at Constance.

For all of her bravado, Constance saw the truth. There had been other men. Of course there had.

She gave Minnie's shoulder a hard squeeze and the girl turned to face her. "Before the nurse comes," Constance said, "isn't it time you told me the truth? You have good reason to be worried about this test, don't you?"

Minnie sniffed and tossed her hair around. "Tony ought to be worried about a test. When does he take his?"

Constance had to admit that she didn't know. In truth, no mention of such a thing had ever come up at the jail.

"I won't tell the prosecutor," Constance said. "I won't tell the sheriff. But is it true what Detective Courter said? About the men going in and out of the place?"

Minnie shrugged Constance's arm off her shoulder and walked around the room. "Tony stopped coming over," she said. "There was never anything to do or anywhere to go. Half the time, I didn't have any supper at all except what the baker downstairs would give me. It was no kind of life. You wouldn't have stood for it, either."

"And you found someone who had a better kind of life on offer?"

"Some — a few. It was nice to have somebody buy me dinner. Is that a crime?"

Constance didn't bother to answer. This was worse than anything John Courter had implied. "Do you mean to say that Tony didn't coerce you into it? He didn't bring those men around?"

Minnie stared at her, puzzled. "Tony? Why would he? They took me to restaurants, Miss Kopp. To the moving pictures."

"And sometimes they came up to your room?"

Minnie crossed her arms over her chest and stayed stubbornly silent.

"Are you telling me that Tony didn't . . . arrange for any of this?"

"No! Of course not. He never knew." She didn't bother to tell Constance about the night Tony found out. There wasn't time and, anyway, none of it mattered now.

Constance couldn't bear to look at her. Carrie had guessed at the truth, even when Constance hadn't wanted to believe it. She let her eyes drift over to the door as she said, "You understand the difficulty this poses. With your case."

"But you're not going to tell anyone!"

She forced herself to look at Minnie. "That's right. I'm not. Only . . . I don't know how to get you released. If a judge finds out that you invited these men . . . well, that's exactly why they put girls in a place like this."

"But I —"

They were interrupted at that moment by the nurse, a sturdy, broad-shouldered, flat-footed woman with the expression of some-one who had confronted many a crying girl in her examination room.

"I'm Nurse Porter, dear, and you're here for a quick examination." Her voice was low and level. The nurse put a hand on Minnie's arm, but she shook it away. All at once Minnie had the look of a trapped animal about her. Constance backed up against the door to make sure she wouldn't run.

265

"There's nothing to fear," Nurse Porter said. "You're going to go up onto this table, and I'm going to examine you to make sure you're not going to have a baby."

"A baby?" Minnie glared at the nurse. Her hair fell limp around her shoulders. "Is that what you think of me?"

Neither Constance nor the nurse answered. With some difficulty the nurse persuaded Minnie to disrobe and to wrap herself in the white gown. She did as she was told, then sat sulkily on the table while the nurse turned to her cabinet of instruments.

When she had gathered a metal tray together, Nurse Porter came over and took Minnie's arm.

"Now, Miss Davis. I'll be so very quick, and you'll have all the answers in no time. I know how everyone dreads a blood test, so we'll do that bit first, and then you can relax. How does that sound?"

She spoke in a reassuring voice, but Minnie only stared straight ahead and didn't answer.

"I want you to hold your arm out like this," the nurse said.

Constance kept her eyes on her shoes until Minnie yelled about the needle and it was over.

"That's all," the nurse whispered. "There's nothing more to fear. I'm just going to have a look at you now."

Minnie rubbed her bandaged arm and sat up on the table. "Go ahead and look."

Nurse Porter chuckled at that. "Is your bladder quite empty, dear, or do you need the toilet?" she asked.

Minnie shook her head.

"That's fine," the nurse said. "It makes the examination easier if you've already gone, that's all."

First Nurse Porter opened her mouth wide, inviting Minnie to do the same. She grumbled about it but dropped her jaw open.

The nurse probed the roof of Minnie's mouth and looked around the lips and gums. "I see no sores of any kind. That's a very good sign. Now, if you'll lean back on the table and put your legs just so."

Nurse Porter reached down to the side of the table and lifted two metal stands. Minnie stared at them. "My feet are meant to go in those? But —"

All at once, she understood. She looked at Constance in shock. Constance had never seen such a thing, either, and couldn't imagine putting herself in such a position in front of a nurse — or, for that matter, in front of anyone at all.

Minnie had a great deal of trouble maneuvering herself into the necessary position, but it was brought about somehow, and the nurse draped a sheet over her and worked in quick and competent silence. In a low voice, she inquired about the girl's menses, about any episodes of illness or stomach upset, and about the last time she'd seen a man on an intimate basis. Minnie gave only one-word answers, devoid of any emotion.

"No tenderness or swelling of the breasts," the nurse said, mostly to herself.

After a surprised yelp from Minnie, Nurse Porter added, "No enlargement of the uterus. Cervix is pink and healthy. No unusual secretions or sores." With that, the examination was over. Minnie's legs went back down on the floor and she sat upright, wearing a stunned, blank look.

Nurse Porter wrote a few things down in a ledger-book and came around to the side of the table to address Minnie directly. She held a white card in her hand. Constance couldn't see what was printed on it.

"You did just fine, Miss Davis. I see no reason to believe that you are going to have a child. The Wassermann test takes longer. Deputy Kopp will be told the result. Now we must talk about what comes next."

"Next?" Minnie said. "I thought it was over."

The nurse cleared her throat and said, "I'm going to tell you how to conduct yourself so that you need never have these worries again."

"Oh," Minnie said, slumping over. "I know how to conduct myself. But there isn't much trouble to be had in here anyway, is there?"

"Well, you'll be out of here someday, and you must know. The state physician has written a statement that he wishes read to every girl admitted to a New Jersey reformatory. You are to listen carefully."

"Go ahead."

The nurse held up the card and began. "If you were to ever have any sort of relations with a man again, a child is the almost certain outcome. Do you understand?"

Minnie nodded but couldn't bear to look at Nurse Porter, who continued, "If you are so unfortunate as to give birth to an illegitimate child, you would be almost certainly forced to put it away in an institution of some sort, only to hope and pray that it may die soon — and generally, they do. If it does not die, the existence of that child would forever hang over your head like the sword of Damocles and you'd live with the constant terror of being found out. Please nod and let me know that you've heard."

"Oh, I heard," Minnie returned.

Constance couldn't catch a breath herself. The nurse couldn't have known that she herself had once been prepared to abandon a child to an institution. She'd never once thought, much less hoped, that the baby could die. Something froze inside of her at the thought. She looked over at the nurse, who was standing, grim-faced, with her eyes fixed on the card.

"A venereal infection could cost your health and even your life. If you were to have a child, the infection would almost certainly ruin the child, and this says nothing of the disease's spread. Any man who would pursue an unmarried woman is almost certainly already infected himself. You are to refrain from all intimate relations with men, including vigorous kissing. Don't even share a handkerchief with a man. Have you heard every word I said? Tell me yes."

"I don't have any choice but to hear," Minnie said.

The nurse raised an eyebrow at her but continued. "An illicit experience won't just endanger your health, but also your social standing, and your chances of ever marrying or establishing a home. It will condemn you to a life of loneliness. Remember that marriage and love are a woman's whole life. A small minority of women might claim that other pursuits are just as fulfilling, but win their confidence and they will admit to unhappiness and dissatisfaction. A woman who lives without love and marriage is a failure. You don't want that for yourself, do you, Miss Davis?"

"I don't suppose it matters what I want," Minnie said.

Constance couldn't stand another minute of this. "Thank you, Nurse. The state physician has made himself heard."

If Nurse Porter disagreed with any of the sentiments she'd just read, she didn't let on. She put the card away and said, "I'll let you two say good-bye. Miss Davis, stay in your dressing-gown and I'll be back with a uniform."

28

Now they were truly out of time. Minnie sat on the examining table with her arms wrapped around her knees. "How long are they keeping me here?"

"Until your trial."

"And then I'll be right back here."

Constance sat down next to her. "I'll do everything I can. The sheriff wants me to go and speak to your parents again."

"But why? You know how they are."

"They might read about the press conference in the paper. I want them to know that —" She stopped herself, as she'd planned to go back to Catskill to tell them that the accusations against Minnie weren't true. Instead she said, "I want them to know where you are, in case they'd like to write a letter."

"They won't."

"If I can find someone who might take charge of you, I still have some hope of getting you released. Isn't there anyone?"

"I told you before. There isn't."

"And what about this landlord who claims to have seen men going in and out of your room?"

Minnie felt something clutch at her insides. "What about him?"

"If I go and speak to your landlord," she said, lowering her voice to match Minnie's, "what will he tell me? Be honest, now."

Minnie raced through the events of that night. At last, she could give an answer that was both true and useful. "He'll tell you that he saw Tony's brother there once."

"Are you sure?"

"Yes."

"And why would Tony's brother have been there?"

Minnie pressed her lips together. How many brothers did Tony have? She didn't even know. Finally she said, "He came to speak to Tony. They were arguing over something. One of them owed the other money. I don't even remember who started it."

Constance watched her for a minute. Minnie could hardly stand the scrutiny.

"Well, I hope that's all there is to it. I'll speak to your landlord and make sure that's his story. If it is, the prosecutor won't have any evidence of . . . of that sort of wrong-doing to use against you. But, Minnie —" Constance reached over and took the girl's chin, forcing her to look up.

"I'm listening. You don't have to make me look at you."

"Are there any other witnesses? Anyone who might come forward and claim —"

"No!"

Constance pressed on. "What I mean to say is this: Might the prosecutor find any of these men? Might he compel them to testify?"

Minnie had to think about that for a minute. How would anyone ever know?

"No. Anyway, why would they admit to it? Then they'd have to go to a reformatory."

No, they wouldn't.

Constance couldn't bring herself to say it, but she knew it to be true. The nurse knocked at the door and Constance said, "Please, Minnie. Be a good girl. If you get any kind of a bad report while you're in here —"

"I won't."

Minnie clearly wasn't in the mood for a sentimental good-bye. Constance brushed past the nurse and strode outside. Once she was free of the place, she practically ran for the train.

274

29

Minnie had been given a bed squarely in the middle of the dormitory, which meant that no matter which way she turned, a girl was eyeing her from the next bed. At last she rolled onto her stomach, pulled the blanket over her head, and tried, without success, to push away the memories of those last few weeks in Fort Lee when everything went wrong.

Could anyone blame her for being lonely? Even before Christmas, Tony had stopped coming around as much. She could see that he'd grown bored with her — and if she wanted to admit the truth, he'd probably lost interest after that first night. She knew as soon as she met him that Tony liked to have a good time with girls but wasn't about to settle down with one.

Still, he did help her, by signing his name to the lease and passing her off as his wife. He came around often enough to make the story look plausible to their landlord, and carried the rent money downstairs himself once a month, even when he contributed so little to it. Apart from that, Tony showed little interest in taking up with Minnie on any sort of permanent basis.

What did that matter? There were other men. Minnie soon found that the Park Avenue boys who came up to Catskill for the summer weren't any different from the dentists and lawyers of Fort Lee. They just wanted a little company.

That explained the man with the crinkly smile waiting outside the jute mill that day. He was a salesman with a new line of gaskets and belts on offer. He'd just paid a call at the mill and was wondering where he might find dinner when Minnie bumped into him.

He delivered his line easily, about Minnie looking like a girl his sister used to know. Minnie, for her part, happened to know a nice quiet restaurant at the edge of town. So it began.

In this way, Minnie got by. It wasn't too different from anything she'd done in Catskill. None of the town girls thought anything of accepting a dinner or theater tickets from an admirer, and why should they? They hadn't a dime of their own. How else were they to meet anyone, or to entertain themselves? Their mothers had antiquated ideas about dances and church socials, which didn't cost a thing as long as you had a dress and a dance card, but nobody did that anymore. People went out in public for their entertainment. Entertainment cost money. Boys had money and girls didn't — especially in Catskill, where the girls' parents insisted on keeping what little wages they earned at the mills. It was as simple as that.

Minnie didn't go to bed hungry anymore, and sometimes she didn't go to bed alone. She never invited a man upstairs the first time. She had her standards. She wouldn't invite a young man of limited means — she had one of those, in Tony, and didn't want another — but he couldn't be too old, either. If there was anything the least bit fatherly about him, she couldn't bear the idea. She would let him buy dinner and give him a kiss when he presented her with a little bundle of steak and rolls to take home. But a man with a little gray around the temples, a man who probably had a daughter himself at home — a man like that couldn't come upstairs and put his hands on her. He couldn't.

As it happened, though, that left plenty of

men who could. Young men of twenty-three with their father's money in their pockets. Men in their thirties with their name on a door-plate somewhere, and a secretary who looked a little like Minnie (or so they said), and an automobile that took them right out into the countryside, anytime it wasn't too terribly cold for a drive — men like that could come upstairs, and she was glad to have them. They banished her loneliness, they pushed away the emptiness, they lit her up like a candle. In their company she felt whole again, and splendidly alive. With each one of them she could see, for just one night, a different version of herself, another future in front of her, a day when contentment and satisfaction never left her. They had that to offer, however fleetingly, and she took it.

She loved to see how large they looked, in their suits and coats, turning around in her shabby little room, wondering aloud how she managed to keep body and soul together in a place like that. Some of them brought her gifts: bracelets, perfume, stockings, and she was always delighted, and never thought twice about accepting them.

She couldn't wear the jewelry — Tony would notice eventually, and it would furnish him with the perfect excuse to skip out on her for good — so she wrapped those gifts in a handkerchief and kept them hidden under her mattress until that morning the police knocked on the door. She wondered if anyone had discovered them yet, tucked between the boards in the bathroom ceiling. She wondered how long it would be before she could retrieve them, and how much money they would fetch.

Nothing she did felt, at the time, like the calculated maneuver it appeared to be now, in hindsight. An arrest has a way of clarifying things, of casting a prism of criminal intent over actions that, at the time, seemed reasonable and entirely justifiable. Why shouldn't Minnie have left home, if she wanted to? She was sixteen and old enough to work or marry, so what was the crime in wanting to live on her own?

And was it her fault that the mills didn't pay enough to put dinner on the table? Although she hadn't wanted to go back to factory work, Tony had encouraged her and she'd agreed. He had a friend who earned twelve dollars a week at the jute mill, which was quite a bit more than she'd ever made in Catskill. But when she went to speak with the girls' superintendent, she was offered only half that. She was bold enough to ask why and was told that the men had families

to support. Someone must have been looking after Minnie, the girls' superintendent
suggested, and it was good of her to want to
earn a little extra, but she wouldn't want to
take a salary away from a family man, would
she?

Minnie tried to say that no one was looking after her, but it was too awful, and she
couldn't bring herself to utter another word.
She took the job, and the wages that never
quite paid her rent, because she couldn't
find anything better and she couldn't go
home.

What was Tony to her, once he'd helped
her settle, however precariously, in her little
room? He came around on a Thursday night
now and then, expecting her to play the wife
and cook him dinner, but he'd been eating
his mother's good Italian cooking and
Minnie couldn't put anything on the table
that pleased him. He claimed not to be able
to afford to take her to the moving pictures.
When she offered to pay, one Saturday after
she'd just collected her wages, he looked
disgusted and said that he'd never let a girl
spend money on him. It was a question of
honor.

But where was his honor when it came to
looking after her? He obviously felt that he'd
done his duty. He never said a word about a

280

future for the two of them, not that Minnie was too certain on the subject herself. And if he ever wondered what she did, on all the nights he wasn't with her, he didn't ask.

Then one night — early one morning, really — she heard his footsteps on the stairs just as a sheet music salesman from Pittsburgh was putting on his shoes. There was no place for him to hide, nothing for him to do but to stand and face what was coming to him.

No matter how indifferent Tony might have been toward Minnie, he couldn't take the sight of another man in her room. He threw the salesman down and would've given him a good pounding, except that the man scuttled over to crouch in the corner, to Minnie's everlasting embarrassment, and Tony just laughed at him. But then he turned and took in Minnie — half-dressed, caught in a lie — and he tore the place apart. He threw every picture off the wall, broke a chair, and smashed dishes — while Minnie screamed at him to stop.

All the shouting and banging on the walls rousted the neighbors, including their landlord, the baker downstairs, who had just come in to light the ovens. Minnie would've been evicted on the spot, except that Tony was flooded with remorse. When the landlord demanded to know what was going on, Tony pretended that the salesman was his brother, and that they were fighting over some feud in the family. The landlord relented and they were allowed to stay on one condition: that they furnish some proof they were married.

That left Tony and Minnie alone in their room, huffing and panting. Minnie spoke first.

"This is your fault."

Tony laughed at that. "I didn't invite a fellow upstairs for the night."

"If I lose this place, where am I to go?"

"You should've asked him that."

This was getting her nowhere. She would've been perfectly happy to never see Tony again, but where was she to go? She thought about the little bundle of jewelry she'd hidden away, and wondered how far that would get her. She'd been holding on to anything of value she owned against the day she'd have to save herself. Had that day come? Or was there something worse around the corner?

"Get a marriage license and show it to our landlord," she said, "or I'll pay a visit to your mother and tell her everything."

She'd never met an Italian man who wasn't terrified of his mother. He went off

282

in a huff, but she knew he'd be back.

A few days later, he walked right in without knocking.

"I thought you'd be out with one of your fellows," Tony said.

"I don't have any fellows," Minnie said.

Tony stood across the room, with his back against the door. "Well, my sister moved back home, and she's got a no-good husband and two babies. They want me out of the basement."

"But you can't stay here!"

"Of course I can. I just paid the rent."

Minnie felt a little knot inside of her, but she stood very still. She ticked off the choices in her head: *Go home. Stay here. Run away.*

"I thought we couldn't stay unless we were married," Minnie said.

Tony reached into his pocket and pulled out an envelope. "It's a marriage license, just like you said. I even signed your name."

So this was how it would be. He had every right to stay. She was free to leave.

But somehow, neither of them did. One night turned into a week, and a week turned into two. They slipped into some semblance of a sham marriage, with Tony paying the rent and Minnie burning the potatoes at dinner every night.

It was nothing that Minnie wanted. She didn't love him. She was starting to hate her life in Fort Lee as much as she'd hated Catskill. But she couldn't seem to put more than a dollar or two together at a time, and where would she go, anyway? What could she do that was any different from this? Work in a different factory, in a different city? What was the point of it?

When she didn't come up with an answer herself, one was forced upon her. Here it was: a metal cot in a dormitory, surrounded by a dozen girls who were just like her.

30

Through the church's narrow windows, Edna could see the ladies from the Preparedness Committee lining up chairs and putting out leaflets. No one else had arrived and she didn't like to be the first to walk in. Instead she went around behind the church and found herself in a dismal little cemetery, bereft of the comforting canopy of trees, without so much as a bench or a ledge where she might sit. Two of the graves were new; it gave her an uneasy feeling to see the dirt mounded up so lightly. She would have preferred a more solid barrier between the dead and the living: a carpet of grass, a thorny rose-bush.

Edna reached in her pocket for the leaflet she'd picked up at the train station. She'd been carrying it every day, until it was creased and creased again, but she hadn't shown it to anyone. The idea of someone like Edna boarding a ship for France seemed so far-fetched that she couldn't bring herself to say it aloud. She could only hold the notion in her imagination, like a dream she was in danger of forgetting, until tonight, when any girl in possession of that leaflet was invited to come and join the effort.

She took three turns around the cemetery, staying just out of sight until she heard voices and knew that a few others had arrived. It was early in the evening by that time, at the blue hour just before winter's early sunset, when the lights dimmed and the lamps inside the church glowed yellow through the windows. She walked around to the entrance and was met by a woman at a card table taking down names. Edna gave hers and accepted another copy of the leaflet she already had.

As she looked around the room, she at once felt uneasy and out of place. If there was another factory girl present, Edna didn't recognize her. This was a convivial crowd of well-to-do young women in fur-trimmed coats and good hats. Were these the women who went to war? None of them looked particularly suited to it.

Along one wall was a table filled with trays of cookies, sandwiches, and teapots, but Edna noticed that no one else took anything to eat and thought that perhaps it wasn't done in their circles.

She was standing in the very back of the room, uncertain as to whether she ought to stay or leave, when she felt a hand on her elbow. She turned to see a cheerful, round face, framed in blond curls. The woman wore a plain dress-suit of gray wool twill, but Edna had the idea that it had required some effort to find anything so somber in her closet.

"Are you Edna?" she said. "Oh, I know you are, because I ran over and looked at the list after you signed in. You have what my father calls a seriousness of purpose. You belong with us, I just know you do."

Edna couldn't help but feel cheered by that little speech. No one had ever come right out and told her that she belonged anywhere.

"I want to do my part" was all she could think to say.

"And you will! I'm Ruby. How rude of me. Come sit with us right in the front. I insist. You're my guest now." She put her arm through Edna's, and they walked to-gether like sisters to the very front row, where Ruby deposited her in a chair along-side several similarly polished young women. "Make friends!" she called, and ran to the refreshments table, returning almost

287

instantly with two cups of tea and enough cookies to pass around. "No one ever eats at these things, and I don't know why. It's such a waste. If we're not going to eat them, we should send them to France, shouldn't we?"

That provoked a round of easy laughter among Ruby's friends, and then it was time to bow their heads and hear a prayer for the fighting men in France. After that, a woman introduced only as Mrs. Roberts took the podium and gave a short speech. She spoke in a resonant voice accustomed to elocution.

"There are those who insist this isn't our country's fight. There are those who say that our duty is to our homeland, and that the best we can do is to fill a barrel with old coats and send it over. But every woman here knows better."

She gave a definitive nod as she said it, and was rewarded with a chorus of applause. Edna looked around at all the young and beautifully turned-out women in the room and wondered again if she had a place among them.

"Then there are those who do their part by rolling bandages and sending cheques to the relief groups and knitting socks. That's just fine, for those who want to do it. With such terrible shortages, every dollar makes a difference. The men freeze in the trenches and the hospitals run out of supplies. The needs are endless, and there are those who want to put themselves to the task of meeting those needs. That's fine work, but every woman here wants to do more."

Another cheer, louder this time, went around the room. Edna felt herself swept up in it.

"And we can do more, but we must train and organize and prepare ourselves. Everyone here must consider carefully what she has to offer. Paris is overfull of women who are eager to help but haven't the training. So I ask you: Can you dress a wound? Can you run an automobile? Can you work at the telephone switches? Because this is what the English and the French are calling for. If you can knit, stay at home and do it from here. If you can go around and collect donations, then by all means do that. But if you have something to offer the soldiers" — here a little laughter went around the room — "other than your pretty little face and a kind word, but something of substance, then you are wanted in France, and we shall be sure that you go."

Edna stood with everyone else to applaud, although she didn't know, at that moment, what she might do to be of service to France. She couldn't dress a wound or run an automobile.

A stack of cards went around, and they were asked to mark the skills they had to offer. Edna was relieved to find a dozen or more boxes she could check, from canning and cooking, to sewing, to factory work and the operation of small machinery. She was surprised to see that Ruby and her friends marked almost nothing.

"Why, we've never had a cook who would let us anywhere near the kitchen," Ruby said, as she watched Edna fill in her card. "I don't know how you managed to learn all of it."

"It isn't difficult," Edna said, "if you just want a chop in a pan and some potatoes."

"That'll suit the soldiers just fine, I imagine," Ruby said. "But you know, in spite of all her talk, Mrs. Roberts won't stop any of us from going. She just wants us to take a few Red Cross classes first, and that's no trouble. When would you like to sail?"

"Sail?" Edna hadn't considered that she might just step on board a boat and go.

"Well, you have to pick a date. Oh, you haven't turned your card over." Ruby flipped the card around and showed her the reverse. On it were four dates over the next few months, along with the names of the ships and, next to that, two numbers:

$100/$50

Edna wasn't sure at first what it meant, but the idea was starting to dawn on her. Now she understood the fur collars and the velvet hats.

"Is this — is this the cost?" she asked, a little tremulously.

"Why — yes, for the passage. It's always something around a hundred dollars, but they change it all the time. And then fifty each month while you're there, because of course the relief organizations raise funds to feed the refugees, not the volunteers. But you only have to put up one month in advance. They'll just send us home if the rest of the money doesn't arrive!"

That brought another laugh from her friends down the front row, who were all busy conferring with one another over dates. Edna tried to restrain her shock, but it must have shown.

"Oh," said Ruby, reaching over to put a hand over hers. "We don't all have fathers paying our way. I hope you didn't think that. Some of them flatly refuse."

"I wasn't sure," Edna mumbled.

"Not at all," Ruby went on. "Some of us are raising the money ourselves. We hold little parties, and ask every guest to sign on for just one dollar for every month we'll be away. Fifty of those, and you're ready to go! Have your mother invite her friends. Ladies like that can always put a dollar toward a good cause."

"My mother —"

"Yes, exactly!" Ruby said cheerfully. "Now, I want to sail in April, and I want you to be my bunk-mate. Won't we have the best time? Can you be ready to go by then?"

Edna felt a little dizzy at the idea of it. A hundred dollars for the voyage, and fifty a month after that — it would cost seven hundred dollars for one year in France! She had no idea that she'd be expected to pay her own way. She didn't earn anything close to seven hundred dollars in a year, and she spent most of her paycheck on room and board. The whole business was impossible.

Ruby was leaning over her expectantly. She had the prettiest blue eyes and a perfect little nose. When had anything not gone according to Ruby's wishes?

"You will, won't you, Edna? Say you'll come with us in April. You'll speak to your father and mother, and arrange it all?"

Seven hundred dollars. The war would be over before she saw seven hundred dollars. But hadn't Ruby said that she only needed to raise the first month's fee? Would they really send her home if the money didn't arrive for the second month? A hundred and fifty dollars sounded almost manageable. She couldn't imagine where she would get it, but wasn't she obligated to try?

"Of course I will," Edna heard herself say. At just that moment, she almost believed it.

31

Constance didn't say a word about Minnie's confession when she returned from the reformatory. Sheriff Heath hadn't asked, and she didn't see it as her obligation to repeat every word an inmate said to her. There seemed to be no way, under these changed circumstances, for Constance to help Minnie, but she didn't want to make things worse for her, either. A girl who pretended to be married to one man while going around with two or three more was exactly the sort of girl who ended up in a reformatory. Constance felt certain that the punishment was too harsh, and unjustly penalized the girl for a crime that required a man's willing participation as well. But what was she to do about it? For the moment, she could stay quiet about what she knew. That, at least, was within her power.

She'd spent too many nights at the jail lately and desperately wanted a proper bath, but by the time she returned from the reformatory, it had been too late to go on home. So she spent another night in her cell and would have started for home in the morning, had not a guard come up the stairs to inform her that her sister was waiting for her outside.

"Which one?" Constance asked as she stuffed her feet into boots still wet and stiff from last night's snow.

"The unpleasant one," the guard said. All the guards loved Fleurette because she flattered and teased them. They'd hardly ever seen Norma, but she nonetheless had a singular reputation among them.

Norma insisted on waiting outside, so Constance threw on a coat and met her in the driveway. She was standing apart from the jail, looking up at it grimly. From underneath her mackinaw, an old gray sweater bunched up awkwardly around her neck. She hadn't exactly dressed for a trip to town.

Norma was not a woman inclined to go out for the purpose of talking to anyone, her sister included, which was why she so rarely turned up at the jail. Once or twice she'd sent Constance a postcard, always with a cryptic message pasted across it. She used to send such messages via pigeon-mail, but both Constance and Fleurette refused to accept messages from Norma's birds anymore. It displeased Norma to resort to postcards, but there was no other way.

She cut them from newspaper headlines, and Constance and Fleurette were meant to puzzle out their meanings. "Good Works Not Promises" would arrive if Constance had agreed to help with some chore and then stayed away for too many days in a row. "Lunch Refused" turned up one day when Fleurette insisted on making her version of Italian soup, which was nothing but boiled macaroni in chicken broth and smothered in grated cheese, along with, as Norma liked to say, enough garlic to defeat the Germans.

But this, apparently, didn't warrant a postcard. "What's the matter?" Constance asked as she walked across the drive.

"Was Fleurette here yesterday?"

"Well, I wasn't here myself yesterday, but someone would've told me if she'd been by. Why?"

In the time it took Constance to answer, a chilly understanding crept over her.

"She didn't come home last night," Norma said.

Constance took her by the arm and pulled her toward the jail, but Norma refused to go.

"Are you sure? Couldn't she have stayed overnight with Helen? What did she say when she left?"

"Nothing. She left sometime around noon yesterday while I was in Ridgewood," Norma said. "I assumed she went to Mrs. Hansen's. That's where she always goes. Why would I have thought otherwise?"

"You wouldn't," Constance said, with a panicky sort of impatience.

"I spent all afternoon putting that back fence together and went to bed with a hot water bottle around eight. I was going to stay awake until I heard her come in, but the next thing I knew it was morning. I checked her room right away. She definitely hasn't been home since yesterday."

Constance choked on the blustery morning air as she tried to get some sort of answer out. Minnie Davis's predicament was all too present in her thoughts. She'd only just been imagining what she'd do if Fleurette ran off like Minnie did. One part of her mind was busy denying that any such thing could ever happen, and another part was already organizing a search party.

"There isn't any note," Norma said. "And I haven't seen evidence of any other kind of trouble. No letters or postcards from men, no cigarettes, no liquor —"

"Liquor and cigarettes! What exactly do you think she's been up to?"

Norma raised an eyebrow. "We don't know, do we?"

"Norma! We do know! We know exactly where she's gone. She ran off with May Ward and that man — her husband . . ."

"Freeman Bernstein. And he should go to jail, if he's put her into his vaudeville troupe without our permission. I've looked through all our directories and I don't see his name. I suspected right away that he was operating under the shadow of some sham corporation. They all do that on Broadway."

"What do you know about what they do on Broadway?" She couldn't believe that she was arguing with Norma over how show business managers conducted their business.

"I knew enough to find this," Norma said. She pulled a card out of her pocket and handed it to Constance. It was the portrait of May Ward she'd signed the night of the audition. On the back was the name of the portrait studio and the line: "With the Compliments of Theatrical Amusement Company, Leonia, New Jersey."

"Then we'll go to Leonia," Constance said.

She turned back to the jail, and this time

she grabbed Norma by the arm and jerked her along, causing Norma to stumble and lose her hat. She had only just cut her hair — she always did it herself, as she hated for anyone to touch her head — and the curls stuck out in every direction. Even her hair had a sense of outrage about it.

"None of this would've happened if you'd listened to me and refused to give her the five dollars," Norma grumbled, as she put herself back together and went unaided to the door.

Constance saw no reason to answer that.

"Oh, and I found this on the floor in your bedroom."

Constance turned around. It was the tin where she kept her money hidden away. Norma hadn't found it on the floor — Fleurette wouldn't have been that careless. Norma had obviously been through her drawers before and knew right where she kept her money.

Constance took the tin but she didn't have to open it. She knew as soon as she saw it.

The tin was empty. She had seventeen dollars saved, and now it was gone.

32

They found Sheriff Heath in his office. Deputy Morris sat across from him. "I thought you were going home this morning," the sheriff said when he saw Constance, "but as long as you're here, do you remember a man we brought in —"

But then he saw Norma and stopped.

"Fleurette's gone missing," Norma said.

Deputy Morris turned suddenly in his chair. Fleurette was such a pet to him.

"She isn't missing," Constance assured him, "but she's gone off with a vaudeville troupe without a word to either of us. We're on our way now to speak to the man responsible. I believe there might be cause for an arrest, so . . ."

Sheriff Heath settled back into his chair. There was something odd in his expression that stopped her.

"On what grounds would we be making an arrest, Deputy Kopp?" he said.

"Wouldn't the Mann Act have something to do with it?" Norma blurted out. "Transporting a woman across state lines for immoral purposes? Isn't that what you go around arresting people for these days?"

Sheriff Heath ran a hand over his mustache and said, "I'd like to know what Deputy Kopp has to say about a woman complaining to the sheriff because her sister has gone off at the age of eighteen to find employment for herself."

Constance sighed and dropped into a chair. "I'm not proposing that we bring charges against Freeman Bernstein until we know more. Only that the situation might call for some stern questions from someone in an official capacity. I thought you might take us in the wagon."

Deputy Morris and Sheriff Heath exchanged a look that suggested they understood things that she did not. She bristled at it but stayed quiet. Already she could see that it had been a mistake to try to bring the sheriff into this.

"Let's start over," Sheriff Heath said. "If she didn't leave word, how do you know where she's gone?"

Constance reminded him about the audition and showed him the photograph.

There passed another maddening look

between Sheriff Heath and Deputy Morris, after which the sheriff said, "In that case, would you say that a girl of eighteen should be permitted to join a troupe after having auditioned, in public, with the full knowledge and approval of her family?"

"We didn't approve," Norma put in crabbily. "I didn't. This man can't be trusted. The entire operation is suspect. I've seen Freeman Bernstein. He's something of a huckster. You know the type."

"I'm afraid I don't," Sheriff Heath said. "Deputy Kopp asked me about Mr. Bernstein when this whole business started. As far as I know, he's done nothing criminal. I can't go running down to Leonia just because a deputy of mine happens to have a grievance. And speaking of deputies, mine are needed at work."

"Not today!" Norma said. She gathered her coat around her and looked at Constance expectantly. But already Constance could see the weakness in her case.

"The sheriff's right," she said. "We already have too much trouble with the police interfering with girls in situations like this. Fleurette wasn't lured away or conned." It made her shudder a little to hear herself describing Fleurette in Minnie Davis's circumstances, but she pushed on. "She went on her own. It's the only thing she's ever wanted to do."

"But we don't know anything about it," Norma said. "If she was working at a factory, it would be another matter. We haven't any idea where she's sleeping tonight."

"That may be true, but we've no reason to think it's a matter for the law."

Now Constance felt foolish for barging into Sheriff Heath's office. None of the other deputies went running to him every time they had a problem at home. It was true that if she looked at Fleurette's situation as one of her own cases, she'd find no evidence of wrongdoing, nor any reason to think that the girl ought to be brought home against her will. It had been nothing but fear and instinct that sent her running to the sheriff's office.

Constance also blamed herself for being swayed by Norma's resolute suspicion of Freeman Bernstein. Norma never liked anyone upon meeting them for the first time, and she was particularly mistrustful of a man who had designs on any of the Kopps. There was no way, as she thought back on it, that anyone in Freeman Bernstein's situation could win Norma's trust and admiration, even if the audition hadn't been a sham. Why, then, had Constance given any credence at all to her opinion?

She hated to turn against Norma and give the impression that she would stand with Sheriff Heath rather than her sister. But she couldn't please them both.

She looked back and forth between Norma and Sheriff Heath and then said, "You're right. I'll go down to Leonia and settle this myself, and you won't hear another word about it. In fact, I'll be close to Fort Lee, so I'll stop in to speak to Minnie Davis's landlord while I'm there."

Sheriff Heath looked resigned to it and waved them out of the room.

33

Freeman Bernstein kept his office in a building of pink brick that filled most of a city block on Broad Avenue in Leonia. Norma spotted him walking out the front door when they were still half a block away. She ran ahead to catch him and Constance lagged behind, as she was limping along in the same wet boots, now dried to a stiff and blister-inducing form.

At the sound of Norma's footsteps, he turned around, wearing a bemused expression and puffing on a pipe.

"I'm sorry, my dear," he said as Norma caught up with him. She wore the split riding skirt that she refused to describe as trousers, and her mackinaw flapped along behind her as she ran. She couldn't have looked anything like a woman with aspirations for the stage, but he said, "The auditions are over, and we've filled all the parts."

"I don't want to audition," Norma said.

"I've come to get my sister back."

He patted his pockets with comic exaggeration and claimed not to have any sisters on his person at present.

By then Constance had caught up with them. Mr. Bernstein looked her over with great interest. "Have you brought a lady policeman with you?" He seemed transfixed by Constance's badge.

"She's my sister, too," Constance said, "and we've reason to believe that she's traveling with your wife's troupe. She left without a word. We must know where we can find her."

Now he was grinning broadly at her. "You're that lady deputy at the sheriff's office, aren't you? They sure do like to put you in the papers. Why don't you girls come up to my office and we'll talk about it."

Before either sister could say a word, he linked elbows with them and marched them back down Grand Avenue and through the wide double doors of the building.

Norma and Constance were not the sort of women to be swept up by a man and led down the street, but Mr. Bernstein proved to possess an irresistible force. He wore a lively checkered suit in a fashionable cut and walked with the lanky grace of a dancer. His face was deeply lined and easily contorted into any expression, so that when he raised his considerable eyebrows, great lines of befuddlement or curiosity came into being across his forehead. When he smiled, there weren't two dimples, but three or four, plus a single one in the center of his chin. Now that she saw him up close, Constance had to admit that he was one of the most interesting-looking men she'd ever met. He smelled good, too: as he pulled them along, they were enveloped in the fragrance of good tobacco smoke, a barber's tonic, and whatever cream or salve he used to slick down his curly hair.

There was also just a hint of some liquor about him, but it wasn't so overpowering that Constance believed him to be a drunk. She was introduced to the source of it soon enough. He whisked them upstairs and deposited them into leather chairs in his office, where he presented them with two dainty glasses and a bottle of sherry.

"We couldn't possibly," Norma said, with her arms crossed in front of her.

"Oh, you could. It's very easy. You just splash a little into the glass and take a sip every now and then." Mr. Bernstein grinned. He had eyes more green than brown, and after he removed his hat, Constance saw a little red in his hair. There was some Irish in his family line somewhere.

But Norma waved him away, and Constance explained that she was on duty, although she wouldn't have taken any regardless. There had never been liquor in the house after their father left, apart from a little medicinal brandy that their mother kept hidden away.

"Yes, you're on duty. The lady deputy," Mr. Bernstein said as he flopped into the chair behind his desk. "Is it really you? It must be. I've never seen a woman better suited to it. We ought to put you into the pictures. What do you think about that?"

"She doesn't think anything about it at all," Norma said. "We've come to see about our sister. It was irresponsible of you to hire her on without speaking to her family first. We are her guardians, and it is our duty —"

"Oh dear!" Mr. Bernstein's eyebrows lifted in an expression of mock surprise. "Did I hire a girl of fourteen? I'd never do it deliberately. Tell me her name and I'll send her home tonight."

"She's eighteen." Constance put an arm on Norma to settle her down. "We only want to ask after her welfare, and to make sure that she is, in fact, traveling with Mrs. Ward. She left us no note. It was irregular of her to go away without telling us."

Mr. Bernstein wasn't listening. He'd been riffling through a drawer in his desk, and after a few minutes of searching, he pulled out a crumpled newspaper clipping describing Constance's capture of an escaped fugitive in December. It wasn't Carrie's story, which told the truth. It was one of the others.

" 'Lunatic Captured on the Subway Steps,' " he read. "I know just the fellow who can play the lunatic."

"He only pretended to be a lunatic," Constance said. "He's nothing but a common criminal."

"All the better, because my fellow will only be pretending, too! Now, I'd like to hear you deliver that line again, about him being nothing but a common criminal, if you wouldn't mind standing over by the window and giving it your very best. Here, try it like this," and to her astonishment, Mr. Bernstein stood, put a hand on his hip, and delivered the line in a falsetto that sounded nothing like her.

Constance did not get up from her chair, but just sat and stared at him. When he saw that he wasn't going to get any applause, he sat down again and said, "I just have to know. Did you really put him in a halter hug? If you can show me that maneuver, I'll have you on the stage in a week."

By this time Norma was thoroughly fed up and snatched the newspaper story away from him as if it belonged to her. "She didn't come here to audition for a part. If you won't tell us anything about our sister, we'll go straight to the police. Her name is Fleurette Kopp. Is she with Mrs. Ward or not?"

Mr. Bernstein arranged his face into something that looked like sincerity and said, "I do apologize, miss. I can see that you're both very worried about her. She has joined our little company, and I can assure you that she's perfectly safe. But if I can give you girls some advice —"

Norma was on her feet, glaring down at him. "You may not give us advice. You may give us the touring schedule so that we might know where on God's green earth our sister has gone off to, and make certain for ourselves that no harm has come to her, because no one else seems to be looking out for her except the two of us."

Mr. Bernstein took a deep breath and motioned for her to sit down. Constance tugged on her elbow, and she returned to her chair reluctantly.

"Ladies, I'm only trying to warn you. I've been in this game for fifteen years, and I've seen this a thousand times if I've seen it once. A girl grows up with dreams of being on the stage, and then one day, she gets her chance. But her mother won't let her go. What mother would, when she can keep her girl at home and have an extra pair of hands about the place? So the girl goes off anyway, and it isn't long before her mother and father turn up, furious, and make all kinds of noise. Maybe they even bring the police and have the girl arrested for moral depravation or disorderly conduct. But what do they think is going to happen after that? Do they think they can bring her home and put her on the straight and narrow? Do they think that a couple of years in one of those reform homes is going to make a proper lady out of her? I can tell you right now that almost every girl in the theater has spent some time in a reformatory over the years. It only makes them more rebellious and more ambitious. So what do you intend to do about your sister, Miss Lady Sheriff? Are you going to go fetch her and drag her home, so that she can sit around and watch while you go out and get into all kinds of danger? I know what you lady officers do. They have you going in and out of dance halls and amusement parks. I bet you've seen the inside of an opium den, and a disreputable house full of girls for hire. Why is it all right for you, but not for your little sister? No. You girls should go on home and forget all about this. Just wait it out, and be glad to have her back when the tour is over. When she does come home, I suggest you listen with interest to what she has to say about it, and treat her like an adult. I hired on a strict old German lady as chaperone, and a tough-looking fellow to be a guard and a lookout, and I did that so that I can look ladies like you in the eye and promise that no harm will come to anyone under the employment of Freeman Bernstein. It would ruin my reputation, and I can't have that. I'm a businessman. Can you understand what that means?"

At long last he finished. He sat back, put a match to his pipe, and drew on it, looking quite satisfied.

Norma turned and gave Constance a brief look that only a sister can read. It conveyed utter fatigue over the audacity of a man who dared lecture two women he'd never met about matters he couldn't possibly understand. It told Constance that Norma had hardly listened to a word of his harangue, and had instead put the time to better use in making a plan that the two of them would carry out together.

It was only the faintest flicker of a glance, but Norma didn't change her views readily. Constance knew quite well what she was likely to say and do in almost any situation. So she sat quietly and waited for her sister's plan to be put into motion.

Norma managed her own version of a polite smile and rose from her chair. "Thank you, Mr. Bernstein. You've made some awfully fine points that my sister and I hadn't considered until now. It was good of you to take the time to put it before us so clearly. Would you mind walking us downstairs? I'm afraid I might lose my way."

He jumped to his feet, the pipe bobbing between his teeth. "My pleasure! It was a delight meeting you both. I only wish every worried sister or aunt or mother would come and speak to me before they go chasing after their girls. It's no trouble at all to set them straight, as you now understand."

He came around the desk and held his elbows out so that they might walk out the way they walked in. Norma waited until they were across the hall and halfway down the stairs before she said, "My handbag!"

She turned and ran back up the stairs.

"The door's unlocked!" he called after her. Then, turning to Constance, he said, "Does she need any help?"

"She'll be fine," Constance answered. "Are you down here in Leonia because of the moving picture business? There seems to be a new studio opening every week."

That was all the encouragement Freeman Bernstein needed to deliver a lecture on the advantages of motion pictures over stage acting and the lucrative possibilities for a manager like himself who could put actresses and dancers before the camera, which was to say nothing of prizefighters, war heroes, dogs with special talents, lady deputies, miniature men, and any other human oddity or public figure of note.

This brought him back to the idea of putting Constance in the pictures. "Why, just imagine what audiences would make of a girl chasing a bank robber down the street and making an arrest! It'll be the most thrilling stunt to ever happen in a theater. Of course, if we want to make a successful picture of it, the girl would have to marry the bank robber. Or — well, she could marry the police chief, or the sheriff, or whoever put her in the job to begin with. That sounds about right. No, I like it better if she marries the crook. Have you ever thought about that, Miss Kopp? Marrying one of them? After they get themselves straightened out, of course. Or maybe it works out that the crook wasn't really the crook after all. Maybe the girl arrests the wrong man, and when she finds out, she feels so bad about it that she falls in love with him, and they get married. How do you like that? 'The Wrong Man.' That's what we'll call it."

Constance wouldn't have been able to take much more of that, but fortunately she didn't have to. Norma's footsteps came down the hall, and soon she was back in the stairway, her handbag tucked under her arm, and a barely concealed look of satisfaction on her face.

34

Thinking that Mr. Bernstein might get suspicious and demand to look inside her handbag, Norma had instead secreted the sheet of paper into her bosom. But he'd been too bewitched by his idea for a picture about a lady cop who marries the crook to notice. "I've got a better title!" he shouted as they walked away. "We'll call it 'Captured!' Subtitle: 'She Captured His Heart.' "

Once they were around the corner, Norma extracted the handbill and looked over the cities listed. "She's in Scranton tonight. I don't think we'll make it in time. We should go directly on to Bethlehem and meet her there."

Constance took the bill from her. At the top was a familiar slogan: "Pretty, Vivacious, & Versatile! May Ward and Her Eight Dresden Dolls — The Most Elaborate Girl Act in Vaudeville, Employing Beautiful Costumes and Special Scenery." Below that was a list of cities, dates, and theaters. After Bethlehem came Allentown, Harrisburg, and Pittsburgh, followed by a list of stops in Maryland and Washington, before turning north again to Philadelphia and back to New York City.

"We'll get her before she leaves Pennsylvania," Norma said.

" 'Get her'?" They'd reached the train station by then. Constance looked over the timetable while Norma folded the bill and tucked it away in her handbag.

"Well, isn't that why we're going?" Norma said. "To find her and bring her home?"

"I don't remember agreeing to go anywhere. We know where she is now, and we have assurances that she's safe. We could write to her in care of the theaters in any one of those cities if we wanted to. We might even be able to put a telephone call through."

Norma snorted. "You're not seeing the situation clearly, which doesn't surprise me at all, because you've always been blind to trouble where Fleurette is concerned. Mr. Bernstein has shown us what kind of man he is."

"I don't know what you mean."

"He took one line out of a newspaper

article about you and tried to turn it into cheap entertainment. He'd put his own mother on stage, if he could rent the theater at a discount and sell tickets for a quarter."

"But what do we expect Fleurette to do if we turn up at the theater, in front of Mrs. Ward and all the other girls, and insist on bringing her home? Is there any possibility that she'll be glad to see us? Could you imagine her coming along willingly? And how do I explain that I'm allowed to go wherever I want, and to do as I please, even if that means wrestling with a criminal, but she can't stand on a stage and sing a song?"

"You don't do as you please. You're being paid to do a job. You follow orders. Anyone would agree that your work is thoroughly unpleasant and should be making you miserable, and probably will, once you've been at it long enough."

Norma had a maddening way of derailing a conversation. Constance wondered suddenly if she'd ever had a straightforward talk with Norma about anything. She couldn't recall one.

"Never mind about me," Constance said. "We must think about what we're doing."

"I've already thought about it. You're the one who can't make up her mind."

It was true; she couldn't. She had half a

mind to grab Fleurette by the collar and drag her home, and the other half — well, she still wanted to grab her by the collar, but she told herself that she knew better, and that it wouldn't do any good.

"The minute we turn up, it's over," Constance said. "Fleurette won't forgive us for it. We'd better be certain, and I'm not."

Norma dropped onto a bench along the platform and folded her arms across her chest. "I said I don't like that man."

"Yes, you did."

"There's something untrustworthy about him."

"So you've observed."

"I know I've heard his name before, in connection with some scandal or another."

"I'm surprised you don't remember."

"I will."

"Until you do, I think we ought to stop and ask ourselves the question: Are we prepared to follow Fleurette around for the rest of her life and disapprove of everything she does, or are we going to behave like modern women and let her go her own way?"

"I suppose you're the expert on how modern women behave."

"Well, I know I'm expected back at work. Is that modern enough for you?"

The train arrived and Norma swept her arm toward it. "Go on, then."

35

Norma boarded a northbound train and Constance took a rickety little trolley down to Fort Lee to see about Minnie Davis's landlord. The trolley rolled along at such a maddeningly leisurely pace that she wished she'd walked. She'd had to squeeze herself into a narrow wicker-work seat meant for a much smaller person, which made for an unpleasant ride, and she fumed over her predicament the whole way.

While it was true that Constance was furious at Fleurette for going away, she was mostly furious at her for going away at that particular moment. Had she only run off a week earlier — or, who knows, a week later — Constance felt she would've been able to think clearly about it. But she was unsettled over the Minnie Davis case and the uncomfortable truth that Minnie had tried to keep from her. Was Fleurette hiding something, too?

It was obvious that Fleurette felt emboldened to go away precisely because of the
kinds of cases Constance had been strug-
gling with at work. Constance tried to think
back over what she might've said about
them in Fleurette's presence.

She was fairly certain she'd delivered a
lengthy speech about how petty and selfish
it had been of Mrs. Heustis to try to keep
Edna at home, and what a mockery she'd
made of the police and courts by involving
them in a family matter. (Had she really
said that, and then gone running to Sheriff
Heath the minute Fleurette disappeared?
She had.)

It seemed that she also had sharp words
for Mr. and Mrs. Davis, and she felt the
need to repeat them at home. Fleurette
must have been terribly emboldened to hear
that Constance believed it to be Mr. and
Mrs. Davis's own fault for driving young
Minnie away.

Constance also might have said that if the
Davises couldn't offer Minnie some kind of
life that satisfied her, they deserved to lose
her.

Yes, she definitely said something along
those lines.

Who, then, could blame Fleurette for
thinking that she had every right to accept

the very role for which, as Sheriff Heath pointed out, she did audition, with the full knowledge and consent of her guardians?

Did Constance ever once voice an objection to her auditioning, or to accepting the role — on the unlikely chance that there really was a role, and it was offered to her?

She did not.

There seemed no rational reason, then, for Constance to be alarmed over Fleurette's new venture, or to go chasing after her. She probably shouldn't, in hindsight, have gone to interrogate Freeman Bernstein, although she did have some obligation to make sure Fleurette was, in fact, with the company.

But the trouble was that she couldn't separate her worries over Fleurette from the outright state of alarm she'd been thrown into at the reformatory. Seeing Minnie sent away so abruptly, and hearing at last the hurried confession that she'd suspected all along — all of this had her worked into such a nervous state that she hardly knew where Minnie's situation ended and Fleurette's began.

Constance stepped off the streetcar in Fort Lee and found the bakery where she'd first seen Minnie. She stood across the street and looked up at the little window on the second floor, which was now covered over in newspaper, perhaps to make ready for another tenant. She couldn't help but admire Minnie for making some stab at a new life, even such a modest life as this one. As for the men who might have come in and out of that room, Minnie was right. If there were no men in evidence — no other party to accuse of a crime that took two to commit — then she deserved her freedom as much as they deserved theirs.

It was an uncertain legal argument and an even shakier moral premise, at least in the eyes of Bergen County's elected officials, but Constance was emboldened by the idea. Her spirits surged even higher when she opened the door and breathed in the heavenly fragrance of a bakery that had not quite reached the end of the day's operation.

Constance knew bakers to keep early hours and was relieved to find Minnie's landlord, Mr. Elliott, still there. Apparently one of the ovens had failed, and he was pounding at it with a wrench in between groans and curses.

The other oven worked just fine, and a late batch of popovers had just come out. A girl behind the counter sold her two, with powdered sugar. She took them in a little brown bag and tried not to think about the cloud of steam that would be released if she bit into one right at that moment, before they were allowed to cool. There was nothing like a popover directly out of the oven.

But that would have to wait. When she told the girl that she needed to see Mr. Elliott on sheriff's business, he threw down his wrench and came over. He looked every bit the part of a baker: rotund and heavy around the shoulders, with massive hands that knew how to pound down a rising loaf of dough or punish an errant oven. He seemed a little gruff about the interruption and guessed right away the nature of her business.

"You know that girl left without paying the rent," he said by way of greeting. He stood behind the counter, wiping his hands on his apron.

"She can hardly pay it now. She's behind bars."

"Deserves it."

"I understand you've agreed to testify against her. I take it you've spoken to someone at the prosecutor's office."

"Course I have. I want my rent money."

Constance feigned regret. "Oh dear. I'm afraid you've been misinformed. This isn't a case about the rent, and you won't get paid."

"What do you mean, I won't get paid? I'm

going to tell the judge —"

"It's a morality charge. I can assure you that the proceedings have nothing to do with the payment of rent. You'd have to speak to your city clerk about that." Constance didn't know who one might speak to about collecting late rent, but thought that a city clerk sounded convincing.

He snorted at that. "Well, I might as well tell the judge anyway. That girl was no good. Had a different fellow up there every night."

"Did she? How many fellows, exactly? The judge will ask, and you'll be under oath."

The baker looked over at the girl behind the counter, who Constance took to be his daughter. "Go on back there and pull out those rolls." He looked at the sack in Constance's hand and said, "You'll ruin them if you wait."

"I know. But tell me first: How many men did you see? Are you going to be able to describe them?"

"Describe them? I don't live on the premises. I only caught that one fellow because I'd come in to light the ovens."

"Who was he?"

He shrugged. "I just saw him run out. Tony chased him down the alley. He was plenty mad."

"What did Tony say?"

He sighed and rubbed his forehead with his sleeve. "Well, he claimed the fellow was his brother, but what do I know?"

"Exactly!" Constance said, with enormous relief. At least this part of Minnie's story was true. "What do you know? Was the man Tony's brother, or wasn't he?"

She reached in the bag, unable to wait any longer.

"Aw, hell. Is that what the judge is going to ask?"

She nodded, her mouth full of powdered sugar and a flaky golden crust that almost took her mind right off her business. It made the baker smile to watch his popovers disappear.

"Well," said Mr. Elliott, a note of resignation in his voice, "I promised I'd say my piece in court, so I suppose I'll have to."

When Constance was able to speak again, she said, "That's just fine, Mr. Elliott. It's entirely up to you. The first session starts at eight o'clock. The prosecutor will let you know what day to appear."

"Eight? I've got a bakery to run! You don't expect me to close my doors just to go tell a judge that I don't know what I saw, do you?"

She shrugged indifferently. "Sounds like a wasted morning to me. What did you say you had coming out of the oven next?"

327

36

They were the worst potatoes Minnie had ever seen. The skins were green, they were soft and withered, most were pitted with bruises, and all of them sprouted roots. She tried to cut away the worst bits and was left with a meager pile of white potato-flesh and a much larger mound of peels.

"Don't let Miss Pittman see that," Agatha said, and quickly brushed the waste into a bin.

"But we can't be expected to eat it," Minnie said.

"Oh, you'll eat worse. There's bugs in the flour. You'll see them in your dinner rolls."

"Agatha!" called out Esther from across the kitchen. "Don't be like that."

"But it's true," Agatha persisted. She had plump lips and a smile wider on one side than another, and she spoke with a lisp. Minnie liked her because of it. She allowed Agatha to take her by the elbow and lead her to the flour-bin, which pulled out from a cabinet in the pantry.

"See here. Bugs." She reached in, took a handful of flour, and let it fall. Little brown bugs the size of fleas scampered to bury themselves as they landed.

Minnie believed a show of strength to be the best course of action. "They're only weevils. You can sift them right out and feed them to the chickens."

"The chickens!" Agatha screeched. "You're not a city girl, are you?"

"I wanted to be," Minnie said, "and that's what got me into trouble." She went back to her potatoes and tried to be less discriminating with her knife. Agatha was scrubbing pots and Esther, the eldest and most senior resident of the state home, was boiling down ham bones for soup.

"What *did* get you into trouble for, exactly?" Agatha asked.

"No, let's try to guess," Esther said. She turned around and squinted at Minnie, as if she might divine the answer. "You ran away from home."

"Of course she did," Agatha said. "You don't even need to answer that one. But then what happened? You ran away from home and you found a man to take you in."

"He didn't exactly take me in," Minnie

said. "I persuaded him to rent a room for the two of us."

"Oh, that's much worse," Agatha said. "Don't tell it to the judge that way."

"That's right," Esther said. "You never want anything to be your idea. I'm here because I kept insisting that no one else was to blame. The judge believed me, and thought that any girl who lived such a wicked life of her own accord ought to be locked up and stripped of her inheritance."

"You didn't really have an inheritance, did you?" Minnie took another look at Esther and tried to picture her as the daughter of a rich man. She did have a pretty little chin and a turned-up nose, and eyes that might be made to look dramatic with a little effort. Minnie could imagine her in silk and furs.

"Ten thousand dollars would have been mine on my twenty-first birthday, but now a judge has hold of it, and I might never see it again, unless I marry the sort of man who won't squander it."

"What's the point of ten thousand dollars, if not to squander it?" Minnie returned.

"Oh, I agree entirely," Agatha said.

"Well, I'll be squandering it on a husband, if one will have me after five years at the state home," Esther said.

"I don't think you'll have any trouble," Minnie said.

"Even the feeble-minded are marriageable with ten thousand dollars on offer," Agatha said.

"Feeble-minded! Don't call her that!" said Minnie.

Agatha wiped down the last of her pots and said, "Oh, that's the name they put on you. You'll find out, after you're here for good. There's a man who comes around and interviews you. We know all the questions and the best way to answer, so you won't have any trouble."

"Well, I suppose Esther had some trouble, if she was called feeble-minded."

"Oh, no," Esther put in. "Feeble-minded is the best one. Below that is lunatic, imbecile, and idiot." She struck a pose, as if making a dramatic recitation. "The feeble-minded girl is marked by glibness of tongue, a bold and confident manner, and an attractive physical appearance. She has the passions of a grown woman and an experience of the life of the underworld."

"Well, that sounds — like a very clever girl," Minnie said, to agreeable laughter from the others. "You seem to know quite a bit about it."

Esther wiped her eyes and walked across

the kitchen to whisper, "I stole his little book and copied down the best parts so we could all learn them. I'll give you the questions. As long as you answer them correctly, he'll put you down as feeble-minded. If you're at all worried that he won't, just remind him that you have the passions of a grown woman. He's quite susceptible to persuasion."

"Then he's the feeble one," Minnie said. "Do you serve less time if you're feeble-minded?"

Agatha and Esther looked over at each other, calculating. "I don't think so," Esther said at last. "But you won't get sent to the lunatic asylum or to the industrial school. That's where they put the imbeciles, so they can be trained for a lifetime of pasting cardboard boxes together. And you know they give them an operation so they can't have babies."

"No!" Minnie gasped.

"Of course," Esther said. "They don't want another generation of idiots and imbeciles. It runs in families, apparently. Be very careful not to say anything about your relations that might raise suspicion. Don't mention drunkenness, laziness, unexplained deaths, spinsters, anything like that."

"My mother died when I was young, and

I was never told the cause," Minnie said.

"Invent something blameless," Agatha said. "Could she have been trampled by a horse or thrown from a train?"

"Agatha!" Esther called. "That's awful."

"I'll think of something," Minnie muttered.

They worked in silence for a minute. Minnie hoped very much that no one would ask her father and stepmother about her. Mrs. Davis never hesitated to say that Minnie and Goldie were bad girls, through and through. How might she elaborate on that, if given the chance? Minnie could quite easily imagine Edith Davis fabricating all sorts of lies and nonsense about her, her sister, and her mother, and Mr. Davis nodding grimly along.

Five years in a reformatory was bad enough. A lifetime in a box factory — and an operation — that was something she'd never imagined.

"What happens when you go to court?" she ventured to ask at last.

"Oh, it all depends upon who's going to speak for you," Agatha said. "What are your parents going to say?"

"They won't be there," Minnie said quickly, and very much hoped she was right.

"Have you any kindly schoolteachers or

sympathetic aunts?"

"None." She said this boldly, as if it were a badge of honor. That won a laugh from the other two, and Agatha's line of questioning became a game.

"Then what about a softhearted shop-keeper or a compassionate clergyman?"

"I haven't any of those, either."

Esther joined in. "Perhaps a lenient land-lady?"

"The very opposite," Minnie said.

"Then what about a sweet-tempered supervisor," Agatha said, straining for another alliteration, "or . . . or a merciful matron?"

"Merciful matron!" Esther cried out. "Are there any of those?"

Minnie thought about Deputy Kopp and wondered how merciful she could be after what Minnie had confessed. They'd parted in such a hurry that she couldn't begin to guess as to Constance's state of mind.

"I might know one," Minnie said, "but I haven't given her any reason to be merci-ful."

"Jail matrons can't do anything for you anyway," Agatha said.

"Oh, but this one can," Minnie insisted. "She helped a girl go free just before I was arrested. Just an ordinary factory girl. She told the judge that the charges were base-less, and he believed her."

Agatha and Esther both turned and looked at her thoughtfully.

"Are you sure?" Esther said.

"She told me herself," Minnie said.

"Then you'd best go to work on that matron," said Agatha.

37

GIRL SHERIFF'S GOLD BADGE
Constance Kopp Also Has
Gold-Plated Handcuffs
and a Title

HACKENSACK, N.J. — Miss Constance Kopp, who has been detecting things ever since she aided in convicting Henry J. Kaufman, a Paterson silk dyer, of sending threatening letters to her in 1914, has been rewarded by Sheriff Robert N. Heath, whose unofficial assistant she has been, with a gold-plated badge, a gold-plated pair of handcuffs, and the title of Under Sheriff. Henceforth Miss Kopp can prove that she's an honest-to-goodness detective.

Her last feat was to obtain a

336

confession from Miss Minnie Davis of Catskill, N.Y., whose charges have resulted in the arrest of young Anthony Leo of Fort Lee, and nearly a dozen of his friends, the former on a white slavery charge. County Detective John Courter and Chief of Police Patrick Hartnell of Fort Lee discovered Miss Davis' plight and rescued her from a house in Fort Lee where she said she was detained against her will.

Now Miss Kopp wears the badge and carries her handsome handcuffs in her handbag.

"I'd like to see those gold-plated handcuffs," Constance said.

"So would I," said Sheriff Heath. "This isn't Miss Hart's story, is it?"

"Of course not. It isn't her paper, anyway. This must be someone who was at the press conference. What sort of confession do they think I've obtained?" Constance said.

"I'd like to know about the dozen white slavery suspects they've arrested, as we don't seem to have them upstairs. But they spelled John Courter's name right, and

337

that's all that matters to him." Sheriff Heath leaned back in his chair. "What happened at the bakery?"

"The landlord didn't see a thing. Tony's brother had been over, that's all. They got into some sort of a fight and the brother ran off. I don't think the landlord's going to testify."

"You're making it difficult for Detective Courter."

"He doesn't have a case. He should let them both go."

"He likes to win cases."

Sheriff Heath was sorting through a box of mail and tossing letters at her. She had only to glance at the postmarks to see that they came from the usual far-flung places where her admirers lived: Pie Town, New Mexico; Burden, Kansas; and Chance, South Dakota. Norma would answer them, and all the others that were sure to follow, as the loneliest men in the world read about her gold-plated badge.

Sheriff Heath said, "I don't suppose Miss Davis had anything more to say on the way to the reformatory."

It wasn't easy for Constance to keep the truth to herself, but she thought it in the girl's best interests. She said, "What could she possibly tell me? She wasn't held against

338

her will or misled, except for the promise of marriage that went unfulfilled, but you already know about that."

"Mr. Courter would like to know how Anthony Leo convinced her to go off with him in the first place. Was she drugged? Does she remember a handkerchief going over her mouth, or a powder being slipped into a drink?"

"Of course not!"

"Then how did it happen?"

"Are you asking me why a girl would give up her factory job and the bed she shares with her sister to run away with a handsome man on a river-boat?"

He made a face at that and put his letters down. "It's the prosecutor asking these questions, not me. But I wouldn't mind knowing why a girl would give up a decent home for a furnished room rented under a false name, and an empty promise to go along with it."

"Her parents are very strict. I saw it myself. A girl like that — she starts to earn a little money, and she doesn't want to hand it all over to her father. She wants something for herself, in exchange for all the work she's putting in down at the factory. Something that belongs to her. She doesn't want to live her whole life for her parents."

Constance had to fight a little shudder as she said it. Who was she talking about, Minnie or Fleurette?

"She could get married," the sheriff said.

"She tried to."

"She didn't try very hard."

"All right," Constance said with a sigh. "I can't explain sixteen-year-old girls to you. What's to become of her?"

"It's Mr. Courter's idea that if Minnie won't cast herself as the victim, he'll decide that she went willingly into a life of depravity, and formally sentence her to the reformatory. He'll try to make an example out of her."

"She doesn't belong there. It'll ruin her."

"She's sixteen years old and she ran away from home. That's exactly the sort of girl who goes to a reformatory."

"But Edna Heustis ran away from home and no one sent her away."

"Miss Heustis was found working at a steady job and living in a good Christian home, or at least that's what you told me."

"Yes, and Miss Heustis had a chance to make her case in front of a judge. Minnie deserves the same."

"Are you going to argue in favor of releasing a sixteen-year-old girl, with no assurances as to her welfare? Even Judge Seufert won't go along with that. If she hasn't already been taking favors from men, she'll fall into it easily enough. She'd have no other prospects and no one to look out for her."

Sheriff Heath finished his sorting of the mail and dropped another stack in front of Constance. "Besides, John Courter's running for my office. He thinks a few cases like this will put him on the side of all that is good and righteous in Bergen County."

"He wants to be sheriff?"

"I thought you knew."

"I knew he was running for office. I didn't know he wanted to be sheriff." She felt considerably deflated at the prospect of having to watch John Courter campaign against Sheriff Heath and toss insults at him, although she had no doubt that Sheriff Heath would win. Nor did she think she could persuade Mr. Courter to do the good and decent thing for Minnie Davis and drop the charges.

"Talk to her parents again," Sheriff Heath said. "She's going home or she's going to the state home. Put it to them like that, and try to get them to think sensibly about it."

"I'm not sure the Davises go in for sensible thinking, but I'll try. I should check up on Edna, too."

"Go ahead."

She took up her stack of letters, and then she saw it.

A postcard from Fleurette.

38

By now you know it, or if you don't, you're no kind of detective at all. I've gone off with May Ward & Dresden Dolls — I'm now quite the doll myself — know all the songs & am learning the dance steps — This is the kind of life I love and you know it — not to worry, there is a Mrs. Ironsides and a Mr. Impediment to keep us straight, and they do, usually —

F.

"This doesn't tell us a thing," Norma muttered.

Constance sat at the writing desk in their parlor. Norma stood over her and peered at the postcard through her ill-fitting steel-rimmed spectacles.

"It tells us that she has a chaperone, and that she's keeping busy with work that she enjoys. What else would you have her tell us?"

Norma shook her head. "There's something about this Bernstein. You're too trusting of him."

"I'm not trusting of him at all! He proposed turning my life into a moving picture, and told us how to run our own household, and what we ought to think of him, and how we ought to regard Fleurette, as if he knows a thing about her. But I don't have to trust Freeman Bernstein, as long as I trust Fleurette."

"Well, don't try to tell me that you trust her," Norma said. "This is the girl who ran away without so much as a word of goodbye. What would you think if I did that?"

Constance found the idea momentarily cheering, but didn't say so. Instead she looked up at Norma, who was still standing over her, waiting for an answer, and said, "She's always wanted to be on the stage. If we weren't going to allow it, we should've told her before now. She's having the time of her life, and it isn't our place to stop her."

The Eight Dresden Dolls usually slept four to a room, which meant two to a bed. With

344

Fleurette added to the company they now slept three to a room, a state of unexpected luxury that had the effect of ingratiating Fleurette to the entire company.

She had, of course, paid the cost of the third room, at the rate of a dollar a night, although there was no discussion of her having it to herself. Charlotte and Eliza eagerly volunteered to share the room with her. There was likewise no debating the sleeping arrangements: they each took a bed, and Fleurette slept on a cot.

"You're the smallest," Eliza said. "Look at how perfectly that little cot fits you!"

It wasn't mean-spirited, or at least Fleurette didn't take it that way. She was absolutely giddy over the fact that she was there at all, as she'd half expected to find her sisters standing in front of the Hotel Jermyn, blocking the entrance. Sheriff Heath would be nearby with his motor car, looking on approvingly as Constance arrested a few mashers on the sidewalk for good measure before dragging Fleurette bodily back to Wyckoff.

It was tiresome to even think of it. How dull and predictable they both were, Norma with her war-mongering and her silly birds, and Constance with her blind crusades for justice and her petty grievances against the sheriff's enemies. Other girls had sisters who loaned them dresses and introduced them to the younger brothers of promising young men. Why didn't she have sisters like that?

To her relief, Norma and Constance hadn't been lying in wait outside the hotel. Once Fleurette had been swept upstairs with the rest of the troupe, leading a fleet of porters who wheeled cartloads of trunks and bags, and once she'd settled into her room with Charlotte and Eliza (trying to look as blasé as they did about every cunning detail of the room: the tiny sink in the corner, the little gilt-edged mirror, and the vanity with a neat stack of free writing paper) — once she was settled, and saw that she really had triumphed in launching herself into a new life — a monumental task came to her, in the form of billowy armloads of costumes in need of mending.

"You'll have to stitch our names into these terrible old petticoats," Eliza said. "We're supposed to wash them ourselves, but we get them hopelessly mixed up anyway."

"The sleeves are too tight on these shirtwaists," said Bernice. "The costume change is so fast that we rip them. Do something about the sleeves, or do something about May's favorite number. One of the two isn't going to survive another week."

"A few of us are slipping out after Iron-sides falls asleep tonight," Charlotte said, and Fleurette's hopes flew around wildly. "I wonder if you can bring up this hem by a couple of inches so I don't look like a schoolgirl when I wear it." There was no mention of Fleurette going along when they snuck away. It was only her first night with them, so she didn't dare ask. As it was, she had more than enough mending to keep her occupied.

May Ward, of course, kept a suite to herself, down the hall and around the corner from the Dolls and Mrs. Ironsides. (Mr. Impediment wasn't allowed on the women's floor but stationed himself in the lobby, within easy sight of the elevator, and paid the hotel porters to keep watch when he couldn't.)

Mrs. Ward liked to keep a room apart from the girls, they told her, because she "comes and goes at irregular hours, and keeps ir-regular company."

It was easy enough to guess at what that meant. Fleurette wondered how May Ward managed to slip past Mr. Impediment, or wasn't he in charge of watching her, too?

There was no performance on the first night owing to the late hour of their arrival, but on the second night, a maid knocked at her door around five o'clock. The Dolls had gone ahead to the theater, and Fleurette stayed behind to finish what mending she could before the show started. Seeing the Dolls perform every night was to be her great reward for a day spent in a cramped hotel room, bent over a sewing machine that rocked back and forth on the unsteady vanity. It didn't matter if the Dolls went running around to shops and arcades all day without her, or snuck past the chaperone at night, as long as she was with them at the theater and could somehow be a part of the show, even from backstage.

The maid had a little card for Fleurette, with a note from Mrs. Ward summoning her to her room. Was this another audition? Was she to be put on stage already? The maid didn't know and said only that she was to come quickly.

There was no time to do anything about her hair or to find a better dress among the half-unpacked trucks and piles of frills in need of mending, so she slipped on her shoes and followed the maid down the hall. At Mrs. Ward's door, the maid knocked and went on her way.

"Florine!" called a raspy voice from inside.

"It's Fleurette." She hoped she didn't sound impertinent.

"Well, hurry up and help me with this!"

Fleurette let herself into what must've been the hotel's most lavish suite for women. There was a woven carpet of royal blue and gold fleurs-de-lis, wallpaper of a matching blue and gold stripe, heavy mahogany chairs, three electric chandeliers, a marble fireplace, and, in the room beyond, an enormous brass bed with a heavy brocade coverlet tossed over it. May Ward was nowhere in sight.

"Come on through!" she called.

Fleurette followed her voice through the bedroom and into a bathroom as elegant as anything she'd ever seen. Never had she imagined that so much marble and brass could be rallied together in the service of hygiene, nor had she ever seen herself reflected in so many mirrors at once. There were two or three on every wall.

But she wasn't there to admire herself in the mirror. Mrs. Ward sat on the edge of the bathtub, with a bucket of ice next to her and something clear and pungent in a glass.

Her eyes were red, her face flushed, her hair in wild disarray. "Oh, there you are. What's the use of having a seamstress if I can never find her?"

"I was only just —"

"Never mind. Look, I stepped on this

349

damned frock. Stitch it up, will you? There's a motor car running downstairs and gasoline is dear." She glided to her feet and twirled around. Fleurette gasped when she saw the damage. Mrs. Ward had, for some bewildering reason, already put on her costume for the opening number: a filmy gown meant to emulate a Greek goddess, with layer after layer of impossibly frail chiffon. It had been rent apart and sewn back together in three or four places. One of these ineffective patches had given way when Mrs. Ward stepped on the hem.

From down on her knees behind the actress, Fleurette mumbled, "I didn't bring my kit."

May spun around, tossing ice cubes as she did. "Didn't bring your kit? Why'd you think I called you? Here, the hotel must have something awful you can use," and she ransacked the drawers until she came up with a little wooden box holding needle and thread. Fleurette did what she could with it, but warned her that the entire piece should be replaced. "Or just let me take off this outer skirt, and switch it with one of the inner layers," she offered.

As soon as Fleurette snapped off the thread, May spun around in front of the mirror, gleeful. "Oh, that's just fine. Anything can be mended, can't it, Florine? Here, I want to see what you can do with this old thing." She pulled a shimmering beaded gown of pale green and gold from a hook and tossed it at her. "I keep losing the damned beads. There's a whole handful of them in a little dish on the dresser. I'll send someone down to your room to pick it up when I'm back from the theater."

"Do you mean — tonight?" Fleurette saw hours of work ahead of her, and no hope of watching the show from backstage.

May Ward turned around and laughed, still effervescent from her drink. "Yes, of course! Tonight! There's some sort of affair in the ballroom with an undersea theme, and I must look the part. Won't it be perfect?"

The dress sat heavily in Fleurette's arms. It weighed almost as much as a small child, owing to the hundreds of glass beads clinking merrily against each other. It was a beautiful piece of work, something she would've been thrilled to put a needle to, even a week ago.

Why was she bothered over missing a single night at the theater? There would be another night, and another after that.

"It certainly will be perfect," she told May Ward, "after I finish with it."

39

Three women were booked into the jail within a few hours of each other: a mother of four accused of drunkenness and neglect, a woman charged with poisoning her husband with mercury, and a domestic cook caught stealing her employer's kitchen utensils. It took Constance an entire day to get the women booked into the jail, showered and de-loused, issued uniforms, and settled into their cells. She'd been neglectful about supervising chores and had to issue some stern words of warning when she saw that the other inmates hadn't cleaned their cell blocks.

At the end of the day, she realized that she hadn't had a chance to look in on Edna Heustis and thought it best to call so that she could file her report. The sheriff's office was unaccustomed to doing its business by telephone, but it was becoming more of a necessity, particularly lately, as the Freeholders scrutinized the cost of running two automobiles and insisted that the deputies find ways to get by without them.

Cordelia Heath was once again occupying the sheriff's office. She sat at his desk, paging through a city directory and addressing a stack of envelopes.

"He's out on a call," Cordelia said, without looking up.

"Pardon me, Mrs. Heath. I just needed to use the telephone. Sheriff's business. I'm to report on a girl . . ."

Cordelia pushed the telephone to the edge of the desk. "Go ahead. You don't have to tell me about it."

As Constance spoke to the operator, she glanced down at the sheriff's desk and saw that Mrs. Heath had opened a folder containing a campaign advertisement for his 1912 campaign for sheriff. Next to a formal portrait was a description of his platform: "Honesty — Efficiency — Economy — Social and Spiritual Betterment of Prisoners."

"That's a fine platform," Constance said, while she waited for the operator to put her call through.

Mrs. Heath looked up and said, "It was good enough for sheriff, but it won't do for Congress. We're going to need a new picture and a new platform."

"Congress? But I thought he was running against John Courter."

She gave a polite little laugh. "A sheriff can't succeed himself in office. Didn't you know that? My husband's running for Congress. I'll leave you to your call."

She gathered up her letters and bustled out. Constance found herself alone in the office, staring out the open door into an empty hallway.

Congress?

The possibility — no, the certainty — that someone else would occupy Sheriff Heath's office come November settled over her in one awful moment. How had she not realized that the sheriff was leaving?

Cordelia had always wanted to go to Washington. She had ideas about a particular kind of genteel life as a congressman's wife that had something to do with silver teapots, bone china, and a husband who didn't spend quite so much time in the company of criminals. Sheriff Heath had said so himself. Constance just didn't think he'd ever agree to it. What was she to do, once he was gone? Sheriff Heath had given her a life beyond anything she could've imagined. She had a position, a title, and a place of authority. But there was no reason to think that the next sheriff would let her keep any of that.

Mrs. Turnbull came on the line, and Constance gathered herself together to make her inquiry. She was assured that there had been no trouble from Edna. But when Constance asked to speak to her, Edna couldn't be found.

"I didn't see her go out," Mrs. Turnbull said. "One of the girls thinks she went to church."

"On a Tuesday night?"

"It seems peculiar to me, too," Mrs. Turnbull said. "She comes home by curfew. That's all I know."

"And she won't tell you what she's doing?"

"She's been very secretive about it, to tell the truth," Mrs. Turnbull said, "but it's no concern of mine, as long as she behaves herself."

"Well, I'm obligated to report on her welfare. I believe I ought to come up and speak to her."

"You're welcome to try. She won't tell me a thing," Mrs. Turnbull said, and rang off.

Constance sat alone in Sheriff Heath's office and tried to picture another man behind that desk.

And what was this about Congress? She

couldn't imagine Sheriff Heath without his badge.

Perhaps it was best that telephoning hadn't worked. A trip out of town didn't sound so bad at the moment.

She went the very next day. Before she left, Constance was pleased to receive a reassuring letter from Miss Pittman at the reformatory: the results of the Wassermann test were in, and Minnie Davis was free of disease. Miss Pittman added that Minnie was settling in well, and that she seemed to be a good worker. Minnie herself would not be permitted to write letters for the first month, she explained. Constance very much hoped that there wouldn't be a second month.

She went first to Catskill to speak to Minnie's parents, and sat once again in the grimy sitting room, among the odor of strangers' clothing in need of mending. The Davises did not make their home a pleasant place to be, and it was easy for Constance to sympathize with Minnie's opinion on that point.

The New Jersey papers were not circulated in Catskill, but Edith Davis had managed to get her hands on them regardless, and had a stack of clippings sitting on a little side-table under a darning egg. She lifted the egg and pushed the papers toward Constance with one fingernail, as if they were too filthy to touch.

"I knew from the time she was a little girl that she would come to this," Mrs. Davis hollered.

Goldie hadn't said a word since Constance had come in, and even then she spoke quietly from her chair in the corner, without looking up. "You didn't know her when she was a little girl."

"Oh, I knew about her, and that mother of hers!" Mrs. Davis shrieked, and offered no further explanation.

Constance had hoped to win over Mr. Davis, who was sitting in his dusty overalls examining a bandage on his left hand. She leaned forward and said, "Please understand that the prosecutor has no evidence. These accusations of your daughter entertaining men — you've every right to be outraged to see such a thing in the papers, but Mr. Courter said those things against Minnie without first bothering to find out if they were true. I can assure you that no such charges will be filed."

"He must've had a reason," Mr. Davis said. "Anyhow, it's no concern of ours. She don't live here no more."

"That's why I've come to speak to you. Minnie needs a good home. The prosecutor has sent her to the girls' reformatory in Trenton. If she doesn't have a respectable place to go, she could be sentenced there for several years, and I know you wouldn't —"

"A reformatory!" Mr. Davis said. "It's worse than we thought."

"It doesn't have to be," Constance said hastily. "If the judge had a word from you, she might be able to come home."

"No, no. If it's as bad as all that, the reformatory is the only place for her. We should've sent her years ago," said Mrs. Davis.

"But it's meant to be a punishment for a crime, and I don't think —"

"If there wasn't a crime, she wouldn't be in jail," Mr. Davis said. "Go on back to New Jersey and tell that girl I said to repent."

Constance looked to Goldie for help. For a long-limbed girl, she'd managed to make herself very small. She sat with her legs crossed, her arms folded over her chest, and her chin down. As soon as she realized Constance was about to speak to her, she bolted out the front door and down the street.

"You heard me," Mr. Davis said. "Go on,

now."

Constance stood and looked down at the two of them, as gray and miserable as the dingy furnishings and piles of mending that surrounded them, and understood that she was outmatched. If a case could be made to the Davises to take their daughter in again, she clearly wasn't the one to make it.

"I've never seen parents so hardened against their own child before," she said. "You've put your principles above your family, and you'll be the poorer for it."

"It isn't for you to judge," Edith said. "Go on, like he said."

She left Catskill in a downtrodden frame of mind. She hated to hear a father speak so approvingly of putting his own daughter away. It was becoming all too easy for parents to turn their unruly children over to the state. Some of them regretted it once their tempers cooled, but by then it was too late: once a child was sent to a reformatory, a remorseful parent couldn't do a thing about it. Constance had heard of mothers who pleaded to have their daughters back, because they needed the help at home, or even because they were moving away and didn't want to leave anyone behind. None of that mattered. Every sentence was served in full.

But it didn't seem that the Davises would ever want Minnie back.

She stopped next in Pompton Lakes to see about Edna Heustis, arriving at Mrs. Turnbull's boarding-house just as the girls were sitting down to supper. A maid brought her into the dining room, where five boarders looked up at her with expressions of friendly curiosity.

"Did they make you take a test to become a lady officer?" asked Fannie, a freckle-faced girl with hair the color of butter.

"Do they only let you arrest other girls, or could you arrest a man?" said Delia. "I might nominate a man for the honor."

Just then Mrs. Turnbull walked in with a covered dish. "If you're here to see Edna, she works a split shift tonight, so she gets home a little later than the other girls. She isn't in any trouble, is she?"

"Not at all. I said I would look in on her, that's all."

"Then you might as well wait for her, and let me fix you a plate."

The only other supper on offer would have been something cold from the jail kitchen a few hours later, so Constance accepted and sat down with the girls. She took the opportunity to ask each of them in turn if their mothers and fathers were bothered by the fact that they'd gone to work and lived on their own. Two of the girls said they hadn't any parents and had been under the care of an aunt or some other relation, who had been all too happy to see them grown and looking after themselves. One of them said that her father was "no good" and her mother "not much better" and that she left home as soon as the factory would hire her on. She hadn't heard a word from her parents and hoped not to. The other two were a bit vague in their answers, but gave her to understand that they had reached some accord with their families and lived in a state of uneasy truce, sending more money home than they would like, and less than their families wished to receive.

"After we pay the rent, there's hardly nothing left," Pearl said.

"You get all your meals and your laundry," Mrs. Turnbull shot back. "Nothing's stopping you from living with your mother."

"Then she'll take all my wages."

"Did you expect to make your fortune at the powder works? Clear these plates."

Constance jumped up and helped the girls with the dishes. Just as she finished, the door opened and Edna Heustis walked in wearing her factory apron and cap. When she saw Constance, she stepped back uneasily, wrapping the corner of her apron around her fingers.

"I've only come to check on you," Constance said. "Can we go upstairs?" Edna scampered up the stairs ahead of her and opened the door to her room.

"Is something the matter?" she said, when they were alone.

"I only wanted to see you, and to know that things have worked out for you. The judge asked me to check on your welfare, remember?"

"Oh." She sat down heavily on the bed. "I'm fine. I took a split shift, because it pays a little more, and in the middle of the day I come back here and help with the cleaning, for a reduction in my rent. I haven't the time to get into any trouble."

"You look exhausted," Constance said.

"I'm not," she insisted. "I'm only trying to earn a little extra."

"Why? What's happened?"

"Nothing! It's not illegal to work a few extra shifts, is it?"

"Of course not," Constance said, "but you sound a little desperate. If something's the matter, you ought to tell me."

"I'm just — I want to raise money for the war." That was as much as Edna could bring herself to say. She was afraid that if she told the deputy what she intended to do, she might be prevented or her parents might be told.

"That's good of you, Edna, but I don't want you to wear yourself out. Are you sure there's nothing else? Sometimes when a girl is desperate for money, there's another reason for it."

"What do you mean?" She looked alarmed.

"No trouble with a man?"

She laughed. It was an unexpected sound in the room. "Of course not!"

"It's not so outrageous as that."

"I suppose not, in your line of work."

Constance looked around the room and saw the pamphlets on relief efforts and the Red Cross leaflets. "Are you going to learn some nursing?"

"I might," Edna said.

Constance looked her over appraisingly. "You'd do well. You're sturdy enough."

You're sturdy enough. After Constance left, Edna sat alone in her room, fingering the Red Cross's list of nursing courses. She was exhausted from the longer shifts, and so far, the rewards had been so meager as to hardly be worth it. She might manage to save fifty cents here, and a dollar there, but it would never put a hundred dollars in her pocket for the voyage over, much less the monthly sum required for her room and board.

To make matters worse, Ruby and her friends on the Preparedness Committee seemed to be faltering in their desire to rush off to France. They were fretting over family obligations and social affairs they couldn't miss. Their mothers disapproved, a few of them said, and their fathers weren't so sure they'd put up the money after all.

It was such a game to them. They made an entertainment of holding teas to solicit donations, and of fashioning wool flowers into corsages that their friends might buy to fund their wild plans. Meanwhile, Edna, having no friends with money to spare, worked every shift she could, taking time off only when the Preparedness Committee held its meetings. The Red Cross courses were about to begin, and when they started, she'd have to choose between the extra earnings and the coursework required of every volunteer. It was an impossible choice — she couldn't do without either.

But to give up would be worse. Her job at the factory, her room at the boarding-house — it had seemed so exciting at first, so liberating, but now she saw how it might go on forever, if she couldn't find another course for herself. Any girl her age would be thinking of marriage. She couldn't bear the idea of marrying a man who stayed home from the war, and she wasn't particularly interested in marrying one if he was only going to run off to fight and might never return.

The drumbeat of war was growing louder. What else was there for her, if she didn't go to France?

40

Constance returned from a walk to the druggist, having gone in search of a mustard plaster for Providencia Monafo's cough, and found Norma waiting at the prisoners' entrance. Constance thought wearily that this was the second time in a week that she'd turned up at the jail.

What, she wondered, was stirring Norma into such unexpected and uncharacteristic action? It stood to reason that Fleurette's sudden departure (she refused to call it a disappearance) would cause Constance no end of worry — she, having borne the child for nine months and run away in secret to bring her into the world, had more than a sisterly interest in her well-being. She worried about Fleurette — she would never stop worrying about her, naturally — but her occupation demanded that she look at the matter from the perspective of a woman of the law. Through the eyes of her profession, Fleurette had done nothing wrong. Constance believed it only right to adopt that view.

Norma, on the other hand, had seized upon Fleurette's situation and worried the life out of it, like a dog with its prey. She was often like that when she got hold of something she considered unjust or improper, but never before had she taken one of her causes so far. Constance had grown to count on Norma to be that domestic presence who sat in the parlor and disapproved of things. She did not, however, like to find Norma disapproving of things at her place of employment and wished she knew how to discourage the habit.

"I don't know why you wait around out here," Constance called to her from the end of the drive. "The guards would've let you wait inside."

"I worry for anyone who finds the inside of a jail comfortable."

"I worry for you, coming into Hackensack the way you do. I don't recognize you off the farm. It's like seeing a goat in town."

"Goats have more business in Hackensack than you might believe." Norma said things like that because she had to have the last word on any subject, but particularly on the subject of farm animals.

Constance looked over her sister with a feeling of discouragement. Norma had pinned on an old green felt hat of their mother's and wrapped around her neck a red and white knitted scarf that their brother, Francis, had worn when he was a boy. Below that was a tweed riding suit bearing multiple patches, and the boots she wore to muck out the barn. It had the overall effect of a disguise rather than a suit of clothes, and Constance told her so. Norma ignored that and reached into her pocket.

"We've had another postcard from Fleurette, but that's not why I'm here."

"Let me see it." As Norma didn't seem to want to go inside, Constance led her to the garage, where they could be out of the wind and ensured of some sort of privacy. The mechanic had just left, and the wood stove still had a few sticks burning.

The postcard showed a hotel in Allentown with a theater next door. On the reverse she'd written:

```
I hadn't any idea the Dresden
Dolls  were  so  thoroughly
adored! Last night an admirer
of May Ward's took us all out
for lobster bordelaise — if
```

you can imagine it — but you can't because we've never had lobster for dinner — nor have you ever tasted Roman punch, but I have — only a sip! Frau Ironsides had it taken away and ginger ale brought in its place, but in Champagne glasses so we could pretend.

F.

"She's torturing us with that talk of Roman punch, but I'm not going to let myself be bothered by it." Constance handed the card back to Norma.

"I'm not here over the postcard," Norma said impatiently.

"Then what is it?"

She thrust out a rolled-up headline. It was exactly the sort of thing she liked to tie to the leg of a pigeon and send home, except that Constance wasn't at home. Pigeons couldn't be trained to deliver messages to the jail unless they'd been raised there, a possibility that Constance very much hoped would never occur to her.

KIDNAPPED GIRL FORCED
TO WRITE LETTERS

As it was only the headline, cut out with pinking shears, Constance had no choice but to say, "Aren't you going to show me the rest?"

Norma pulled it from her pocket. "It concerns a girl who was drugged with chloroform at a train station." Here she paused and lifted an eyebrow in anticipation of Constance's response.

"Yes, I heard you. You needn't make a dramatic recitation out of this." (Only one year earlier, Fleurette had been threatened with just such a kidnapping. It was not an incident that Constance was ever likely to forget, but Norma thought it her grim duty to remind her of it at any opportunity.)

Norma lifted the clipping to better see it through her spectacles and continued. "She was taken away to Chicago, but made to write to her parents as if she'd only run off to visit an aunt in Rochester. The kidnappers contrived to have the letters smuggled by train to Rochester to be posted."

"Very clever, those white slavers."

"She was gone for a year. After she escaped, she said that she'd tried to conceal secret messages in the letters, but no one in her family noticed them."

"What sort of messages?"

"Having the first letter of each line spell

out C-H-I-C-A-G-O and so forth." Norma made it sound like Constance was out of step for not knowing such tricks.

"I've never known Fleurette to go in for secret code. You're the one they should kidnap. You'd send back all kinds of codes and hidden messages."

"You wouldn't know what to do with a hidden message if I sent one."

"I don't even know what to do with this newspaper story, so I suppose you're right. If you mean to suggest that Fleurette is only sending these notes under some sort of threat from kidnappers — well, I just can't go along with that."

Norma buttoned her collar up under her neck and made ready to leave. "That's fine, because I've already taken care of it."

"How?" Already Norma was walking away. Constance followed her outside and waved away a guard who'd been sent downstairs to fetch her. She practically had to shout, as Norma was walking so fast.

"Norma!" Constance called. "What did you do?"

She turned around and fluttered her hand in the air a bit regally. "I turned the matter over to Belle Headison."

41

Norma and Belle Headison as co-conspirators! How had this been brought about? They'd never been introduced, so far as Constance knew, but she must've said something about Mrs. Headison at home, Paterson's first policewoman being a noteworthy topic. Still, it was astonishing that Norma would take it upon herself to go and visit anyone for any purpose, much less to enlist the help of a perfect stranger in a family matter.

Although as Constance considered it, she had to admit that the two were almost a perfect match. Norma couldn't be bothered to muster Mrs. Headison's sense of moral outrage over the generalized threat to virtuous womanhood that lingered in the air, but she more than outpaced Mrs. Headison in vigilance and suspicion of individual shady characters.

Norma, in other words, had no moral mission, other than to identify those particular parties whom she found lacking and to gather evidence against them — particularly when they interfered with her family. Mrs. Headison, on the other hand, ran a crusade. Put together, they were a dangerous combination.

It was also true that Mrs. Headison was altogether stiff and rigid in her way of thinking, and believed that the best answer for every girl was to be picked up by the scruff of the neck and delivered back home to her mother, to resume her crochet-work and laundry duties. She had little sympathy for a girl who wanted anything else. If Edna Heustis had fallen into the custody of Mrs. Headison, she surely would have been made to resign her position at the powder works and return home to her mother.

And now, thanks to Norma, Fleurette had become Mrs. Headison's latest target. Constance wouldn't wish that fate on any girl, much less her own.

It was conniving of Norma, Constance thought, to make such an announcement and then walk away, stomping down the gravel drive toward the approaching trolley car, when she knew that Constance was needed at work and couldn't chase after her. The reason the guard had been sent to fetch her was that a woman had just been arrested on a swindling charge, and it fell to Constance to register her, put her through the bathing and de-lousing ritual, and issue her a clean set of clothes.

She would've put the guard off and run over to Paterson to speak to Belle Headison that minute, but apparently the inmate was kicking up quite a fuss and none of the other guards wanted to listen to her. Constance had no choice but to put that business aside and tend to her duties. The swindler thought she might fight Constance over the removal of her clothes and the humiliation of a jailhouse shower, but she soon found herself outmatched and submitted to a vigorous scrubbing and a caustic hair rinse. "I suppose it's for everyone's good if the bugs are got rid of," the swindler muttered, and Constance praised her for her community spirit.

As soon as she had the inmate settled, she went directly to speak to Mrs. Headison but found her office empty. A note pinned to the door said she wouldn't be back for the rest of the day. Constance's shift at the jail was over by then, so there was nothing to do but to go home and face Norma.

Constance found her next to the barn, tossing pigeons in the air. Her friend Carolyn Borus was standing across the road, watching them flutter up into the sky, circle around, and come back to land on the roof of their loft.

Mrs. Borus had arrived by horseback. She wore a smart riding costume and high boots. Her chestnut bay nibbled at a pile of hay behind the barn.

"Your sister has the most remarkable ideas!" she shouted to Constance.

"Yes, I've been noticing that lately," Constance called back.

Mrs. Borus scrambled out of the little gully alongside the road and walked over. "She believes she can predict the fastest flyers by watching their flight pattern as they take off. Have you ever heard of such a thing? She's been keeping records for weeks now. We'll know for certain when we run our test flights, but I think she's onto something."

Norma reached into the pigeon loft, took two more birds in her hands, and tossed them up. This time neither Carolyn nor Norma bothered to watch their flight.

"Those two are slow, but it's only fair to let them try," Carolyn explained.

"How are yours faring under this system, Mrs. Borus?" Constance asked.

"Oh, very well. I'm about to leave for

Columbus for our next test flight. And then it's Chicago after that. I wish you could persuade your sister to come along. It isn't easy to manage a dozen pigeons by myself."

"If I go, there's no one to give an accurate time when my birds return," Norma said. "Constance is never at home. Even if she was, her timekeeping is unreliable."

"That's true," said Constance. "I shouldn't be trusted with a pigeon clock." She had long ago understood that the only way to be dismissed from pigeon duty was to make a mess of the timekeeping. It was wonderfully effective: Norma never asked her to do it anymore.

Mrs. Borus took her horse from around back and led it down the drive. "I'm leaving on Friday. You have time to change your mind."

After she rode away, Constance followed her sister into the barn. Norma took up a rake and started mucking out the chicken coop.

"I don't know what made you think Mrs. Headison should get involved in any of this," Constance said to her, now that pigeons and trains were no longer their topic of conversation.

"She seemed quite willing," Norma said.

"But she's a Paterson policewoman. We

might not know exactly where Fleurette is, but she's certainly not in Paterson."

Norma pushed a wheelbarrow of feathers and old pine bedding out the door and deposited it on what was to be their summer vegetable garden. "It doesn't matter where Fleurette happens to be. Mrs. Headison has friends in every city. She has only to wire the Travelers' Aid Society at each stop on the tour and ask them to keep an eye on May Ward's theater company. They're all too happy to do it, those women. They love an assignment."

The idea of a Belle Headison in every city across America gave Constance a case of nerves. "But they're not to follow her around and watch her every move, are they? They've been given the general idea that a theater troupe is in town and that they might be on the alert . . ." She trailed off, as the likelihood of her version of events seemed ever more remote.

"Oh, no," Norma said as she pushed the empty wheelbarrow back into the barn. "They've taken up the assignment with tremendous enthusiasm. They're going to attend every show, and watch at the stage door, and keep an eye on the hotels, too."

"Norma, you didn't! Why have you let Freeman Bernstein set you off like this? I never thought I'd be the one to defend a man like him, or to stand up in favor of Fleurette's going off with a vaudeville troupe, but that's exactly what's happened, isn't it? You put me on the opposite side of this. You, and now Mrs. Headison. I'm going right over there tomorrow to insist that she call this off."

"Go ahead and try," Norma said. "She won't be called off. She's a woman of principles."

Norma went over to the barn stove's metal chimney and pounded on it, which released a great cloud of ash all around her. "I thought so," she muttered, and went to work clearing the chimney and sweeping up the ashes.

Constance stood looking down at her, at her broadcloth overalls smeared in mud and dusted in wood shavings, at the back of her head, where her hair stood up in a mess of brown curls, and at her heavy shoulders, working the short-handled broom.

There was a song Fleurette used to sing, a man's song, about how some wives were like anchors and others like balloons. It occurred to her that the same must be true of sisters.

She had never once thought of Norma as a balloon.

Was she an anchor? She felt like one, at that moment. She even looked like one.

42

The next morning, Constance went directly back to Mrs. Headison's office, fueled by indignation and the wild uncertain fear that Fleurette would discover what Norma had done and turn her back on them for good. It seemed inevitable that their time together was coming to an end. Fleurette was eighteen and would find work for herself or find a husband, or perhaps one and then the other, but in any case, she wouldn't want to live with her sisters forever.

Constance was only just starting to realize what that meant. It meant that she and Norma would be alone, just the two of them. There was no future for Constance that didn't have Norma in it. The thought of it made her glum and broody.

It was in this state of mind that she arrived at the Paterson Travelers' Aid Office and at last found Belle Headison there, banging at a typewriter. She sat straight as a ruler, perched on the very end of a little wooden stool on wheels, with her silver hair in one of those spartan buns that pulled at her ears and at the corners of her eyes.

She jumped up when she saw Constance. She was a tightly wound, energetic woman who always seemed about to break into a run. She spoke too loudly and stood too close. Constance was forever backing away from her.

"Deputy!" She rushed over to take her hands. "I had the pleasure of meeting your sister, and now you've come to pay me a visit. How many more Kopps are there, apart from the girl who's gone astray?"

"She hasn't gone astray," Constance said. "And we have a married brother in Hawthorne, but I don't suppose you'll run into him."

"The Kopp intelligence in a man. That is something I'd like to see. Or did your mother save it all for the girls and forget to keep any for the boy? I know some families like that."

"Francis does just fine. But I've come to apologize for my sister Norma. I'm afraid she's sent your colleagues off on a frivolous errand."

Mrs. Headison gave a little gasp. "Frivolous? Not at all! If she's fallen in with the theater crowd, there's no guessing what might happen. I'm sure I don't have to tell you that the primary sources of moral decay in this country are the theaters, the dance halls, and the saloons. Those girls are left to run amok and — well, you know all about the trouble they get into. Every night when the play is over, there are calls for dates and you know very well the class of men from whom they come. The girl in this situation finds it difficult to keep her honor behind the footlights. The stage atmosphere makes for a loose holding of the bonds of virtue."

Mrs. Headison was a little winded after that speech, and so was Constance. There was no talking her out of her opinions. Constance knew better than to try.

"It is distressing what can happen," she said, "but today I'm only here about one particular girl, and that is Fleurette. I'm afraid Norma gave you the wrong impression. She hasn't fallen in with a bad crowd, or put herself in harm's way. I've always told her that she has every right to go out and find work for herself, and that's exactly what she's done. There's nothing wrong with it."

"I was made to understand that she snuck away, under cover of night," Mrs. Headison said.

"It doesn't matter when she left, or how.

She writes home faithfully and we have every reason to believe that she's safe. I don't want her thinking that we've set a gang of spies upon her, and I certainly don't want to put the ladies at the Travelers' Aid Societies through any extra difficulty on our account. You may let them know that the concerns over May Ward's theater troupe are unfounded, and that we have no reason at all to suspect anything untoward."

Mrs. Headison looked a little crestfallen at that. "Nothing at all untoward?"

"No. I'm so sorry she bothered you. If you would just put out a wire —"

Suddenly Belle seemed to have a new idea. "But your sister was under the impression that Miss Fleurette was being pursued by a show promoter who wants to put her on the stage and exploit an unfortunate scandal at whose center the three of you found yourselves last year. I thought I'd be doing all of you a favor."

Constance was shocked to hear her talk that way. Had Norma really said all of that to a complete stranger? She felt her face go red and she had to swallow hard to get her voice back.

"It was a scandal for the man who harassed us and was found guilty. My sisters and I did nothing to humiliate ourselves.

That's a fiction that Norma has invented for herself. The difference between Norma and me is that I do not go around charging people with crimes I believe they might someday commit. I hope you regard your duties as I do mine."

"Well, I . . ."

"Good. Then let's not keep these ladies on an assignment that has no merit, when there is surely more serious work to be done, and girls in real distress who could use their help."

Mrs. Headison wouldn't look at Constance after that, but she nodded and went over to her desk to write something down.

"Thank you," said Constance. "Now, I wouldn't want Fleurette to find out about our misunderstanding . . ."

"Misunderstanding?" Belle Headison sounded bereft.

"Yes, because that's all it was. It would only upset her to think we didn't trust her, and we do."

With her eyes still on her desk, Mrs. Headison said, "Oh, it's never the girl I mistrust, but the hands she might fall into. Take that white slave case of yours. What's to become of that poor girl?"

"Yes, I saw you at the press conference."

"Mr. Courter invited me. I hope you don't

mind."

Constance minded very much but tried not to let it show. "Minnie Davis insists that she left home of her own free will. It would be the worst sort of exaggeration to call it a white slave case."

Mrs. Headison shook her head pityingly. "I wouldn't be so sure. I had a girl just like her a few months ago. Claims she ran off willingly, and found a man who might get around to marrying her one day, except he never did."

"What became of her?"

She seemed surprised that Constance would even ask the question. "Why, I had her sent to the state home on a charge of social vagrancy. I'm sure you'll do the same with Miss Davis."

"I'd like to try to put girls like her on a better path," Constance said. "Some of them never meant to do wrong. Don't you think they can be saved?"

"Saved for what?" Belle Headison seemed genuinely puzzled by the question. "They'll never marry. No employer would have them. There's no telling what social diseases they might be spreading among the men in this county, just before we're about to send our boys to war. Can you imagine? No, I think it's in everyone's best interest to keep them away from society until they're much older, and not such a trap for healthy young men. Besides, we don't want a child born to a morally degraded mother. We'd have an entire generation of degenerate and feeble-minded children. I'd lock Minnie Davis up until she was quite past childbearing age. Wouldn't you?"

43

Constance took the trolley as far as Main Street in Hackensack, then decided to walk the rest of the way to clear her head. It was one of those blindingly bright afternoons that was always accompanied by a high wind in winter. The men walked with their hands clasped down over the tops of their hats, and the women felt around for pins and straps and ribbons. Every shop awning snapped and shook like a sail. A strip of bunting had worked loose from the Odd Fellows Hall and flew high above the second-story windows, tethered by a single fraying knot at the base of a flag-pole.

From across the street, she spotted Sheriff Heath coming out of the *Bergen Evening Record*'s office. He paused for a minute in front of Mr. Terhune's shop and looked in the window. There were a few other men admiring whatever was inside. Constance stepped up next to him and saw that it was a motorcycle.

"It looks like a terribly clumsy bicycle," she said.

"It's quite a bit more than that," Sheriff Heath said.

"You're right. It's probably noisy, too."

"I'll tell Mr. Harley you're not impressed."

"Are you planning to take Mrs. Heath to Washington on one of those?"

He turned to her and tipped back the brim of his hat. He had a way of leaning in and squinting at her sometimes, as if he were trying to read small type. "What do you think? Congressman Heath?"

It took her breath away, the way he put his ambition out before her like that.

"I thought Sheriff Heath sounded just fine."

He shrugged and said, "So did I. But the law says a man can only serve as sheriff for one term in a row. I could run again someday, if Washington won't have me."

"Oh, they'll have you. Why wouldn't they?"

He turned and they walked together toward the jail. "I'm up against a brick-maker. There's less to dislike about him."

"Well, I'd vote for you," Constance said, although she didn't like the idea of voting him out of town.

"Then I wish you could," he said.

"I didn't think you wanted to go to Washington."

They passed a barber shop, a druggist, and a hardware store. Every man coming in and out wanted to stop and shake hands with the sheriff. Constance could see him as a politician, making promises and giving speeches. He would miss the crooks, although he might find some in the capital.

After that business concluded, he said, "The local party nominates the best man for every office. They put me up for sheriff and I was glad to have the chance. Now they've put me up for Congress. Mrs. Heath believes I can win. She intends to make my campaign a success. I'll let her run the whole thing if she wants. It's good to see her taking an interest."

That was as much as Sheriff Heath was going to say about his marriage, but Constance understood. It was better between them when Cordelia could be on his side, and have a cause to rally around. She was miserable living in the sheriff's quarters, and who could blame her? Of course she preferred a nice home in Washington.

By now they'd reached the jail. She followed Sheriff Heath into his office.

"One of our guards has an aunt in Atlanta," he said as he settled behind his desk. "You've made the papers again."

Constance groaned and dropped into a chair across from him. "Why would they bother about me all the way down there?" She took the article from him. It had been folded several times, and was heavily marked with underlining and exclamation points by the guard's aunt, who apparently thought the whole business appalling.

From the very first paragraph, Constance found herself agreeing with the aunt.

Constance the Cop is a real police officer, stout-hearted and daring. She does not hesitate to venture into a physical mixup with the sterner sex in the pursuit of her duty. Also does she operate the "halter hug," which, though it may sound rather enticing to the imaginative masculine reader, still it has proved to be just as distressingly effective to the culprit as a regular wrestling strangle hold. For Constance's arms are both lithe and muscular, and while they unquestionably could be shaped to tenderer ends have, nevertheless, the compressive power of steel cables when hardened by the call of duty.

She couldn't bear to look at another word and tossed the paper back to him. "I feel sorry for Atlanta if it must send all the way to New Jersey for its entertainment."

The sheriff spread the story across his desk. It took up the entire front page of the Sunday magazine, and two more pages inside. "You've made quite a sensation, Miss Kopp. I don't recall a reporter from Atlanta visiting us here in Hackensack."

"That's because he was never here!" She turned the paper around and ran her finger down the lines of type. "He copied most of this from other papers. There's a long bit about the Kaufman case, and quite a lot about von Matthesius, all pulled from other reports. And he fabricated all the quotes himself." She pointed to a line at the end of the story from a New York police officer who, the reporter claimed, witnessed her capture of a fugitive at a Brooklyn subway station last year: "Gee! I seen some A1 strong-armed performers in my time, but that chicken cop's got somethin' on all of 'em!"

The sheriff was a man who valued dignity and sobriety above all else, so it took some effort to hide his amusement. "Are you quite sure he made that up?"

"Oh, please don't tell me that women officers are being called 'chicken cops' behind our backs."

He held up his hands in mock surrender. "If they are, I'm not going to be the one to tell you. How'd you get along in Catskill?"

"Poorly," Constance said. "Please don't remind me again that the only reason you hired a woman was to get the female population in line. Whatever magical powers I possess are wasted on the Davises. Isn't there something else we can do for her?"

"Well, I don't know what it will mean for Miss Davis, but the case against Anthony Leo is falling apart. If she won't testify against him, then it's nearly impossible to make a case that he took her forcibly over state lines. And thanks to your efforts, the landlord has told John Courter that he hasn't anything useful to say in court about men sneaking in and out of the place. He won't be testifying."

"But that has to be good news for Minnie, doesn't it? If Anthony Leo's to be released, surely she will be, too."

"We'll know in another week or so. He's

going before the judge and you're to bring Minnie back from Trenton for the day. They might dispense with her case at the same time, I don't know." The sheriff was sorting through the morning's mail on his desk. He held out a handwritten note to her.

"It's Carrie Hart. She was just here looking for you. She says it concerns Fleurette."

44

The note instructed Constance to meet Carrie at the library if she returned within the hour. Constance hurried back downtown in the direction she'd just gone, but stopped short as she pushed through the library's double doors.

Carrie was sitting at a table with Norma, their heads bent over a newspaper.

The shock of seeing Norma out on her own in public was beginning to wear off, but she couldn't guess as to how Norma managed to keep turning up at the side of Constance's professional acquaintances. Had she ever introduced Carrie and Norma? Surely not. She rushed over, bewildered, and sat across from them.

"What's this about Fleurette?" she whispered. "I wish you wouldn't scare me like that."

"Why didn't you tell me that your sister's gone missing?" Carrie asked.

"She isn't missing," Constance hissed, although she could see from their pitying expressions that her version of events held no interest. To Norma she added, "I can't seem to turn around without you showing up with another hare-brained scheme. What's the matter with you?"

Norma spoke with a note of grim triumph. "She didn't go off with May Ward."

"That's nonsense," Constance said. "Of course she did. We have postcards from her! Freeman Bernstein told us she joined the company."

"Look." Norma pushed the newspaper across the table.

"Why are you reading the *Scranton Times*?" But then Constance saw the notice about May Ward's show. The entire cast was listed. There were eight Dresden Dolls, and Fleurette was not among them.

It unsettled her, but she didn't want to admit it. "What does this tell us?"

Norma snorted. "I don't know why you have to be so thickheaded. She isn't there. If she ever was with the troupe, she's run off."

"Or she's been kidnapped," Carrie put in, a little too eagerly. "Norma told me about the hidden messages in the postcards."

"She hasn't been kidnapped," Constance

said crossly. "Norma, I can't believe you'd involve Carrie in this nonsense. Of course there aren't hidden messages in the post-cards."

"We just haven't found them yet," Norma said.

"Oh, you mustn't blame her," Carrie said. "I was here a few days ago to work on a story, and I overheard Norma asking after the Pennsylvania papers. She gave her name to the librarian and I introduced myself. I've never met the other Kopps!"

"What a shame," Constance mumbled.

"Well, they don't take the smaller papers here," Carrie continued, "but of course, we take everything at my office. I told her to meet me here this morning and I'd have exactly what she's looking for. And here it is! Now, where do you suppose Fleurette has gone?"

"Harrisburg," said Constance. "It says right here that Harrisburg is the next stop on the tour, and I have every reason to think she's with them. There could be any number of reasons why she isn't listed with the company. Maybe she's an understudy. She said she hadn't learned all the steps yet."

"She didn't tell us she was an understudy," Norma said.

"She might not have wanted to. Or maybe

the paper had an old notice, printed before Fleurette joined."

Carrie and Norma exchanged a maddeningly conspiratorial look. "That isn't all we know," Norma said, regally.

Constance waited, although her outrage was beginning to simmer over. At war inside of her were twin emotions: fury at Norma, and terror over the idea that Fleurette really had disappeared.

Carrie leaned across the table to deliver the news. "This Freeman Bernstein. Norma was right. She did remember him from the papers. He's the one who ran that pleasure resort up at 110th Street a few years ago. Did you ever see it? It was right on Fifth Avenue."

"I don't go in for pleasure resorts," Norma said, as if anyone needed to be reminded of that, "but I did read about this one. Carrie found it in her archives."

"It was called Midway Park," Carrie continued. "Mr. Bernstein meant it to be a little Coney Island right in the city. Female trapeze artists, calcium lights blazing all night, a merry-go-round, and a brass band — you can imagine the way the neighbors complained, but he had a few thousand people through there every night. Anyway, he was putting all these little buildings up, and one of them fell over in a storm and hurt a few people. That was enough to get it closed down. A few months later, he formed a new corporation under a new name and went right on to the next venture."

"That's what he does," Norma said. "Every few years, he's running a new scheme under a new name. You remember Beulah Binford and the murder scandal down in Virginia? He tried to put her on the stage after the trial. Can you imagine making a show of that mess?"

Norma started shuffling through a stack of clippings. Constance slapped her hand down on top of them. "Norma. I can see what you've done. You've put together an entire file of grievances against Freeman Bernstein, and you've enlisted the help of a reporter who surely has more important work to do. It's bad enough that you'd pull Belle Headison into this. I can't believe you're bothering Carrie with it, too. I can't take a step in this town without finding someone else you've enlisted into this nonsensical scheme of yours."

Norma didn't bother to answer and went back to studying her newspapers. Carrie smiled brightly and said, "Oh, this is a far more interesting story than anything you've given me. Courthouse duty is dull, but this — this is perfect! 'Woman Deputy Rescues Sister.' "

"We don't know that she needs rescuing."

"Of course she does," Norma said.

Carrie sat back in her chair and watched the two of them, clearly amused.

Norma shuffled her papers around. "You admit it looks suspicious."

"I don't like Fleurette being gone any more than you do, but we mustn't turn it into a criminal case."

"Well, I won't be satisfied until someone has laid eyes on her and can report back that she's being looked after. We really don't have any idea."

"Fleurette is not being forced at knife-point to send home cheerful postcards, if that's what you think."

"I know exactly what I think. You're the one who refuses to see the facts."

Norma was staring at Constance rather ferociously, waiting for some sort of answer, which never came, as there was no way to respond to a statement like that. Finally Norma hoisted an eyebrow and said, "I've waited long enough. Carrie and I are getting on a train and you can't stop us."

Norma on a train? Norma, for whom a trip to Hackensack was once exotic?

Constance blamed Carrie for this. She'd fanned all of Norma's wild notions about kidnappings and secret plots, and failed to see that her mistrust of Freeman Bernstein was founded on nothing more than a generalized contempt of any outsider who tried to interfere with her family.

But now there was this grain of doubt, this disquieting possibility that something really had gone wrong with Fleurette. What if she really had disappeared, or fallen in with bad company? What if she really was stranded somewhere, and very much in need of rescuing?

Constance wasn't about to admit that Norma might be right. She said, "I can't seem to stop anyone in this family from getting on a train. But if you're going, I'm coming with you, if only to intervene before you make fools of yourselves."

"You don't have to. Stay home if you don't like it."

"I don't like it, and I'm not staying home," Constance said.

That's what passed for a compromise with Norma.

45

"You're up early," Fleurette said from behind a mouthful of pins.

"I haven't been to bed." May Ward tried to sound gay about it, but her voice cracked. It was six in the morning, and they had a train at noon. Her room smelled of spoiled wine and stale cigarettes. Dresses and stockings were flung over every chair and heaped on the floor around her bed. It was no wonder her wardrobe was in such poor repair: she was always stumbling over skirts, crushing beadwork, and snagging hooks and buttons. Never had Fleurette seen such fine dresses so thoroughly abused.

"I can't match this metal thread, of course," Fleurette said. "I'm just going to put a few stitches in the shoulders and a few under the arms. That should hold until New York, if you're careful. I'll look for the right thread when we get there."

"Do whatever you have to do. I don't care

about metal thread."

"Oh, but a dress like this? We must. It really should go back to Paris to be fitted. I want to do the very least that's required to hold it together until . . ." Fleurette's voice trailed off as she drew close to the gold filet lace that attached at the shoulder and draped so languidly down the back. She remembered looking, as a child, at butterfly wings up close and realizing that those brilliant patterns were made up of tiny scales, like miniature feathers, each attached by some filament too fine to see. That was how this dress was made. To go at it with a No. 12 needle — her smallest — was like attacking it with a sledgehammer.

"Are you sure this sort of slouchy thing is the style? I don't feel quite upright in it. And where's the waist? It just sort of — falls down."

"If it comes from Callot Soeurs, it's the style," Fleurette mumbled. She never expected to touch a dress like this. It seemed to be made of spun gold, and it did drape in the most bewitching manner. There was almost nothing to it: just a loose chemise with a belt slung around the hips, tied with two gold tassels at the end, which Fleurette guessed (correctly) were meant to hang carelessly down behind one hip or the other, like an afterthought.

The arms were bare. A corset was superfluous — although Fleurette couldn't convince Mrs. Ward of that. "I've worn every kind of beautiful dress on every kind of stage, dear," she'd said, "and let me tell you, things don't always stay where they're supposed to. I'm going to require some kind of boning if I'm to go flitting about in this little thing. It looks like I'm wearing nothing at all."

Fleurette made the last of her temporary stitches and stood back to check her work. The dress was all wrong for May Ward. The colors — gold lace and pearly silk — matched her complexion and her hair too closely. In this case, the dress was the picture and the woman merely the frame. It begged for dark hair and olive skin. And it had been cut for a taller, lankier woman, which was why Fleurette had been obliged to take in the shoulders, and why Mrs. Ward insisted on her corset.

"Are we finished?" May Ward asked. "I'm about to drop."

"Let me take this off you before you do." Fleurette went to work on the eyelets in the back. "I didn't know one could buy a dress like this outside of New York."

Mrs. Ward laughed wearily. "It was a gift.

I believe the previous occupant ran out West with a cattleman."

"I don't think I'd leave this dress for a cattleman," Fleurette said.

"Nor should you." She stepped out of the dress and turned around to face Fleurette. In her ordinary muslin underthings, she could've been anyone. "Tell me something, Flora."

"Yes, ma'am." Fleurette had given up trying to teach Mrs. Ward her name. She stood with that dream of a dress in her arms, looking at the pale and freckled body that had somehow earned the right to wear it.

"What kind of girl begs for a job as an unpaid seamstress? You aren't running away from someone, are you?"

"No! Of course not."

Mrs. Ward put a hand on her hip and cocked her chin. "There's not a horrible father back in Paterson, or a shrewish mother?"

"I just wanted to work. You saw our act. I want to be on the stage, ma'am."

May Ward looked puzzled. "What? Oh, yes, your act. That was darling. Now, I can't persuade Mr. Bernstein to pay you. He's a detestable old thing and I'm very nearly through with him myself. But you might as well stay on for the rest of the tour. I'll see to it that the company pays your expenses, and I'll slip you a few bills when I can. Will that do it?"

Fleurette was very nearly out of money. This was the first mention of her staying on. She tried to conceal her relief, as Mrs. Ward did not go in for sentiment. "Yes, of course. Thank you."

"Just don't tell Freeman." She went to work at the buttons on her corset. Fleurette knew that was her signal to leave, but she had very little time alone with Mrs. Ward and hated to miss her chance.

"I know all the songs, too," Fleurette ventured, her hand on the doorknob.

May Ward was climbing into bed. "What's that?" she said, yawning.

"The songs. I know all the songs. If you need another girl."

From under the covers came a muffled laugh. "The last thing I need is another girl. Send a maid in at eleven, will you?"

46

Sheriff Heath was not at all pleased to hear that Constance had decided to go after Fleurette — or, more to the point, to go after Norma, who was going after Fleurette.

"If you genuinely believe she's in trouble, there's nothing stopping you from telephoning the police," he said. "People do it all the time."

"But I can't be certain," Constance said. "If I send the police after May Ward's troupe and there's nothing wrong — well, Fleurette would never forgive me."

"If there's nothing wrong, you ought to stay here and do your job."

"But if I don't go, Norma and Carrie will chase after her on their own, and that would only be worse."

He held up his hands in a sign of defeat. "I've never seen three sisters get each other so hopelessly mixed up. Don't take more than two days. Anthony Leo goes before the judge on Friday, and you're to bring Minnie Davis back."

Even the girl's name stabbed at her. If she could think of a single thing to do for Minnie, she would've stayed in Hackensack and done it.

"I'll be here," she said.

Constance, Norma, and Carrie stood under the candy-striped awnings at the Harrisburg train station. Norma was dressed for traveling, in an old-fashioned tweed suit that smelled of camphor, and a sturdy felt hat upon which she'd made one concession to fashion, by arranging three plum-colored pigeon feathers into a little fan shape and tucking them into the brim. Constance had to admit that it looked smart on her. Carrie, naturally, looked the part of the city reporter, in a slim blue suit and a double-breasted wool coat. She summoned a porter with an elegant snap of her fingers.

The Hotel Columbus was their destination. According to a woman they'd met on the train, it kept a floor for women and put out a reasonable lunch for forty cents. As it was only a few blocks away, on Walnut, the porter wheeled their bags over rather than bother with a taxicab.

On the way, Constance thought it best to

remind Norma of the promise she'd made. "If Fleurette is found safe . . ."

"Yes," Norma said moodily.

"And it appears that the circumstances are as they have been described to us . . ."

"We've been over this."

"And if there is no sign of any wrongdoing that can be observed by the three of us . . ."

"I know!"

"Then I will never hear the name Freeman Bernstein again. You'll drop the matter forever."

Norma refused to look at her.

"Forever," Constance said again.

"Yes, that's what I said." Norma didn't like being made to say it again.

"And I'm a witness," Carrie said cheerfully.

"But you're not a reporter," Constance put in. "Not on this trip. I don't want Fleurette to know that we went to spy on her."

"I'll only write a story if there's some trouble. Not that I'm hoping for it."

"All a reporter does is hope for trouble," Norma said. Constance didn't bother to remind her that she was the one who'd involved Carrie in the first place.

The hotel was a dun-colored brick affair on a busy intersection, with a cigar shop on the corner and the hotel entrance off to the side, out of the fray. The porter knew his business and took them directly to the ladies' desk, where an officious-looking woman introduced only as Miss Lydia took down their names and offered a suite with two large beds, a fireplace, and a view to the river. They took it, even though it meant that Constance would have to share a bed with Norma, who snored.

It was then that Norma decided to play the part of the detective. She wasn't very good at it, and it embarrassed Constance to watch, especially with Carrie standing back, observing, with a wry little smile on her face and a notebook in her hand.

"My friends and I enjoy the theater and wonder what might be on offer," Norma began, sounding stiff and unconvincing. She approved of the arts generally but took no interest in any particular occurrence of it.

Miss Lydia nodded and started to shuffle through the papers on her desk. Norma added, "Something we wouldn't be ashamed to tell about back home."

Had Norma ever been ashamed in her life? Constance had never even heard her use the word.

Miss Lydia found the card she'd been looking for underneath her blotter. She raised a pair of spectacles to her eyes to read it. "You might enjoy a choral concert at Fahnestock Hall."

Norma would enjoy nothing less, so Constance said, "That's exactly what I had in mind."

Norma eased her heel back on Constance's shoe and said, "But we want to hear about everything before we decide."

Miss Lydia looked up at the two of them and said, with a cheery lilt in her voice, "Then I suggest Mr. Howe's Travel Festival. There are to be film studies of the Indians and of the Swiss Alps. It can be quite broadening to see those places you might never — oh, and it includes 'curious examples of crystallization, adventures in the insect world, and logging in Italy.' "

"Absolutely perfect!" Constance crowed.

"There must be something else." Norma sounded a little anxious.

Miss Lydia read down the page. "I don't suppose you'd want to look at *The Birth of a Nation.*"

"I hear there's been some trouble about that," Norma muttered, before Constance could accept on her behalf.

"Yes . . . well, there's not much more." Miss Lydia ran her finger down a column of type. "*Fruits of Desire* involves a laborer,

410

a capitalist, a humanitarian, and a socialist, along with a society woman, and a woman who gives it all up for love."

"I'd rather not know what they get up to," Norma said.

Miss Lydia said, "Nor I. Now, if it's a comedy you're after, May Ward and Her Eight Dresden Dolls are at the Orpheum."

"May Ward is precisely who we're after," Constance said, earning another jab from Norma.

"My sister's an admirer," Norma said. "She always wanted to go on the stage herself, but she's too tall and it frightens the men. I thought it would come as an advantage to be able to be seen from so far away, but she's plain, too, and nothing can be done about that."

Miss Lydia looked up at them with half a smile, probably hoping to catch Norma in a joke. But Norma stood over her, as dour as ever, and said, "I wonder if May Ward signs autographs. I don't want to wait out by the stage door all night for nothing."

It was then that Miss Lydia gave the information Norma had been hoping for. "You won't have to follow her far. Mrs. Ward and her girls have always stopped over at the Hotel Columbus. They'll be just down the hall from you. You'd better go up

411

if you want to be ready for the theater at eight. I'll have three tickets at my desk when you come down. You'll find the theater just around the corner on Locust, so you'll have no need of a taxicab."

They took the keys and went on upstairs. Their room was at the end of a long hallway carpeted in a pattern of parrot tulips. The bags had been sent up ahead and they passed the porter on his way out. Norma handed him a coin whose value she kept concealed from Constance, but which almost certainly wasn't enough.

"Why am I the admirer of May Ward, when you're the one who dragged us all the way here to see her?" Constance hissed at Norma when they were out of earshot.

"You don't seem to understand anything about detective work," Norma said. "Everything you said made her more suspicious."

"There was no need to play the detective," Constance said. "You could've just asked her straight away whether May Ward was in residence here or not."

"She wouldn't have told me," Norma said, and proceeded to mutter about it as they unpacked their things and shook out the dresses they'd brought for the theater. Fleurette had made both of their dresses, of course, which left Constance feeling all the more guilty and unsettled about what they'd come to Harrisburg to do.

Carrie worked on her hair in front of the mirror. "Are you sure you wouldn't like me to pose as a theater critic? I could interview May Ward and her Dolls, and find out for myself if Fleurette's with them."

"Bringing a reporter along only makes this look more suspicious," Constance said. "I don't want any of us to be seen. We're here to make sure that Fleurette is safe, and then we're going to scurry away and no one's ever going to know."

They hadn't any idea how many rooms May Ward might have taken, or where they were in relation to theirs. Norma kept running to the peep-hole and looking out when she heard footsteps go by.

"You can stop looking, because they're already at the theater getting into costume," Constance said. "We'd better see about some dinner before we go."

Norma was at the window now, watching the people below going past. She was breathing noisily, and a little cloud of steam was making an impression on the glass. "We can't risk going into a restaurant. We'll be spotted — if Fleurette's here at all, and I don't think she is."

"Fine, then I'll order something cold on a

tray."

"I detest anything cold on a tray," Carrie said.

Constance considered that and said, "Maybe they'll send up some soup."

The hotel did a little better than that, but not much. The first course was a delicate affair of thin soup and spongy bread that satisfied none of them. Norma was critical of her baked tomato and picked at the boiled chicken, which she said tasted as if it had ridden on a train.

"I don't understand why anyone bothers with a city," she declared.

Constance didn't try to understand that remark or to answer it. Carrie wrote it down and Constance begged her again not to make a story of them.

They waited as long as they could, to make sure every member of the theater company would be out of the hotel, then went downstairs and out into the blue, lamp-lit night.

47

Harrisburg was a disaster. Fleurette didn't have a dollar to her name. May Ward's way of arranging for the company to pay Fleurette's expenses was to put the Dolls back into two rooms, which meant two girls to a bed, two beds to a room, and a cot on the floor for Fleurette.

This made Fleurette decidedly less popular with the Dolls. Just when she thought they might ask her to sneak out with them at night, in the unaccounted-for hours between midnight and five, when Mrs. Ironsides slept, she found herself abandoned again.

"We'll clear out so you can work" was how Bernice put it. They were gone all afternoon, and only stopped in for a few minutes before leaving for the theater. After the show, they intended to return once for a change of clothes and run right out again.

"If Ironsides comes around to check the

beds tonight, you'll cover for us," Eliza said.

"What would I tell her?" Fleurette asked.

"Tell her Charlotte had a telegram. It's her grandmother."

"No, we already used that one," Charlotte said.

"Oh, then it's her elderly aunt. The one who raised her. Say that we ran off to the train station to see about sending Charlotte home to her dear old aunt."

"But that's a terrible excuse," Fleurette called as they gathered their coats and made ready to leave. "It's too easily checked, and what happens when Charlotte doesn't get on the train?"

"Say that Roberta has a headache and we went out in search of a powder" came Charlotte's voice, out in the hall now, floating along in their wake.

It was just as well that they'd left. There was no room for her sewing machine unless she dragged the cot onto one of the beds and piled atop it all the combs and brushes and powder puffs that littered the writing desk.

She'd spent far too long on May Ward's Parisian frock, considering she was planning to pull out her own stitches and replace them when she found the metal thread. Still, it had been impossible not to take extraordinary care with the job, handling the dress as delicately as she could, and looking long and hard at the fabric before finding the right place to put the needle. She wanted to be entirely sure that her stitches could be easily undone and re-placed, perhaps by more skilled hands, without any trace remaining of her repair.

Once it was finished and returned to Mrs. Ward ("toss it anywhere," the actress had groaned, having not yet recovered from a wild night, but Fleurette couldn't toss it anywhere, and hung it on a fabric-covered hanger she'd improvised with a pillowcase) — once she was finished with that, she had a mountain of costumes waiting for her. The decision to keep Fleurette on for the rest of the tour had led the Dolls to raid their trunks once again, and to pull out their most-hated costumes for a complete renova-tion.

"I look like a shepherdess in this dress," Roberta complained, about her shepherdess costume, and the others agreed. "If only you could take out every single ruffle and make it more of a city girl's dress, we won't look like such children. Make them look like that dress of May's you were showing us."

"That dress of May's came from one of

the very best houses in Paris," Fleurette said. "There's no way to make something like it without —"

"You'll think of something," Eliza put in. And the entire troupe — all eight of them — deposited their ridiculous and cheaply made costumes with Fleurette, who had no choice but to take one apart to see what, if anything, could be made from it. She had one night to finish the work: the Dolls had persuaded Mrs. Ward to let them skip a costume change so that they might all have new dresses at once for the following evening's performance.

By five o'clock, she had one of the dresses taken apart and pinned back together. The Dolls popped back in before leaving for the theater and heaped praise on the new design, which was thoroughly modern, with a daring hemline and a low waist, but still slightly pleated so the skirts would move when they danced.

"It's just perfect," Roberta declared. "Can you do all of them tonight? May hates to skip a costume change. If you can't do them in one night, don't do them at all."

Fleurette promised to try, although it seemed impossible. The way to go about it was to take all the dresses apart, spread them out in a row, then put each one back together in precisely the same manner. First she'd cut away the petticoats, then she'd stitch in a new band around the waist from some of the old petticoat material — such a cheap and telling way to drop a waist, but the audience wouldn't notice — and then she'd put the skirts back on, giving each one a few even pleats. Something had to be done about the sleeves as well, but she'd save that for last.

It was a dull job, once she knew how to do it. For the rest of the evening, she worked in silence and solitude. The drudgery of her time with the company had started to tell on Fleurette. She felt diminished by the long hours in a dim and stuffy room, especially as that room was entirely unsuited to the kind of work she needed to do. She had no work-table, no iron, poor lighting, and no proper mount for her machine.

The Dolls treated her more like a servant than a compatriot. They hadn't seen her act back in Paterson and knew nothing of her theatrical ambitions, as she so rarely had a chance to tell anyone about them. She'd expected to be with them all the time: out about town during the day, and at the theater every night. She'd imagined herself backstage, helping with costume changes and perhaps working out new dance steps alongside them, not left alone in a hotel room with more work than she could possibly finish.

For the first time, she allowed herself to feel a little sorry over her predicament, and just the slightest bit homesick. She hadn't realized it, but she had a certain shorthand with her sisters that no one else seemed to understand. Anytime she tried to say something cutting or clever to one of the Dolls, she'd be greeted with confused stares. And no one was the least bit interested in indulging her, or looking after her, or seeing to her comfort in any way. Her cot was creaky and flimsy. The only food she could afford — train station sandwiches and tea and toast at the hotel — was bland and dispiriting.

She gave in to her misery and recounted every single thing she missed: her bed, her hot baths, her sewing room, her pleasant afternoon job at Mrs. Hansen's, the company of Helen and the other girls, and even her sisters. Her old life, which had once seemed so weighty and oppressive, now felt rich and warm and familiar. It rushed back at her like a dream and Fleurette, already so tired and bleary-eyed from her work, found herself blinking back tears.

But that wasn't to be the worst of it. She was halfway finished — every dress taken apart, every one of them missing its skirt — when she heard a popping sound, smelled smoke, and looked down to see an orange flame flicker to life and then expire along the fabric-wrapped electrical cord of her sewing machine.

48

The theater was overfull. It had warmed so quickly that women were already fanning themselves with their programs and men were putting fingers under their collars. There was an air of whiskey and merriment in the audience, and a thrilling undercurrent of anticipation.

The lights went down and May Ward stepped out in front of the curtain to the ravenous applause of the audience. She wore an old-fashioned dancing frock buoyed by so many frothy layers of petticoats that it seemed to bounce around on its own. On her head was an elaborate poke bonnet trimmed with an arrangement of silk flowers, feathers, and bows. She stood perfectly upright, but the bonnet swayed precariously.

The pianist played a little melody, and people started laughing and clapping before a word came out of Mrs. Ward's mouth. Constance didn't recognize the song until another girl, presumably one of her Dresden Dolls, flitted across the stage with an enormous stuffed canary attached to a stick. The bird came to rest in the very center of May Ward's bonnet.

Norma slumped down into her seat and put a hand over her eyes.

"You're the one who insisted we come all the way to Harrisburg to see this," Constance whispered.

"We came to find Fleurette. I'd hoped never to hear this song again," Norma said.

Norma had banished the song from the house at the height of its popularity a few years ago. Fleurette used to sing it all day long, and would beg one or the other of them to take the bird's part. They both refused, although they knew the lines by heart.

Here it came, whether they wanted it or not. The pianist gave his cue and May Ward sang:

On Nellie's little hat, there was a little bird,
That little bird knew lots of things, it did
    upon my word;
And in its quiet way, it had a lot to say.
As the lovers strolled along;

May Ward was possessed of a bright and

clear voice that rang out like a bell. She embellished every line with a theatrical trill. As she began to skip around in a pantomime of a lady out for a walk with a man, the other girl scampered along behind her, making sure the bird bounced jovially up and down on her hat. She plunged into the second verse:

To Nellie, Willie whispered as they fondly
    kissed,
"I'll bet you were never kissed like that!"

The girl made the bird flutter on its stick and sang, in her best imitation of a bird's voice,

"Well he don't know Nellie like I do!"
Said the saucy little bird on Nellie's hat.

Carrie laughed and clapped along with the rest of the audience. Norma shot Constance a look of despair. It was a highly infectious song, which explained why they used to hear it coming out of every music shop in Paterson. May Ward didn't write the lyrics, but she was the one who made it popular, which was why her face decorated the sheet music.

She sang each verse in the same grand

manner. Norma kept her head in her hands, trying, no doubt, to forget the lines as soon as she heard them.

"Oh, it's twelve o'clock," said Willie as he
   took her home;
"I'll bet you're never out as late as that!"

The girl wiggled the bird around and sang its line:

"Well he don't know Nellie like I do!"
Said the saucy little bird on Nellie's hat.

Constance thought it might never end, but it did, eventually. May Ward collected her applause, as did the girl and the bird.

They disappeared into the wings. After a little shuffling, the curtain rose to reveal a stage set meant to look like the front of an old half-timbered European-style shop. From the awnings hung dolls, pots and pans, drums, masks, puppets, toy horns, and other such props meant to recall a Main Street department store.

One girl after another ran out on stage, costumed in ordinary street attire and shop aprons. The Dresden Dolls were almost impossible to distinguish from this distance: one saw only brightly painted lips, pink cheeks, and enormous eyes lined in black. Constance watched anxiously for a glimpse of Fleurette, but none of the creatures on stage answered to her description.

"Haven't you seen her yet?" Carrie whispered.

"She must be in the next number," Constance said.

"She isn't here," Norma mumbled.

The next number, called "The Cash Girl," concerned itself with the affairs of a department store cash girl (played by Mrs. Ward) in want of a husband. She found her happiness in the affections of the store detective, but only after pretending to steal a pair of gloves to win his attention.

One girl, dressed as a doll in the toy department, sang "The Tale of an Old Rag Doll," and another, playing the part of a girl shopping for her first party dress, sang "The Girl in the Looking Glass." May Ward herself performed "The Moon Song" at the end, under an enormous celluloid moon, in the arms of her store detective.

It wasn't a bad little play, but there was something shopworn about it. Constance was growing a little frantic over the fact that she hadn't seen Fleurette.

The next number, "The Garden of Love," was filled with the kind of silly romantic songs that Fleurette loved. "Put Your Arms Around Me" was performed by May Ward and four Dresden Dolls, none of whom were Fleurette. "Hands Up" seemed to have six of the ensemble on stage at once. Still they didn't see her.

Constance fidgeted in her seat and contended with an avalanche of explanations and excuses, none of which bore up for long: Fleurette was new to the company and would probably only take a few small parts alongside the entire ensemble. She had been given a solo, as she so often had back at Mrs. Hansen's, and would appear on her own in the next number. Maybe, Constance thought, she would only be brought out on stage for the grand finale.

But the truth made itself known to her eventually. Fleurette wasn't there.

More than once she counted eight Dresden Dolls on stage together. Fleurette was never among them.

Norma had stopped looking at the stage and was glaring at Constance. She was letting her have the first word, but only so that she could contradict it.

"There's an explanation," Constance whispered.

"There's always an explanation. The jails are full of people with explanations. She's going to have to do more than explain."

"Well, the first thing we have to do is to find her," Carrie put in. "She might yet be with the company. Let's go around to the stage door before the crowds get there."

She led the way out of the theater, just as the final encore ended. Once outside, they slipped around the corner and into the alley. It was dark back there, with only a single lamp at the stage door. They had just enough time to get themselves situated behind a row of ashcans before the theatergoers started to trickle around to the alley. Soon there was a crowd of young men and women pressed shoulder to shoulder, many of them waving autograph books.

Finally the door opened and the porter — the man Fleurette called Mr. Impediment in her postcards — stepped outside, gave the audience a disapproving frown, and yelled for them all to stand back. Then, to the accompaniment of squeals and shouts from the crowd, May Ward stepped out in a pretty white fur wrap and a hat to match.

She stood alone at first to collect applause and whistles for herself, and then she turned around and waved for her chorus girls to join her. One by one they popped out of the stage door, each with a winter coat over her costume and a hat trimmed in feathers and flowers. Mr. Impediment saw to it that autographs were signed in some orderly fashion, and that the more ardent male admirers were held back and prevented from slipping notes to the girls.

But still there was no sign of Fleurette.

"She could be ill tonight," Constance whispered to Carrie and Norma. "Maybe she's back at the hotel, and one of these girls is an understudy."

Norma pushed her coat up around her neck and said nothing.

"Or maybe Fleurette is the understudy, and she wasn't needed tonight," Carrie suggested.

Norma shook her head. "She never said anything about being an understudy."

"She might have neglected to mention it," Constance said. "There's only so much room on a postcard." She didn't believe that herself — it didn't seem like Fleurette to run away just to be an understudy — but she was desperate for an explanation.

Two black motor cars nosed down the alley and lined up at the stage door. The figures of May Ward and Her Dolls crowded into the machines. Constance thought she might have seen someone else climb in with them — or had she only imagined it?

"She's not here," Norma said.

"If we hurry we can have another look at them back at the hotel," Carrie said. They made haste down the alley and around the corner, which put them back at the hotel just before the motor cars arrived.

By this time Constance was in a state of panic. Was it possible that Fleurette really had disappeared? She wanted one more look at the company before she decided.

"I'll follow them upstairs and try to take a peek in their rooms in case she's there," Carrie said. "She won't recognize me."

Norma pulled Constance across the lobby to the opposite corner, where a sort of reading-room had been assembled around a fireplace. She took the only chair available and told Constance to hide inside the telephone booth.

"You know I hardly fit inside a telephone booth!" Constance complained. But Norma had settled into her armchair and taken up a newspaper, which she intended to use for concealment.

"If you don't think she'll spot you because you're holding a newspaper, then you have no idea what you look like most of the time," Constance said.

"I don't think she'll spot me, because I don't think she's here," Norma returned.

"Keep that to yourself." Constance

couldn't bear to imagine where else Fleurette might be.

She perched awkwardly on the little stool inside the telephone booth and arranged the brim of her hat to fall down over her eyes — although if Fleurette was there, she would, of course, recognize her hat as easily as her face. By that time, Constance wouldn't have minded if Fleurette had walked into the lobby and spotted her, if only to put an end to the uncertainty.

She had only just settled into the telephone booth — if anyone is ever actually settled into a box of glass and wood no larger than a coffin — when May Ward made her grand entrance, sweeping into the high-ceilinged lobby and causing a stir the likes of which only a woman of her celebrity could bring about. Almost every man in the lobby rushed over to her at once. They tried to take her arm, they held out their cards to her, and they even offered to help with a little bag she carried. The room was filled all at once with their jokes and laughter. Constance had never before seen one woman create so much excitement on her way to the elevator.

The porter was doing his best to keep the men away from Mrs. Ward, but he also had the eight Dresden Dolls to attend to, each of whom attracted their own small following. They were all still brightly painted and dressed in their costumes, and resembled tiny island-nations of feminine charm, each one beribboned and bejeweled and leading her own band of loyalists.

An older woman in a plain brown coat followed behind with the two chauffeurs, who struggled under the weight of bags and hat-boxes. Constance took the woman to be Mrs. Ironsides, the chaperone. She was keeping a sharp eye on all of the girls and snatched away a note that someone tried to pass to one of them.

The Dolls gathered around the elevators. One of the hotel porters was summoned to help swat away their most ardent admirers, who had mingled in with the crowd with the obvious intention of trying to follow them upstairs. In the course of sorting out who belonged and who didn't, one elevator landed, and then another, and the Dresden Dolls all stepped on board with their entourage. Somehow Carrie managed to creep on board with them, showing her hotel key to prove she was a guest.

Only Mrs. Ward remained, surrounded by young men eager for her attention. She continued to sign autographs and laugh and flirt while her mountainous porter waited sullenly at the elevator.

Constance slumped over in discouragement. She squinted at her reflection in the
brass telephone and marveled at the mess
she was in. The lobby had grown quiet as
the last of Mrs. Ward's admirers drifted
away. Constance allowed the brim of her
hat to fall down over her eyes, and wished
she could simply disappear rather than go
and confront Norma over what they were to
do next.

She was, therefore, not prepared for a
sharp knock at the glass. She jumped and
lifted up the brim of her hat with the
expectation of seeing Norma waiting for her
impatiently.

But it wasn't Norma. It was May Ward.

49

No one, apart from her own sister, had ever glared at her so ferociously. May Ward had a look in her eyes that put Constance into a cold sweat. The actress's lips were as red as a poisonous berry, her cheeks as white as death, except for a flaming streak on each side that looked more like war-paint than a lady's blush.

Constance stared at her for what felt like an eternity, before realizing that she couldn't keep the glass door between them closed forever.

When she pushed it open, May Ward leaned inside and gave her a whiff of imported perfume, gin, and a costume that needed laundering two days ago.

"Who sent you?" she demanded.

Constance's first impulse was to lie. "I'm sorry, ma'am. I'm awaiting a call. The operators were told to put it through here. I believe there's another booth upstairs."

But she wasn't interested. "You are not here to make a call. I saw you watching us, and you're not the first one I've seen following us around. You work for Freeman, don't you? It's just like him to send a lady detective."

Constance was too panicked to answer, so she took the opportunity to look around the lobby. Mr. Impediment was standing nearby, in a spot that had probably been chosen for him by Mrs. Ward. Norma's armchair was turned away, but the upper edge of her newspaper stood at attention.

"I'm not a private detective," she told Mrs. Ward. "You might speak to the hotel manager if you believe someone's following you." Constance was trying to make it sound as if Mrs. Ward were the paranoid one, when in fact it was her heart that was hammering, and her neck that had grown hot under the collar.

"I don't need to see any manager," she spat. "You tell Freeman that I will not have hired men — or hired women — watching me. I've gone along with the chaperone, and the porter, but I will not have a spy trailing us from city to city. Go on back to Trenton, or wherever he dredged you up. If I see you in Pittsburgh, I'll have you arrested."

She spun around and marched off before

Constance could gather her wits about her. She and the porter stepped into the waiting elevator. Constance wriggled out of the booth and ran after her. "If I could only ask you a question —"

Mr. Impediment put up his hand. "Come any closer and I'll call the police."

"But I am —"

The elevator door closed and they were gone.

Norma dropped her newspaper and rushed over. "What on earth did you do to get yourself spotted?"

"Nothing! I sat as still as I could, and my face was mostly hidden underneath my hat. You were the one calling attention to yourself, with that newspaper held up like a signal flag."

"I was behind a column."

They stood, glaring at each other, both of them with high color in their cheeks and a kind of frantic agitation that kept them looking over each other's shoulders.

"It's time to go to the police," Norma said.

There was something about the way she said it that hit Constance in the soft spot right under her sternum. The finality of it slammed into her.

Carrie emerged from the elevator and met them with a shrug. "I have their room numbers. They're around the corner from us. I couldn't get a look inside the rooms, but I didn't hear anyone else in there."

Norma told Carrie what had happened. They both stood staring at Constance. By some unspoken accord, it was up to her to decide how to handle this. "Go on upstairs," Constance said. "We probably should go to the police, and ask a few questions of Mrs. Ward, but I just want to sit here for a minute and think about it."

Carrie said, "I'm going back to the theater. I might see if the ushers know anything."

Constance thanked her for that. Norma stood with her arms crossed for a minute, her jaw working back and forth but no words coming out.

"Go on upstairs," Constance said. "For once, just go."

Norma, miraculously, did as she was told.

Constance sank into an armchair by the fireplace, overcome with discouragement, but she was not to be left alone with her thoughts, because a woman sitting by herself in a hotel lobby with nothing along the lines of a magazine or a bag of knitting to occupy her is quickly taken care of. A man in a red uniform with gold braid on the shoulders rushed over and offered to bring her any sort of delicacy from the hotel's restaurant.

He suggested a pot of tea or a Turkish coffee. He thought she might like a bread pudding in wine sauce or a slice of Boston cream pie. There was something called a Biscuit Tortoni whose virtues exceeded his powers of description, but she understood it to involve eggs, cream, cherries, and coconut.

He believed she would find it restorative. Constance hesitated for a minute, as she was too miserable to take a bite of anything, but then decided that she should defer to his expertise.

Soon there was a dainty table alongside her, and a cup of good coffee, and not one but two desserts, neither of them diminutive. The pastry chef, he explained, insisted that she try them both.

At that very moment, Fleurette stepped off the elevator. If it hadn't been for the waiter half blocking the view, Fleurette would have seen Constance reaching for the coffee, then wiping a spot of heavy cream off her wrist.

But Fleurette didn't see her. Constance lifted a hand to the waiter, which he understood to mean that he should stay right where he was. People who work in hotels have that kind of intelligence about them.

Fleurette took no notice of the two of

them, or of anyone else in their corner of the lobby. She was headed straight for the front desk. Under one arm she carried something bulky and heavy that became visible only when she hoisted it onto the counter.

It was a portable sewing machine.

Fleurette spoke to the man behind the desk for only a minute, and then took a claim ticket and left the machine with him. She was back on the elevator and out of sight so quickly that Constance thought she might have dreamed it. She sent the waiter away, and took a bite of the Tortoni.

Fleurette was safe. There was nothing the matter with her that Constance could see. She hadn't been kidnapped, she hadn't run off, and she wasn't out having a wild time late at night with the fashionable theater crowd. In every way she looked like an ordinary working girl.

And now Constance understood why Fleurette hadn't been listed with the cast. She wasn't on the stage at all.

She finished her dessert — there seemed no reason not to, in light of the foregoing events — and crossed the lobby to speak to the man behind the front desk. He had a long, narrow face and the tiniest round spectacles.

"I saw a young lady come through here with a sewing machine a minute ago," she said. "Is she the hotel seamstress?"

"No, ma'am," he said. "That's May Ward's seamstress. She needs her machine fixed before morning, so a fellow's coming to look at it tonight. That's how these theater types are. Get a man out of bed in the middle of the night over an electrical cord."

He offered to ring the housekeeper if she needed something mended, but Constance waved him away.

"I'll take care of it myself," she said.

50

"It doesn't look like she's having any kind of life. As far as we know, she didn't even go to the theater last night. Do they have her locked in a room sewing every night?"

Norma was trying to put on a show of protest, but she knew she'd been defeated and only wished to argue with Constance over it for the next several hours while they were stuck on a train together.

Constance tried to summon up some pity for Norma. The world must have been a very frustrating place for her, on account of the way it refused to yield to her ideas. Constance tried to speak more gently. "Fleurette went of her own accord. This is the life she's chosen. We must consider the matter closed."

Norma said, "I don't know why she would lead us to believe that she's on the stage when they'd only hired her on as a seamstress."

"Only?" Constance said. "That's exactly why. She probably wanted us to think that this was something — well, quite a bit more than what it actually was. She could've been trying to make us proud of her. Did that ever occur to you?"

"I don't like the idea that she's lying to us."

"Well, we lied to her, too, by sneaking out here to follow her around. I'm not sure which is worse. And I want to remind both of you that we won't ever tell Fleurette what we did. She'd be furious if she found out we followed her."

"Then we're to listen to her stories of her splendid stage life, and pretend to believe it?"

"Let her have her little fiction. It's harmless. She's always lived half in a fantasy world anyway. Don't pretend to be shocked by Fleurette telling made-up stories. And, Carrie, I want you to promise me that this stays out of the papers."

"Oh, there's no danger of me getting a story out of this," Carrie said dispiritedly. "Good girls doing what they're supposed to don't make the paper. And you're not giving me much of a story in Minnie Davis, either."

Constance wanted very much to keep

Carrie out of the courtroom when Minnie was brought back for Tony's trial. "She might testify that she was shown a forged marriage license, but you're right. It doesn't amount to much."

"And nothing ever came of the male visitors she was to have entertained in the evenings?"

"The landlord was the only one to ever say anything about that, and when he was asked again, he couldn't recall anyone but Mr. Leo's brother."

"So there was nothing to those claims?" Carrie said. "They sounded about right to me."

"Not at all," Constance said, not trusting herself to say more.

"Then I don't have much of a story."

Norma rattled her newspaper and cleared her throat loudly. "I wonder about people who can't find anything decent to discuss when in close proximity to others on a railcar."

Carrie picked up a magazine and Constance stared out the window. At least she could return to work secure in the knowledge that Fleurette was safe. She was so relieved that she was entirely willing to forgive her for lying over what, exactly, her role was in May Ward's troupe. She wasn't even bothered about the money Fleurette had taken from her bureau. If anything, Constance wanted her to have funds of her own while she was away from home.

Norma, on the other hand, worried her more than ever. Constance had no reason to doubt that her concern for Fleurette was genuine. Her mistrust of Mr. Bernstein was the sort of thing that, Norma being Norma, she really couldn't help. But late the previous night, after she'd given Norma and Carrie the news that Fleurette had been found, and they'd finally gone to sleep, the most discouraging idea came over her. Was Norma overreacting, or was she simply so bored that she cooked this up to give herself something new to do?

Until last year, Norma had always been the busiest of the three of them. She looked after the barn and the animals, she climbed up on ladders to attach window sashes and pound on roof shingles, and she chased after Constance and Fleurette if they didn't do anything about spring cleaning or summer canning. She was in charge of the household and, truth be told, took on much more than her fair share.

Constance didn't know how she had any time at all left for her pigeon hobby (*hobby* being a word that Norma loathed and would never allow to be employed in reference to her pigeons), but somehow she managed to keep herself occupied on a full-time basis with those birds as well. It didn't seem like much of a life, but Constance wasn't the one who had to live it.

She had long ago figured out that Norma kept pigeons because she had to have command of something. She'd always been like that, even as a small child. She used to follow Francis, Mother, and Constance around, telling them to do all the things they were already doing. "Scrub the lamps," she would say as Constance went through their rooms and took the glass globes off to wash the smoke out of them. "Put the rags out the window," she'd tell Mother, as she was already waving them around to shake off the dust. She always said those things with a grisly determination unbecoming of a five-year-old, as if it were her dreaded duty to inform her family as to their tasks.

For that reason it was a relief when she took up pigeons, and they became the recipients of her endless orders and drills. Better a flock of birds than the other members of her family, everyone reasoned.

But things had changed lately. Constance was away from the house almost every day and most nights. When she was home, she couldn't be counted upon to do much of anything in the way of chores. Fleurette couldn't either, as she'd been spending all of her time at the theater. Constance hadn't considered it before, but Norma now ran the household by herself and passed most of her waking hours alone, with only the burbling of those birds for company.

With her pigeon society diminished, she and Mrs. Borus had taken up with this group that was arranging long-distance pigeon races, but that wasn't much to occupy her time in the winter. Her world was getting smaller. Constance wondered if she even understood how small it was. She seemed to be allowing the most petty worries and complaints to overtake her. Increasingly, she latched on to illogical and far-fetched threats and waged useless battles for the purpose of proving some obscure point. It seemed absurd, as Constance thought about it, that she'd managed to bring about this ill-advised trip to Harrisburg to spy on Fleurette.

Constance sat across from her on the train and watched her work her way through a stack of newspapers and magazines, noisily and boisterously. She snorted at the paper, quarreled with it under her breath, wrote notes in the margins, crossed out the things she disagreed with, and even smacked it once or twice.

This is the woman I'm tethered to for the rest of my life, Constance thought as she watched her. She wished all the more that Fleurette would come home, even as she contemplated yet another reason why she might not want to.

51

Minnie Davis had not been idle. The reformatory's program of kitchen work, floor-scrubbing, and laundry kept her hands busy (Miss Pittman did not approve of idleness, gossip, or novel-reading, so their days were filled with chores), but her waking thoughts were consumed with the far more pressing matter of her own liberty. The prospect of enduring five years in confinement was unbearable. Hadn't she left Catskill to shake off the strictures of home life and factory work? At least in those days, she could wander down to the boardwalk; at least she could dance and flirt and play games. But to be deprived of any small pleasure or privilege in life was intolerable. And who would she be, at twenty-one, released from the reformatory and kept under the supervision of the courts?

She'd be a failed woman. A criminal, a ward of the state. She'd be someone who didn't matter at all, to anyone.

At first, she thought only of escape. The reformatory's buildings were clustered together in the center of an open expanse of lawn, fringed in woodlands. According to Esther, the forbidding metal gate at the front didn't extend all the way around. She'd find nothing but split-log farmers' fences if she ran out the back way.

"But you won't like your chances against the farmers," Esther whispered. They were on their knees together, scrubbing the dormitory floor. "The reformatory pays a reward if they catch a girl trying to escape. And they all keep dogs. You can hear them in the woods."

Esther was right. Minnie heard them howling in the middle of the night, most likely over a possum. What would they do if they caught a whiff of a girl on the run?

The punishment was worse for runaways, if Esther was to be believed. "They send you to the state prison," she told Minnie, "and you don't get out when you're twenty-one. You'd be in a real jail, for as long as they want to put you there."

Still, Minnie was tortured by an urge to run. She was always looking for an escape route, watching the staff's routine, staring off into the brittle winter woods in hopes of divining some way through. She hadn't a dime of her own, but already she'd started squirreling away anything that might be of use to her if she saw a chance to flee: a dull but possibly useful butter knife, a tin of potted meat, a bar of soap.

She was storing up something else, too: any account she heard of a girl who'd been set free. Such stories circulated like underground currency. They had to be traded for something else of value. Minnie would recount a wild night in the city with Tony (which never happened), or tell about the vindictive wife she'd met in the Hackensack jail who'd put her husband's eye out with a fire poker because of the way he kept looking at her sister (entirely invented, but effective), and in exchange, she'd hear tell of a girl who fooled a judge, bribed a neighbor to pose as her aunt, or volunteered for missionary work, only to escape on her very first night away from the reformatory.

The missionary work interested Minnie the most, as she felt herself incapable of fooling a judge and hadn't any money with which to pay a bribe.

"How did she do it?" Minnie wanted to know. "Was it a church that offered to take her?"

The girl in possession of this story, who

everyone called Red although it was not her name, shook her head. "It was a lady policeman just like the one who brought you. She knew a group doing good work out West and arranged to have a few girls sent there. But they all ran away, and that put an end to it."

Minnie couldn't imagine Deputy Kopp sending her out West to be a missionary, but there was a nugget of an idea in there. In the days that followed, as Minnie scoured pots and ran bed-linens through the wringer and waited in line for her soup, she worked over the possibility, rubbing it down and polishing it smooth, like a stone between her fingers.

52

Edna rarely saw Ruby and her friends at the Red Cross classes. Several of them already knew how to speak French and didn't need to learn to count and name the parts of the body: *un deux trois quatre cinq, main jambes oeil épaule pied.* They dropped in on the cooking classes only sporadically, claiming that anyone could follow a recipe, although Edna found the lessons on toast water and onion gruel to be a fair reminder that cooking for invalids and soldiers would require inventiveness and practice, and that family dinner recipes might have little to do with it. One night they boiled down a restorative jelly of port wine and cloves meant to warm a soldier drained of blood, and on another night, they baked sea-pies in mess tins, so that they might be carried to the front and eaten later. They learned how to cook without utensils, and how to wrap meat in clean grass and roast it in a clay pot.

The exact circumstances under which those dishes might be served, or those rudimentary French words spoken, were difficult for Edna to imagine, but she did what she could to commit each evening's lesson to memory. There was something bracing about being in a classroom, even if the church basement was nothing like the school-rooms back in Edgewater. She liked the daily practice of learning something new. It gave her a sense of forward movement, even if she wasn't yet going anywhere at all.

Most days, she wasn't sure that she ever would go to France. She never did confide in Ruby the impossibility of raising the funds for her passage, but Ruby guessed at it soon enough. The wealthy young women who organized this endeavor had already secured pledges for more than they needed and persuaded a few of their donors to redirect their contributions to Edna. When Edna protested that she didn't want to accept charity, they were quick to remind her that the charity was directed at war relief, not at her. For that reason she agreed to the donations, but they weren't nearly enough — a dollar a month here, three dollars a month there. She persisted only because she couldn't think of a single other thing to do.

One night, after a course on purifying and storing river water, she was surprised to come home and see Dewey Barnes waiting on Mrs. Turnbull's porch.

"I hope you haven't been out here for hours," Edna said. She fumbled for her key and stood a little apart from him. He seemed to belong to some other epoch in her life. She feared being dragged back into it if she stood too close.

"I went to the train station and found a bar that was just a little more welcoming to a male clientele," Dewey said. "Your landlady told me you'd be back from your church meeting around now. I didn't mind waiting."

He shifted awkwardly from one foot to the other. She couldn't invite him in and wasn't sure she should ask him to sit down. There was only a single bench, damp and dirty, and she thought it might give the wrong message if they sat together.

He coughed into a gloved hand and said, "Now listen, Miss Edna. I didn't come all this way to stand on your porch at ten o'clock at night. I'd been hoping to take you for a little supper and speak to you privately, but they tell me you're away most every night at that church. I suppose you're lonely, is that it?"

If she told Dewey, he would tell her brothers. She still had the vague idea that someone — her parents, the lady deputy, perhaps even that judge back in Hackensack — could stop her from going to France. So she told no one.

"The church does good work for the war," she said. "Knitting and bandages."

He nodded eagerly. "That's fine, that's good."

There came another terrible pause. Edna couldn't shake the feeling that she'd been caught doing something she shouldn't.

Dewey pressed on. "Yes, well, I know you're missed back in Edgewater, and I suppose I came to ask if you've given any thought to when you might be coming home."

She looked up at him and met his stare for the first time. She took in his flat, friendly face, his wide and unsuspecting eyes, and the easy, complacent smile with which he greeted the world. Dewey Barnes, at your service. He would be forever at the service of the woman who would have him.

The question hung in the air a little too long, and Dewey's expectant features fell. Still Edna felt obliged to answer him squarely and not leave him guessing.

"I don't believe I am coming home,

Dewey."

"But — you can't stay here forever! Pompton Lakes is nothing but a factory with a few boarding-houses around it. I should know — I've had time to inspect the premises. There's no future for you here. Unless — but surely you haven't — I mean — you haven't taken up with one of those factory boys, Edna?"

She turned away and looked off across Mrs. Turnbull's porch railing and down the narrow street, which ended in darkness. With Dewey standing before her, offering warmth and good cheer and his constant, sturdy presence, she felt more alone than she ever had. What was she rejecting, and why? The idea of going to France had made the world seem so vast, and her own life so limitless. But now she saw that world shrinking again. There was only the factory, and the chores at the boarding-house, and the courses on war-work in the stuffy dark basement. None of it seemed as if it would actually take her anywhere.

And now — did she really mean to send Dewey away? With him standing in front of her, offering himself to her, she softened toward him a little. Dewey Barnes would take her to the pictures and on picnics in the summer, and quietly endeavor to make her life as agreeable as it was within his power to do. Wasn't that a way forward?

But she'd been silent too long. Dewey took it to mean that she had, in fact, fallen for someone at the factory. He ducked his head down, pushed his hat on, and turned to go.

"It isn't another man, Dewey," she said. That was enough to make him stop on the porch steps. "Only . . . I'm sorry, but there's just nothing between us. I didn't mean for you to ever think there was."

It stung her right through the chest to say it, but she couldn't think of any other way. It wouldn't be fair to make him wait or let him hope.

Her words had the effect she intended. He looked her over one last time. The depth of sorrow in his eyes took Edna by surprise.

"All right, Miss Edna. My mistake."

He was gone before she could change her mind.

53

At last Minnie was transported back to the Hackensack jail for her court proceedings. She felt freer behind those steel bars than she ever had at the reformatory. Here was her chance.

Constance did what she could to tidy Minnie's hair. The girl had nothing to wear but the plain jail uniform issued to all the inmates, but Constance had smuggled in a fresh shirtwaist and tried to make sure Minnie looked scrubbed and wholesome.

"Just be respectful," Constance whispered. "Take a minute to think before you answer whatever questions they put to you. And don't try to talk to Tony. Don't even look over at him."

Minnie nodded, wanting very much to seem agreeable to anything Constance asked of her.

"Your landlord won't be testifying against you. As far as I know, they haven't a single witness who can claim to have seen men going in and out of the place. But, Minnie, if you lie . . . it puts me in a terrible position if you lie. You understand that, don't you?"

Minnie saw her opportunity, and took it. "All of this puts you in a terrible position, doesn't it, Miss Kopp?"

Constance sat back and stared at her. "What do you mean by that?"

Minnie swallowed hard. She'd practiced these lines. "Only that . . . well, surely you didn't become a lady deputy just to see girls like me put away. I'm not a criminal, am I?"

Constance leaned over and looked through the bars of Minnie's cell to make sure no one was within earshot. "You have to admit that you put yourself into this situation," she whispered. "And I'm not the judge. But you know I'd do more for you if I could."

Minnie took Constance's hands. "Oh, but, Miss Kopp, you can! Just put me with one of the other girls you've helped. Someone who's in a better situation than me, and might look out for me. And then someday I could do the same for some other unfortunate girl. Don't you see? At the reformatory they told me about a lady officer who did something like that out West. Couldn't you try it here?"

Minnie's hands were so cold that Constance wrapped hers around them instinctively. "I don't know who told you that," Constance said, "but I don't have an army of girls out there waiting to take someone in."

The gate to the fifth floor opened and a guard's footsteps approached. "But you don't need an army!" Minnie whispered. "Just one."

"Sheriff wants the inmate over at the courthouse," the guard called out. Constance gave her one more worried look and led her out of her cell.

They found Sheriff Heath waiting for them outside the courtroom. He was a man who worked very hard not to let his expression betray him, but Constance could tell that something had gone wrong.

He looked over at Minnie. He hated to say anything in front of an inmate, but there was no choice. "They've released Mr. Leo."

"Released him!" Minnie squealed. "Then he's free, and so am I."

"I'm afraid not," the sheriff said. "The prosecutor dropped the charges against Mr. Leo for lack of evidence. The baker refused to testify."

At least Constance had done something right. "What about the false marriage license?" she asked.

"That's only a fine, and his parents paid it." Sheriff Heath looked a little pained. "Detective Courter had enough doubts about Mr. Leo that he thought it best to drop those charges and focus his efforts on . . . on Miss Davis."

Minnie watched the two of them, puzzled. "But — if there's no evidence, they're going to let me go, too."

"Miss Davis, the prosecutor has recommended that you be sentenced to the reformatory until you're twenty-one." The sheriff would never tell an inmate that he was sorry about a sentence imposed, but his voice was full of regret.

"Where were we when all this happened?" Constance demanded.

"Apparently Mr. Courter met privately with the judge about dropping the charges."

The door to the courtroom opened and a bailiff looked out at them. "It's our turn," Sheriff Heath said.

Constance marched in furiously, dragging Minnie behind her. She practically shoved the girl into a chair. Detective Courter was already there, with another man from the prosecutor's office, and the judge was seated.

She was too impatient to sit through any preliminaries. "Your Honor, it has come to my attention —"

"Miss Kopp!" said the judge, obviously pleased to see her. "I have on my desk your report about Miss Edna Heustis. I could not be more pleased to see that she has continued to lead an upright life as you assured me she would. I'd like to see more cases like that. I even took the report home to show Mrs. Seufert, who thought it a fine piece of writing and an instructive tale. She's going to read it to the ladies at her club — without the names, of course, but only to show what can be done along these lines if we put some effort into it — and she'd like to have you over for dinner. I don't know if I've ever told you about the wonders Mrs. Seufert can work upon a roast duck, but you're to find out for yourself, at your earliest convenience."

Constance's anger was considerably deflated by the prospect of Mrs. Seufert's roast duck. Surely if the judge was feeling this friendly toward her, he might be willing to make a favorable ruling for Minnie Davis.

"Thank you, Your Honor. I'd be delighted." She risked a glance over at Detective Courter, who, she assumed, had never been invited to one of Mrs. Seufert's dinners. "Miss Heustis is as respectable and hard-working a young lady as you might hope to meet. We've done right by her."

"I do admire that girl," the judge said, a little fondly, as if speaking about a favorite granddaughter.

"If we can get to the business at hand," Detective Courter said.

"Yes." The judge shuffled the papers on his desk. Constance turned around to look at Minnie, who was pale and frightened and fidgeting with the lace at her wrist. It was a moment for desperate ideas, and Constance groped for one.

"Now, didn't I send this girl to the state home already?" the judge asked.

"That was only a transfer of custody until the trial," Detective Courter said. "Your Honor, Minnie Davis was found in a furnished room with Mr. Anthony Leo, posing as his wife although the two had no intention of marrying. Other men were seen coming in and out of the place. Although she is only sixteen, Miss Davis is already morally compromised and would be best served by a sentence of five years at the girls' reformatory." He passed a paper to the judge and put a folder under his arm as if the matter was concluded.

"Sit back down, John," the judge said. "I'd like to hear what Miss Kopp has to say, and I want to hear from the girl herself."

"But isn't it customary for the sheriff's office to be removed from matters such as —"

"Thank you, Mr. Courter," the judge said briskly. "Miss Kopp, I suppose you've gone around and done your bit here, is that right?"

Constance stood and said, "Yes, Your Honor. It's well known by now that Mr. Leo possessed a forged marriage license, which implies that Minnie Davis did have some expectation of marriage. As for male visitors, there's no evidence of that, and no witnesses to testify to that effect."

"Your Honor," Detective Courter said, a bit scornfully, "Mr. Leo and Miss Davis were caught by police, red-handed, as it were."

"Yes . . ." The judge looked down at the papers on his desk.

Constance was afraid she was about to lose him. "To my knowledge, no men have been brought in on a debauchery charge involving Miss Davis," she said, "and Mr. Leo was just released. I believe the act you're describing takes two to commit. Without anyone else having been charged, I see no justification for putting this girl into an institution until she's twenty-one."

Judge Seufert looked up at her in surprise. "That's a novel argument. What about it, John? Where's the other half of this duo?"

"Well, I —"

Constance plunged ahead while she had the chance. "I know that the courts would rather not release Miss Davis on her own. She and her parents are on difficult terms, and neither wishes to live under the same roof with the other. But that's not a crime, and she shouldn't be deprived of her liberty over it."

"I don't see that you leave me another choice, Miss Kopp," the judge said.

She risked another look over at Minnie, who had her eyes in her lap. "There is another way, Your Honor. Miss Davis would like to share a room with Miss Edna Heustis."

Minnie gasped and stared up at her.

"I know that Miss Heustis would keep an eye on Miss Davis and exert a beneficial influence over her. I will take her to the powder works myself and see that she gets hired on, but I anticipate no trouble with that, as she already has factory experience and is accustomed to hard work. I'll speak to the landlady on her behalf and make sure Miss Davis is allowed to pay her rent after she's collected some wages. The landlady runs a strict house and will no doubt help to keep Minnie in line as well."

Detective Courter made noises of protest, but the judge waved him away and looked down at Minnie. "Miss Davis, you don't deny that you ran away from home and lived with a fellow as man and wife outside the bounds of marriage, do you?"

Minnie kept her face very well composed. "No, Your Honor, but it was a mistake, and I didn't understand what could happen. Now that I know, I would never do it again."

"Didn't your mother ever tell you what could happen?"

Constance had to intercede on Minnie's behalf. "I've been twice to see Miss Davis's parents. It's a hardscrabble home with very little time for motherly advice, but they do know right from wrong."

"Is that true, Miss Davis? Do you know right from wrong?"

"Yes, Your Honor." Minnie was standing now, with her shoulders back and her hands clasped prayerfully in front of her. "I'm sorry for what I did, and I only wish it hadn't landed me in jail."

"Everyone wishes they hadn't landed in jail," the judge said gently. "Do you suppose you could live a good and quiet life, and

466

make yourself a decent marriage someday, and stay out of trouble with the law?"

She took a deep and unsteady breath and nodded. "I do, Your Honor. I'll do just as Miss Kopp says. I won't be any bother to anyone."

He turned to Sheriff Heath, who'd been sitting quietly off to the side. "Bob, do you have something to say?"

The sheriff stood and said, "I hired a lady deputy because I needed someone to take an interest in the female inmates and find ways to guide them to a better life. There's no need for this girl to become a ward of the state, at a substantial cost to the taxpayers, when she can be put to work. We both know that Deputy Kopp will see to it that Miss Davis behaves."

Judge Seufert looked at Minnie thoughtfully for a minute and said, "Miss Davis, I'm going to release you under the condition that you report to Deputy Kopp in the manner she prescribes, for a minimum of six months, to be extended at her discretion. She'll be writing quite a few more of those reports, and you'd better hope I enjoy them as much as I did the first one. If we see you again in our courts, you won't be treated so kindly."

Minnie nodded and whispered her thanks.

Constance took her out of the room before the judge could change his mind. Detective Courter was still sputtering furiously. As she left, she could hear him and the judge arguing over it.

Minnie looked a little green, and Constance wondered suddenly if she was really prepared to live up to her end of the bargain.

"I expect you to be grateful for the chance you've been given. I'm going to have to ask quite a lot of Edna. You must be grateful to her, and make it easy for her. Can you do that?"

Minnie nodded but didn't dare speak for fear she'd ruin it.

Constance pushed open the courthouse doors, and they stood on the steps. Minnie took a deep breath of damp winter air and shivered as it went through her. She took Constance's elbow to steady herself.

"Will I have to wear handcuffs on the train to Pompton Lakes?" she asked.

"Not this time," Constance said.

54

Minnie stood in Mrs. Turnbull's drab sitting room, with its dusty old lamps and rickety card table in the corner, and tried not to fidget while Constance explained their purpose.

"We've come to ask if Edna would be willing to share her room with another girl."

Mrs. Turnbull clapped her hands together and looked Minnie over with genuine interest. "That's a fine idea!" she cried. "Edna's about to work herself to death. You can share in the rent and each pay your own board. It's the smallest room, but you won't mind, will you, dear? We can just squeeze in a cot. I suspect it'll be more comfortable than the place you've been sleeping." She gave Constance a meaningful look as she delivered that last line.

Constance didn't want to tell too much about Minnie's situation, so she merely said, "Miss Davis was being held as a witness. She was never charged with a crime herself. Owing to the amount of time that has passed, she lost her place at the jute mill in Fort Lee and had to give up her room. All she needs is a fresh start. If I can get her on at the powder works, I hope you'll be willing to wait on the rent until after she's been paid."

That was satisfactory to Mrs. Turnbull. Constance took Minnie quickly out the door and over to the factory to make sure she could find a place for her.

"Show them what a good worker you'll be," Constance whispered as they walked into the enormous brick building that housed the fuse workshop. Minnie looked around with wide eyes, taking in the long row of machinery and the girls in their white caps working quickly and silently.

"It reminds me of the knitting mill back in Catskill," she said. "The machines are almost the same."

"That's good, then. You've already had practice."

Mrs. Schaefer was down at the other end of the room talking to one of the girls. "There's the superintendent," Constance said. "Do your very best."

When Mrs. Schaefer came around, Constance told her that Minnie was a good worker who knew her way around a knitting machine and a jute mill. Minnie obliged and said that it all looked very familiar.

"We're always looking for girls with experience," Mrs. Schaefer said. "You wouldn't believe how many runaways we get. Girls who have never worked a day in their lives and want only to get out from under their parents and to do as they please. We're not in the business of helping girls to go against their parents and run wild. There's no fraternization with the men, and I want you in a good reputable boarding-house if you're not going home at night."

Constance said, "You won't have any trouble from Miss Davis. She has every reason to work hard and to do well. She's to room with Edna Heustis. I'd like a word with Edna if she can be excused."

Mrs. Schaefer seemed satisfied with that. "If you two girls can help each other, and stay out of trouble, I'll put you on the line."

Edna was plainly nervous when she saw Constance, but when the matter was explained to her, she agreed at once to share her room with Minnie. The two girls shook hands solemnly, and Constance reminded them that she would be back to look in on them.

Mrs. Schaefer took Minnie off to be

outfitted for her uniform. While she was gone, Constance told Edna what she hadn't wanted to say in front of them.

"I know your room's awfully small as it is, but it'll save you both a little money. And to be honest, I'd like you to keep an eye on her."

Edna nodded, wide-eyed. "Has she done something terribly wrong?"

"No, of course not. She's had a difficult time, but it's nothing you haven't heard before. I took quite a risk and, honestly, this is the only chance she's going to have. I'm asking for your help, Edna. Do what you can to be a good influence on the girl, and promise me that you'll send for me right away if she starts to go even a little bit wrong."

Constance was worried that Edna would be furious with her for putting her with a girl like Minnie, but Edna seemed pleased to be entrusted with the responsibility and said that she would do what she could. "She'll learn to like it here, just like I have."

Edna seemed so sure of herself, and so accepting of the very little that life had given her. If Constance was being honest, she would've admitted that she put her sympathies in with Minnie, who wanted so much more than factory work and a rented room in a small town. But there was nothing she could do for Minnie's ambitions, other than to win her a small measure of freedom.

"I'll be back to check up on you," Constance promised. "You're both my responsibility, and I want to see you do well." She said her good-byes to Edna and told her to walk home with Minnie and get her settled.

The five o'clock bell rang just as Constance left. As she walked back to the train station, she could hear dozens of girls calling to one another, their voices clear and free in the cold air.

It was impossible to move a cot into Edna's room. Instead, after much grunting and moaning and pushing and shoving, Edna's brass bed went out and two cots went in. "I hope you girls get along," Mrs. Turnbull said when she saw the arrangements. "You hardly have enough room to turn around."

After she left, Edna and Minnie sat on their cots and faced each other. Minnie's ambition was to sneak away that very night, or perhaps the next, and to go straight to New York, where she would take on a new name and a new life. But then Edna said the most remarkable thing, and Minnie stopped thinking about New York all at once.

What Edna said was: "It's just like the Army."

Minnie gave her a puzzled look.

"I mean, with the cots. You can almost imagine us in a military camp outside of Paris."

Minnie shifted around on her cot and took in the rest of the room. Edna's war literature was everywhere: there were leaflets on the wall, brochures on her bookshelf, and lessons and diagrams scattered across her floor, all of them having to do with bandages and signal flags and uniforms.

"What is all of this?" Minnie asked.

Edna watched as Minnie picked up a brochure and paged through it. Although Minnie was only sixteen, she had a certain swagger about her that Edna envied. Minnie was, as her mother might have said, brash: She was tall and broad-shouldered, she talked loudly, and she waved her arms around for dramatic effect. There was something larger than life about her. She picked up Edna's things as if she owned them. She seemed like a girl who knew what to do.

It would be impossible to keep a secret from Minnie. Finally Edna said, "This . . . ah . . . it has to do with the war."

Minnie looked up at her, her mouth hanging open. "The war?"

"Yes. In France."

Minnie rolled her eyes; that much was obvious. "What about it?"

"I . . . well, I intend to go. To serve. In France."

Minnie looked up abruptly and dropped the pamphlet. She leaned forward toward Edna, her elbows on her knees.

"You? By yourself?"

55

"I am not going out there in front of his spies." May Ward was only half-dressed, having ripped another seam in her haste and carelessness. She was leering at the audience from behind the curtain.

"But no one's spying on you," Fleurette whispered. She was frantically trying to stitch the seam without stabbing Mrs. Ward with the needle.

"You just haven't seen them. It's someone different in every town, but I can always tell one of Freeman's operatives. They're all the same breed of stocky matron like you see standing around in cheap dance halls. You wouldn't know about that, would you, Florine?"

"Oh, I can imagine," Fleurette said. She'd been trying very hard not to think of home, but at the mention of stocky ladies in dance halls, a warm wet lump came up in her throat and she had to push it down.

Mrs. Ward had taken her drinks too early in the day, which was always a disaster, as it made her drowsy right before the show. Fleurette tried to chase after her with coffee, but May simply waved it off and felt around in her bosom for a little vial of reviving powder she kept hidden there.

But tonight the powder was all gone, and the coffee made her violently ill. She was on her knees, ostensibly to allow Fleurette to make the repair to her dress, but it soon became clear that she couldn't get back to her feet unaided.

Three pairs of dance slippers appeared around them. Fleurette looked up to see Bernice, Eliza, and Charlotte looking down at them.

"She can't go on tonight," Bernice said.

"Of course I can," May Ward spat.

"Is she still on about the men following her everywhere?" asked Eliza.

"They're not men. They're very unattractive ladies," said May.

Charlotte bent down. "No one's following you, ma'am. But it's time for the show."

Mrs. Ward's eyes were half-closed. Her head lolled over to one side, and she mumbled something incoherent.

Bernice said, "Let's get her onto the divan. Fleurette can sit with her until the

477

show's over."

May Ward jutted her chin up to make a protest, but no words came out.

"How are you going to do the show?" Fleurette asked.

"I'll take her part," Bernice said. "I've done it before."

"But you'll only have seven Dolls."

"It doesn't matter, as long as we have an even number. Charlotte will sit out with you. We're already late. Help me get into her costume."

With all of the Dresden Dolls gathered around, they managed to move Mrs. Ward to a little divan backstage and to relieve her of her costume so that Bernice could scramble into it. They wrestled Mrs. Ward into a kimono, whereupon she fell quickly asleep, as limp as a rag doll, her arms and legs draped lifelessly. Before Fleurette knew what was happening, the show had started, and she and Charlotte were by themselves on the floor, watching the actress sleep.

Charlotte rubbed her neck. "I can't wait to go home," she said, as the opening bars of "The Bird on Nellie's Hat" drifted backstage.

"Home? Isn't there to be another tour after this one?"

"Oh, no. Mrs. Ward's leaving the stage for

the moving pictures, haven't you heard? This is our last tour. I'm going home to give singing lessons to little rich girls."

"Don't you want to get on with another act?"

Charlotte ducked down so that she could see a bit of the stage between the curtains. Fleurette turned to watch, too. Bernice was acquitting herself quite beautifully in the role of May Ward.

"Not really," Charlotte said. "I don't want to be a chorus girl when I'm old like Bernice. She's been doing this for ten years. Can you imagine?"

"But you wouldn't be a chorus girl forever," Fleurette offered. "You'd have your own act."

Charlotte laughed. "Like her?" She nudged May Ward, who was snoring faintly now.

"She doesn't seem to enjoy it as much as I thought she would," Fleurette said.

"She's too high-strung for this life. Maybe she'll do better in the pictures. She won't have to travel around as much, and there won't be so many people everywhere. They get her too wound up."

"I always thought I'd like to have so many people around," Fleurette said.

"What do you mean?"

"Well . . ." She turned around again and peeked at the sliver of audience she could see from her vantage point. "To be in front of a crowd like that. I used to dream of it."

"Have you ever been in front of an audience that size?"

"Nothing like it," Fleurette said. "We had a little theater back in Paterson, but it was nowhere near as grand as this."

Charlotte was sitting with her knees drawn up to her chin. She studied Fleurette for a minute and then said, "You've learned every single number, haven't you?"

Fleurette nodded, her eyes still on the stage.

"Then why don't we both go?" Charlotte stood up and held her hand out. "May's not going anywhere. Let's throw a costume on you and get you out there for the next number."

56

Minnie didn't run off on her first night in Pompton Lakes, or on the second night, or the third.

She had her reasons, of course. On the first night, she was simply exhausted over the day's events and the sudden turn her life had taken. She thought she'd do better on the run if she'd had a good night's sleep first, and a chance to consult the train-tables. It was also true that she hadn't a penny to her name. Originally she'd planned to lift a dollar from Edna's purse — just enough to get her out of town — but then she met Edna, and couldn't do it. She told herself that it was only the difficulty of rif-fling through Edna's purse in such close quarters, but there was more to it than that, even if she wasn't quite sure, at first, what it was.

On the second night, she was bone-weary from her shift at the powder works. She'd had no difficulty in learning the machine, but she was out of practice and had trouble keeping up. She nearly fell asleep over her supper. By the end of the evening, she remembered that she hadn't managed to put her hands on a dollar or a train-table, so thought she'd stay just one more night.

On the third night, it occurred to her that she might as well wait and collect a week's pay, thus remedying the money situation without taking anything from the other girls, who, she could see, needed every penny to get by.

Still, something else was keeping her in Pompton Lakes. She found Edna's war talk to be strangely intoxicating. Boarding a ship for France sounded infinitely more interesting than boarding a train for New York. She had an idea, already, of how things would work out for her in New York: from the minute her feet hit the pavement, she'd be looking for a way to earn some money, or someone who wanted to spend his money on her. The "someone" would inevitably disappoint. Relations would sour. Work — whatever work there was to be had — would be tedious and unrewarding. She'd be in a city overfull of riches: theaters and tango rooms, dining palaces and smart cafés, dress shops and perfumers. But none of it would be hers. She'd be forever on the outside, trying to maneuver her way in.

But what of France? Here was unexplored territory. She knew nothing of Paris, or London, or of the German front. What did that matter? It was a new world over there. Men were taking up arms, marching against the Germans, and living in the most un-imaginable conditions in trenches along the front. Women were working, too — not in factories, necessarily, although there must have been factory work for those who wanted to do it — but in hospitals, Army camps, and training schools. There were women working telephone switches and driving ambulances. Even in the grips of a military campaign, there was a lawlessness about it that Minnie found both terrifying and riveting.

And Edna wanted to be a part of it! Minnie had never in her life met anyone as thoughtful and purposeful as Edna. She was such a slight, mousy girl, with so little to say, but a steel cable of resolve ran through her. The notions of duty and service and country came as naturally to her as breath-ing. She was entirely sure that Europe had to be saved from the Kaiser, and that the Americans were the ones to do it.

"Yes," Minnie tried to say one night, "the

Americans, certainly. But — you?"

"Well, I'm an American, aren't I?"

There was no arguing with that.

Minnie found herself attending the meetings of the Women's Preparedness Committee with Edna. Soon she was sitting next to her in classes on bandage-rolling and soup-making. Late at night, they practiced their French.

"You don't have to help me study," Edna said.

"Deputy Kopp said that I was to follow your example," Minnie said. "Besides, I ought to keep busy. I ought to do whatever you're doing." She'd been avoiding the other girls in the house. She saw herself in them, and saw how easy it would be to run around with them, and fall into their ways. She hadn't entirely abandoned the idea of running off to New York — she'd only postponed it, one night at a time — but she didn't want to risk being sent back to the reformatory over a silly dalliance with a man in Pompton Lakes.

She would study her French verbs, instead, thank you. And — here was another surprising truth — she would study Edna. Edna was becoming a source of fascination for her. She had the most astonishing ideas about the world, and her place in it. Here was a girl who could see ten miles down the road and ten years ahead, and who knew exactly the way forward, and was prepared to go, unwaveringly, through the hell of war if that's where her convictions led her. Minnie had never met anyone like her.

She tried not to think about the fact that Edna would be leaving, or to wonder what would become of her after Edna was gone. When Edna and the society girls talked about their upcoming departure at the meetings, Minnie turned her head away and pretended not to hear.

57

Two postcards arrived from Fleurette in a single day. The first showed a stately theater in Philadelphia. On the reverse she'd written:

What a grand city! — and they adore May Ward here. They adore me too, as I had the biggest laugh of the night last night. We've been held over for two more shows, which means we won't get the break we were promised. It's no matter, as Mrs. Ironsides drags us around to museums and spoils our liberty.

F.

The second came from a hotel in Baltimore.

One of the girls twisted her ankle, another burned her neck quite badly with a hair-iron, and Mrs. Ward is convinced that we're cursed. Tell Norma the parks here are full of pigeons who can't be bothered to do as they're told. She ought to come down and take charge of them.

F.

Constance didn't know what to make of Fleurette's claims of success on the stage. Was it really necessary for the girl to lie to them so deliberately? At least she continued to write, and gave no indication that she knew that she'd been spied upon. Norma, astonishingly, had lived up to her end of the bargain and not said another word about Freeman Bernstein, or about their ill-advised trip to Harrisburg. Some measure of domestic tranquility had settled over the Kopp household. When Constance was at home, she and Norma lived together peaceably, or at least in a spirit of resignation, having given up trying to change the other's ways.

Things had calmed down at the jail, too, with Minnie Davis packed off to share a room with the ever-trustworthy Edna Heustis. Constance was more than a little pleased with herself for having put those two together. She'd already forgotten that Minnie had suggested it, and had begun to think of it as a program of her own invention, which might prove useful for the Democratic candidate for sheriff — whoever that might be, as he had not yet been named — in the campaign against John Courter.

She was, in other words, enjoying a rare moment of tranquility, both at home and at the jail. That was not to last. On a Monday evening in the middle of March, Constance walked into Sheriff Heath's office and found herself face-to-face with a ranting, gesticulating, furious Freeman Bernstein.

He was pacing around the room, still in his coat and hat, gloves in one hand, ranting about a misappropriation of taxpayers' money, abuse of power, and something called a writ of *melius inquirendum,* a term unfamiliar to the sheriff, judging from the way he raised his eyebrows in despair upon hearing it.

When he saw Constance in the doorway, Sheriff Heath said, "Mr. Bernstein, I believe you've met Deputy Kopp. I know she's eager to hear your complaint and to see it settled, but I wouldn't want you to have to repeat yourself after you've just given so thorough an account, so perhaps I will —"

"Nonsense, Sheriff!" Mr. Bernstein interjected. "She'll hear every word of it. Or perhaps she can tell it all to me, as she's the cause of it — she and that disputative sister of hers."

It occurred to Constance briefly to defend Norma, but then she decided that she agreed with him on that point. Instead she took a place by the window.

"May I first say," Constance told him, "that whatever has happened, it wasn't sheriff's business. You and I have met but once, and I wasn't on duty and hadn't come in any official capacity. I don't like to see the sheriff's time taken up with a personal matter."

"Nonsense!" Freeman Bernstein shouted. He threw his gloves down but picked them up straight away, most likely so that he would be able to throw them down again. "Kopp is always a cop, no matter where she goes and what she does. Isn't that right, Sheriff?"

Sheriff Heath nodded glumly and tried again to put in a word. "What we expect from our deputies, whether on duty or off —"

Once again, Mr. Bernstein wouldn't let

489

him finish. "Yes, yes, just as I said. And your lady deputy thought it best to use her powers to conduct an unwarranted investigation of my wife, and to follow her personally into Pennsylvania, and to employ a veritable army of matrons in every city on Mrs. Ward's theatrical tour, who trailed my wife and her company from hotel to theater to restaurant and back again and managed to scare the wits out of her at every turn. Do you know how high-strung these actresses can be, Sheriff? Do you?"

Sheriff Heath made to answer, but Mr. Bernstein went on without pause. "And don't go lecturing me again about evidence and *testimonia ponderanda* and that nonsense. My wife described Miss Kopp perfectly, which was not difficult, as all she had to say was that a very large woman was squeezed into a very small telephone booth and was regarding her suspiciously from under the brim of an unfashionable hat. Anyone who has ever seen Miss Kopp would recognize her from that description."

Constance resisted the urge to defend her hat and instead said, "Mrs. Ward is a famous actress. It's natural that people would want to watch her and to follow her from place to place. There's no law against it."

"That's enough of your legal gibberish!"

Mr. Bernstein bellowed. "My wife is under the misapprehension that I am the one having her followed. She's so angry about it that she's fired me as a manager, and refuses to come home at the end of her tour. She says she's going to take a flat in Manhattan and hire new representation. I want something done about it immediately."

He slapped his gloves on the back of the chair again, but with less ferocity this time. Then he dropped into the chair, panting. Sheriff Heath saw his opportunity.

"Mr. Bernstein, I appreciate the difficulty you find yourself in. But you must understand that I have a jail full of actual criminals. I simply can't expend the resources of this office on the resolution of marital complaints. If you're not able to convince your wife that she isn't being followed, might you like to consult a doctor about it, or a lawyer? I'm acquainted with an attorney in Paterson who knows his way around a marital dispute, and I'd be happy to send you to him."

"A lawyer?" Freeman Bernstein was on his feet again, reinvigorated by outrage. "The only lawyer I need is the one who's going to represent me at the courthouse when I make a complaint of kidnapping."

"But who's been kidnapped?" Constance

called as Mr. Bernstein flung open the door and made ready to take his dramatic exit.

"My wife, of course. If you say that she wasn't being followed and that everything she's told me is false, then I can only assume that she is being prevented from coming home because she's being held at gunpoint and forced to write these vicious letters. She must be in the hands of white slavers, or worse. I'll go to the courthouse right now and make my report. That fellow in the prosecutor's office is always going on about white slavers. He'll want to hear about this one."

"Mr. Bernstein, do not forget that it's a crime to file a false report," Constance said. "I don't see how this could benefit you."

She'd never seen anyone as animated as Freeman Bernstein was at that moment. His cheeks were red, his eyes were bright, and every line in his face was contorted into any expression of outrage. He might have even grown a few inches taller, or perhaps he was standing on his toes.

"It will force you to go and fetch her!" He jabbed a finger in Constance's direction. "They'll send the lady deputy, won't they? Of course they will. She's your responsibility now, Deputy Kopp. You'll have to go and get her, and to talk some sense into her.

Isn't that what you matrons do?"

She didn't like being poked by this man. "What about you? You lure girls away with the promise of putting them on stage, and give them nothing but drudgery instead."

He stared at Constance, his mouth open, and then burst into laughter. "Lure them away? When have I ever had to lure a girl onto the stage? They follow me around day and night! They beg me!"

He wiped his eyes and gave the sheriff a knowing smile, hoping for some commiseration. Sheriff Heath just stared blankly.

"But . . . Fleurette auditioned to be a Dresden Doll, and you never put her on stage."

Mr. Bernstein put his hands on his hips and cocked his head at her. "Fleurette. Do we have a Fleurette?"

Constance was almost yelling by now. "You said you did! That's why we came and asked you. And yes — I saw her. I mean —"

"Aha!" he said. "You did follow her! I knew it. Well, you saw her. How did your sister do on the stage?"

"She isn't on the stage. She's your seamstress."

Now he seemed to understand. He paced around, a finger on his chin. "Oh, yes. Flo-

493

rabelle. Little girl. The one we saw in Paterson."

"Yes!" she said. "You filled her head with ideas about how talented she was and promised her a place with the troupe."

"I never did!" He turned to the sheriff and raised a hand as if to take a vow. "Honest, Sheriff. I never did. I thought the girls had a nice little act, but they're amateurs. We wouldn't put somebody like that in our show. She's not vaudeville material. I told her so. She chased after me and asked for a seamstressing job, but I said I couldn't carry one more girl. She offered to work for free, if only I'd put her on as company seamstress. Said she'd share a room and promised not to eat much. She only wanted to show us what she could do. I felt sorry for her and decided to give the little darling a chance, but I never said I'd put her on stage. I suppose she's done a fine-enough job. I haven't heard a thing about her."

Sheriff Heath saw the expression on Constance's face and stayed quiet.

"Are you saying that you never told her that she could perform with May Ward?" she asked.

"Of course I didn't!" Mr. Bernstein said. "Listen, Miss Lady Deputy, your sister's a sweet little thing, but she's unschooled.

How long has she been at that academy — a year?"

"A little over six months," Constance admitted. "But all her life, she's always danced, and she sings at home, and —"

He sighed. "Do you know how many girls I meet every year who like to sing and dance at home in front of their adoring mothers and sisters? What we do takes training, ma'am. Years of it. Your girl likes to prance in front of a mirror, but that's not enough. I'm sure she's a fine seamstress. Tell her to stay with that."

"You don't know a thing about her!"

Sheriff Heath stood up and said, "Thank you for coming to see us, Mr. Bernstein. I hope you're able to work out matters with your wife peacefully."

But the sheriff was rewarded with another look of contempt. "Peacefully? You don't know my wife, sir."

"But by your own admission, there's no evidence of a kidnapping."

He was worked up into a fury again.

"Really? We'll see what the prosecutor has to say about that!"

He tossed a scarf around his neck in the very picture of theatricality and stormed out, slamming the door behind him. Constance opened the door just a crack to make sure a guard had hold of him and was ushering him out. Once she was reassured on that point, she dropped into a chair across from Sheriff Heath.

"Miss Norma certainly knows how to make an enemy," the sheriff said. "I don't believe I've ever met anyone with such an imagination. He told me that Norma riffled through his office to find May Ward's tour schedule. I said that sounded outrageous even for a Kopp sister."

"Oh, I'm sorry to say she did riffle through his office," Constance confessed. "But it's not impossible to learn an actress's tour schedule. It doesn't prove anything."

Sheriff Heath sat back in his chair, looking a little downcast at the realization that Norma stood guilty as charged. "I thought the worst offense was you watching May Ward in a hotel lobby, and that hardly sounded like a capital crime, especially since she seems to see ladies following her everywhere lately. She's obviously imagining things."

"Oh, I'm afraid she's not." Constance told him that Norma had gone on her own to speak to Belle Headison and set her army of matrons on the march. "I tried to put a stop to it, but I suspect that Mrs. Headison didn't listen to me."

He groaned. "Then you really did send someone to spy on her in every city?"

"I didn't. Norma did."

He rolled his eyes in the general direction of the ceiling and thought about it. "I warned you not to go. I made it very clear that I didn't want any sort of family trouble interfering with your duties. I don't believe he'll make any progress with the prosecutor's office next door, so we don't have to worry about false charges being filed. If I know temperamental wives, Mrs. Ward will be back home within the week. Go on upstairs, and don't let me hear another word about Freeman Bernstein."

Constance would've liked nothing better, and told him so. Upstairs, she made her rounds of the female section, feeling just as downtrodden and dispirited as every inmate serving penance behind bars, and called lights-out early.

The next morning, as Constance went down to supervise the laundry chores, Sheriff Heath came marching down the corridor toward her. "It's your lucky day, Deputy. Freeman Bernstein is a man of his word. I never would've believed it, but he's filed the charges. As you seem to have brought this on yourself, I'm sending you to New York.

You're to rescue May Ward from the white slavers who are alleged to have captured her."

58

Freeman Bernstein was all too happy to furnish the address where his wife might be found, and the names of her captors. He told the prosecutor that she had given the information to him during a telephone call made under duress. Constance was to go to the office of her attorney, Arthur Basch, and if she wasn't found there, Mr. Bernstein was quite confident that she could be picked up at the Gaiety Theatre, where her new manager, Siegfried Wallace, kept an office. Constance had warrants for both men. Sheriff Heath had arranged for a Detective Cook from the New York Police Department to meet her and help in serving the warrants, as she would be operating under New York's jurisdiction.

"You and I both know this is nonsense," Sheriff Heath told Constance, "and I don't like to waste a detective's time. But in the unlikely event that you find them up to some sort of criminal mischief, I want everyone in sight arrested."

Detective Cook was waiting for her in front of the Equitable Building on Broadway. He'd brought another officer, Campbell, along with him. In their uniforms, the two men were almost indistinguishable — both square of jaw, broad of shoulder, quick to grin, and eager to offer a pinch of tobacco to Constance, and then to laugh and elbow each other in the ribs when she refused.

Having two officers along put Constance in a tricky spot. It seemed to her that the only way out of this mess was to tell the truth: to confess to Mrs. Ward that she was Fleurette's sister, that Fleurette had run off without telling her, and that Constance had acted out of a maternal sort of fear over what might happen to a girl traveling with a vaudeville troupe. She would assure Mrs. Ward that it was only Fleurette she'd been spying on, and hoped to convince her to keep the truth from Fleurette in the name of family harmony.

Constance had no idea how she might do any of that, especially with two officers tagging along who weren't supposed to know that she was the cause of all the trouble. She found herself hoping that Mrs. Ward had, in fact, been kidnapped, although she knew there to be hardly any chance of that.

The detectives showed little interest in the case and only glanced at the warrants.

"She's upstairs with her lawyer?" said Detective Cook when he looked it over. "That's all they have up there. Lawyers and bankers and insurance agents." He waved his hand at the elaborate stone building towering over them. "Used to be a nice little place down here. It burned down — they put up this eyesore. Throws a shadow over Broadway like you ain't never seen. It's freezing down here now. You never do see the sun, and you know why? You know what's up there, on the top floor? Bankers' club. Costs a hundred and fifty dollars just to join, and that's before you order your rib-eye."

"What's the rib-eye cost?" Campbell asked.

"They don't even put it on the menu. I went up there once, just to see. Told 'em it was an inspection, but I was only there to have a look at that menu. No prices, just steak and peas and something they call potato croquettes, because they're too fancy to admit to frying a potato."

The men had a good laugh at that. Constance tried to join in, but every time she said a word, they dropped their grins and stared solemnly at her. At last she gave up on the pleasantries and said, "I believe I'm to go in first, gentlemen, in the hopes of surprising them and taking Mrs. Ward into my confidence."

Campbell nudged Cook in the ribs. "Send the girl in first. That's how they do it now," he said. "Doesn't bother us, miss. There's only one way out of those offices. You go on in, and we'll be right there to catch 'em if they run out. I'd loan you my revolver, but I might need it myself."

"I carry my own." She got a whistle from the detectives for that.

"We don't let our ladies go around with guns, do we?" Detective Cook said to Campbell.

Campbell shrugged. "She's from New Jersey. You gotta have a gun out there."

Constance felt stodgy doing it, but she told the men to spit out their tobacco and go to work. They followed her through the massive doors and into a grand marble lobby, where they called for an elevator and soon found themselves in the tiled corridor outside Mr. Basch's office. Every door held a pane of full-length frosted glass with the occupant's name in gold leaf. The men lined up along either side of the door.

"Mrs. Ward will want to speak privately,"

she told them in a low voice, although, of course, it was she who wanted to speak privately to Mrs. Ward. "I'll send the others out here to you. Don't make too much of a fuss until we sort it out."

"Yes, Chief," Detective Campbell whispered for the benefit of Detective Cook, who chortled at the joke.

Constance ignored him and went in without knocking. Mr. Basch's office was filled with cigarette smoke and the sound of ice clinking in glasses. It was a fine room, with painted linen on the wall and good deep carpet. Mrs. Ward was draped over a leather chair in as extravagant an evening dress as Constance had ever seen off the stage, with a dropped waist and a low neck and some sort of gold lace that shimmered like metal. She wondered if she was looking at Fleurette's handiwork.

Behind the desk was the man Constance took to be Mr. Basch. He wore a good pinstriped suit and had a perfectly square, cleft chin that made him rather painfully handsome. Another man sat across from him. He jumped up when she walked in and extended his hand.

"I suppose this is our lady cop. We were told to expect you." He was a thin man, almost entirely bald, with a showy mustache and a red bow tie. "Siegfried Wallace. I'm Mrs. Ward's new theatrical manager."

At that May Ward glanced lazily up at Constance, took a sip from her glass, then turned again and startled. "She's not a cop! She's the detective my husband hired. What's the idea?"

Now everyone was staring at Constance. She could only assume that the officers in the hall were listening with great interest as well.

"I'm afraid you've made a mistake, Mrs. Ward," Constance said, with loud and clear authority. "I've never been hired by your husband. I'm here on sheriff's business and I'd like a word with you alone."

"I'm her attorney," said Mr. Basch. "Send Siegfried out, but I'm staying here."

"If I'm to manage her, I ought to know what I'm in for," said Mr. Wallace. "I'll stay as well." Both men leaned against the wall, apparently enjoying themselves, leaving May Ward and Constance staring at each other.

Mrs. Ward was defiant. She put her fists on her hips and pursed her lips. "I don't know who you are, but I know that my husband threatened to send the police after me under a charge of kidnapping if I wouldn't come home. That's nonsense. I'm thirty-five years old, and I've been all over the world on my own. I'm no more likely to be kidnapped than you are. Go on back and tell him that I have every right to hire a manager and see him anytime I like in the course of conducting my business."

"I thought she was twenty-nine," Mr. Wallace said, in the manner of a vaudeville stage whisper. Mr. Basch laughed. Constance couldn't have been more grateful for the grave error they committed, for it gave her an opportunity.

"Go on out of here, both of you!" May cried. "I won't have you making jokes about my age or anything else. Remember who pays you. Now, go on up and have a drink at that club of yours. I'll take care of myself. I don't know why I bother with either one of you."

May Ward stood her ground. The men skulked out of the room. Constance slammed the door before Mrs. Ward could hear them register their surprise upon stumbling into the arms of the awaiting officers. She heard only the faintest scuffle and assumed that the men did a fine job of taking their captives down the hall in quiet dignity.

Mrs. Ward dropped into her chair again and lit another cigarette. "I don't intend to say a word to you," she said, "but I couldn't stand the sight of either one of them. They're useless, managers. Worse than husbands."

Constance sat down gingerly in the chair next to her. "You don't have to say anything," she said. "I'm the one who's come to speak to you. I've a confession to make, and an apology to deliver, if you'll let me."

May arched an eyebrow and blew a stream of smoke at Constance. "Where'd you buy the badge, at a toy shop? Why did my husband hire you?"

"He didn't. I'll tell you the truth if you'll let me. Your husband's not at fault. I am."

She laughed. "Well, he's always at fault. Let's not go making excuses for him."

"He didn't hire me," Constance said, "and I'm not pretending to be a lady officer. I'm a deputy sheriff in Hackensack. Your husband swore out a complaint of kidnapping in front of a judge, and I do have warrants to arrest both your attorney and your manager."

"Fine! Take them both!" She waved her hand dismissively and took a long drink.

"I hope it won't come to that." Mrs. Ward was making it awfully hard for Constance to get the truth out. "I'm here to tell you that I'm the cause of all these troubles. I did follow you to Harrisburg, but it wasn't because of your husband. I was trying to keep an eye on my sister."

At that she threw her head back and shrieked. Constance only hoped that the men outside wouldn't hear and rush in. "Your sister? Who is she?"

"Fleurette Kopp." There it was. She swallowed hard and hoped for the best.

At first Mrs. Ward didn't seem to recognize the name, but then she gave another high-pitched squeal and said, "Flora? Florine? The seamstress? Our little seamstress? You were worried about her?"

"I . . . well . . . my other sister was, really. Norma. She tends to make a big fuss over small things and . . . ah . . . well, she was sure that Fleurette would get into trouble."

"How would that little girl ever get into trouble? She's hardly looked up from that sewing machine. I couldn't believe she wanted to come on for no pay. Our wardrobe was in shambles, but we would've made do."

"I believe she hoped to impress you, Mrs. Ward. She wants to be on the stage someday."

May Ward cackled at that and slapped Constance's arm playfully. "What is she, five feet tall? She's too short for a chorus line and, anyway, she can't dance. But she's done an awfully nice job with our costumes. I hope you'll tell her that."

Constance hated to hear a perfect stranger talk about Fleurette that way. "Tell her yourself," she said stiffly. "I haven't seen her in some time."

"Well, she'll be home in another week or so. We only have our New York engagements and then we're through. But you still haven't told me what you were doing in that phone booth. You looked ridiculous, by the way."

"My other sister, Norma, insisted on following Fleurette to make sure she was safe. I knew she would be, but . . ."

"But you went, too." Now Mrs. Ward was enjoying the story. She leaned forward and filled her glass from a bottle on the desk, then offered it to Constance, who declined.

"I went to keep an eye on Norma, and to stop her from embarrassing Fleurette on her very first time away from home. I never meant to alarm you, truly. Of course, we were trying not to be seen."

She gave a loud barking laugh. "Let me give you a piece of advice, Mrs. Deputy. Everyone can see you. You might make a good cop, but you're a terrible spy."

Constance smoothed down her skirt, which looked awfully drab next to Mrs. Ward's shimmering silk dress. "Yes, well. I'd like to apologize for setting you against your husband, who, as you can see, had no part in this."

"Why didn't you tell that to the judge? Why did you come all this way, with warrants and everything? Oh . . . I see. You don't want to have to admit to a judge that you're the cause of all this fuss." She seemed altogether too gleeful about it.

"It's not just the judge," Constance said hastily. "If it made the papers, Fleurette might find out that we followed her. That's why I've come here today. I must ask you to forgive me, and to help me, although I've given you no reason to want to."

But she'd stopped listening when Constance mentioned the papers. "Trouble in the papers? Why, there's nothing better than trouble in the papers. Let me tell you something, lady." She slammed down her glass and leaned woozily toward Constance. "Trouble in the papers is the only thing that's kept my Dresden Dolls going as long as they have. Don't ever believe a word of it, of course, but don't run away from it, either. Trouble in the papers sells tickets."

She was spitting, and her eyelids fluttered erratically. Constance was beginning to worry that she was too far gone to listen to reason. She wondered if she could get that glass out of her hand.

"Thank you, Mrs. Ward. It's just that my salary depends upon my staying out of the papers. I've come to ask you if you . . . if you . . ."

May was staring at Constance now, interested to hear what might be on offer. Constance took a deep breath and went on. "I've come to ask if you wouldn't mind coming back to New Jersey, just for one night, so that we can put an end to these charges, and —"

"I'm not going back to that man, after what he's done!" she cut in. She waved her arm and in doing so, flung her glass off the corner of Mr. Basch's desk, and the bottle along with it. Both bounced and rolled on the carpet, but did not break. The gin spilled, which, Constance thought gratefully, solved one problem.

"Oh, damnit, the drink's gone," May muttered.

Constance leaned over and took her forcefully by the wrist. "Mrs. Ward. Your husband's done nothing wrong. Do you understand what I've come to tell you? It was all my doing. Now I only ask that you keep this from Fleurette. Can you do that? Can you promise not to tell her that it was her sister who stirred up all the trouble?"

She burst into laughter and nearly toppled over in her chair. "You want me to go home and patch things up with my husband, and keep a secret from my own seamstress, all so that you don't have to be ashamed of your own bad behavior?"

"Oh, I am ashamed," Constance said. "I'm nothing but ashamed. The trouble is that I don't want Fleurette to be ashamed of me, and I don't want to lose my place at the jail. It's very well for you to get to sing and dance on the stage, but the best that a woman like me can hope for is to keep my badge and to be of some use to the sheriff."

She couldn't believe the way she was debasing herself before this vain, drunken woman, but she was getting a bit frantic. If she didn't bring this to a satisfactory close soon, the police officers would rush in, or Mrs. Ward would fall asleep from drink. She was working against a clock.

But May seemed suddenly to compose herself. "Why should I help you, after what you've done?"

"That's just it! You have no reason to. I can only ask —"

"No, no." She jumped up and tottered around Constance in a circle. "No, no, Mrs. Lady Policeman. You're asking me to do a favor for you, and I'm telling you to offer

511

me something. I work for wages, just like you. So what do you have that I might like?"

At first Constance thought she was after money or jewelry. She patted herself down and May laughed, dancing over to her lawyer's desk and standing behind it, framed by the window. Constance had the feeling she was practicing a part.

"I don't want that enormous uniform of yours, or that terrible hat."

"If you're asking for money, Mrs. Ward . . ."

"I'm not."

"Or some favor to be delivered later, if you find yourself in legal difficulties . . ."

"That's nice, but I might never need it, and then what good would it do me?"

This woman was definitely a puzzle. Constance wanted nothing more than to send her back to her husband and let them drive each other mad. "I can't imagine what else I could do for you," she said, but then, all at once, she could.

"Actually — just a minute — if you like to be in the papers, I do know a lady reporter who's always eager to write something sensational. She could do a terrific write-up about you and the Dresden Dolls. Would you enjoy that?"

May Ward laughed and clapped her hands

together. "It's perfect! Let's send for her. Only I have an even better idea about what the story should be."

Constance slumped down in her chair in relief. "Anything you like. Anything at all."

59

THE LADY SHERIFF RIGHT ON THE JOB

She Serves Warrant on the
Alleged White Slaver
"Victim" Laughs at Her
Husband's Charges —
Only New Movie Manager

NEW YORK — Constance A. Kopp, the Lady Sheriff (strictly speaking the Under Sheriff) of Bergen County, N.J., bustled into police headquarters last night and said she had a warrant for a man for white slavery and wanted the assistance of the New York authorities.

Detective Cook was assigned. They went to the office of Lawyer Arthur G. Basch, where quite a party awaited them. In it was Siegfried Wallace, theatrical manager, upon whom the Lady Sheriff promptly served the warrant. There was also present Mrs. Mary Bernstein, known to the moving picture stage as May Ward, who plays star roles.

May Ward is the supposed victim of Wallace, and the good looking blonde woman who has been many years on the stage burst into hearty laughter at the notion that she had been kidnapped. Her husband, Freeman Bernstein, says she was.

Husband Is "Fired."

Bernstein had been making charges that she had been stolen and had become a "white slave." Smiling at a diamond encrusted hand, she said:

"I told my husband three months ago that I intended to get a new manager — that has been his job. We've been quarreling all the time lately. He left me once — for three nights. I get a big salary in the movies, and the house and all its furnishings at Leonia are in my name.

"Why, he's been charging that I use 'coke' and other narcotics and that I'm practically an insane person, wrested from his charge. I'm ready to submit to a medical examination here and now as to the use of drugs of any sort.

"I'm a woman of more than thirty-five years old, if I have to admit it, and I've traveled many times from coast to coast. Any person trying to kidnap me or make me a white slave would have the liveliest 138 pounds of fighting woman to handle that ever was tackled.

"I have retained Mr. Wallace for my manager, and my husband's crazy mad about it. That's all there is to the story."

The Lady Sheriff insisted that Mrs. Bernstein return last night to Leonia, N.J., and after a bit the actress consented, and was returned home later that night.

Norma gave the paper a loud shake and put it down. "This makes you look ridiculous for going in to rescue a grown woman. I

516

thought Carrie was on our side."

"It was all Mrs. Ward's idea," Constance admitted. "She practically dictated it to Carrie. She was to have a story that made her look wise and worldly, and made me look like a buttoned-up old spinster."

"Well, that's because you are," Norma muttered, and took up the paper again. "What's this about narcotics? I never heard anything about that."

"She invented it. She wants to be accused of wild and decadent behavior so that she can deny it in the papers. People will pay to see an actress who might or might not have an opium addiction."

"I wouldn't pay a penny for that."

"No, she hasn't any hope of attracting you as a patron."

"And how much did she have to pay Carrie Hart to get a mention of her diamond ring put in?"

"That was a condition for giving the interview. One of many conditions."

"I don't know why Miss Hart would agree to print such lies."

"She felt she was owed a good story. She says I haven't given her anything worth printing lately."

Norma sniffed. "She should be a novelist if she wants to tell stories. I don't see anything I'd consider news here."

"The news is that May Ward agreed not to tell Fleurette the truth, which is to say that I've found a way out of the mess you put us in."

Constance didn't expect any gratitude from Norma over that and didn't get any. "I never put you in any mess."

"May Ward wouldn't have spotted me in a hotel lobby if you hadn't insisted on —"

"I thought we agreed not to speak of Freeman Bernstein again," Norma put in.

"You're the one reading the paper."

Constance had come home to see if they'd had word from Fleurette — and there was one postcard, telling nothing they didn't already know and promising to be home in a few days. Constance also wanted to square her story with Norma so that they could have some hope of not arousing suspicion when Fleurette did return.

"Fleurette will want to know all about your visit with Mrs. Ward," Norma said.

"With any luck, she won't know anything about it," Constance said. "May says that the girls don't bother with the papers and only read magazines. If she does see it, Mrs. Ward has promised to say that I behaved entirely within the bounds of my profession and that Freeman Bernstein is to blame for the entire misunderstanding."

"We're counting on an awful lot of people remembering how to lie to Fleurette," Norma said.

"I'm counting on Fleurette being too self-absorbed to notice what anyone's saying if it doesn't pertain directly to her."

"Then it might work." Norma went back to the stack of letters she'd been reading. "I've fallen behind in your correspondence. Here's a man who runs an African lion ranch in Arkansas. He says women make better lion tamers, as long as they have the nerve to stand up to the lion."

"Stand up to it?"

"Yes, apparently, if a lion attacks, the thing to do is to stand your ground. You're to roar right back at it and wave your arms in the air. A timid person runs, but that's what finishes them. A lion will always win a foot-race."

"It doesn't say that," Constance said, and snatched the letter from her, but it did.

"Here's one you might consider," she said, taking up another.

Dear Under-Sheriff Kopp,
  I suppose you will be promised to someone else by this
time, but if you're not, mine

is the best offer of its sort you will get so you might as well take it. Out here in Nevada the sheriff spends his time chasing down claim jumpers and horse thieves as you might expect, but there is the more ordinary breed of criminal as well, including girls who, from time to time, must be locked up for their own good and the general health of the men in this town. I'm sure I don't need to explain that further, for a lady sheriff knows all about social hygiene and the ruinous diseases that are the natural result of sin and debauchery.

I've made my jail impervious to scorpions and rattlesnakes, which is no easy feat, but it must be done if I am to persuade a woman to give herself to me in marriage and to take charge of a woman's duties at the jail. As the sheriff's wife you would see to the cooking and the laundering and a bit of farming, which would be no extra trouble at all, as we harbor only 25–30 men at a time plus a girl or two. Our inmates hardly eat a thing, nor do they expect much in the way of pressed trousers, which is to say that looking after their meals and such wouldn't be any more work than a wife's ordinary obligations.

I had a housekeeper tending to all this but she's dead now and I took it into my head that rather than put the expense on the taxpayers of hiring another, I ought to find a wife. We don't see a lot of women in Duckwater, but there you were in the newspaper and I knew this would be a much better place for you than that jail in New Jersey.

Send a line at once that I may make ready to receive a wife —

    Your ever-hopeful intended,
      Sheriff Q. R. Greenville

"I wish you wouldn't read them aloud," Constance said.

"Dear Mr. Greenville," Norma pronounced as she wrote. "It brings me great displeasure to inform you that Miss Constance Kopp is an abysmal cook who cannot manage to put toast on the table for her two sisters, much less feed a couple dozen criminals, nor is she to be trusted with laundry or, for that matter, the planting of potatoes or the overseeing of a few laying hens. In fact, I find little to recommend in her for matrimony, as she is neither tender nor sympathetic, she cannot manage a bank-book, and her looks have already gone. I'm afraid she would disappoint in every way. Please take comfort in the fact that I intercepted your letter in time and saved you the regret and heartache that an association with Miss Kopp would inevitably bring."

"That's just fine," Constance said. "Answer the rest along those lines."

60

Minnie was pocketing shortbread at the refreshment table when Ruby came rushing up to her. Ruby was pale and pretty, and when she'd been crying, it showed. Her face had the shattered look of a handful of crumpled rose petals. "Where's Edna? Quickly, I have only a minute."

Minnie looked around and saw her across the room. Ruby ran over and Minnie followed.

"Edna!" Ruby gasped. "Listen to me."

She took Edna's arms and pulled her away from the other girls. Minnie stood nearby, unsure if she was allowed to listen.

"Daddy won't let me go," Ruby said. "He's absolutely set against it. He said he never knew we were serious about it or he wouldn't have allowed any of this to go on as long as it has. And I'm not the only one. He's going around to all the other fathers and, one by one, the girls are being told to stay home and knit." Her voice broke when she said it, as if knitting were the worst punishment she could imagine. It would've been funny, if Minnie hadn't felt so sorry for Edna.

"The whole program's done for. They're going to announce it tonight. All the money we've raised is to be turned over to the Red Cross. That's the end of it."

Edna's face was a mask. Her little mouth was set in a rigid line. Minnie wanted to go over and put an arm around her, but she didn't dare.

"Oh . . . I suppose it's better that I didn't have to hear it announced in front of everyone," Edna said in a monotone. "It was good of you to tell me first."

"But that's not all of it!" Ruby said. "I came to tell you that my passage is paid for, and Daddy doesn't know about it, so he won't try to get the money back. You might as well take it. You can leave in a few weeks!"

"But — what am I to do on my own? I can't just go without a group."

"Oh, of course you can. There are so many groups. Just go to Paris and appeal to Mrs. Wharton. She's running all kinds of relief programs."

"Mrs. Wharton?"

"Yes, the novelist! She prints her address

in the paper. She expects Americans to come to her. She's begging us to."

"Just — go to Paris? But I haven't the money to stay once I'm there."

"Mrs. Wharton will find the money. Or someone like her. It isn't as hard as all that."

Minnie edged a little closer. Ruby looked over at her.

"Plenty of other girls already paid for their passage, too," she said to Minnie. "I'm sure at least one of them can keep a secret from their father."

That night, Edna and Minnie walked home under a deep purple sky and a half-moon that hung low on the horizon. They meandered along, too lost in conversation to bother with the most direct path to Mrs. Turnbull's.

"I have some money," Minnie said. "Or rather, I have a few trinkets hidden away. I've been meaning to go and collect them. They're just little things, but I can sell them."

"You're only sixteen," Edna said, "and, anyway, I don't think Deputy Kopp would allow it."

"She won't have a thing to say about it, once we're on the boat." Just picturing it — Minnie on the deck of a ship, looking out over the rail at the receding skyline of New York — thrilled her like nothing she'd ever imagined before.

"But it's going to be awfully hard work," Edna said, "and dangerous. You mustn't go just to have a gay time in Paris. I want to do my duty as an American, and that means I'm going to the front."

"I want —" Minnie stopped herself. What she started to say was: *I want to go wherever you're going.* But what would Edna think of her if she said a thing like that?

In the short time she'd known Edna, Minnie had come to see her for the extraordinary creature that she was. Edna was singularly focused on the war and her duty to it. Edna would dress wounds and hold the hands of soldiers while they screamed in surgery. Edna would peel potatoes and carry dinner through the fields, under cover of darkness. She would learn to drive an ambulance and work the semaphore flags and whatever else needed doing in service of a call that she heard more clearly than anyone Minnie had ever met.

But she needed someone by her side. Edna had an endless reservoir of determination, and all the high ideals in the world, but she didn't know how to bluff, or play a trick, or talk her way into a room where she wasn't invited. She was constitutionally unable to lie or cheat or hide anything — money, jewels, the truth. Minnie could do all of that, and while she didn't know much about war, she was fairly certain that something in that line might be called for.

Minnie would get them to Paris. She would find Mrs. Wharton. She would get them on a train, or in a soldier's auto heading to the front. She would see to it that they were fed and housed. They would go through the war together. They needed each other. She was sure of it.

Minnie reached out to stop Edna, and they turned to look at each other.

She couldn't bring herself to tell Edna that she'd never understood what it meant to put her life to a purpose outside herself, until now.

And she couldn't say that something had always been missing, and she'd always wondered who or what it might be, until now.

That something, improbably enough, was Edna.

Minnie had never felt protective of anyone before, but she was prepared to stand up for Edna, and defend her, and watch out for her. She couldn't say any of that either.

What she said, at last, was "I'm an American, too, aren't I?"

61

She came back to them on a Sunday.

The horse's water trough had rusted through and Norma's attempt to patch it with a sheet of metal failed. She hated to buy a new trough, owing to the expense. Constance had to take her through the previous year's ledger-books to show her that repairs took their financial toll in the spring, and it was to be expected. That led to grumbling over the inadequacy of the Sinking Fund that Norma had established, and the need to further trim their sails to replenish it. Constance told Norma she had every confidence in her ability to make the numbers come out right. Norma did not find that reassuring.

The trough sat on a rather complicated wooden stand of Norma's own invention. It took both of them to wrestle the old one out of the stand and get the new one, which was of a slightly different size, properly situated.

Constance was in a foul mood owing to the fact that Norma had dragged her out of bed at six o'clock for a day of chores, when she'd come home prepared to do nothing more than sleep and read a book in the bath. She hated to be mucking about in the barn before noon, when the cold leached out of the floor boards and the frost clung to the roof.

They did what they could for the trough. The horse seemed satisfied enough with it. Constance was relieved to see Carolyn Borus drive up before Norma could inflict some other domestic tedium on her. Carolyn came running out of her motor car, waving a letter at them.

"We're sending a message to the White House!" she called. "There's a nationwide effort underway to deliver letters to President Wilson by messenger pigeon. Twenty pigeon-keepers in Washington have signed on. We're to write a letter, and the birds will be sent here by train for us to release back to the capital. What shall we say to the President?"

Norma pulled off her gloves and took the letter. Constance read it over her shoulder.

"Only a few dozen pigeon societies have been chosen to receive the birds, and ours is one of them," Carolyn said.

"Let me make sure I understand," Constance said. "To send a letter by pigeon to the White House, it must be raised in Washington and transported here by train, because of course they can only fly home to the place they were born."

Norma looked up at Carolyn with an expression of apology for her slow-witted sister.

"Of course," Norma said irritably. "How else would we do it?"

"And then you will attach the letter and it will fly back to its loft near the White House."

"Exactly."

"Whereupon the letter will be removed and delivered to the President."

"It's a simple-enough plan and I don't know why you pretend not to be able to follow it."

One of the chickens kicked up a great fuss, and Constance looked over in time to see her raise herself slightly out of the straw and lay an egg. The Leghorns always complained the loudest. After she settled down again, Constance said, "I follow it just fine, but if you're trying to demonstrate some efficiency in transmitting messages, I'm afraid the post office has you beat."

"We aren't doing it for the sake of efficiency," Norma said.

"She's right," Carolyn put in. "The idea is to make a sort of spectacle of it and to put us in the public eye. We want the President and his generals to see the speed and secrecy by which a bird can deliver missives in wartime."

"We do need a spectacle, which means you'll have to ask Carrie to write a newspaper story," Norma said, "although my name won't be in it, and she won't be allowed to fill it with lies."

"That's just fine," Constance said. "She'll be delighted. I'll leave you to your letter-writing."

She tried to disappear back into the house, but Norma had a list of chores that required four hands. After a little more discussion with Carolyn, Norma sent her on her way so they could finish.

It was only a few minutes later that another motor car arrived and Fleurette disembarked. Mr. Impediment hauled a trunk out and deposited it upon their porch, along with more hat-boxes, handbags, and wraps than she possibly could've left with. He tipped his hat to all three of them and drove away, leaving Fleurette anchored to her spot in the drive, staring at Norma and

Constance.

What a sight they made! There was Fleurette, in a little day dress of blue and white foulard, with pearl buttons at the neck and a matching set along her hatband — and here was Norma in her muddiest old divided skirt and a sweater that must have belonged to Francis, and Constance in the corduroy number that was her night-dress at the jail, which she'd brought home to wash but ended up sleeping in once again instead. Neither of them looked as though they'd seen a comb or a powder puff in their lives, while Fleurette's hair was done to a high gloss and she wore a shade of claret-colored lip-stick that seemed to have been made for her.

She didn't look like a little girl dressing up in her mother's clothes anymore. She hadn't in some time, really, but that realization was made all the more startling by her sudden and unexpected appearance in the drive.

Fleurette spoke first. "Did I see Mrs. Borus go past?"

"She was just here with some very important news," Constance said. "Norma's pigeons are going to Washington."

"Not my pigeons," Norma said. "Other pigeons. Constance still doesn't understand it."

Fleurette drew closer and Constance managed to get an arm around her. "I sent you postcards," she said.

"Yes, and we found them very thrilling," Constance said. "All that lobster and Champagne."

"Not so very much Champagne," she said. "And four girls to a room. I didn't tell you that part. I awoke every morning to Charlotte Babcock's feet on my pillow."

"I don't suppose they let you out to have any fun at all?" Constance asked, trying to sound sympathetic. "Mrs. Ward must have so many admirers. I'm sure you had invitations."

"Oh, we had our wild times," Fleurette said. "Men can't resist a girl on stage. But I was too exhausted from doing two shows a night. It's quite a different pace than Mrs. Hansen's. One has to adapt to a life on the stage."

She squirmed away and released a cloud of some new perfume — lilies of the valley, maybe, or jasmine. It was expensive, whatever it was, and a mighty battle waged in Constance's mind between the forces that wanted to know who had purchased it for her, and those that believed it better to leave that question unanswered.

Constance followed Fleurette into the house. Norma washed her hands at the pump in the barn and came in behind them.

Fleurette looked around at the dim parlor and sighed. "Nothing's changed around here. Nothing ever changes. I've gone off and traveled all over five states, and seen new faces everywhere I go, and learned a dozen new songs and performed to thousands, and what's new around here? Absolutely nothing."

Norma and Constance busied themselves bringing in Fleurette's bags, which were still piled on the porch. She'd obviously grown accustomed to having someone else carry her things. Constance thought it might not be such a good idea to give the impression that she'd be taking on those duties, but she did it anyway. Norma raised an eyebrow at Constance just once, when she spotted a new red and gold embossed hat-box with a tag attached bearing May Ward's name. It must have been a gift. As far as Constance could tell, Mrs. Ward had kept her secret.

"I suppose you've been down at that gloomy old jail all this time," Fleurette said. "Did you arrest anybody while I was gone? Did you catch a thief, or a murderer?"

"She found a job at the powder works for a girl," Norma said.

Fleurette let out a bright and dismissive laugh. "Is that all they pay you to do — put girls into factory jobs?"

Norma said, "Just yesterday we had a letter from a moving picture man inviting Constance to make a picture about a lady deputy who rescues girls from white slavers."

"I wouldn't like to see a picture about that," Fleurette said. "Write them back and tell them she has a younger sister who's so pretty she's been threatened with kidnapping. Perhaps I can go missing and you can come to my rescue."

Constance tried very hard not to look at Norma. "That sounds awfully dull."

"Not as dull as this old farmhouse." She unpinned her hat and handed it to Constance, the way she might pass something to a valet.

"I could arrange to have someone shoot at us again, if you'd like that better," Constance said. "Or aren't you about to go right back out on tour?"

Fleurette wandered into her sewing room. She ran her hand over her sewing machine, and the bolts of fabric, and all the spools of thread hung on pegs on the wall. "I wouldn't mind sleeping in my own room for a while, with all my things," she said, a little quietly.

Constance carried her bags upstairs, quickly, before she could change her mind.

HISTORICAL NOTES
AND SOURCES

Readers of the first two books in this series, *Girl Waits with Gun and Lady Cop Makes Trouble,* might already know that Constance, Norma, and Fleurette Kopp were real people, and that the events in these books are based as much as possible on the real events in their lives. I encourage you to read the historical notes in those books if you'd like to know more about their background and family history.

As with the previous two books, I rely on fiction to fill in the gaps in the historical record. In some cases, I moved dates around or altered minor details to help tell a more cohesive story, as I'll explain here.

In early 1916, Constance was working as New Jersey's first female deputy sheriff, and one of the first in the nation. In those days, women in law enforcement were rarely given a gun, a badge, and arrest authority, much less paid the same as a man. This makes Constance's experience fairly unique. It's not exactly clear when Constance received her badge, but it was first reported in the *New York Times* on February 13, 1916. She was then the subject of major newspaper profiles nationwide, which (according to papers) brought her a flood of marriage proposals and other mail.

Edna Heustis was arrested on March 9, 1916, and released on March 14 after a short investigation by Constance. Judge Seufert really was the judge on the case, and much of what Constance said to the judge comes directly from the newspaper account cited below. Edna did leave her home in Edgewater to work at the DuPont powder works plant in Pompton Lakes. My description of her work at the plant was based on newspaper accounts from the era and other reports about the working conditions at textile and munitions plants.

Although her mother's name, Monvilla, is unique, I had some questions about the genealogical records I found for Edna, so her family is entirely fictional. (I did find a passport photo of an Edna Heustis who more or less matches her description, which you can see on my website: www.amy stewart.com.) Mrs. Turnbull's boarding-house is fictional, but based on nonfiction accounts of similar establishments from the era.

Everything that happened to Edna after her arrest is entirely fictional. I owe a great debt to Mary Roberts Rinehart's wonderful novel *The Amazing Interlude* for her descriptions of young women preparing to go to France. I was able to correlate her fictional account with many nonfiction accounts to describe how small civic groups came together to sponsor women going overseas — and the way those efforts could fall apart as well-heeled families decided they weren't actually willing to let their daughters serve.

Edith Wharton did run war relief programs in France during World War I, as did many other private citizens and charities. Eager volunteers did turn up in Paris with little in the way of money or concrete plans, so Edna and Minnie's situation was not unusual.

Minnie Davis was arrested on January 23, 1916, in Fort Lee, where she and Anthony Leo were living in a "shanty" on Main Street and posing as man and wife. He really did work aboard a steamship on the Hudson, and she really did work at the Catskill knitting mill until she ran away. Newspapers reported that Leo was part of a "white slave ring," but there's little information beyond that.

I was able to find more biographical details about Minnie. Her parents' and sisters' names are correct; Edith really did work as a seamstress; and I suspect that the Davises were a blended family because of some discrepancies in ages between family members. Everything else about the family is fictional.

I don't know exactly how the Minnie Davis/Anthony Leo case was resolved, so the details are largely fictional. I drew from many different nonfiction sources from that time to tell the story of how so-called "white slave" cases were prosecuted. Girls were sent to reformatories for years over morality crimes, with little access to due process or a competent defense. (The right to a free attorney was established through a series of Supreme Court decisions from 1931 to 1966.) Also, it was common at that time for witnesses to a crime (including victims) to be held in jail until the trial. Witnesses received slightly better meals than inmates, as reported in Bergen County newspapers of the day.

Sheriff Heath really was running for Congress as a Democrat, and John Courter was running for sheriff on the Republican ticket. I know very little about Cordelia

Heath's life, so she's mostly fictional. John Courter's political stances are mostly conjecture, based on the few insights into his thinking I could find in newspapers from that year. However, his perspective on "morality crimes" is very typical of politicians of his day, and some of his lines about the Mann Act come from other political speeches of that time, as cited below. He was very much a political foe to both Sheriff Heath and Constance.

I also don't know anything about what Fleurette and Norma were up to at that time. Norma's interest in pigeons is entirely fictional, but the efforts she and (the fictional) Carolyn Borus were participating in — long-distance flights to prove the worthiness of carrier pigeons for war work, and an effort to send letters to the White House by carrier pigeon — really did happen.

A handful of newspaper clippings show that Fleurette was auditioning for singing competitions. Although her connection with May Ward is entirely fictional, the final scene, in which Constance was sent to New York to arrest Mrs. Ward after Freeman Bernstein claimed she'd been kidnapped, really did happen a little later in 1916. I simply fictionalized the events leading up to that moment. Most of the details about

Mrs. Ward's act, and her husband's history, are true. I do portray May Ward as something of a drunk, and that is entirely fictional.

The other female inmates of the Hackensack jail are all based on real women who did commit the crimes described, but not necessarily at that time or in Hackensack. Providencia Monafo really did shoot her tenant, and Josephine Knobloch was arrested during a labor strike and refused to pay her fine. Both women would have been inmates at the Hackensack jail at around this time.

"Girl Sheriff, a Real Lecoq" ran in many newspapers around the country, including the *Evening Telegram* on March 5, 1916. The passage on p. 39 about prison reform actually comes from another lengthy profile about Constance that appeared in the *Passaic Journal* on March 19, 1916, under the headline "Bergen County Has New Jersey's Only Woman Under-Sheriff." The text of Edna Heustis's war recruitment pamphlet was adapted from a few lines in Helen Fraser's 1918 book *Women and War Work.* Mrs. Roberts's speech on p. 288 was inspired by this book and several similar speeches recounted in newspapers from 1916 to 1918.

"There's a Little Bit of Bad in Every Good Little Girl" was written by Grante Clark and Fred Fischer, and recorded by Billy Murray in 1916.

"She Pushed Me into the Parlour" was written and composed by Alf Ellerton and Will Mayne in 1912.

The letter from lawyer Edwin Bagott proposing marriage appeared in a slightly different form (and to a different woman) in the *Galveston Daily News* on August 23, 1904.

The incident on the trolley actually happened to pioneering Los Angeles policewoman Alice Stebbins Wells and was described in *Policing Women* by Janis Appier.

John Courter's speech includes well-circulated lines from popular speeches and writings of the day. The bit about the ice cream parlor can be found in Ernest Albert Bell's 1910 book *Fighting the Traffic in Young Girls* and was a frequent refrain of United States Attorney Edwin Sims, who was instrumental in the creation of the Mann Act. Other lines from Courter's speech come from Jane Addams's *A New Conscience and an Ancient Evil* (1914). In those days, ideas were circulated not by

Twitter, but by pamphlets, books, and speeches reprinted in newspapers. It was not at all uncommon for speakers to repeat lines they'd read in such sources; think of it as the retweeting of the day. This was very much part of how the hysteria over so-called "white slavery" spread. For more on this subject, I recommend David J. Langum's *Crossing Over the Line: Legislating Morality and the Mann Act* and Jessica R. Pliley's *Policing Sexuality: The Mann Act and the Making of the FBI.* Many of the descriptions of the State Home for Girls in Trenton came from the 1936 book *I Knew Them in Prison* by Mary B. Harris, including the fact that "colored girls," to use the language of the era, had to carry their chairs to dinner because the state hadn't allocated enough chairs. Miss Pittman's chilly line "We weren't prepared to receive colored girls" was precisely the language used at that time to describe segregation and the exclusion of African American girls from social service organizations. The description of the house meant to look like George Washington's headquarters at Morristown, the chipped plaster in the punishment rooms, and the cage in the attic with the rats crowding around all come from Harris's book.

The speech Nurse Porter gave to Minnie comes from *Sex Knowledge for Women and Girls: What Every Woman and Girl Should Know* by William Josephus Robinson, published in 1917.

Esther's description of how girls are defined as "feeble-minded," "idiot," "imbecile," or "lunatic" can be found in many mental health publications of the era. I drew particularly on a 1914 University of Texas bulletin, *Care of the Feeble-Minded and Insane in Texas.*

"Girl Sheriff's Gold Badge" appeared in the *New York Times* on February 14, 1916. I replaced County Detective Louis Nestel's name with that of John Courter.

The Hotel Jermyn in Scranton and the Hotel Columbus in Harrisburg were popular hotels in their day, and I tried to render their details faithfully.

Belle Headison's rousing speech on how difficult it is for girls to preserve their honor "behind the footlights" comes in part from the 1914 book *The White Slave Traffic Versus the American Home* by Mabel Madeline Southard.

Thanks to Barbara Gooding's *Images of America: Hackensack* for the bit about Terhune's Harley-Davidson showroom.

The account of Freeman Bernstein's failed Midway Park can be found in the *New York Times* on June 25, 1908, "Two Caught in Ruins as Building Falls," and June 24, 1908, "Court Urged to Close Midway Park at Once."

Callot Soeurs was a Parisian design house run by four sisters. The gold dress May Ward wore was one of their designs (although it was fictional that May Ward wore it).

The entertainment on offer in Harrisburg, including Mr. Howe's Travel Festival and the controversial film *Birth of a Nation*, all come from February 1916 theater listings in the *Harrisburg Telegraph*.

"The Bird on Nellie's Hat" was written by Arthur J. Lamb and published in 1906 with May Ward's image on the cover of the sheet music. It would be worthwhile to search online for videos of this song being performed — particularly the version sung by Miss Piggy.

The building where May Ward was arrested was, in real life, the Equitable Building, at 120 Broadway, which really did cast such a shadow that people complained. The situation brought about new zoning requirements designed to let more light into city streets.

Several newspapers gave conflicting accounts of May Ward's alleged kidnapping, but they all agree that her husband, Freeman Bernstein, made the allegations and that Constance was sent to rescue her, make arrests, or otherwise sort out the mess. These events actually took place in September 1916. "The Lady Sheriff Right on the Job" ran in many newspapers, including, on September 30, 1916, in the *Wichita Beacon.*

ABOUT THE AUTHOR

Amy Stewart is the award-winning author of seven books, including her acclaimed fiction debut *Girl Waits with Gun* and the bestsellers *The Drunken Botanist* and *Wicked Plants.* She and her husband live in Eureka, California, where they own a bookstore called Eureka Books.